MW01463465

COLLAPSE

EPOCH'S END
BOOK 5

MIKE KRAUS

MUONIC PRESS

COLLAPSE
Epoch's End
Book 5

By
Mike Kraus

MUONIC
PRESS

© 2021-2024 Muonic Press Inc
www.muonic.com

---

www.MikeKrausBooks.com
hello@mikeKrausBooks.com
www.facebook.com/MikeKrausBooks

No part of this book may be reproduced in any form, or by any electronic, mechanical or other means, without the permission in writing from the author.

CONTENTS

Want More Awesome Books? v
Special Thanks vii

Chapter 1   1
Chapter 2   11
Chapter 3   19
Chapter 4   26
Chapter 5   37
Chapter 6   48
Chapter 7   58
Chapter 8   76
Chapter 9   83
Chapter 10   98
Chapter 11   105
Chapter 12   115
Chapter 13   127
Chapter 14   137
Chapter 15   151
Chapter 16   168
Chapter 17   175
Chapter 18   186
Chapter 19   205
Chapter 20   219
Chapter 21   230
Chapter 22   244
Chapter 23   255
Chapter 24   261
Chapter 25   268
Chapter 26   275
Chapter 27   281

WANT MORE AWESOME BOOKS?

Like Mike Kraus? You can buy direct from him at shop.muonic.com or you can find his books on Amazon and Audible.

Find more fantastic tales at books.to/readmorepa.

If you're new to reading Mike Kraus, consider visiting his website (www.mikekrausbooks.com) and signing up for his free newsletter. You'll receive several free books and a sample of his audiobooks, too, just for signing up, you can unsubscribe at any time and you will receive absolutely *no* spam.

SPECIAL THANKS

Special thanks to my awesome beta team, without whom this book wouldn't be nearly as great.

Thank you!

CHAPTER ONE

Medic Saanvi Patel
Nuevo Laredo, Mexico

A chill wind whistled through the loose-boarded buildings of the criminal containment center southwest of Nuevo Laredo. Tumbleweeds blew against the chain-link and razor wire fence encircling the holding area, a dilapidated block of houses and businesses stretching in a rectangle the length of a football field. Plywood shutters battened tight slammed in their wooden frames, thudding to the wind's pulse while haggard trees that had once provided shade were trimmed back to allow more precious sunlight to gift its fragile warmth.

In the backyards, the dirt had turned cold and hard from the bitter temperatures slicing their way in from the north, the sparse grass brown and withered and rough. Burn barrels filled the yards, refugees huddled around them, hands raised, faces pressed close to warm chilled extremities. Furniture arms and legs stuck up from the crackling flames as they burned whatever they could scavenge to stave off the freezing winds. In the southern section of the camp on the street's north side sat a boarded-up restaurant and an old-style pharmacy topped with a sign out of the 1950s. Its face bore the image of a smiling woman with curly black hair, the word *Farmacia* stretched across the top in faded red lettering.

The camp's inhabitants were refugees from the north, singled out as troublemakers by the Army officers in Laredo. Prisoners strolled briskly between the ramshackle buildings, an urgency in their step as they threw furtive glances through the chain-link at the guards on the other side. Many still wore the lightweight clothing they had brought from the States, inadequate to handle the brutal chill moving in.

Whispers twisted through tight alleyways where refugees protected dwindling supplies, bartering and organizing out of sight as rumors of a break-out gained traction. Reluctant guards milled around the fence line, rifles slung on shoulders, black beanies pulled over brows, hands tucked deep into pockets as they huddled inside thick Army coats, their cheeks glowing red in the punishingly stiff wind. Gusts of warm breath blew from covered lips before fading to nothing as they walked with brisk movements to generate heat, attention focused on the supply tents and mess hall where a smell wafted out that could have been cooking meat, beans, or something else the company officers had scrounged up.

The command center and barracks were located outside the fence on the west side, made of a warehouse and prefab buildings dropped off by helicopters weeks earlier. Soldiers had assembled them so fast that almost nothing worked - the lights were spotty, the vents loose and leaky, and the laboring HVACs clacked away, barely holding the temperature inside above 50.

Captain Jennifer Godwin stood in her office wearing a heavy Army coat, staring north at the more modern buildings of San Miguel Village, ones that might have offered more comfortable living conditions, though her commanders had been adamant about keeping the criminal elements away from the adjacent neighborhoods. Poor planning combined with a frantic shuffle of resources and insufficient logistical support had led those who had preceded her to throw together the camp in what was-in her opinion-the worst possible way.

The phone in her breast pocket buzzed, and she pulled it out, placing it against her ear.

"Godwin."

The voice on the other end was her staff sergeant. "Captain, we've got word on the transports for the remaining prisoners."

"Go ahead."

"They won't be coming in on time. In fact... they won't be coming in at all."

The captain's shoulders slumped, though she managed to refrain from clicking her tongue. "What do you mean they won't be coming in at all? You requested those transports days ago."

"Yes, ma'am."

"So, what's the problem?"

"They've been re-routed to carry supplies into southern Mexico to support relocation operations there."

"Who ordered it?"

"A general placed an emergency request, which allowed him to assume control of the vehicles. It's part of the new resupply directives straight from Washington. High-ranking commanders take precedence--"

"I know what the directives say." Godwin stepped to the desk and pressed her fingers against the aluminum surface, hand in the shape of a claw. "It's still unacceptable, Sergeant. We've got our own relocation efforts happening. These prisoners need to be moved pronto."

"I know, ma'am."

Throat tight, fingers pressing harder on the desk, words coming out clipped, frustration slipping through. "So, what the hell am I supposed to--"

Knuckles rapped on the office door, drawing her eyes. "Who is it?"

The door popped open, and a red-haired private poked his head inside. "Sorry to interrupt, ma'am, but something's come up."

"What do you need, Swanson?"

The private entered and shut the door quietly behind him, addressing the captain in a low voice. "It's the dozen Canadian refugees we picked up the other day. They're still in limbo in the processing warehouse, and they're causing a distraction for the troops. This morning we caught one of our soldiers sneaking them supplies from our own stores."

Godwin sighed wearily. "They shouldn't even be here. If we can't find a record of them, kick them out of processing and release them. Have the offender detained if he hasn't been already – I'll deal with them later."

The private took a step closer. "Let them go, ma'am? Like out into the desert?"

"That's the gist."

A strained grimace broke across the soldier's face. "But, technically, we can't let them go, according to the new border agreements."

Godwin placed a hand over the phone and lowered her voice to match the Private's. "I don't care what the new agreements say. They change all the damn time, and I'm sick of it. We don't have the supplies to care for refugees that aren't ours, so out they go. Do it now."

"Yes, ma'am." The private looked as though he was about to turn away, then spoke again. "But if the higher-ups find out--"

Godwin's knuckles hit the desk with a sharp crack, the reserved strike stopping just short of damaging her hand. "Do what I tell you and let me deal with the repercussions. That's an order – dismissed."

"Yes, ma'am."

The private turned on his heel and exited the office in a hurry, leaving the door hanging open. Another shadow shifted in the hallway, coming hesitantly forward as the captain lifted the phone back to her ear.

"Are you still there, Sergeant?"

"Yes, ma'am."

"As I was saying before, keep working on those transports. I want replacements inbound as soon as possible. I don't care where you get them. The prisoners need to be gone within the week. Is that understood?"

"Yes, ma'am. I'm on it."

Godwin ended the call and slipped the phone into her pocket, eyes darting toward the hallway as the shadow moved in, knuckles rapping gently on the door.

"What is it?" she snapped, then her expression deflated, shoulders sagging with relief when she saw who it was. "Oh, thank heavens. Please come in and shut the door behind you. Lock the damned thing, too. Weld it shut if you can."

Private Saanvi Patel stepped into the room in a soft shuffle of boots and a light chuckle, pivoting to push the door home with a click before spinning to greet her superior. "Good to see you again, Captain Godwin."

"At ease, soldier." The woman slid her backside onto her desk and shook her head with a defeated sigh. "It's good to see you, too, Patel. Been a while. Where have you been?"

"I was on a special project back in Virginia when Asheville got hit with some aftershocks. We hitched a ride on an Osprey that crashed a few miles north of here. Hoofed it the rest of the way in with some refugees."

The captain nodded. "I heard something about that. Miracle you survived the crash. What are you here for?"

"The commander put me in charge of prisoner health, and your camp was on my schedule today, so I'm here to report what I found."

"Right, yes. He said we'd be getting a visit from a medic. That's great. Best thing I've heard all day."

"Why's that?"

"I'm happy to see a friendly face and not someone who needs something from me."

Patel's dark eyes shifted, taking in the captain's drawn features, cheeks gaunt with weight loss, the corners of her mouth pulled into a perpetual frown. "If you don't mind me saying, you look a little stressed." An apologetic scoff quickly followed. "What I mean to say is, I'm surprised to find you here. When we last talked, you mentioned you might be heading south to take part in the fighting."

The captain spun off the desk and circled to sit in a chair. Ripping open the drawer, she produced a bottle of amber whiskey and two glasses and slammed them on the desk, nodding to the seat on the opposite side.

"Drink?"

The medic took three steps and sat with an emphatic grin. "*Yes.*"

Godwin poured the drinks and slid one glass over to the private. They raised their glasses in toast, then sipped. Patel relaxed back with a soft smack of her lips, the whiskey burn adding color to an otherwise cold and dreary day. After a pause and a swirl of her drink, the captain finally got around to answering the question.

"I *had* intended to go south and fight, but they reassigned me here when the truce-surrender, whatever-came."

"That explains it. Not having fun here?"

"You'd think this would be a pleasant spot to lie low for a few months, but we're one of many under-supplied refugee camps sprouting up, and there'll be a lot more. All I do is field a million questions from clueless guards about every little thing. Trust me, I'm not getting the best the military has to offer."

"Sorry to hear it."

The captain blustered. "Well, except for you. I've been asking for a competent medic, and it looks like they finally sent one."

"I appreciate that."

"And how are things in the camp?" The captain's voice sounded strained, even after relaxing with a drink. "I mean, how are the refugees?"

Shoulders stiffening, back straightening, the private started with a nod. "Ah, yes. Of the 247 refugees here, you have a low rate of infectious disease. I found three cases of the flu, and those folks have been quarantined, but there's no signs of anything that would spell trouble for you."

"That's good news."

"On the non-disease side of things, there is a man in the northern part of the camp who needs his leg reset if he ever wants to walk again."

"When can you do it?"

Patel had another sip of whiskey and gave a head shake. "No can do, Captain, not with my level of experience. I'll call a specialist to have a look. It would be helpful if I had your signature on the order."

"You've got it." Godwin's expression turned dark. "For what my word's worth. It feels like command tossed me into a dark hole to rot.

They keep undermining my authority at every turn. We might not get that doctor for months. What else do you have for me?"

"I'm a little concerned about the cold, captain. Quite a few refugees were underdressed, and I assume they entered camp that way. Don't you have anything to give them?"

Godwin felt her chest squeeze as a weight pressed on her shoulders. "I wish I could, but there's barely enough winter gear for the soldiers and guards here. If I haven't mentioned it already, we're low on supplies."

"You might have said something to that effect," Patel replied with dry smile, the words respectful as she danced around the real reason for her visit. "What about transporting them somewhere else? Surely, they've got warmer camps farther south to place them."

The captain drained the rest of her drink and set the glass down hard with a wince. "I sure as hell would've if I could. I've scheduled three separate transports to come get them, but they never make it."

"Why not?"

"They keep re-directing them for other operations, leaving me S-O-L."

"I understand," Patel nodded before she polished off the rest of her whiskey and rested the glass in her lap. "It's just that I'm hearing the temperatures are falling faster and farther here than they originally thought. It could be well below zero within the month, and from what I can see, the detainees are burning everything they have to keep warm. Chairs, tables, beds, pieces of plywood from the walls."

"It's a sad situation,"

"What about letting them go? At least they'd have a chance to settle in a better climate. I hear there are plenty of fertile valleys left in Central Mexico. I just don't think it's right to leave them--"

"Between you and me, I agree with you, but it doesn't matter what we *think*." The captain's tone held frustration and a touch of resentment. "We can't simply release them, because many are criminals. They even moved a few here from a minimum-security New Mexico jail. And while it might seem cruel to keep them in the cold like this, it's our job to guard them no matter what our personal feelings. Don't worry, the transports will make it here before the weather gets too cold, and I'll see the *refugees* are relocated to a safer place."

"Are you sure?"

"You'll just have to trust me."

Patel nodded affirmatively but stiffly, her agreement hiding her fear. Placing the glass on the table, she stood to go. "I'll return in three days to check on things. In the meantime, I'll put in that order in for a specialist right away. You'll have the paperwork within the day."

"It was good to see you, Patel. Stop back in and see me." Godwin rose with her, posture slightly more relaxed than before. "We'll have another drink."

"I look forward to it."

"And if you need anything, come ask. I'll do my best to make it happen."

"Thanks, Captain."

With that, Patel turned and left the office, shutting the door quietly behind her. Her feet carried her through the prefab command center, relief and uncertainty causing her stomach to twist with a slight case of nausea. It was good seeing Jenny again, though alarm bells of concern rang in her head for the detainees – refugees, whatever the spin was – in camp. The cold was coming fast, and when it arrived, there'd be nothing anyone could do but freeze.

She stepped out into a heated tent that was draped over the captain's prefab housing where six guards sat inside the enclosed space with a large kerosene heater blasting warm waves of air. Light, scruffy beards lined their jaws and Patel frowned. Any good commander would snatch them to attention and make them dry shave in front of everyone for the lack of hygiene, though then again they also wouldn't be drinking on duty, either. *The small things go first,* she thought, *and signal the coming downfall of the larger ones.*

Instead of guarding the captain's building, two soldiers played cards at a table while the other four huddled around a computer tablet. One of the card players removed a flask from his jacket and poured whiskey into a cup of tea, stashing the liquor away before taking a surreptitious sip. The lights strung across the ceiling flickered and the electric heating unit in the back corner hitched and puttered on, ozone and oil smells hanging heavy in the air.

With a shake of her head, Patel stepped through the tent flap into the blustery afternoon. The wind bit her cheeks, freezing her nostrils shut, causing her nose to wrinkle as she clutched her coat tighter around her shoulders. Brisk steps carried her into the south lot where a dozen older model Humvees sat parked side-by-side along with a pair of M1161 Growlers. The vehicles had mismatched parts, fenders different shades of green and beige, dents in them, balding tires half flat.

The two guards at the entrance gave her a cursory glance and then returned to hovering over a burn barrel, hands out, fingertips cut from their gloves. Far from standing carefully at guard, watching for signs of trouble, their eyes focused downward, breaths coming out in tired puffs as they tried to stay warm above all else.

Behind them stood a massive pile of wood beams and broken furniture, old skids, boxes, and crates. Raising her gaze to the next block, she spotted a handful of soldiers busting through walls with sledgehammers, piling the salvaged wood off to the side. Without proper heating and shelter, they'd resorted to taking apart the town to stay warm, matching the detainees in desperation.

She pivoted left, looking over a low row of shrubs, across the dirt lane to the holding block and its chain-link razor wire fencing. Three guards leaned against the fence, talking, laughing with shivering lips. Her eyes came to rest on five figures standing around a crimson burn barrel, one man staring back in her direction. Tall and wide-shouldered, he wore a heavy brown coat with the hood pulled over his face. Patel glanced around to make sure no one was watching, then she shrugged and shook her head, hoping her disappointment showed in the gestures. The man tapped on his wrist, and she replied with a nearly imperceptible nod. With a slight turn, she strode over to a soldier holding a leash as he huddled in his coat, staring north up the road.

"I've got her now," she said as she came up, reaching for the lead. "Thanks."

The soldier gave up the leash without question or comment, then returned to his placid, shivering watch. The German Shepherd on the other end of the lead whined and licked her chops happily as Patel led her away, the pair angling around the south side of the holding block. The animal's fur was fast growing back over her wounds, the fire-burned sections looking less gnarly, making her seem less like a hell hound and more like a family pet. The dog walked with a slight limp, sad eyes glancing worriedly across the street where the man stood by the burn barrel, watching them go in stiff silence.

CHAPTER TWO

President John Zimmerman
Air Force One, Southeastern United States

Crisp air circulates through the cabin as the fuselage of Air Force One shudders and dips in the rough currents. President John Zimmerman barely acknowledges it, his face caught in a look of disbelief. He stares at the dark oaken surface of his desk as it reflects the comfortable but bright overhead lights. A smaller version of the one in his office, it boasts a full communication suite with three pop-up screens, enabling him to watch multiple situations at a time.

The cabin is long and wide, the top half stark white, cut sharply in two by a line of dark trim with blue paint reaching the floor, its roundish walls giving it a high-tech, bubble-like appearance. His shoes rest on a soft navy carpet that covers the decking, shifting and groaning as the plane absorbs the wind's abuse.

His most trusted staff members are assembled in three chairs facing him: Secretary of State Rita Cortez, General Mark Davidson, Chief Scientist Rick Manglor and the President's assistant, Maxine.

The other staffers sit in the forward compartment, tapping away at their laptops as they relay information back and forth with the various U.S. agencies.

Another brush of turbulence gives the cabin a rough shake, jostling them from side-to-side as if the plane is slipping on an oily piece of plastic. Rita shifts uncomfortably, clutching her stomach with pain on her face.

"So, that's it, then?" Zimmerman asks, expression dour. "There's no way we can stop the anomaly? It's done?"

Rick clears his throat and raises his finger. Hair standing up straight, shirt loose and coffee stained, blue eyes wild with lack of sleep, the man has reached the height of dishevelment. "Actually, Mr. President, we may have sped up the freshwater surge."

"You'd mentioned that as a potential risk," he nodded, "and I agreed we'd take the chance, anyway. Can you tell me how much the freshwater influx has accelerated?"

Rick shrugs, mouth moving but no words come out. When he finally speaks, it's after a nervous sigh. "That's difficult to say, Mr. President, though the North Atlantic Drift must be completely disrupted or at least sluggish beyond immediate repair. We'll know more as we gather additional readings. I think it's safe to say the cold will advance faster than we predicted. Already, they're reporting minus 10 degrees in spots on the Texas-Mexican border, and those temperatures will trend downward over the next few days."

"How low can we expect to go?"

"Arctic levels. Something like an average of minus 21, give or take."

General Davidson shakes his head, his face red with growing anger. "How could your people could have screwed this up so badly? I heard the bombs were useless except to split the crevice open like a damned wound!"

"They were the best figures we had to work with," the scientist argues, jaw tightening, "based on the current modeling we had."

"Yes, and to get that modeling we had to lose a nuclear sub and over 22 research vessels, warships, and equipment we could have used elsewhere."

"I didn't authorize the plan," Rick snarls, lack of sleep putting an edge on his demeanor. "I just put the data together to the best of my ability. And I don't have to answer to you--"

"Stop it." The President's voice growls, cool yet stern enough to grab the men's attention as he looks across at them. "I gave the go-ahead for the operation and I take full responsibility for what happened. I won't tolerate any in-fighting - we gave it a shot, and it didn't work. Blame me for it, and let's move on. Rita, Mark, tell me about Cuba."

The general recovers his composure, lifting a notepad from his lap, scanning the words. "The operation was successful, sir. Our forces overran the island in record time after communicating to the Cuban officials that it was a no-win scenario for them. They had one chance to surrender before we annihilated them with extreme prejudice.

"Our pro-American influences in Havana encouraged the Cuban general to submit at 0900, with only a few shots fired. We're setting up strategic defenses as we speak. That includes the takeover of every naval and air force base in the country, putting boots down. We've got thirty thousand troops on the ground and more incoming. The area outside the capital is secured, and most of our required infrastructure is installed at the OSH. That's the Offshore White House."

"What's it look like in the water?"

"Three carrier strike groups and 23 submarines guard the coastline."

"Very good, Mark. That's the kind of progress I want to see. Any word on civilian casualties?"

"Less than a thousand, sir, and most of those were from two missile malfunctions that hit a town near Cabañas during the first phase of the maneuvering."

"Finally, something working out in our favor." John sighs, the tension in his voice lifting ever so slightly. "Looks like we've got a place to call home for the next couple months."

"Yes, sir."

"What about the nuclear missile silos back on the mainland? Are we in any danger of losing them?"

"Of our four thousand missiles, we moved fifteen hundred to our secure military site in Mexico. For the other silos and launch solutions, we have teams on site to guard and monitor the equipment. They're mostly underground, with enough supplies and power to last five years, though I can't say it's too pleasant of a life."

"Make sure we stay on top of getting those troops relief as soon as things settle and figure out how to support them for the long term in all aspects."

"Yes, sir."

The pilot alters course and guides Air Force One in a more southerly direction, guarded by a pair of F-22s flying just out of sight in the clouds. As the officials settle in for the long trip, the President monitors their position on his in-flight tracker, their path taking them past Tampa, the plane easing over the Gulf of Mexico toward Havana.

John glances out the large port windows as winds and rain beat down on them, followed by several close lightning strikes. An hour and a half later, the Cuban coastline comes within sight, and the pilot calls for landing instructions.

They make a pass over Havana and turn toward the runway as uniformed United States soldiers ready the city for its new occupants. Swarming the streets in Humvees and camouflaged SUVs, they herd citizens from areas around the capital buildings to camps on the edge of town. Military checkpoints pop up on every block, soldiers occupying boarded up homes and apartments, using whatever means necessary to subdue the understandable anger and resistance on the part of the civilian population.

The thriving city, usually blaring with music and food and life, has completely shut down. Steel doors slam to the pavement, closing tourist establishments as vendors fold their carts and hide them. Revelers pause and scatter in the wake of the United States military machine, massive and ominous and efficient as it assumes control of the Cuban capital.

Air Force One's wheels touched down with a heavy impact, causing the president's desk to shudder as Rita Cortez groans with relief as the flaps lift, bringing the jet to a screeching halt at the end of the runway. As they taxi to a secure part of the tarmac, the president stands and paces behind his desk. The passengers have gone quiet except for General Davidson, who has been on the phone during the landing.

The burly man hangs up and places the phone in his lap with a nod to his commander in chief. "We're good to go, Mr. President. The checkpoints are all setup, and we've got complete control of the airport and surrounding buildings."

"Fidel Castro must be rolling over in his grave." Rita's brow arches in sour amusement.

"Good," General Davidson quipped back. "Hook up a couple of power leads and let him spin."

The President glances around with a hesitant grin as the staffers up front turn in their seats, some standing to stretch, awaiting his word with uncertain, fearful expressions.

"Look, this will be hard." He comes to stand behind his chair. "We're in a foreign country that we've just occupied and taken control of. Our families are 2,000 miles away. But things will get better. We'll seal the capital and bring our loved ones along soon after. Once we're settled in, we'll bring our resources to bear, and the Cubans will view us as friends, and they'll join us on our trek south to freedom. Together, we'll transform the Southern Hemisphere into something amazing, you'll see." The words sound strange as they come from Zimmerman's mouth, speaking of things that would have been unimaginable at any other time in history.

"Thank you, Mr. President," someone said from the back. Others echo the sentiment, and Maxine gives him a warm smile and a confident nod.

Coming around to sit on the edge of his chair, he turns to his chief scientist with a hopeful expression. "Rick, how long can we stay here before the temperatures force us to move?"

The man cleared his throat, voice raspy, eyes plagued with weariness. "We're estimating a couple months at most, sir. It's plenty of time to push through to the ultimate objective."

"I agree with him on this one," Mark adds. "Our advance teams are making significant headway in both prepping for the Navy's arrival and working to block others interested in the area."

"Good work. That's excellent news." John taps his fingers on his desk, looking between the pair. "I never doubted either of you for one second. Let's keep pushing."

In the ensuing pause, Rita slides a folder across the shiny surface toward him. "This might be a good time to review these documents."

Thin and seemingly harmless, the folder lays on the desk like a brick, unmarked and oppressive, the President regarding it as though it's poisonous to the touch. With a heavy hand he pushes it back.

"I'll... review it later. For now, I just want to get settled in."

"As you wish, sir." The Secretary of State takes the folder back and rests it in her lap.

The cabin pressure changes, and the door comes open with a whoosh, drawing Zimmerman's eyes toward the anterior fuselage as speakers above them crackle with static before a deep, professional voice fills the space.

"Attention passengers, this is your captain. Be advised we're ready for the President and his staff to disembark. Please do so at your leisure."

Nodding, Zimmerman stands and sweeps his hand toward the front of the plane. "Okay, folks. You heard the man. Go on and find your rides. I'll stay here for another minute or two."

The staff rises in a bustle of noise and motion, grabbing their briefcases and laptops before filing forward. As each leaves, the cabin grows quieter, dropping the president into a thoughtful silence that fit his mood. Rita and Rick exit, leaving just General Davidson and his personal staffer, Maxine, on the plane. The assistant stares at him, waiting for an order while the general toys with his phone.

"You can go, too, Mark. No need to hang around."

"Negative, sir. Protocol dictates that I stay with you at all times until the security level falls."

"Oh, yes. Well, I could use a drink." Zimmerman stands from his desk and strides to a serving table with glasses on top and a mini fridge beneath it. "Anyone else? Never mind. We'll all have a drink, and that's an order."

"You won't get an argument from me, sir," Davidson says as the pair follow him over.

The president pours two fingers of whiskey in each glass, adding ice cubes to Maxine's, then he presses a button and watches as a cover in the fuselage slides aside to offer a view of the bustling airport and city beyond.

Turning, he hands a glass to each, then lifted his in a toast. "Here's to new beginnings."

"Hear hear," Mark says, while Maxine only nods, eyes remaining locked on him.

Glasses clink and are tossed back, the president draining most of his, enjoying the delicate burn as the sweet liquor coats his throat and makes flames in his belly. Maxine sips hers while the general takes it a step farther and downed his with a single swallow, then holds up the glass in his large hand for another pour.

"We drink like this at every new beginning, we won't be able to function."

Chuckling, Zimmerman obliges him, and the three turn to capture what they can of the city through the vista window.

"We're involved in quite an operation here." With one arm folded across his chest, the president holds his liquor in front of his face, swirling the contents thoughtfully as the general agrees with a dignified grunt.

"No other administration has ever even imagined attempting something like this," Maxine says, her tone tracking the president's train of thought.

"Yes, but what's the cost, Max? We're annexing entire countries, forcing innocent people out of their homes, sometimes at gunpoint from what I hear."

The general grunts again and Zimmerman's eyes drift over the beautifully constructed historic blocks of Havana. "People from a different century erected those buildings. Will their ancestors, the citizens of this city, today, really see us as friends? Or will we still be enemies, and I'm just blowing smoke up my own backside?" With a light scoff, he shakes his head. "Likely, the latter."

"I'd say you're right on that point," Mark adds, already halfway through his second drink.

"So, does that make us the good guys or bad guys?"

"Probably a little of both."

"And that's how we justify what we're doing."

Maxine's eyes move back and forth between the two. "You're both good men. The best I've ever worked for. While none of this is ideal, it has to happen, and that's the bottom line. To be honest..." The words trail off as she draws her drink toward her stomach, retreating a half step.

"What is it, Max?"

"No," the woman curls in on herself. "It's not my place."

Zimmerman shakes his head, his mood lighter from the whiskey and open to ideas. "Please, speak your mind. You've never held back before."

The staffer glances up at General Davidson, who only shrugs. "Might as well."

"What I'm trying to say is that while your talks have been upbeat, I can't help but think things will get worse before they get better. The people of Havana won't welcome us with open arms. I expect there to be rebellion and fighting, and it'll happen no matter where we go."

Zimmerman's expression turns sour but amused. "So, I *have* been blowing smoke up my own backside."

The general winces with a knowing nod. "We've considered all that, and I'm right there with you, Maxine. People won't roll over just because we ask them to. I guess we were hoping things would go smoother than expected."

Zimmerman nods, part of him wanting to disagree with them, another part saying they are than right – they're spot on. "So, we're the bad guys, after all?"

"Not the bad guys." Maxine shrugs and downs the rest of her drink in one gulp. "Just the *strongest* guys."

CHAPTER THREE

Specialist Lance Morales
Santa Fe, New Mexico

The transport bucked and bounced along the icy road, trundling over swaths of densely packed snow that had slipped beneath the earth movers' massive, modified snowplows. After Albuquerque, they'd hopped on I-25 where the LeTourneau L-2350s, spread across all four lanes, their thirty-foot-wide plows cutting through the frozen drifts with jaw-rattling grinding sounds that caused Morales to cover his ears with his arms at every opportunity.

The turbocharged aftercooler diesel engines churned in a single collective growl as they sent sheets of snow and ice flying off to the sides in twin arcs of blinding whiteness twenty feet high. They caught tangles of trees and debris and crushed them together, wood bending, shrieking as it washed over the guardrail. The plows slammed aside cars and SUVs, moving big rigs with the sounds of cold, crunching metal and the smooth sliding of rubber wheels across ice. The trucks spun and smacked the guardrails and medians, trailers falling to pieces as their contents scattered in the road, no obstacle too large to withstand the sheer force delivered by the powerful machines.

From the back of the transport, Morales stared at the passing landscape, a nightmare of winter white that carpeted every inch of ground, suffocating trees, bending them, snapping them in two. Icicles the size of cave stalactites hung from the larger boughs, their shiny points forming a crystal wall above the tree line. One cracked away and plunged into the waiting snow like a dagger, piercing the white all the way to the frozen ground beneath it.

His gaze followed crests of ice-covered hills, the frosted, crusted edges sharp and glistening in the grayish midday sun as gusts of sleet blew through the air behind them in dervishes of whistling wind and stinging flakes of ice. Smith gave him a light punch in the arm and gestured upward. Lifting his eyes, the soldier looked up to spot a V-shaped flock of geese, their honks masked by the plows' incessant grinding.

A heady wind gusted through, briefly disrupting the formation and several animals fell out of place, drifting back and forth on the air current before falling dangerously low to the point Morales didn't think they'd catch up. One did a slow spiral downward and disappeared out of sight behind the tree line and a second animal nosedived and plummeted, wings barely flapping in the frozen sky.

"Jeez," Morales said with a heavy head shake.

"They migrated south too late!" Smith shouted. "They can't make the flight. Probably exhausted."

"Dying as they fly. Nature is completely screwed. At least here."

"I can't argue with that." The lieutenant's constant grin faltered, the corners of his mouth dragging downward.

"You think we'll ever see another summer?"

Smith's gaze dropped to the road where the convoy followed, spread out across a pair of lanes as it curved around the last bend out of sight. More vehicles had caught up to them after Albuquerque - Humvees and APCs for defense, bearing massive snowplows themselves in case they needed to split off or one of the LeTourneaus crapped out. Huge army supply trucks and troop transports trundled behind those along with tractor trailers carrying heavy bulldozers and backhoes. The convoy was moving at a leisurely 20 to 30 mph, though to Morales it sounded like they were going much faster as miles of I-25 slid beneath the heavy machinery, the vehicles sticking together on the cleared road.

Captain Jones, sitting in the front seat with the driver, shoved open the hatch door and shouted back with a clipped tone. "We're getting out at the next exit, folks. Be prepared to work." Then he slammed the door shut again with a clack.

One LeTourneau fell behind the other, switching from a side-by-side position to in-line. The entire convoy began a slow shift off the exit ramp as the resounding vibrations of the plows lowered in pitch, grinding over a different type of pavement. They merged into a single long line on the narrower ramp, taking a right toward an unknown town, following the LeTourneaus like ducklings behind their mother. Massive snowdrifts all but covered the one-story buildings, gas stations and stores identifiable only by parts of signs jutting up from the layer of white. A steak house sign stood tall on the right side of the road, the bull's head mascot just visible, a dusting of powder caught in the glass etching to give it a highlight. Side roads were impossible to navigate, blanketed in six or eight feet of snow topped in a hoary, crusty frost they could have walked on.

"There's no way we could handle these roads without the GPS and those big plows." Smith gave a low whistle.

"Yeah, this is insane," Morales agreed, voice filled with awe, finding it hard to believe anyone could have survived the deep chill lying over the land. His eyes shifted, moving up a snowbank the plows had added to, where he could barely see the tops of trees that were twenty feet high. "I wouldn't be able to tell where the streets are without the tree lines, and even those are almost buried or they just blend in so damn well amidst all this white."

A quarter mile along the two-lane highway brought the LeTourneau's grinding to a sudden halt, the grating, ear-bending sounds stopping, leaving a deafening silence hanging in the air for a moment before the murmuring began. Truck doors opened and slammed shut and a moment later, Captain Jones came around the rear and leaned over the tailgate, the lower half of his face covered in a wide, green scarf.

"All right, men. Everyone out. Let's go!"

"Where are we, cap?" Smith called as the soldiers filed out and climbed down onto the plowed pavement.

A swirl of icy snow whipped into Morales's eyes, the gust invading his bare skin through the small gaps in his clothing. With a shiver, he thrust his hands deeper into his pockets and walked away from the truck, turning to stare past the gargantuan plows that dwarfed everything around them. An extensive field of white stretched off the left side of the road, lumps of buildings bulging like soft pillow mounds, the connecting driveway buried in an intimidating crust of hoarfrost.

"It's a FEMA storage facility southwest of Santa Fe," the captain responded with a grin, "one of the big three in the United States. We're standing next to six large warehouses atop a nest of underground bunkers. How's that strike you?"

Smith came up to stand by Morales, gesturing at the field of white before scratching his head. "That's great, cap, but how do you expect us to reach it? I don't think we brought any sled dogs with us."

Jones gave his lieutenant a hard slap on the shoulder. "That's what you're for, soldier. We're going to dig our way to it, then uncover the buildings and secure the supplies. I'm told great treasures lie below ground. Let's break out the maps and start cutting smaller paths between the buildings. Lieutenant and the specialist, you're with me."

"Yes sir, cap," Smith said, throwing a glance and an elbow at Morales. "You heard the cap, we're bringing this warehouse back to life."

The team leads, specialists, and drivers gathered at the front of the truck, hovering over the warm hood and idling engine, a facility map spread out before them. Morales stared at the layout and glanced back often to marry their current position to what was on paper in his mind. Serious for once, Smith put his finger on the warm map, tracing a path from the road up to a pair of smaller squares that represented buildings. "Let's send one heavy up the main street with an excavator behind it, clearing the lot while carving out some of the side lanes. Once we have an idea of what's there, we can bring in the APCs to do the bulk of the work with teams of shovels and picks to finish the details."

"Spot-on, Smith." The captain raised his voice and spun his finger in the air. "Let's make it happen."

The second of the massive LeTourneaus backed up ponderously while another team unloaded the excavator from its place on a trailer bed before trying to get it started. Being twelve degrees below zero without the windchill didn't help matters, forcing the crew to warm the engine with heaters before it finally started, the throaty diesel sputtering and complaining the entire time.

Morales, rated to drive the excavator, climbed into the cab and followed the LeTourneau up the main road as it cleared a path to the buildings. He worked the joysticks gingerly at first as the hydraulics warmed up, using his bucket to catch piles of snow the bigger truck left behind, carving around the edges to widen the path between the lines of grass. Once the main plow reached the parking lot between the first two buildings, Morales uncovered the beginnings of a pair of side roads that encircled the grounds.

The excavator's tiny heater clattered away inside his cabin, giving a hot edge to the oil and hydraulic reek coming off the machine. After a while, a fine sweat coated his brow, and he tossed back his hood and cracked one of the windows to allow in some cold air for ventilation.

While the LeTourneau pressed deeper and APCs with smaller plows drove in behind them, two hundred bundled troops with shovels and picks in hand took up the rear, watching the machines work while they stayed huddled in groups, chatting amongst themselves. The APCs took up where Morales left off, shoveling the side roads to provide access points for machines and men around the warehouses. Following the first earth mover into the lot, he chipped away at one warehouse with his bucket, eyes narrowed at the front of the building, looking for the door. The steel teeth crunched through hoarfrost and snow, dumping massive amounts off to the side. Someone beeped, and he turned to see a dump truck had edged in behind him along with a second excavator.

Joining forces, the two diggers focused on one area, moving tons of snow and ice, dropping it into the truck bed with heavy crunches and white powder billowing everywhere. They filled the first dump truck, and it pulled off only to have another replace it. Morales reached as high as he could with the bucket, knocking off dangerous overhangs that might break off and hurt the soldiers working below. With the parking lot nearly cleared, the second LeTourneau drove up and made quick work of what snow remained before joining its brother at the next lot over. As the APCs and other heavy gear pressed by, cargo trucks idled in parking spots, waiting to be filled with supplies from inside.

Soon, the excavators reached the walking path and the stiff, frozen bushes along the building's front. Morales used his bucket to tap at the top edge of the wall, causing a section to break away and reveal the dirty beige cement beneath it. Once the dangerous spots up high were removed, a hundred soldiers swarmed the building with axes and shovels, chipping away like a group of coordinated dwarves working deep in the mines of Moria. Wheelbarrows were filled with snow, carted across the road, and dumped and within an hour, the soldiers reached the wall and were working their way toward the door.

"It *must* be here somewhere," Morales murmured, backing his machine up, parking it with the engine idling.

He climbed from the cab and grabbed a shovel from a tired soldier, stabbing and hacking at the stubborn snow along with the rest. The sharp edge of his tool banged a support pole for an awning, and he worked feverishly to dig beneath the narrower space. Stepping back, skin icy with frozen sweat, Morales let a few men finish the job, watching as they cut a swath to the front door where their tools tapped against the glass.

Captain Jones jogged up with a half dozen soldiers, Smith included in the bunch. The lieutenant handed Morales a flashlight, and he leaned his shovel against the wall and joined them. A security specialist went to work on the keypad adjacent to the door frame, opening the cover to reveal a faint green glow of numbers.

"The place still has enough electric for the security doors and some lights," Morales said to his friend. "They must have seriously strong batteries."

"And probably almost dead in this cold," Smith added.

Three seconds later, the door's deadbolts popped, and Captain Jones traded places with the specialist, pulling the door handle to release a gust of stale, warm air from the building that brushed across Morales's cheeks.

The soldiers filed in, flashlight beams cutting to the end of a dark hallway where a thick, steel door awaited them. Emergency lights radiated a dim glow, illuminating wooden doors and another cross hall. With an eager grin, Jones led them toward the metal door, pushing past the offices and janitor's closets, the soldiers following in a scuffle of boots, their hard rubber soles squeaking on the wet tiles. Morales kept close, shining his light into the cross hallway that ran the length of the building in both directions. They went straight for the metal door, though, hacked the security panel, and popped those locks as well. Jones, shaking with excitement, threw it open and strode inside, the soldiers filing in fast behind him, their shuffling boots suddenly echoing as if standing in a cavernous chamber. Flashlight beams pierced the gloom, pointing in all directions to chase away the shadows.

Morales stepped in last, having to push between Smith and the captain with an aggravated sound, trying to get a good view. He lifted his own flashlight beam, shining it across the open warehouse, stopping in his tracks as he stood, gaping with the rest of them.

CHAPTER FOUR

Tom McKnight
Nuevo Laredo, Mexico

"Shouldn't she be here by now?" Barbara whispered the question as they stood on a street corner on the holding facility's north side.

"Yes, but let's be patient. She'll be here any minute."

Shadows surrounded the niche between a crumbling concrete wall and a stubby pine tree, already showing signs of encroaching cold, its leaves brown and wilted where they hung from sagging branches. The sun still offered no relief from the chill, hidden behind the late day clouds, the air turning bitter and biting with sharp, unforgiving teeth. Tom watched refugees as they hustled between buildings, passing the pair with furtive looks, meeting their stares with equally hard ones, causing them to turn away and hurry past.

Barbara glanced over her shoulder. "I'm just worried about the kids. They shouldn't be left alone, not with these strangers around. And I'm not referring to the guards, though they're bad enough as it is."

"Sam's in charge, honey," Tom replied, looking toward the end of the street where three refugees whispered over a burn barrel filled with branches and twigs gathered from tree trimmings. A woman moved off, hustling into the thick clusters of ramshackle buildings and Tom tried to push aside the thought of trouble, shifting uncomfortably. "She's been through a lot the past few weeks. She can hold her own and then some. She'll keep them safe, trust me."

Barbara settled back, leaning against the tree with a pensive, glassy-eyed expression. "Oh, I know the kids are more than capable of taking care of themselves, especially Sam and Linda. I'm just worried about the long-term effects this will have on them."

Tom snorted. "Well, considering our youngest two kids lived through a firefight, saw their neighbors killed, and had to perform first aid on their mother.... Oh, don't forget they were kidnapped, too—"

"Twice!" Barbara scoffed.

"Oh yes, kidnapped twice, that's right. And Linda shot a man and tried to kill another by drowning *and* shooting him." Tom chuckled dryly. "Yes, I'd say you're right. There might be a *few* underlying issues we'll need to address down the road."

Barbara smiled at Tom's trademark sarcasm, then her expression fell. "And Sam lived through a stint at sea on a lifeboat, had to try to burn people alive to survive, watched her friend die before her eyes.... Oh, Tom, our children have experienced an entire lifetime in just a few short months, more than we ever did."

"Okay, fine. I guess they'll all be equally messed up." Tom put on a smile, though his eyes brimmed over with tears and he swiped at them with the back of his sleeve. "I'm just sorry about everything that happened to you and Linda and Jack. If I could have figured out Keith's game sooner, none of this would have happened. I'd have put the bastard six feet under and spared everyone the horrors he's inflicted."

"You can't blame yourself, honey," she replied, her tone soft. "You couldn't have predicted any of this. We'll just have to help our babies the best way we know how." Barbara came off the tree and threw an arm over his shoulder, chest and thighs pressing against him. A warmth flowed between them, her physical presence like a bombshell. With shut eyes, he gently bumped his head into hers to return the affection.

"I wouldn't worry about the kids too much." The voice broke from the other side of the fence, a shadow against the chain link. "They bounce back pretty well, especially when they have great parents."

Tom looked up to see a woman's slight form standing in military fatigues, a black beanie on her head, heavy Army coat smothering her waifish shape. In her hand, she gripped Smooch's leash, the dog prancing on impatient front paws, tail sweeping leaves and loose gravel across the pavement as the shepherd's dark, baleful eyes stared up at the pair, a soft whine repeating in her chest. Unable to stifle a brief grin, Tom glanced both ways before jamming his hands into his pockets and casually approaching the fence with Barbara at his side.

"Smooch!" Barbara said, keeping her voice quiet as she knelt and put her fingers through the chain link to accept excited licks from the animal.

Tom gave a terse nod. "Good to see you, Saanvi."

"You too, Tom. How are you guys holding up?"

"Same as before. Food's low, and it's getting colder by the hour. Not to mention the unsavory types we're locked in here with."

"Tell me about it," Patel replied hesitantly.

Tom gave her a stony stare. "What is it?"

The medic shifted from one foot to the other. "I got a meeting with Godwin, and she mentioned there are inmates from a minimum-security correctional institute in there with you."

Tom's jaw tightened. "What else did she say? Is there any way she can move us?"

"The camp is a total shitshow." Patel shrugged apologetically. "Forgive my French. Godwin is an outstanding commander, but she's losing control of things." Patel inhaled and let out a heavy breath, glancing left and right, lowering her voice even though there was no one around. "The guards are just... not good. Morale is dangerously low across the board. And her own commanders are undermining her authority at every turn. There won't be a transport to take you south anytime soon."

"So, we're going to sit here and freeze?" Barbara asked from her knees, fingers rubbing Smoooch's ears.

Hand already gripping the fence, Tom squeezed as a trapped

feeling rose inside him. "Did you ask her about letting everyone go?" "I mean, if she can't take care of us, then we have to be set free."

"That's what I told her, but she still wouldn't bite. Seems she's going to hold on to you until the last possible minute."

Raising on his toes, the weight of his glare pressed on the medic. "But what if that's too late?"

"It won't be," she replied, unaffected by the pressure. "She'll get the transports here, and they'll take you south to plead your case at another camp."

"That's an entirely different concern," Tom said, wondering how far their enemies were away from the holding facility. "I expect Keith and Banks to show up at any moment. If they do, and we're not gone..." The thought dangled as anger swelled in his chest, imagining their smarmy grins as they approached from the other side of the fence, the *free* side.

Patel frowned knowingly. "I haven't forgotten what you told me about those two and why you had to escape them."

Barbara stood and straightened "Can you help us escape?"

"That was going to be my next question," Tom said.

The medic leaned slightly away from the fence. "You know I can't do that. I've got a duty--"

"If you can't break us out of here, we'll be condemned to a death sentence," Tom argued with a glance back. "Not just us, but our kids, too."

"I don't appreciate the pressure tactics," Patel replied flatly, soft expression turning as hard as a statue. "I'm doing the best I can, given the circumstances. And you *did* hijack a military aircraft. That's hard to look past, even given your situation."

"C'mon, Saanvi... it's not our fault the plane crashed when it did. And it wouldn't have mattered if we were on it or not. I'm sorry... I don't mean to put pressure on you. You've really come through for us, and we appreciate it."

The medic's cheeks slackened into a rounded shape once more, eyes softening in rich brown color. "I know it's not your fault, but you're asking me to undermine my commander and friend. Not only is it wrong, but they could throw me in the brig for it... or worse."

Barbara moved closer to Tom as the wind picked up. "They wouldn't shoot you for something like that, would they?"

"Absolutely, they would," the medic said. "I haven't heard of that happening myself, but things are constantly changing. It's getting scary."

"They would definitely shoot someone," Tom agreed. "Particularly if that person's blatantly going against orders. Plus... us civilians are under martial law. Laws don't exist anymore, not like they used to."

Patel stepped back to the fence, eyes imploring. "Look, I'm on your side, but I've got my family to worry about, too. They're only protected because of my service. If I betray that by helping you escape..." The thought remained unfinished, along with a sense of inner turmoil.

"No, we can't ask you to do anything that would threaten your family." Barbara strained to keep an understanding tone. "But things are getting desperate in here. Every day we stay is another day of danger."

"I'll think of something." The medic's fingers reached out to rest on Barbara's where she clung to the chain link.

"There's something else, Saanvi." Tom glanced back to make sure no refugees stood within earshot. "Another reason why you have to hurry."

Face pressed closer to the fence, she nodded. "I'm listening."

"There's talk of dissent in the camp."

"What? Like, refugees planning to break out?"

"That's right."

"How many?"

"So far, less than a dozen, but the numbers are growing with the worsening conditions. They've got a couple of rifles, so the rumor goes, and they're preparing to fight. They could be part of the criminal element you were referring to."

"When will they make their move?"

"No clue, but you can expect violence sooner than later, and that timeframe will be shortened as the problems with food and weather compound. You mentioned the guards weren't so good."

"Morale is down, and they're not expecting a fight, for sure. They're disobeying orders, a few have even abandoned their posts, gone AWOL."

"Then do what you have to do, for your sake, too." Barbara pleaded. "But don't forget us. Please."

"Right, I won't." The medic's head shook, breath coming fast. Then, with a single deep sigh, she settled down and shifted to Tom. "I *really* appreciate the information. I'll run it up the chain and work hard to get you guys out of here."

"Thank you, Saanvi." Tom nodded, forcing a smile. "Anything you can do would be helpful."

With a faint nod, she looked around. "I'd better go."

"Right," Barbara said, falling to her knees in front of Smooch. "And we'll see *you* later, girl."

The dog whined and pawed at the chain link, then tried to press her muzzle through. Tom reached down with a genuine grin and stuck his finger in a gap to accept licks and nuzzles from the loyal animal.

"And we appreciate you taking care of our girl," he added. "If not for you, she'd be out wandering the desert alone, or dead."

"That part isn't a problem at all," Patel chuckled. "I've always loved animals, and she's a wonderful dog. I suspect it's because she has great owners."

"And receives plenty of love," Barbara smiled. "Thanks again, Saanvi. We owe you so much."

"No worries. Talk to you soon."

With that, the medic turned away, making a kissing noise to get Smooch to follow. At first, the dog was reluctant but allowed herself to be led away. Tom watched their only hope of escaping the holding facility without getting shot walk off.

Barbara clutched the fencing. "Think she'll help us?"

"No clue," he said with a shrug. "It's a lot of pressure to put on a young woman. If she goes to her superiors, they could stop the rebellion, though it might make us targets of the other refugees if they suspect we snitched."

"So, we need to watch our backs."

"Big time."

Hands interlocked, the pair retreated into the depths of the camp, avoiding people, working south through the back alleys and yards. They climbed over rubble from a missile strike and at the far end of the block they circled to the front of the crumbling pharmacy where the kids stood around a burn barrel, rubbing their hands close to the fire.

"There they are," Linda cried in relief.

"Yay!" Jack crooned, skipping over to embrace his mother.

Tom gave them both a hug, then headed to Sam. "How'd the watch go?"

The young woman broke from the barrel to stand nearby, arms folded, a serious expression on her face. "Fine, mostly. A few people came by wanting to share the fire, but I got them to go away. No sign of the *group*."

"Okay, good. I don't want us associating with them, especially now."

"I know, Dad. You told us, like, a billion times."

"Really? A whole billion? That's a lot. It might take me several days or weeks to say anything a billion times."

Sam rolled her eyes. "You know what I mean."

Tom quickly sobered, brushing off an amused chuckle as he ushered her toward the pharmacy door. "Okay, let's get inside. It's going to be dark soon, and we don't want to be out here in the cold."

Jack was the first one in, opening the boarded-up glass doors and moving into the sales floor. Tom had left the bell on the door as an alarm, and it jingled as they entered. The dated decor was from the 1950s with old posters for pharmaceuticals like Listerine, Pyrotone, and Placida, Tom estimating they were original prints, probably worth a fortune to the right collectors before the chill. Pictures hung further down on the wall, showing the first owner, Dr. Miguel Ortiz (1958) and the subsequent members of the family he'd passed the store on to; his son, his daughter, and a cousin who was the last proprietor, judging by the date scribbled on the photo.

Despite the store's vintage feel, it appeared to have been well kept with modern products. The rows of shelves were mostly looted of food, though they'd left behind toiletries, cleaners, brushes, and cosmetics. The pharmacy was stripped of valuable drugs except for a couple bottles of amoxicillin that had rolled beneath the counter. There were mild pain relievers, blood thinners, and others with names impossible to pronounce, none of which were of much interest given their situation.

After picking out the place to keep themselves safe from the cold and the other refugees, the McKnights had made modifications to the establishment, boarding up the big pane glass front window and using a pair of empty shelving units as a makeshift barricade for the door.

"A little help with this." Tom nodded to a row of shelving and took a position on one side. Barbara stood opposite him, and together they lifted the entire thing and slammed it firmly against the door. A screech of metal on tile caught his attention, and he spun to see the girls shoving the second set of shelves toward them. The parents jumped out of the way as the kids blew by, bashing the two pieces together with a bang before Sam straightened and dusted her hands off with grin.

"Nice work, ladies."

Tom gave a quick check to make sure they hadn't left any easy entry points and the family retired to the rear of the store, through the pharmacy door, and to an open living space that had been their home the past three evenings. Beds assembled from threadbare covers and army pillows sat on the floor back in the corner next to an old wood-burning stove, the highlight of the establishment and one of the main attractions for choosing the place. A single faucet above a utility tub spouted tap water of dubious quality, usable only after boiling, though better than going thirsty. Aside from their two primary amenities, the McKnights had made use of what pots and pans they found, making meals from meager military supplies plus other bits and bobs they'd scrounged from an adjacent storage room including three expired cans of beans and a tin of dry tea leaves well past the best use date. Still, they were flavorful enough to make hot drinks, and after adding a bit of sugar, perfect for taking the edge off the cold winter nights.

Tom nodded to the stove. "Sam, why don't you get the fire going?"

"I can do that," she said, moving to squat before the door and grabbing the poker from a nearby rack while Tom collapsed on a stool, elbows resting on a makeshift table with a door as its primary surface and two end tables as legs.

"Well, let's get you settled in for the night," Barbara told the youngest two kids. "What do you say?"

"Will you read to me?" Jack asked.

"I'd love to."

The two youngest McKnights pulled off their shoes but stayed fully clothed as they swept back the covers and climbed into the cold beds. Curled up, snuggling side-by-side, the children made exaggerated shivering noises as Barbara turned to a stack of books nearby. A few dozen rat-eared paperbacks had been left behind in the pharmacy, all of them in Spanish, though that hadn't stopped the ritual where his wife sat and read the lines with a questionable accent, the kids growing sleepy to the sound of her voice.

The gentle clatter of Sam's poker rustled in the background and she threw a few pieces of wood into the mix, shoving it around until flames leapt up before shutting the door with a soft clank. Waves of warmth began to pour from the stove as it started to heat up, filling the room, sending a shiver across Tom's shoulders. Barbara's voice read the delicate Spanish words and Tom's eyelids drooped, heart and mind floating in a dozy, exhaustion-induced state. His arms and legs hung loose, relaxed despite him being hungry and sore and worried about the approaching enemies. The nearness of his family was all he needed to see him through it all, the comforting sounds of them going about semi-normal activities, alive, safe and as content as their situation allowed.

Ten minutes later, Barbara's voice faded, and the kids' soft snores filled the room. That alone was its own kind of warmth, and Tom let out a sigh as his wife finished and came to sit across from him. Placing the book on the table, her index finger slipped from between the pages, allowing the heavy cover to fall shut with a gentle thump. The corners of her mouth were tight, though she was still beautiful, green eyes drawing him like a moth to a flame. Unable to resist, he reached out and tucked a lock of sandy dark hair behind her ear, fingers brushing her cheek as his hand withdrew. The gesture drew a shy smile from Barbara, shrinking her age by decades in an instant.

"So, how are you holding up?" he asked.

"I'm doing surprisingly well. I'm worried about things, and sad we lost the farm, but being together is just...." Head shaking, mouth moving without sound, she struggled with the words, then a glance at the kids gave her the resolution she needed. "Having us together is heavenly. Absolutely amazing. As much as I missed you two, I didn't realize *how* much I'd missed you."

He chuckled, hand slipping across the table to cover hers. "I was just thinking the exact same thing. It's crazy how much strength I draw from you."

Barbara bent and kissed the top of his hand, cheek brushing his skin before she straightened. "What do you think about what Saanvi said? Can she help us?"

"She *wants* to help, but I'm not sure she'll come through. There's a lot working against her. She has her own family to worry about, and the penalties if she's caught are pretty high."

"Well, I think we should wait for her. She'll come back with something."

"I can't say I agree with that. I vote we break out."

"You mean, join up with the rebellion?"

"No, that's not what I meant. I--"

Finished with the fire, Sam sat heavily on a rickety crate beside her mother, resting a shoulder against the older woman as the wood creaked beneath her weight. Barbara raised an eyebrow at Tom, eyes shifting to her daughter.

"What do you think?"

A perplexed expression crossed Samantha's face, brow wrinkling in confusion. "You're asking *me*?"

Tom shrugged. "Why not? You're in the thick of this with us, and you're not a little girl anymore. What's on your mind?"

Red rushed to Sam's cheeks, shoulders straightening as she formed a response. "I like Saanvi a lot. She patched us up and takes good care of Smooch. She wouldn't have done any of that if she didn't care. We should wait for her help."

"I'm not saying she doesn't care," he agreed, "or that she wouldn't help us if the opportunity presented itself. I'm just not sure it *will* ever happen. Regardless, we need a plan to break out, just *us*, just in case we need a backup. The weather's getting colder every day. Blowing open the anomaly will fully stall the North Atlantic Drift – assuming that hasn't already happened – putting us on the cusp of an ice age." Tom sagged forward, running a hand through his greasy hair as the weight of his words fell fresh upon his shoulders. "Remember what we talked about in the tunnel, Sam? I don't think it's a possibility anymore. I think it's happening. Right now. We're looking at the end of the Holocene Epoch and the emergence of a new one."

Sam leaned in closer to her mother as Tom continued. "Warmth's hard to come by and food's running low. There might come a day we have to fight the other refugees for it, and that's when things will get *really* ugly."

"You're not wrong, I'll give you that much," Barbara gave Sam a squeeze.

"You make it sound pretty bad, Dad."

"Sorry. I don't want to scare you, but we're we'll past platitudes and assurances." He looked at Barbara. "I need you – both of you – to see what we're facing here. Waiting could mean dying."

"Okay, how about this? Let's give Patel two more days to figure something out. If she doesn't come through by then, we'll blow this popsicle stand."

Sam's head bobbed in agreement, though her heavy exhale quivered with uncertainty, green eyes shifting to her mother as if to gain strength.

"It's a deal," Tom said, reaching out to clasp both their hands. "And two days will give us the time we need to build a foolproof plan. Sounds perfect to me."

CHAPTER FIVE

Specialist Lance Morales
Santa Fe, New Mexico

Sounds echoed deep inside the cavernous warehouse, the sound of footsteps and whispered conversations bouncing off the racks of shelves and concrete walls. Breaths came in frosted spurts as flashlights streaked upward and across the literal tons of frozen supplies, all sealed in boxes or on skids wrapped in plastic. The two massive columns of racks, thirty or forty rows of them, ran in both directions, reaching six stories high to the warehouse roof with more than enough space for forklifts to maneuver.

Smith whistled low. "Jackpot, boys."

"This way." Captain Jones strode ahead to the main aisle, which stretched from east to west, the full length of the facility, taking a right, moving toward a faint white light at the far end. Morales looked up at the frozen racks of products branded as *Rice, Legumes, Freeze-dried eggs, Freeze-dried fruit, batteries, Cold Weather Rations,* and more. Frost covered some packages, making their labels unreadable and barrels of water were stacked to the ceiling, almost all burst open, leaving ten foot icicles as thick as Morales's leg dangling from the shelving units.

Seventy-five yards away, they reached a wide space with a dozen forklifts plugged in, their charging lights as lifeless as the building. Two pickup trucks sat parked against the wall in front of a pair of garage doors twenty-five feet high and the far wall held a smattering of windows, stretching at intervals and illuminated by thin slivers of emergency lighting. Signs for cleaning supply closets, lockers, and break rooms hung on the doors, thin layers of snow and ice covering them all.

Jones angled for the first door on the left as two soldiers anticipated his move and jogged ahead, rifles up as they came to stand on either side of the door, ready to cover the captain. Morales figured none of them expected an ambush given the situation in the warehouse, but caution and training prevailed regardless of the circumstance.

The lieutenant eyed the door, then nodded and one man grabbed the handle and jerked it open while two filed inside, their mounted lights sending beams into the room, cutting through the pitch darkness as they swept the corners.

"It's clear, Cap," one shouted, voice shaky and low. "But you won't believe it, sir."

The captain shot a look over his shoulder at Smith, and the lieutenant shrugged and waited for their leader to go ahead. Jones stepped in, head swiveling, eyes darting around and Morales followed the others into the room, shouldering his way to the left for a better view. Six beams lit the open space, showing cabinets, a refrigerator, a coffee maker, and a sink, water having frozen in the broken spigot, a long icicle reaching down to the drain.

Ignoring the paraphernalia in the room, their lights converged on the center where five forms huddled on the floor. Covered in thick, all-winter coats, gloves on hands, hoods pulled tight over their faces, they sat in perfect frozen stillness in the dark. A shudder streaked from Morales's knees to the nape of his neck at the sight, and he glanced over at Smith who stood stock-still, jaw open.

"This place is a tomb." Smith whispered the words as he stared at the corpses.

Jones stepped closer, reaching for one hood to pull it back, the material cracking like rice paper, taking off a frozen, crackling swath of hair with it. With a disgusted grunt, he turned and addressed the others in the room.

"Smith, take Brozowski and LaPlante and get the bay doors open. Look for survivors while you're at it." The three nodded and left the room with the captain shouting after them. "And see if you can salvage some forklifts from the warehouse area. Warm them up, charge them, and try to put them to use. It'll make this a helluva lot easier."

Morales returned to staring at the dead, strolling around the group, the sounds of the outer doors cranking up comforting him as he stared at the frozen faces, blue cheeks and fleshy noses, eyes open and shiny as glass. Packs of ration bins sat in boxes behind them, snack wrappers and empty containers piled in the corner of the room. A couple of the figures were leaning against each other, others against the wall or desks, their forms slouched over as though they had died in their sleep.

"Look at this, Cap. There's food all around them, so they didn't starve." Morales pointed to a circle of bricks with paper and wood scraps crumpled and charred in the middle. "It looks like they had a fire going, but not for long. Yeah, they must have froze, or died from carbon monoxide poisoning or smoke inhalation maybe, yeah?"

"Or dehydration." The captain kicked a frozen water bottle across the room to smack against a cabinet.

Barely breathing, Morales stepped between two of the dead, leaning over, reaching inside one of the coats to pull out an ID card. "And look. Government IDs. They were probably working in the building or somewhere in the area when the heavy snows trapped them." Blood running cold, he frowned. "They must have huddled in here once the power went out."

"Yeah, that's what it looks like." Jones looked across the stiff figures then spun and pointed at the remaining soldiers in the room. "Get some burn barrels going near the entrance. I want people near a fire every fifteen minutes, and I want men assigned to keep them fed with whatever they can scavenge. You hear me? No exceptions. I won't tolerate any complaints about frostbitten toes or fingers. It'll be so damn toasty around here you'll have sunburns before the end of the day." Chuckles echoed down the line. "Now, get out there and spread the word. Make it happen!"

"Yes, sir!"

Morales followed the others from the break room, glancing back once at the huddled forms, shivering at their dreaded fate. Out on the floor, Smith and the officers had raised the bay doors and were chipping away at the wall of snow and ice piled on the other side. A soldier came in lugging a thirty-gallon tote and slammed it on the concrete, tossing the top to the side. The soldiers flocked to it, hands digging inside for the military grade heat packs, ripping them open, stuffing them into coats and gloves, taping them around legs beneath cold-weather pants. Morales covered his vital spots and jammed two packs into both sides of each boot. Activated by his movements, warmth blossomed in his clothing as he joined Smith at the ice wall.

Taking a pick from the lieutenant, he and thirty other soldiers broke apart the ice as plows and trucks chipped away on the other side. Burn barrels sprung up throughout the warehouse casting a bright orange glow wherever he looked, and at first the fires and heat packs seemed like overkill, but with the bay doors thrown wide open, and the wind penetrating gaps in the snow wall, Morales saw how paltry their defenses truly were against the elements.

Cheeks stinging, fingers growing numb despite the warmth of his gloves, he kept swinging, careful not to get too sweaty. Steel picks and shovels whacked against the ice, and soon the entire floor was filled with loose chunks of it. Wood burned, men shouted, and the powerful diesel machines on the other side dug closer. After an hour, Smith let his pick head drop with a clang, panting as he gestured toward the center of the warehouse. "Come on. Let's take a break."

Not wanting to argue, Morales followed the lieutenant to a burn barrel, resting his pick against the warm metal before ripping off his gloves. Frigid hands up to the fire, he tucked his chin into his coat and focused on getting warm while Smith chatted with a pair of soldiers nearby at another barrel.

"They found more bodies in two of the locker rooms." Smith

removed his own gloves and laid them over his arms, head shaking dismally. "All frozen, just like the ones in the break room."

"They had power to the security systems and lights, but not to the HVAC units?"

"Nope. Without heat, it was only a matter of time till they froze."

Soldiers brought more bins filled with thousands of heat packs and dropped them onto the warehouse floor and Morales and his friend hurried over to exchange their expired packs for new ones. All warmed up again, the pair returned to the wall, attacking it with their tools, cheering with the rest of the men when a bulldozer's teeth broke through, collapsing the massive barrier in an avalanche of crystalline rubble. More bulldozers and wheelbarrows came to haul the chunks away until troops from the other side stepped through to greet their friends with high-fives and nods. Many made a beeline for the burn barrels, stripping off frozen gloves, rubbing hands vigorously in front of the flames as others brought armfuls of office furniture and broken-up pallets, stuffing the barrels full to keep the flames high.

As a path cleared to the outside, the eighteen wheelers backed in, doors thrown open wide to receive supplies and the soldiers stepped aside, gathering around the burn barrels as the machines took up the brunt of the work. Forklifts buzzed to life as six out of the dozen they'd found inside still worked, and drivers steered them into the rows and extracted goods from the tops of the tall racks. Another two forklifts entered from the Army's supply and joined the other six in grabbing pallet upon pallet, trundling up ramps and careening into the trailers, shaking them on their springs, dropping loads at the far end with a bang before backing out to get more.

A chorus of mechanical whines echoed through the warehouse space as oil and fresh electric ozone permeated the air and even with the wide-open bay doors, the stench of diesel fuel filled the air. An occasional crash or clatter of metal resonated as the operators sometimes brushed each other in the crowded lanes, and there were shouts from grunts and officers alike that echoed through the facility as goods were sorted through, selected and loaded up.

When a truck was filled to bursting, it pulled away and got back in line, ready to head out with the convoy. Empty trailers backed in to replace each one, the forklifts swarming around them like ants. Food and medical supplies were the priority of the day - pallets full of vaccines, antibiotics, and anything the cold wouldn't destroy were hauled away to the trucks first.

Captain Jones left the break room and strode across the warehouse floor, eyes on a swivel as he overlooked the operation, sometimes pointing at something to be done, other times shouting into a 2-way radio on his belt. Slowly but surely the racks emptied, and the trucks bulged with supplies, the number of full trucks starting to look more substantial.

The captain spoke into his handheld radio and then listened to the reply, nodding as he absorbed the information. When he was finished, he shouted to those assembled around the fires. "Okay, men, this warehouse is about dry, so let's clear a path to the next one. Smith and Morales, you're on point again."

Charged by their first success, Morales stepped outside between the eighteen wheelers and gathered the drivers to him where they stood beside one of the gargantuan LeTourneaus, one man holding the facility map out for him to find the best way through.

"Right here." Finger tracing a path from their current location and up a service road, he showed them where to go. "Take one LeTourneau along here and into the next warehouse's rear lot. I'll take the excavator and Smith's men and clear the entrance just like before. A two-pronged attack on both sides. Let's go!"

After receiving positive nods from the drivers, Morales stomped into the warehouse, calling soldiers to him as he exited the front of the building and climbed into his excavator. Engine already running, he buckled himself in and flicked the joysticks, jerking the machine to life. Trailing fifty men with picks and shovels, he drove up the pre-plowed path to the next building over.

The teeth of his bucket cracked the ice and snow as he dug toward the entrance. Dump trucks pulled in behind him, and he filled one with tons of frozen debris in just a few minutes. Burn barrels sprung to life, faint orange glows dotting the parking lot, soldiers operating in shifts to cut the path while staying warm. Morales worked himself into a trance, hands shifting with a smooth fluidity only someone who appreciated the machine's power could attain and an hour passed in what seemed like a few seconds as they clawed their way toward another treasure trove. Just as he reached the front walkway, a soldier stepped into his vision and waved for him to stop. He reluctantly stilled the excavator as Smith jogged up, the lieutenant climbing the steps to his cabin, shouting in through the half-open window.

"Hey, we need to shut things down!" He made a cutting motion across his neck with his hand.

"What are you talking about? We just got started!" Morales shouted back, motioning toward the mounds of snow he planned on eviscerating.

"New orders! Jones got word of a spin-up storm heading our way."

"What the hell's a spin-up storm?"

"Sub-arctic freeze, high winds, real bad news. They're ordering us to seek shelter *immediately*. Cap is pulling everyone inside the first warehouse bay, even the rigs."

"All right, man. I'll wrap things up."

Smith glanced at his wrist. "You've got ten minutes to get your butt inside, then we're closing the door. You don't want to be out here when that happens."

Morales nodded. "I read you loud and clear."

The lieutenant jumped off and ran at the soldiers, waving his arms emphatically, pointing toward the first warehouse as he repeated his instructions. The excavator and dump trucks turned and shifted backwards, waiting for everyone to move out of the way. Leaving burn barrels and wheelbarrows behind, the troops sprinted across the icy parking lot to the original building's entrance. Despite a mere distance of one hundred and fifty yards, the going was slow, men laden in heavy winter gear while the machines trundled along after them.

Through the window crack, a snippet of wind cut across Morales's forehead, bringing with it a sting that caused him to stiffen in his seat. While they'd been working in Arctic temperatures for several hours, his skin long having gone clammy and cold, the recent wind was something different. It bit against his skin, sucking the warmth from the cabin, leaving his breath gusting against the windshield. The winds kicked up, brushing the top of his machine, shaking it, rattling metal on metal, drops of ice assaulting the glass, some flying inside, stinging his cheeks until he rolled the window up fully.

As the soldiers entered the first warehouse, Morales continued on, driving the excavator toward the side road the big plows had cut to the rear of the building, but the entire convoy was trying to escape the storm, and traffic was packed tight. He pulled in behind an eighteen-wheeler and waited, the seconds passing slowly, and he sat there glancing nervously at the sky, watching as multi-colored, black and gray and white clouds converged on them from at least three sides. Fighting the urge to abandon the vehicle and make a run for it, Morales remained where he was, leg jiggling up and down nervously until the line finally moved, trucks inching toward the back doors, crawling to safety.

Ice chips sprayed his windows as if trying to break through and shred his flesh and the excavator's framework groaned as a powerful gust of wind shoved against it. In another thirty seconds, the bay doors came into view and he pressed forward, jaw clenched as the brutal winds marched across the rear lot, sending dervishes of snow and ice flying everywhere. Without a watch, Morales didn't know how much time had passed, or how much remained, fingers tapping on the joysticks as his stomach twisted into knots.

"Has to only be two or three minutes before the storm hits us," he mumbled, looking through the windows of the excavator at the rapidly-darkening sky. "Four, at most. I'm a dead man. I won't make it."

The traffic broke as the soldiers got the hang of guiding the trucks through the bay doors. One by one they slipped inside, entering smoothly to disappear from sight. Soon it was Morales's turn, and he maneuvered the excavator into the first bay along the first row of empty racks. Breathing a sigh of relief, he followed the retreating soldier who waved him in and then shifted to point him down the main aisle. As he was making the turn, a forklift flew in from out of nowhere, and he jerked the machine to the right, bumping the rack and shoving it toward the next one, the soldier nodding vigorously and spinning his finger in the air.

Morales narrowed his eyes in confusion. "Again?" he shouted, circling with his own finger. Then he rolled down his window a crack, shouting. "You want me to push them out of the way?"

"Yeah! They're empty! Just shove the bastards aside, or we'll never fit everyone in!"

Backing the excavator up, glancing back to make sure he didn't kill anyone, he angled the machine right, placed the bucket against the rack and nudged it across the concrete floor as it squealed in protest. He bumped the ends of the first two rows together, the groaning racks slamming tight, yet he kept pushing until both curved inward toward row three, then he backed up, shifting to his right again, kicking the excavator forward to zipper the middle section. Above the squealing and clanking metal, shouts went up and forklifts whined, soldiers shoving burn barrels and loose pallets aside to make room for the remaining trucks. A bulldozer flew in behind him and tried to squeeze in beside the next column of racks, its fender clipping the edge of the row, causing it to tip dangerously. The soldier who'd been guiding him screamed for the driver to stop, but the panicked man whipped the wheel and kept his foot on the gas. The first rack shifted and bowed, the thin support rails flimsy without thousands of pounds weighing it down. Somewhere in the middle, the lock-fit pieces snapped apart and collapsed the entire framework against the next three consecutive racks, causing them to fall inward like dominoes.

Soldiers scattered as empty wooden pallets toppled from the higher rows to shatter into splinters. A forklift shot from where it had been tucked in, barely avoiding being crushed as a clatter of metal hit the concrete in a spray of chips and cracks. After six rows, the destructive momentum slammed against a rack bolted to the ceiling and floor, abruptly halting the collapse before it took out half the warehouse. Hands shaking, Morales continued compressing the first column as the last of the trucks filed in behind him. A heavy flurry of wind, snow, and ice chips chased them inside, the brutal winds kicking up like a storm at sea.

Men's hoods blew back from their heads, ears glowing red from the instant frostbite. Still, they bravely guided the trucks in, trying to organize the parking in the freezing chaos. The last of the Humvees and utility vehicles buzzed inside, angling sideways to fit in whatever small space remained. Soldiers grabbed the bay door chains and jerked them hand-over-fist, dropping the massive steel doors as the spin-up storm slammed the warehouse full-force.

Gusts of freezing wind whipped through the ever-shrinking opening, sweeping men off their feet, shoving them together where they toppled in heaps. As soon as the door's rubber lips touched ground, the segmented metal bowed inward, groaning and bulging as wind whistled between every gap it could find.

Morales leapt from the excavator's cabin, boots hitting the floor with a thud. He immediately ran to a man who'd been blasted over by the gale and hauled him backwards until his back struck something hard. Feet sliding from beneath him, half bowed over, his eyes widened as the entire warehouse groaned under the cyclonic pressures. The ceiling made a fluttering, popping sound as if a thousand small stones were hitting it, the big steel I-beams creaking, struggling to hold the superstructure together.

Soldiers turned slowly in the new darkness, flashlights flitting across the walls like fireflies as they stared up at the deadly sounds, gripping each other's arms, half squatting, cowering beneath the immense display of pressure and turbulence. A single, brutal gust struck the warehouse hard, every atom shuddering and quivering as it threatened to fly apart and crash on their heads. The wind faded in a teasing way, rising and falling as it died down. It backed off, petering out, then grew into a steady current that pressed a continuous yet manageable bulge into the bay doors.

Body relaxing, Morales exhaled the breath he'd been holding and he climbed to his feet, gripping the arms of the man he'd been helping and lifted him up, the pair leaning on each other for support. Taking a flashlight from his coat, he shined it into the man's frightened face, jaw-dropping when he saw the edges of his ears and earlobes blackened from the cold winds that had struck them.

"Come on, man, let's get you a medic."

Shaken, he led the frostbitten man through the milling soldiers, striding across the massive bay filled with Army vehicles, arm raised as he called repeatedly for help. Finally, a medic with the Red Cross on his hood took the man off his hands just as Lieutenant Smith approached with his flashlight beam shining in his eyes.

Hand up, Morales scoffed in aggravation. "Knock that off, will ya?"

"Oh, sorry." Smith lowered the light and fixed him with a shaken gaze. "You holding up okay after all that?"

"Yeah, I think so." The constant rattling set his nerves jangling despite the protective mountain of snow around them, protecting the warehouse as much as it was pressing against it. "I just hope the place holds up."

"It probably will."

Morales gestured at the wall with the doors, leading Smith away from the chaotic bustle of men and machines. "Why do you say that?"

"I'm thinking this isn't the first storm that blew through." The lieutenant's gaze shifted along with his flashlight, lungs drawing a deep but uncertain breath. "And it didn't fall on *them*."

Morales turned and followed the beam into the gloomy break room where the lonely workers were still huddled together in a circle around their cold fire, frozen water bottles and discarded food wrappers scattered everywhere, their forms passive and immobile. Stomach sinking with raw dread, he looked to his friend, sharing a look of impending doom.

CHAPTER SIX

Keith
Houston, Texas

The stubby-looking Bristol Freighter with its fat nose and high cockpit taxied toward them, swinging its wide body around as the massive twin propellers buzzed, vibrating the air with sheer power as the Hercules 734 air-cooled piston engines prattled and thundered, the smell of oil and fuel permeating the air. The fuselage was coated in camouflage that was worn from age, and spare fuel tanks mounted under the wings. Beneath the high cockpit was painted the languid form of a leggy pin up model wearing a flowered dress, legs gently crossed and staring across the runway with wide blue eyes. Dark locks flowed over her silky pale shoulders, her pouting red lips poised in a kiss and above her was scrawled *Lucky Lady* in perfect comic-style lettering.

"How do you know these people?" Banks repeated herself, the corners of her mouth drawn into an uncertain frown. They were standing outside a hangar at the end of the runway, a black SUV behind them with a pair of burly MPs keeping guard.

"We worked together on a few unofficial missions in countries nobody's ever heard of." Keith shrugged nonchalantly. "They're rough. *Very* rough, but they can get the job done."

"How can they do what we can't?"

With a scratch of his head, Keith stepped from the hangar's protection, pulling his coat tighter around his shoulders, shivering as he gestured for Banks to follow. "They've got resources, experience and – most importantly – they can do things we might find 'questionable.'"

"Doesn't sound like a smart gamble to me." Banks followed a little behind him, watching the circling plane as it taxied around. "I'm already wishing we hadn't gone down this road."

Keith scoffed. "What other choice did we have? What other road could we have taken? It's not like we have the access we used to. Hell, you can barely get anyone to get you a coffee anymore."

A growl came from deep within Banks' chest. "I get it. But I still don't like it."

"I understand." He folded his arms across his chest. "But have no fear, this group is the best I've ever worked with. As long as we deliver on our end, we won't have any problems."

The freighter pulled within thirty yards of Keith and Banks and drew to a stop, the props spinning down as the back door behind the wing flipped open. A set of stairs uncurled and hit the ground with a clack on the hard, cold concrete and four figures began to descend the steps. The first was a short, stocky man in rough travel clothes of brown and green, his entire form filled with a cocky confidence, his gaze searching around, taking in everything with a keen, practiced eye. A tall, lithe woman came out next, a bright blonde ponytail bouncing against her leather-clad back. The outfit hugged her slim form, complimenting long legs and slender hips, and her neck bore tattoos of digital code tracing up the side while exotic, flowery scent drifted off of her, detectable even in the strong winds.

The next was a slight-framed man dressed like the first, only he wore his light brown hair slicked fashionably back with an expensive pair of sunglasses perched on his nose. A massive shadow filled the exit as the final figure emerged, pausing at the top of the stairs. His thick, sloped brow turned slowly, the gray eyes beneath it scanning his surroundings, settling on Keith and Banks, sending uncomfortable shivers down both of their spines. His shoulders stretched a tattered wool sweater tight, suspenders taut against his body, tree trunk legs covered in combat fatigues which were tucked into thick boots.

"What the hell is *that* thing?" Banks whispered as she shifted, taking an involuntary step back. "He's not even wearing a coat."

"That *thing* is a Dmitri." Keith whispered back to her, then smiled as the group drew closer, hand reaching to shake hands with the first man who had emerged from the plane.

"Hello, Serge. It's been too long."

Serge's gaze raked over the pair as he accepted the handshake, searching for weaknesses and making judgments and assessments in seconds.

"It's good to see you again." The man spoke perfect English, though his European accent was thick with mysterious inflections, hiding his exact origins.

Keith nodded to the others as they approached. "Lena and Mikael," he said, giving them a genuine smile in spite of his twisting insides. The woman gave a terse nod, and the man with the slick blonde hair grinned wider. Looking beyond them to the massive pair of stomping boots, Keith's smile faltered a hair as he called out.

"And how could I forget you, Dmitri, my big Russian friend?" The giant grunted as he came up but didn't smile or otherwise show an iota of emotion, standing behind his comrades with his massive arms crossed over his chest.

"Long time, no see, Keith." The woman's accent was also thick, words bubbling from the back of her throat with a slavic edge, the unique tattoo on her neck twisted elegantly as she stood next to the leader with her feet shoulder width apart.

"Too long," he agreed, gesturing at the lieutenant colonel. "Everyone, this is my boss, Colonel Banks. We need your help."

"Why else would you have called?" Serge asked. "No one ever calls us to do shots or have beer."

"That's true," Keith laughed as the tension hung on a proverbial tightrope.

"Who is this Banks?" One of Lena's fine eyebrows arched above her tinted sunglasses. "What do you do?"

"That's not important," the Colonel replied stiffly. "All you need to know is that I'm good for the payment we promised you."

Keith cringed internally as the tall woman stepped forward, lifting her glasses to reveal a pair of sea-green eyes that bored into Banks, the women eying each other carefully.

"It matters to me," Lena replied, tone accusative. "While you don't wear their uniform, I smell US military all over you." Her nose wrinkled, lip curling as she made sniffing noises in Banks's direction.

"Is that supposed to be an insult?"

"It is not a compliment, for sure."

"What she is asking," Serge said, "is are you active military?"

"What if I am?" Banks heaved a disappointed sigh. "Keith, I thought you said these people were tough."

The lithe woman sauntered up to the lieutenant colonel, mirroring her stance, fists on her hips and sunglasses perched on her forehead. "We are not afraid. But we don't work with scum." The giant behind her grunted his agreement, and the other two men spread out a bit, watching Banks and Keith closely.

Banks spread her arms and shrugged. "If you want to get paid, you'll work with me. If not, you can get back on your plane and head back to wherever it is you came from."

Keith edged toward the pair, hands up in a conciliatory gesture, trying desperately to defuse the situation. "Guys, this is a black ops mission. Strictly off the books. What does it matter if we're Army, Navy, or attorneys for the IRS? Especially under the current circumstances. We have what you need, so let's get on with it, eh?"

"Lena, it's okay." Serge reached out and took her by the elbow, gently guiding her back to the group before turning to stare down Keith. "A friend of Keith's is a friend of ours. We've been on so many missions together, I think we can trust him. Can't we?"

"I trust no one." The first words from the gargantuan Dmitri dropped like a bomb on the gathering, his tone as deep as a bottomless pit, accent so thick it was hard to imagine that he could speak much more than a handful of words in English or any other language.

"You know me, my friend." Serge patted Dmitri's arm, a calm

expression on his face. "I also do not trust people so easily, but let's at least let them give us the details."

Keith looked at the Colonel, giving the woman a hesitant nod, feeling his blood pressure dropping as the four mercenaries relaxed their stances.

"Okay, then." Banks clapped her hands together one time and continued. "I need a family brought in. It has to be done cleanly, quietly and with no casualties – especially any US troops."

"Who are these people?" Serge asked.

"Their names are Tom and Barbara McKnight, and they have three children. They're currently somewhere south of the frozen zone, though not sure where. I do have a solid lead for you to start with, though."

"What are they, special forces, or agents of the US government?" The swarthy Mikael spoke, his youthful voice lilting upward like a musical note. "Do they have something you require?"

"The man is a scientist." Banks replied. "An engineer, to be exact. The woman is his wife."

Mikael scoffed and the group – minus the giant – shared amused glances amongst themselves. "So, no challenge for us? Just a routine civilian pickup? Keith, why the hell do you need us for such a simple job?"

Banks's tone lowered ominously, tinged with a hint of aggravation. "They've proven... tough to bring in."

"Oh, really? Who did you send after them?" Lena scoffed. "How can *children* provide any challenge?"

"They got past *me*, okay?" Keith replied, annoyance bubbling in his chest as he relived his experiences with the McKnight's in a flash of remembrance. "Their kids are no joke, either. They're all resourceful and slipped through my fingers a few times."

"Not hard to do given your condition," Serge snorted at Keith's bandaged hands.

Lena looked him up and down. "Are they good at fighting?"

"No."

"Can they shoot?"

"They're not marksmen."

"How did they evade you?" She chuckled. "Please, tell us, so we can be prepared to lose like you."

Bandaged fists clenching at his sides, wincing from the pain, he fought to grant them an even-keeled reply. "My hands were tied much of the time, and they got lucky."

The mercenaries' eyes stuck to him, dancing with amusement, holding back snickering laughter and even the giant's mouth was pulled tight in a thin, quivering grin. Just when Keith thought they'd give him more grief, the woman retreated behind Serge and folded her arms across her chest.

"To be clear," Banks continued, "I need them brought in alive, though if the goods are damaged it's no skin off my nose."

"At least we get to have a little fun," Mikael stated flatly.

"Let's talk payment." Serge gestured. "Do you have what we discussed?"

Banks stepped forward, drawing an envelope from her pocket, handing it to the leader who took the package and passed it to Lena. She opened the unsealed top and removed a slip of paper with codes and an old-style set of keys. Holding those in one hand, she retrieved a handheld computer from the inside of her coat and thumbed in the codes. The group stood in uncomfortable silence as she looked back-and-forth between the page and the results on her screen until she finally nodded, folded everything up, and placed the bundle in her jacket.

"The information appears accurate. These are the coordinates to a bunker we have previously known about, and the access codes and keys appear to be legitimate."

Banks nodded smugly. "As promised, that'll lead you to King's ransom of weapons, ammunition, and medical supplies. And that's just the upfront payment. You'll have access to nine more bunkers once you bring in McKnight and his family."

"Am I to understand that this is probably one of those 'sensitive' missions too dirty for even our American friends?" Serge smiled, his dark eyes shifting between the two. "One that cannot be tied back to them?"

"That's right," Banks nodded. "It must be done with the utmost secrecy and discretion."

"Sounds good to me." Lena shrugged and shifted her stance.

"Easy peasy, as you Americans say," Mikael added with a laugh, Dmitri grunting his agreement from the back.

Serge stepped forward and offered out his hand, but Banks hesitated. "There is... one more thing."

The merc leader dropped his hand, his smile following suit. "What is it?"

A gust of icy wind blew between them, snatching at Banks's words. "You'll need to take Keith with you."

"Excuse me, what was that?" Serge leaned in, feigning confusion.

"You heard me. Keith goes with you."

Keith's face blanched and his blood turned cold. The group of east European mercenaries were used to working solo, and they weren't particularly fond of him – or anyone, really – despite Keith's earlier business dealings with them.

"We do not need middle management looking over our shoulders," Serge said with a snide sneer in Keith's direction. "No deal."

"Then you won't be getting the supplies." Banks shrugged casually. "Though from what I hear, things aren't exactly going well in your part of the world. Sure would be a shame to miss out on so much you could sell off to the highest bidder."

Lena stepped forward and gave Keith a rough shove on the shoulder, snarling at him. "Is this your doing, you snake?"

The agent absorbed the blow, stifling a reflex to return a swing, hands thrown up in exasperation. "No way! I had nothing to do with this! I didn't even know, I swear!"

"Then why?" Serge shifted his eyes to Banks, folding his thick forearms across his chest. "Why would you require him to go with us? I thought you didn't want our work to be traced back to you?"

"We have the codes. Let's raid the bunker." Lena's thin lips curled with resentment. "One bunker for our trouble, time and wasted fuel. That should cover it."

"I'll change the codes," Banks smiled coldly, "and ensure you never see the outside of a cell – or a grave – again. In spite of rumors to the contrary, our military machine is fully functional. I'm sure a few teams would love an excuse to get away from dealing with logistics so they can hunt you down. Assuming you were to escape, of course." Keith had to forcibly keep his mouth closed, taking a full step back as he stared at Banks in shock as she opined in a matter-of-fact, almost bored tone of voice.

The dismal sky darkened as clouds moved in, bringing frigid temperatures that hadn't come so far south in decades, or perhaps even centuries. The wind kicked up to flutter hair, sting cheeks, and turn the air sharp – but it still wasn't as cold as the look in Serge's eyes. With a dark chuckle, the merc leader shook his head, forearms flexing with bulging tendons and muscles. The pistol appeared in a flash, taken from beneath his coat, barrel pointing between Banks's eyes. Serge clenched the grip with malevolence, voice rough and angry.

"You threaten us with violence when we came to do you a favor, to take a job you did not want? I should blow your brains across the runway and be done with you." Lena and Mikael chuckled while Dmitri watched them with a stoic expression. "You insult us with your arrogance," Serge growled, putting an exclamation point on his sentiment.

"It is *very* arrogant." The woman nodded to Serge, nudging him with her elbow.

Nonplussed by the appearance of the weapon, Banks merely glanced over her shoulder at a low hill where a pair of Humvees rolled into position, a squat missile launcher mounted on top of one, and a heavy machine gun on the other.

"Go ahead and shoot me." The woman retained her bored tone of voice. "You won't even make it back to your plane if you do, though. And if by some miracle you survive, you'll be hunted down like dogs." Banks shifted her cold blue eyes to the cocky Mikael. "Would that be enough of a challenge for you?"

The blond-haired merc glanced at the Humvees, then gave a hesitant nod. "That would do it."

Serge held his gun steady for a long moment, eyes fixed on Banks, weighing her up, his finger flexing faintly on the trigger, a hair's breadth of movement before he finally slipped it out, resting it on the trigger guard, lowering the weapon as a smile spread across his face.

"You have balls," Serge holstered his pistol. "I admire that in a woman. Yes, we need the supplies." The man waved the pistol in Keith's direction. "And having him along will be no problem. We've worked together before, though not so closely. We will get to know each other better. Who knows, maybe this will be the start of a long relationship."

Banks nodded smartly, still unphased by the entire encounter, treating it like any other normal part of a negotiation. "Excellent. Glad to be working with you fine folks. Please wait out here while Keith gets his things."

The stormy weather deepened as the pair strode back to the airplane hangar, leaving the four mercenaries to close ranks behind them, whispering amongst themselves. When the group was finally out of earshot, Keith hissed at Banks.

"Are you insane?! What the hell was *that* about?"

"I need a man on the inside. You've worked with them before. You're my man on the inside."

"I can't return to the field right now. Just look at my hands." He held them up, fingertips still wrapped from the frostbite he'd suffered. "Losing a few fingers and toes, and almost my nose, should win me a little recovery time, don't you think? I said I'd get you the help you needed, not volunteer!"

"You done?" Banks snapped as they approached the camouflage Humvee where an MP stood near the door. "Because you screwed this up. Royally. You had McKnight in your hands multiple times and utterly failed to hold onto him."

"I—"

"Shut the hell up." It was Banks's turn to hiss at Keith, her eyes blazing with barely constrained fury. "I've taken so much flak because of *your* failures and I'm done with this nonsense. You're going with them. End of story."

Keith lifted his bandaged hands again, a whine creeping into his voice. "I'm not ready to go back out there yet,"

"You'll be fine. I'd send someone else, but we don't have the resources we used to. *I* don't have access to resources that *I* used to have access to, thanks in no small part to your screwups."

"I know, sir, but—"

"There're no buts about it." Banks gestured to the MP who reached into the Humvee's back seat and retrieved a backpack. "I packed you some things. Everything you should need, including a weapon."

At a loss for words, Keith accepted the heavy pack, shrugging it on his aching back, the pain from his gunshot wound and missing fingers lancing through his body.

"You'll also find a sat-phone inside. You can use it to keep me updated on the progress, like last time, though hopefully this time the updates are more encouraging."

"Last time I had to report to you, someone died." Keith's expression turned sour, the weight of the backpack hung from his shoulder like a lead sack.

Banks fixed him with a confused, somewhat disgusted look. "Are you seriously trying to tell me you're feeling remorse over that idiot kid who died?"

"Of course not. Just that distractions happen. I can't always check in on your timetable."

"Keep it as regular as a geriatric who chugs Metamucil every morning."

"But—"

"Or spend the foreseeable future as a guest at a black site. I can arrange that pretty easily if you'd like."

Keith sighed. "No... I'll take care of it."

"You just make sure the job gets done. When this is over, we'll start fresh." Banks patted Keith's back just a little too hard. "And you'll get everything that was promised."

"Right." The agent nodded, swallowing against the dryness in his throat as he adjusted the pack on his back, trying to work out exactly how he'd gotten himself into yet pursuit of the same people he'd already sacrificed so much to try and bring in. He turned from Banks and looked out at the waiting plane where the mercenaries waited for him, four swarthy characters standing in front of the classic airplane with the beautiful lady stenciled on the side. Lena shifted on her long legs, placed her fingers against her lips, and blew him a kiss.

CHAPTER SEVEN

Tom McKnight
Nuevo Laredo, Mexico

Awaking to a biting cold, Tom McKnight blinked away his blurry vision, breath scattering above him in a cloud of moisture that obscured the grungy ceiling above. The constant, ever-present moving of Jack fidgeting in his half-sleep was next to him, the small heels and legs pressing into his side and ribcage while snores from other sleepers assured him that, yes, everyone was still safe and sound. Clenching the blanket to his chin, he resisted getting up and leaving the cocoon of warmth it had taken them hours to create, but it was his turn to take watch.

With a sigh, Tom flipped off the cover and tucked it under Jack to keep the heat from seeping out. He shifted on the makeshift mattress, swinging his legs off the side and grabbing for his boots. Feet sliding into them, he winced at the coldness. The pharmacy was an icebox, smelling of dust, cold wood, and traces of the MREs they'd eaten the previous night. Palms against their cot, he started to rise when his son stirred next to him, shifting beneath the covers, pale face peeking over the top of the sheets.

"Hey, Dad?"

"Yeah?" Tom settled back, wrapped his arms around his knees, and pulled them into his chest. "What is it, Jack?"

"What's a holo... cen?"

Tom chuckled at Jack's mispronunciation of the word. "Well, it's *Holocene,* and that's what scientists call the current geological epoch." He struggled against the fog of morning still lying low over his mind. "Basically, epochs are how they divide time into sections."

"Why do they need to divide it up? Why can't it all be one name?"

Tom scratched his chin. "You know how when you and your sister fold clothes, you put different clothes into different drawers?"

"Yeah..."

"Same kind of thing. There are too many clothes to lump them all together. If you wanted to find a pair of socks you'd have to dig through shirts and pants and everything else. If we didn't have ways of talking about different time periods, it'd be hard to do that, and to tell similar time periods from each other. It's categorization, buddy. Like with animals, plants, stuff like that, too."

Jack looked down at his socks as Tom was talking, tugging at them before he looked back at his father. "So... are we in the top drawer?"

Tom laughed again, nodding. "Yeah, I guess the top drawer could represent the most recent years."

"So, we're the socks and underwear?"

"That would be true. I mean, nothing comes after socks and underwear, right?"

"Right." Jack held his grin for a few seconds before it flatlined. "Is our epoch going to end, Dad?"

"It's not as easy as that, but it sure feels like we're heading into a colder time period. Things are changing very fast. Dramatically fast."

"Will we be like the cavemen and wear furs from woolly mammoths?"

Tom grew serious and leaned in close to Jack's ear, whispering conspiratorially. "I don't think so, but I wouldn't rule anything out."

Jack's eyes grew wide, and Tom laughed, wrapping his arms around his son and squeezing him tight. "That was a joke. There are no woolly mammoths. Now go back to sleep so I can relieve your mom from her shift. I'll send her straight to bed, and it'll be your job to keep her warm, okay?"

"No problem, Dad."

With a groan, Tom stood and pressed his hand against the small of his back, rolling his head around, feeling his neck joints pop as he wandered over to their makeshift table to retrieve a couple of folded blankets. Laying them on his shoulders, Tom shuffled toward the front of the pharmacy, creeping across the creaking floorboards as the wind whistled through cracks in the walls. The dried up, half-inch plywood the previous owners had nailed over holes barely kept the elements at bay, and their attempts to mitigate the cold's incursion had been fruitless for the most part.

Head swiveling, teeth on the verge of chattering, he paused behind the counter where they'd placed a set of makeshift weapons before crossing to the front window, his body heat warming the blankets as he lifted the curtain aside and peered into the road. With no light coming from inside the pharmacy, he remained hidden in the shadows, able to peer outside without anyone seeing in.

As he looked around for Barbara, he spotted a group standing out near the fencing, bundled up and talking amongst themselves, dark shapes emphatically gesturing toward the pharmacy. They shuffled closer, moving onto the sidewalk, their harsh whispers audible through the thin glass pane. With furtive glances, they entered the courtyard, heads swiveling as they approached the front door, Tom's blood turning to ice in his veins. He hefted the pipe he'd taken off the counter and patted his pocket, checking for the presence of a makeshift shiv he'd pieced together from jagged metal wrapped in cloth at one end.

From what he could tell, they weren't carrying weapons of any sort, hands pushed into pockets, heads lowered in reluctant postures and Tom eased back in the chair, hiding the weapons beneath the blankets. The group stopped in the yard, milling around with uncertainty as one middle-aged man in a thick jacket with a faded American flag patch on the sleeve looked over the front of the store. After a long moment he stepped forward and pressed his hands to the glass, scraggly beard dangling from his chin as he peered inside.

"Tom McKnight! I know you're in there. Why don't you come on out so we can have a talk?"

Kicked back in his seat, Tom cupped one hand around his mouth and called through the porous wood in a voice that was softer than a shout. "No thanks, Marty. We can talk just fine like this."

The man on the other side of the glass paused, consulting with the group before returning to the window. "Look, Tom, you know we're getting ready to make our move."

"I figured." He drew a long breath, trying to calm his nerves. "What's that got to do with me and my family?"

"Well, a lot of us are wondering if you'll stand with us or against us?"

"Do we need to take sides?"

"I think you know the answer to that."

Tom shook his head. "So do you, Marty. My family and I are on nobody's side. We're just trying to survive, that's all. Your plans don't concern us, so you can go away now."

"That's where you're wrong. What happens in camp affects us all. Our fates are connected, and we need to be on the same page if we're going to get through this. We need to protect our rights and overthrow these tyrannical government camps." The man's finger tapped on the glass, rattling it in its weak frame. "You know as well as I do it ain't right."

"It's not right," Tom fought to keep his voice calm. "And I don't blame you for being mad, but what you're talking about is dangerous as hell."

"Dangerous? Dangerous?! It's dangerous staying in here, Tom; you know that!"

"True, Marty. But I've got three kids, and I have to consider their safety before anything and anyone else. We wish you all the luck in the world, but the McKnights can't contribute to the cause. We won't stand in your way, but we can't be a part of it. Just be careful, whatever you do. And have a pleasant night, okay?"

Tom held his breath, waiting for shouts, breaking glass and the rattling of the front door as some big oaf threw his shoulder into it, busting through, threatening his loved ones, forcing him to use his weapons to a bloody, violent end. Instead, after several long, tense seconds, the group wandered off, hushed voices muted through the wood and glass. Tom leaned forward and eased back the curtain, watching their shadows follow them into the street where they conferred for a moment before breaking up into smaller groups of ones and twos. Tom released the breath he'd been holding high in his chest, shoulders sagging, the pipe in his hand resting in his lap.

If it had come to blows, he wouldn't have lasted long. The military wasn't treating them well, none of their grievances given an ear and there were too many of them, all upset, cold, and hungry. If a fight was what they had wanted, he'd give them everything he had and then some, but his odds weren't great. A slim shape appeared from the shadows, interrupting his thoughts, circling in front of him in a surprise move and Tom jerked to the side and half-cocked his arm back to strike. When he saw it was Barbara, he relaxed and even cracked a smile.

"Geez, you're getting good at that," he said, voice shaking as he tried to play it off. "I wondered where you were."

A smug but apologetic grin spread on her face. "Sorry, babe. I didn't mean to scare you. I guess I have a lot of practice at creeping around, especially after avoiding Marty and his goons the past few days."

"Yeah, it seems like they're focused on making us join them."

Barbara came to stand next to him, wrapping her arm around his shoulders. "I'm not sure why they even care. We're only two people."

"They consider Sam and Linda potential fighters, too. Jack as a distraction mechanism."

Barbara's expression soured. "They won't be using our children to fight their little war."

"Absolutely not. That's not how Marty's little gang sees it, though. If we're not with them, we must be against them."

"What happens when they come back?"

"I'm not sure." Arm wrapped around her waist, he squeezed her hips against him, resting his head against her side. "We might be able to convince them to leave us alone... or we might have to defend ourselves. Either way, doesn't matter. We need to get out of here."

A wordless silence hung between them for a moment, and Tom couldn't help but hold her a moment longer, feeding off her warmth.

"We'll get through this," she said, hugging him. "We always do."

"I know we will." Patting her waist one last time, he broke his embrace and straightened in his chair. "Go on and get some sleep. We'll discuss our escape plan tomorrow."

"Good night, honey." Barbara leaned close and kissed him on the forehead, then turned and disappeared into the pharmacy's shadowy recesses.

The next morning, a swath of warm sunlight spilled into the room from the clipped back curtains, taking the edge off the chilly air. Still, it was cold. Bone-numbingly freezing. While having no thermometer, Tom estimated the temperature must be dipping into the negative teens and likely lower. At their small table in the pharmacy's rear, the McKnights prepared a breakfast courtesy of the MREs provided by the camp supply officers, Sam sitting next to him heating a piece of pepperoni pizza in a hot pouch and at the opposite side of the table Linda helped Jack get his chili mac started. They were beyond tired of the flavor and texture of the meals, but no one was complaining too much, all happy to have something warm in their stomachs given how bad their situation was.

After Linda poured boiling water from a pan into Jack's hot pouch, she placed the macaroni bag inside and sealed it. The smells of pizza sauce and chili powder hung in the air, underpinned with the smoky flavor of the burning stove. Tom put a gingerbread cookie in his mouth and bit the crisp edge, following the sweet bite with a sip of black coffee that sobered him with its bitter taste. Barbara scraped Alfredo noodles from a pouch onto a chipped plate, digging in with a grimace, taking liberal sips of warm powdered milk from a glass.

"Sooo..." His wife drew out the word as she stirred the noodles in the pouch. "Any ideas?"

"We can try to find some metal cutters," Tom suggested. "We could snip open a section of the fence and slip through in the middle of the night."

"We'd have to trade something to pick up a pair, and that would tip off Marty and his goons." Barbara shook her head, talking around her food. "They'd immediately question our intentions."

"No, you're right," he agreed. "Any signs that we're trying to leave will definitely aggravate them." Tongue brushing against his fingertips, he licked off the cookie crumbs and relaxed, resting his coffee in his lap. "We have to make it look like we're staying put in camp and not show we have a separate plan of our own." He paused for a moment. "We could try to climb the fence."

"Like we did back in the Army camp?" Sam held her pizza folded in one hand, a glass of powdered chocolate milk in the other. "Find some barrels or crates, stack them up, then climb over when the time's right."

"But this fencing has strings of razor wire across the top," her mother replied.

"We got around that by placing blankets on top of the sharp parts," Tom said. "It didn't matter, though. Keith came up with metal cutters and snipped the fencing. But, like you said, that won't work here."

Finishing up her Alfredo, Barbara broke open her chocolate chip cookie pack. "Okay, then. Let's think of something else. Come on, people, get those McKnight brains going. We've been here four days now. Surely there's a way out we're not thinking of."

"The guard situation hasn't changed," Tom pointed out. "They're pretty distracted, trying to stay warm, not really worried about us. And that makes me wonder just how much Saanvi told her superiors, or how much they really care or have control over the situation here. I half expected them to double the troops ten minutes after she walked away."

"Yeah, me too." Barbara looked over at Jack, rolling her eyes at a stack of noodles on his fork that he was balancing precipitously. "Jack, quit playing with your food."

Leaning back in his chair, Tom ran his hands through his hair, interlocking his fingers behind his head. "Aside from getting past the fence, we've got the added problem of finding transportation. The chances of us stealing a vehicle are pretty slim, and we won't survive long, or get very far, without one."

Barbara sighed. "We'll burn that bridge when we get there."

"More like a frozen lake than a bridge," Linda quipped. "It's getting cold."

Chewing her food, Samantha made an uncertain sound, caught somewhere between a grunt and an "um."

"What is it, Sam?" her mother asked. "Did you have something to add?"

She nodded, swallowing her bite and clearing her throat. "When we were out walking the other day, trading up for some supplies, I noticed a weak spot in the fencing."

Tom leaned forward. "Where?"

"You know that burned-out house that caught fire from those people trying to burn tires too close? The one up on the north end of the block?"

"Yeah, I know the one you're talking about."

"When we went by, I saw the fence. It's all black and brittle from the heat of the fire. You can barely see it because it's hidden behind the corner, but I bet we could break through there."

Tom lowered his coffee cup to the table, looking over at Barbara. "I know the exact spot she's talking about. It's around the side where the house presses close to the fence. There's a foot of space to squeeze through, and I'd guess the building is 30 feet long. The yard was littered with junk and burned up trees. Plenty of places to hide supplies until we can break out."

"And I only saw one soldier guarding it," Samantha continued. "That's one guy for the entire section. If we could distract or incapacitate him, we could slip by the defenses and get out."

A slow grin worked its way onto Tom's face, and his eyes locked with his wife. "That might just work. We'll have to scout a bit, but I can't think of a better spot."

"Good." Barbara nodded confidently, leaning across the table and patting her daughter's grease covered hand. "I figured one of us would get it."

"Outstanding work, sis," Linda added with a smile.

"Thanks, guys." Sam's cheeks blushed red.

"Regardless, we'll need to gather more supplies." Tom switched to focusing on the strategic details. "We need makeshift weapons, extra MREs, and more blankets and clothes. Even if Saanvi comes through for us, we'll still have to have them."

"I can help with the weapons." Linda's dark eyes shifted between her parents. "I saw some of that... what's it called? Rebar? It's sticking up from a pile of rubble nearby, and there were smaller pieces broken off, lying everywhere."

"Good, just remember it needs to be inconspicuous," Tom reminded her. "We can't be walking around with baseball bats on our shoulders. Let's focus on things we can conceal in our coats or in our pant legs."

"What about the stuff we came in with?" Barbara asked. "Don't we have supplies in our old packs?"

"We picked up a few things from that last town, but nothing especially good. And the chances are slim that we can get them. Who knows, though, maybe Saanvi can find out where they're keeping them."

Linda stiffened in her chair, dark eyes lifting with excitement. "So when do we get started? Can I come help scout?"

Tom and Barbara shared a look before he replied. "Your mother and I will do that *and* pick up more supplies. You kids will stay here under lock and key."

"Oh, you've got to be kidding me." Linda frowned, pounding her fist on the table with the fork sticking up like a starving child demanding more food. "You can't do everything yourselves."

"We can, and we will," her mother said firmly, standing with Tom.

"We've been locked in here for days." Samantha piled on with her sister. "You guys always say we have to do things as a team. So, let us help."

"Under normal circumstances, you'd be right," he agreed, "but this is a different situation. There are dangerous people in the camp, and they're getting pretty desperate. It's bad enough your mother and I have to deal with them, and we can't be distracted worrying about you guys."

Barbara rested her hand on Jack's temple and brushed his hair from his eyes with her thumb. "You kids are so precious to us, and we understand you've been cooped up in here for days. You're probably going crazy. But this isn't the time to take chances. It's for the best that you stay hidden inside behind the barricade."

With the kids' reluctant agreement, Tom and Barbara bundled up against the weather, layering on extra sweaters and donning their heavy coats and hoods. Tom chose a small satchel with a strap and packed in the bottles of medicine and painkillers they'd found beneath the shelves and in the corners of the store. Included with those items were a pocketknife, steak knife, and a couple paring blades someone had smuggled into camp. After buckling it up, he slung it on his shoulder and met Barbara at the front door. Steeling their resolve, the Tom and Barbara moved the shelving and slipped out into the small grassy courtyard where the wind gusted in angry bursts. Tom held up his finger and listened as Linda and Sam slid the shelves back into place with a slam and once the barrier was reset, the pair nodded to each other and walked left, skirting the south part of the block.

Shoulders brushing, their gaits casual but stiff, they acted like it was just another day in the camp. The usual suspects gathered around burn barrels on every corner and in a few yards as furtive shadows moved in the alleys between houses executing secret exchanges; food for knives, blankets for coal, and whatever could be smuggled in from or past the guards. The McKnights nodded to a few regulars they passed, ones who they trusted marginally, Tom repeatedly glancing toward the center of the camp.

"I don't see Marty or his merry band around," Barbara spoke under her breath, whispering so that just Tom could hear her.

"They've consolidated everything in the center of camp." Tom kicked a rock and watched it bounce into the street and glance off the chain-link fence. "Keeps things away from the guards' prying eyes. I bet they're gathering supplies and weapons for when they break out."

"Well, let's hope we don't run into any of them."

"And try to ignore everyone staring at us in the meantime. Or is it just me?"

Barbara chuckled humorlessly. "No, it's not just you. People are definitely scoping us out."

Smoke drifted by above them, dark tendrils painting over the gray skies, sunlight poking through the taffy-stretched clouds to grace them with a sprig of warmth now and again. The stones from fallen homes had been re-stacked to form new structures, roofs topped with canvas tarps, smoke drifting up from old stove pipes. Garbage blew across the street, plastic bags caught on car tires or lodged in tree branches and large quantities of discarded MRE packages covering the street and sidewalks.

They stopped near a burn barrel on the southeast corner of the block, a half-dozen people crowded around the flames all glancing at them before pressing shoulders together to keep the McKnights from squeezing in. A blue van from the 70s rested off to the side on four flat tires, frame rusted clean through. The side door faced the encampment, thrown wide open, the grayish interior carpet dotted with mold and faded from decades of wear. A man sat in the side door, winter garb hanging off his thin form, his gaze fixated on Tom and his wife, his eyes narrowed and cold. Behind him were cardboard boxes tucked under the seats or covered in old blankets and clothing and a guard stood at each end of the vehicle, hands deep in their pockets, heads up and on the lookout. The pair glanced the McKnight's way and Tom stepped off the curb, striding up to the seller, calling back to Barbara to stay on the sidewalk as he went.

Serious eyes regarded him from a dark-complected face, skin dry and ashy from the intense cold, voice hoarse and cautious. "Tom."

"Hello, Scott. Got any cans for me today? I've got aspirin to trade."

"Aspirin, huh? A full bottle will get you four cans."

"Four? That's robbery. A bottle of two hundred tablets is worth at least fifteen cans of food."

The seller's stony face never changed. "Considering I'm not supposed to be trading with you at all, five cans is a great deal."

"How about 10 cans?"

"Five."

"Geez, man. Are you crazy?"

Scott's expression never wavered, though one corner of his mouth lifted with a slight grin, knowing Tom was bent over a barrel. "Five is a decent trade, risk aside."

With an exasperated sigh, Tom turned away but caught Barbara's steady gaze and the slight shake of her head, then turned back. "I'll give you the bottle for seven cans. And I want a mixed batch. Two corn, one stewed tomatoes, one beans, and two peas. That's as low as I can go, man."

The seller remained still, fiddling with something in his coat pockets, eyes flitting past his customer to peer deeper into the camp, the blue-tinted lips twisting, jaw set as he reached a decision.

"Alright. Seven cans. Never say I did nothin' for you, Tom."

They made the exchange, Tom digging out the full, unopened bottle of aspirin and handing it over for the vegetables. Trade complete, satchel heavier, he returned to his wife, growling under his breath as they walked away from the area.

"He gave us half of what it was worth."

"I have a feeling we'll get a lot more of that in the future."

"I don't understand it. We've been cordial to everyone in camp. I thought we had a pretty good reputation."

A trio of women passed them in the street, striding fast in a heel-to-toe fashion just inside the fence line, each of them bundled up, hooded heads turning in the McKnight's direction. Forcing a smile, Tom gave them a friendly wave.

"Morning, ladies. Hope your day's going well." None of the women replied, continuing their walk in stoic silence, boots devouring the yards in a scrunch of hard soles on the pavement.

"Aren't they a fun bunch," Barbara frowned.

"I'm pretty sure they're spies for Marty."

"Are you serious?"

"Oh, yeah. Pretending to exercise while scouting for guard movements."

"Clever," she admitted. "And here I thought they were just three rude bitches."

Tom chuckled at his wife's raw assessment, then motioned at a group of people circling a burn barrel on the corner of the block near the fence where one refugee stood near the chain link, speaking to a guard.

"Hey, folks." He waved and received a few tentative nods in reply, then nudged Barbara. "Well, not everyone hates us."

At the east gate, they found a line of refugees reaching all the way to the north end of the block. A supply truck had backed up to the fence and a FEMA worker tossing down blankets to a pair of soldiers who in turn handed them out to the waiting refugees. The wary, well-armed guards were dressed for the weather while those receiving the aid wore thick, ratty jackets and jeans with rips, showing dirty long underwear beneath them. Hands were held out, shaking and cold, skin dry and cracked, bodies shivering to stay warm.

"Let's get some things here." They strode to the end of the line and took a spot, moving forward quickly as the refugees got what they needed and returned to their meager domiciles, eager to get out of the weather. Soon, it was the McKnight's turn and Tom stepped off to the side with their contraband, keeping a close eye out for trouble while Barbara collected the blankets with a nod.

Once done, they walked along the north side, coming across yet another burn barrel with two women and a man standing close around it, huddled in thick coats and gloves. The smell of some kind of meat – Tom didn't know or want to find out what it was – drifted through the air, mixing with burning wood and plastic, stinging his nose. Approaching slowly, he raised a hand in a halting wave. A tall, burly woman wearing a thick green jacket with braids of blonde hair hanging from her hood nodded to the pair while her two friends remained silent.

"Hello, Sandy. Things going okay?"

The big lady shifted away from the barrel, offering a brief nod to each. "Tom, Barbara. Still cold as hell, but who's keeping score?"

"Not us." He winced at the sky, glancing toward the fence line where a pair of guards walked by on the other side. "You got anything up for trade?"

"I might, but it's frowned upon to deal with you McKnights."

"That's what I hear. Is that an edict from some great refugee camp council?"

Sandy chuckled. "To be honest, it's all Marty. He put the word out that trading with you folks wasn't the best of ideas."

Tom nodded. "Not surprising. What about you? Do you do everything Marty tells you to?"

Turning from the burn barrel, the burly lady crossed to a woodpile, picked up a 2-foot-long two-by-four, and tossed it into the fire. Flames and cinders twirled up, and a waft of dark smoke blew right into them, causing Tom to turn his head and cough.

"I'm not one to take orders from folks like Marty. The man's just a busybody, and I hate busybodies."

"Sounds like you're willing to do business at least," he sighed, holding her gaze. "We've got medicine and a few other things to exchange for food."

"I can trade with you," Sandy nodded, keeping her voice low, "but I have to keep up airs around here. Can't have anyone in Marty's group thinking I'm going behind his back. You know, when we bust out of here, I'd like to be confident someone won't stick a knife in my back. At the same time, I can't let him kill my business."

"Riding the fence. I understand. What did you have in mind?"

"I'm going to tell you to get the hell out of here and don't come back. You go around the side to the alley marked with an orange ribbon. My sister will meet you in back. She'll have what you need, provided you have something for us."

Tom and Barbara nodded, and Sandy took a deep breath and pointed off to the left, opening her considerable mouth and unleashing a torrent on them. "I told you to get the hell out of here, McKnights! We don't do business with you! Go on, leave!"

Tom and Barbara backed up in a hurry, and not just because they were playing at it; Sandy had a tremendous, booming voice that carried halfway across the block. Boots crunching on debris, they hoofed it around the north end and, sure enough, he spotted a ribbon tied to a construction stick next to a pair of cracked beige houses. The pair angled toward it, peering into an alley cluttered with rubbish and fluttering snow, junk piled up in the corners. Wind whistled through in gusts and gnarly tree branches crowded in from yards, decrepit fingers reaching in to grab at them.

"Ready?" Tom asked.

"Yeah," she replied

Right hand gripping one shiv, he stepped in first, boots lifting over the rubble and garbage, his breathing calm but shallow.

"What are we looking for?"

"No idea."

A low hiss from the left drew Tom's attention to where Sandy's sister waited for them on a patio. A tilted awning covered the space, the sides crowded with old fencing and a stack of tires.

"Ellie?" he called.

"Yeah."

Tom and Barbara stepped through a gap in a crumbled brick wall and approached the patio where the woman straddled a clear plastic bin, stout form hovering protectively over the trade product. Through the side of the bin he could see it was filled with beige colored MRE bags, probably two or three dozen judging by the size of the container.

Tom pointed at the bin. "I see you've got some MREs there."

"That's right," she replied, her tone a few shades less harsh than her sister's. "This is all Sandy's letting me trade to you."

"How much do you want for the whole thing?" Barbara asked, shifting from one foot to the other.

"What'dya got?"

"We've got aspirin."

"What else?"

Tom started to reply that the aspirin was worth its weight in gold, but he backed off, ceding to Barbara and her ability to get what she wanted.

"We've also got these fresh blankets here." She indicated the folded material beneath her arm the soldiers had given them a few minutes ago.

Ellie pressed. "What else?"

Barbara's mouth fell open, and she shot Tom an exaggerated glance of disbelief, though at the same time he caught a hint of craftiness in her eyes and an almost imperceptible grin.

"We've got a good pocketknife, a flashlight, a box of bandages, some gauze, and a bottle of rubbing alcohol."

Despite her stoic countenance, Ellie couldn't stifle the look of surprise that flashed across her face, but she quickly wiped her expression clean. "I guess that'll do. Put it all down on the table."

Tom's insides squirmed as Barbara placed the blankets on an old patio table, the surface warped from the frigid temperature. Next came the pocketknife and flashlight, then the gauze and bandages. Just as she was about to give up the alcohol, she held it back, turning toward the larger woman with a slight stamp of her boot.

"What's wrong?"

"I think this would be a better deal if you had a second bin of MREs by your feet."

Ellie scoffed and shook her head. "We made a deal, lady. You already put payment down."

"Yeah, that stuff is for the one bin. But the alcohol and aspirin… well, that's going to take another bin."

Back stiff, the woman snorted. "You're crazy. We had a trade for one bin, and now you want to change it? The deal's off."

Ellie bent to grab the MREs and leave as Barbara spoke. "Suit yourself, but do you think your sister will be happy knowing she lost out on aspirin and alcohol, which no one else in camp has? Believe me, we checked." Tom's wife nodded, expression turning surer by the second. "Yeaaah, she'd be pretty pissed off if she missed out because you wouldn't play fair."

As the words came out, Tom didn't think they'd sway her, but Ellie stopped with the bin in her hands. After a moment, she raised up, facing Barbara again, her confident look having completely evaporated.

"And don't say Marty and his group have plenty of medical supplies, because they don't," Barbara continued. "We traded them two bottles already, as well as bandages." She held up the bottle and shook it. "This is the last one in camp." With a heavy scoff, she turned to Tom. "Come on, honey, let's go. We'll trade it with someone else."

Satchel open, he played along, shaking his head while she placed their possessions back. "I think Scott would give us a couple cases of canned corn for this," he agreed, both of them starting to walk away from Ellie, who was still standing with the MREs in hand, watching them go with an unsure expression.

Though he kept up a brave front on the outside, Tom was cursing because those MREs were gold. They had a long shelf life and were chock-full of calories, far more than ten cans of vegetables combined, and they were the McKnights' only chance of surviving outside camp.

They'd just reached the collapsed wall and were about to step into the alley when Ellie's voice rang out. "Wait! Come on back. I think we can make a deal."

Barbara grinned and winked at her husband before they turned around. Five minutes later, the pair walked away with two full bins plus whatever else they could fit in the satchel, even picking up a few extra pepperoni pizza MREs for Sam.

"Let's take the back way to the pharmacy," he suggested. "I don't want Marty or any of his people seeing us lugging these bins around."

"Good idea," Barbara said, carrying hers against her hip.

"I know a way that won't take us past their hideout. Follow me."

With a full satchel and heavy bin of food, Tom picked his way toward the block's west edge, stepping quietly through backyards of refugee houses. The state of the homes was abysmal, many half-collapsed or riddled with holes covered by plywood, the once beautiful dwellings with Spanish-style phrasings having become worse than a ghetto. Face lowered, arms growing tired, he avoided making eye contact with anyone, looking away from the faces staring back through the windows. Once they reached the west side of the block, he stepped onto the sidewalk and hustled south.

"That was some brilliant bargaining," Tom said, huffing as he lifted his tote over a group of metal garbage cans scattered on the pavement. "Sounded like you enjoyed sticking it to her."

"I wasn't going to walk away without securing this food. Plus, screw them for joining in Marty's little vendetta against us."

Soon they reached the end of the block and slipped into a path between the bushes where they entered the pharmacy's side courtyard and set the bins on a frost-covered picnic table, hidden from view by the trees. Lids removed, they looked over the meager haul, transferring the MREs from the satchel to the bins, shuffling the meals into order.

"It's not much," he said, "but it'll keep us alive until we settle in somewhere else." They repacked them and hauled them around to the front, eager to get the food inside.

"How can we transport them if we don't have a vehicle?" Barbara asked.

"I have some ideas about that—"

As he rounded the corner, Tom jerked to a halt, almost dropping his bin, shocked to see Marty and a couple of his men nosing around the door. The leader snapped straight, eyes wide with surprise beneath his hood and, jaw set, Tom dropped the bin on the pavement and stepped over it, spreading his legs, shoving his hand into his coat pocket to grip the shiv he'd hidden there.

"What do you want?" Tom's eyes bore into the intruders as he placed himself between them and his wife.

Marty glanced at the bins, raising his bushy gray eyebrows curiously. "Hello, Tom. Me and the boys wanted to have a little chat with you and the missus."

CHAPTER EIGHT

Specialist Lance Morales
Santa Fe, New Mexico

Smoke curled up from the steel containers burning wooden skids, paper, and fuel, filling the air with a charred stench that stung noses and irritated eyes, yet the heat the fires generated was barely enough to keep away the creeping chill that permeated the warehouse. Dark greasy fog rolled upwards to gather in the rafters, covering the ceiling in an ominous cloud of noxious fumes that flattened across the roof to the far side and down the walls, coating everything in soot.

Having rationed their heat packs, the soldiers huddled around the fires in a love-hate relationship with the flames. On one hand, they needed the warmth and on the other the roiling smoke was a promise of a painful, choking death. The warm moisture of their breaths gusted in hundreds of puffs as they tried to draw close without burning their lungs, some keeping their faces buried in their jackets or crooks of their arms to little avail. The building shuddered around them from repeated hits of wind and sleet, the constant creaking like an old ship on the open sea.

Morales rubbed his hands together, leaning in and a little back, looking for a sweet spot where the fumes weren't so terrible. Smith sat next to him, grumbling and complaining as he hugged himself, rubbing his shoulders, gasping softly, hesitant to breathe too much of the toxic fumes. "Well, at least we see what killed the people in the break room," he said. "And we'll be right behind them."

"You don't know that," Morales replied, countering the lieutenant's skepticism with his own blind optimism. "It could have just as easily been the cold."

"I feel it in my bones." The lieutenant doubled down. "Just like back in Reynosa and Monterrey before we got jumped." The man shook his head, cheeks touched with soot, eyebrows dusted with frost. "I got the feeling in my gut, and a few minutes later, *boom*! They hit us."

The men and women of the unit all looked the same, hiding their stony hands, shoulders hunching in claustrophobic fear. With a hill of snow sitting on their heads and no place to go, arguments were growing more frequent, and morale was dropping quickly. Malaise hung over the warehouse and whispers of hopelessness and despair grew by the minute.

"Those were lucky guesses."

"I've never been lucky in my life," Smith said in counter. "I've never so much as won a door prize at a bingo. Nope, I'm all skill and intuition. No luck here."

"And I notice you never complain in front of the other soldiers, just me."

"Take it as a compliment." The lieutenant gave him a mock sneer. "I only complain to the people I like."

"Yeah, right."

A soldier stepped to their steel container and tossed a table leg into the flames, cinders shooting upward in a flare of heat and light, causing an uneven blaze of smoke to pour over them. Smith, choking and waving his hand in front of his face, jerked to his feet, fists stuck out to the sides. "Easy with fire, you idiot," he snapped, scolding the man. "Don't just throw stuff into it."

The soldier opened his mouth to retort but backed off, palms up in surrender, ceding the argument before it turned into something worse.

"That's what I thought," the lieutenant mumbled, glaring at the man's back as he moved to another bonfire and sat.

"Man, you're in a foul mood."

Smith shrugged exaggeratedly, returning to his place next to Morales, hands up to the fire. "I get this way whenever I realize I'm in a slow spiral toward certain death. Also, I haven't had a cigarette in a few hours. I just don't feel like smoking for some strange reason."

"Could it be that we're dying of CO_2 poisoning?"

"That might have something to do with it."

"You should take it as a sign to quit." Morales gave the suggestion with a straight face, a smirk lingering beneath his flat expression.

"Not funny, man. Not funny at all."

A pause filled the air, broken only by the crackling wood and the soldiers' whispered voices. A trembling icy fear gripped his body, and he hugged himself as he stared into the dancing flames, mind drifting to more pleasant things. "I was just thinking of being back home poolside on a hot summer day. Mom's iced tea and all my friends hanging out and soaking up rays."

Smith smirked in a good-natured way as the flames captured his eyes, too. "I was just thinking of Heather Morrison. Had two dates with her before I shipped off to basic. Smoking-hot redhead. That girl could have melted every inch of snow off the building."

An accidental chuckle escaped Morales, and he inhaled a waft of smoke coming off the fire. Fist over his mouth, he choked and coughed. When he was done, he lifted his hand away to see the mucus was a sickly yellow color.

Captain Jones stepped over, gesturing to them. "Smith, Morales. I need you over here."

The pair got to their feet and followed him to where a group stood around a Humvee, surrounded by heaters to keep the equipment from freezing over. Morales reached up and rubbed his nose, an unpleasant crackle of ice and frost rippling across his nostrils as he broke them apart from where they'd frosted shut. He couldn't shake the image of an endless tundra outside the warehouse, an eternity of frostbite and frozen corpses, anything that vaguely resembled summer long devoured by the winter chill. Shaking off the dreadful thought, he focused on what the captain was saying.

With hunched shoulders, Jones gazed across the sea of vehicles. "Look guys, we need to keep these trucks warm. Even with the chemical treatments in the fuel, it's 40 below and getting colder."

Morales nodded with dawning realization. "The diesel fuel will turn to gel."

"That's right."

"We can *not* allow that to happen. And we've got to make sure the fuel trucks stay thawed out, too." The captain leveled his gaze at the assembled lot. "I'm telling you, boys, if we lose the fuel, we're done."

He and Smith branched out along with the other officers, shouting for the soldiers to relocate the burn barrels and metal containers closer to the vehicle fuel tanks. They were too hot to touch, so the men and women were forced to get creative in how they moved them, wrapping chains around them and using pieces of wood or steel racks to drag and shove them into position. Once the burn barrels were repositioned, they grabbed generators and portable heaters and angled them to blow warm air below the chassis, hoping to warm up the underside of the vehicles enough to keep them from freezing over..

"Be careful!" Smith shouted. "Don't let any of the heating elements touch the tanks. And leave the gas caps on. Diesel's not dynamite but I don't think anyone here wants to find out what happens if a cinder flies into a fuel tank."

Smith and Morales teamed up to move their steel container closer to his excavator's fuel tank, using one of the fallen rack bars to shove it into position. Standing close, he placed his bare hands on the engine cover, grinning at the warming metal.

A soldier was assigned to each vehicle to monitor the flames and, crisis averted, the officers gathered back at the captain's Humvee in somewhat better spirits to find Jones sitting with a radio specialist in the front seat, still trying to reach central command.

"It's no use." The man spoke with a growl, head tilted back in frustration. "The storms totally knocked out our signal. We won't be able to call base until it passes."

"How long do you think that'll be?" one soldier asked.

"Impossible to tell," Jones replied. "Our meteorologists just discovered these spin-up anomalies, and they're still studying the behaviors. Could be two hours, or two days."

The soldiers groaned and Morales turned away, hands stuffed into his pockets, looking up the walls to where a faint line of frost touched the smoky ceiling. The oppressive claustrophobia pressed in again as he could swear he could feel the mountain of snow squeezing the warehouse frame, about to crush it like an eggshell and expose the soft insides. A shudder of fear rippled through his chest in gasps and he forced himself to calm down and get his breathing back under control.

A hand landed hard on his shoulder and Smith's voice cut through the panic. "This is tons of fun, right?"

"Yeah." Morales breathed deep, forcing a smile. "What's next on the itinerary? Forklift races? Snowball fights?"

"It's good to know you haven't lost your sense of humor, Morales."

"Are you kidding? How could I *not* be chipper in your delightful presence?"

While they were pulling each other's legs, the back-and-forth continued to ease his panic, driving away the roof's groaning tension. The pair returned to the Humvee, Morales hit with an idea. "Hey, Cap. I just remembered something. What about the LeTourneaus? They're still outside; will they be okay?"

Captain Jones stepped out of the truck, hands on hips as he looked toward the windy bay doors. "Those tanks are insulated with a foot or more of weatherproof material. They should be fine for now, provided the storm doesn't last much longer." He gazed toward the center of the parking area where the tankers sat. "And if we do lose that fuel, we'll just change it out. That's why it's crucial we keep it warm in here."

Morales coughed into his hand, eyes flitting back to the ceiling where the vapor and frost gathered. The continual lung-rattling coughs from the soldiers echoed in the open space, and their bloodshot eyes were another sign of smoke inhalation.

"We need to get this air clean, Cap," Morales said. "I mean, the warehouse is huge, but we're putting out a lot more smoke than we thought we would at the start."

Jones nodded. "Yes, we need to think of a way to vent the area."

"Can we cut some small holes in the roof?" He pointed upward. "The smoke would go right out then."

"Nah. There'd still be several feet of snow and ice to cut through. We'd need guys with chainsaws hanging around up there for a long time to do it."

"What about the shutters and vents? If we could clear those and get the HVAC unit running..." He left the sentence hang as he traced the ductwork barely visible through the thick cloud of smoke roiling above them like a storm.

"Yeah, we'd still get a little ice and snow inside, but most venting systems are built to keep out the elements." Smith flashed a look at the captain before raising his eyes to the roof. "Getting the ventilation going is probably our best bet."

Hands on hips, Jones lifted his gaze. "I agree."

Soon, the dozen officers were staring upward, pointing and discussing where they'd clear the blockage and wondering where the control units might be. The smoke was growing dangerously dense, an oily looking mixture of gases, reminding Morales of the thick black exhaust from an eighteen wheeler's tail pipe.

"Oh, hell, Cap," one soldier said, voice shaking. "It's looking bad up there, man. If we don't freeze to death, we sure as hell're going to suffocate."

Jones raised his shoulders, chest out. "Don't panic, Brozowksi. Just start scouring the place for the control panel to the ventilation units. It's probably in the machine room, off one of these side rooms."

"Even if we find it, we don't have any power," the soldier pressed.

"Maybe Santa Claus will save us," Smith shot back, drawing strained laughter from the troops.

"We can wire up a diesel engine like a generator," Morales suggested. "Splice in some power."

The captain gestured at him. "You hear that? We can use a truck to splice in some power and get the ventilation moving." The red-headed captain scratched his head. "Does anyone have the building schematics?"

"C'mon, man," Smith grabbed Morales's elbow. "Let's try the other end. The machine room must be around there somewhere."

Nodding faintly, he followed the lieutenant, weaving through the tightly packed trucks and soldiers where burn barrels raged to keep away the chill. The troops fed off the fire like fearful vampires, glancing around with bloodshot eyes.

"You really think we can make this happen?"

"It's a long shot." Smith nodded. "Even if we get the HVAC unit turned on, it'll take us a few hours to clear the vents. Hopefully, the storm will let up by—"

Something clattered in the superstructure, cutting Smith off, the metal girders above them groaning as some massive unseen weight shifted. A shudder gripped the building, resonating through Morales's boots, reminding him of a truck with bad brakes coming to a shaky stop. Trails of powdered snow drifted downward like dust and Morales threw his hands out, every instinct in his blood and bones telling him to run, though there was nowhere that was safe. Smith grabbed his arm, gripping hard, pulling him closer as something cracked like a tree branch snapping. Soldiers shouted, crouching, cowering beneath trucks, wide eyes staring up in terror as the building threatened to buckle and crush them all.

CHAPTER NINE

Keith
Somewhere Near San Antonio, Texas

The long stretch of highway wove with gentle curves from east to west across the flat Texas desert, ravaged by the brutal throes of the new winter. Afternoon sun glinted off the crystalline snowdrifts and windswept trees leaned over, bent beneath the withering storms that had blown through. Dense stratus clouds moved swiftly overhead, conflated colors of black and gray forming angry faces that glared across the weather-beaten land. Cacti jutted upward, their thorny tough hides withered in the shrinking frost, scattered among the towns lying off the highway that slept under the snow-covered plains. White-topped roofs bulged, housing the corpses of souls who hadn't escaped, leaving them forever entombed in their frosty graves.

A pair of Stryker APCs blasted along the interstate, snowplows shedding white powder in sweeping wakes off to the sides of the road. The M1132 engineer squad variants were fully encompassing units with eight chain-covered wheels each, their own private network and communications suites, and a full array of external cameras used by drivers with virtual headsets. Each bore an M2 .50 caliber machine gun mounted on top, and though the barrels were locked down they could be brought to life remotely from within the cabin at a moment's notice.

Supported by all-wheel-drive suspensions and powerful Caterpillar C7 diesel engines, the pair of vehicles crushed through the snow at a slow but steady clip, pulling heated and covered trailers, bearing cans of chemically treated fuel to protect it from the brutal chill. Separate from the fuel in the trailers were an abundance of weapons and food crucial to staying alive and well-armed in the rugged landscape for an extended period of time.

The trucks trundled down the highway, slicing through banks of snow, muscling them aside with ease as the big chain-covered tires dug deep for traction, kicking out icy debris in all directions. Keith was in an uncomfortably familiar seat in front of the radio, watching Serge drive using the tactical HUD. The merc wasn't the smoothest driver, but he kept the vehicle stable as they traversed the icy Texas roads and highways.

Mikael lounged in the back, lying between the seats, feet perched upon a stack of duffel bags, head resting on his own pack, arms thrown to the side and enjoying the ride. Lena and Dmitri occupied the second APC that traveled behind them, loaded down with supplies including an array of rifles, rocket-propelled grenades, packs of explosives, electronic equipment, quick rations, and several trunks of cold weather gear.

In addition to everything else, Banks had provided a large container of high quality MREs and high-protein, high-calorie energy bars to keep them going through the next few days. Keith figured the vehicles and supplies were an olive branch, offered by the lieutenant colonel to mitigate being forced to take Keith with them.

"These are very good," Mikael said, waving an energy bar, wrapper half-peeled down and several bites taken out of it. "Maybe Banks isn't so bad, after all."

"I will disagree with that." The merc leader was more relaxed after getting on the road and shifted his attention to Keith. "What is up with her, anyway? Shouldn't someone at her level be able to find one asshole and his family? And don't tell me she's not well-connected. I am very familiar with high-ranking officers across various military structures, and she acts just like one."

"Yes, like her shit does not stink," added Mikael. "I hate officers like that. They are the first to throw you to the wolves while they cover their backsides."

Keith smiled despite himself. It'd been longer than he cared to recall since he'd been alone with the mercenary group, and had forgotten that in spite of their rough exterior, they were more pleasant to be around than Banks or most of her military support staff. Perhaps he was more like them than he cared to admit.

"You're right," he nodded. "She's been in the service a long time, involved with many high-level, extremely dangerous ops."

Mikael laughed. "But I bet she was never actually *on* a mission. She strikes me as the kind of woman who runs *away* from danger."

Keith smiled at the exact depiction. "Another correct statement. The bottom line is that Banks screwed up a recent job, and now she's stuck in a less than pleasant situation."

"She is in the doghouse, as you say." Serge grinned.

"Worse. She's locked in the doghouse and they threw away the key."

The mercenaries broke into chuckles and laughter, shaking their heads and snorting.

"So, she is over a barrel and desperate for us to bring this man and his family in?"

Finger raised, Keith pointed at Serge in a bull's-eye gesture. "Bingo." A small part of him felt guilty for giving up such detailed information about Banks to the mercs, though it was satisfying to hear them laughing at her expense, and to deflect away from his part in the repeated failures to capture and hold Tom and his family. Mikael had been spot on about Colonel Banks's willingness to throw anyone to the wolves. He recalled their conversation after the first APC wreck near Richmond where, despite him being injured and frostbitten, Banks had kept Keith on the job without so much as a by-your-leave.

"She's by the book and formal as hell," Keith said, finding himself almost apologizing for her behavior in spite of himself, "but, in case you didn't notice, there's a lot happening. A lot of moving parts. We've all had to make sacrifices."

"Right." Mikael's feet dangled over the duffel bags, giving Keith a look he couldn't quite process, though it thankfully only lasted a second before the merc got on to another subject. "Speaking of finding our target—Lena, have you made any progress? Can you point us in the right direction?"

Lena's voice filled the cabin through its twin speakers. "Hello, gentlemen. I've infiltrated the U.S. Military's communication systems and am actively searching for traces of our targets."

"That was quick." Keith raised an eyebrow.

"My presence is tiny. Just two little rabbit ears, listening to the data storm. I accessed the remaining functional data centers in the country as well as allied nations not hit by the destruction yet. I'm sending some data to your screen now."

Keith turned to his console and watched lines of text. "I see Banks's mission logs from Asheville, noting the McKnights were there. A short time later, they boarded the Osprey and took off, leaving us hanging." He shook his head. "We already knew that, though. Don't you have something more useful we can use?"

"I can get information from the Osprey's flight recorder."

"But that went down with the crash."

"That is true. However, today's recorders upload data in real-time. While we cannot access the physical device, we have a log of events up to three minutes before the aircraft crashed."

Keith's screen switched to a GPS map with a blinking waypoint. "What am I looking at?"

"That is the craft's last known location."

"That's near San Antonio, Texas," he said, leaning in to study the map, interest piqued. "Hell, that's just a hundred miles from here."

"The vehicle crashed three minutes after that, heading in a southwesterly direction. We can pinpoint their location to within 15 miles of the last transmission."

Using his fingers on the touchscreen, Keith zoomed out on the map to show cities along the Texas-Mexican border. "If they were flying to Mexico, that would put the accident right around here." He drew a circle on the screen, showing the location. "Does this look accurate?"

Lena paused as the network synced between the two vehicles. "Mm. Expand the circle by another two or three miles."

Keith made the correction and sat back, looking from the last known waypoint to the estimated crash site. "How's that?"

"Much better."

"So, after they hit the ground, they would have probably assessed their injuries and kept moving southwest to one of the military checkpoints on the border."

"Are you certain they are alive?" Lena's voice crackled as the wind whipped up a gust of snow, clouding the transmission. "Based on this information – which I am surprised your Banks did not have access to – I would assume they died on impact."

"Banks has fallen out of some favor," Keith replied idly, "and I guarantee you that Tom McKnight wouldn't die in a crash. He's too slimy for that."

"I have doubts," Lena replied, "but either way, our job is complete once he is in custody – dead *or* alive."

"We will assume they survived," Serge interjected. "This black box data does not have information on how hard the crash was, or if it was anything other than a soft emergency landing anyway. Which checkpoint would they have struck out for?" Serge asked.

"There are at least three major ones." Keith pointed at the map. "Laredo, Reynosa, and Matamoros, and another dozen smaller camps along the border wall. We can't be certain which they traveled to or if they even made it. Neither myself nor Banks have access to refugee lists anymore."

"I may be able to hack the camp records."

"That would be useful." Keith absently stared at the screen, imagining which of the McKnights had survived and where they might have gone after the Osprey went down. "We'll start with the last known location of the Osprey and go from there."

Serge snapped the wheel hard to the right, leaning, sending the APC blasting down an exit ramp to hit a connector road to the next highway. With a switch to his forward camera view, Keith watched them swerve through a foot of snow, the interstate outlined by trees sprouting up on either side with occasional glimpses of a guardrail poking above the snowfall.

"At least we're not moving farther north," he murmured. "The snowstorms have been brutal up there, so we need to be careful."

"No problem." Serge shifted the APC's gear and ground on, giving Keith a sly smile. "This is nothing we can't handle. Settle in for the ride."

After connecting to a highway that ran south in the long stretch of endless tundra, Keith spotted rounded white roofs of houses in the distance. A sign for the city stood bent sideways, twisted from the wind, making it impossible to name the place, not that such things mattered much anymore. The town lay in a perfect line southwest from the Osprey's crash site, and his raw gut instinct told him the McKnights must've headed in the direction of the town despite no evidence to back up his belief.

"Let's swing off the next chance we get," he said to the merc leader. "I've got a feeling about this place."

Serge nodded faintly and pressed the Stryker forward, watching the road through his virtual headset. The external front camera mirrored his head movements so he could see in any direction, magnify his vision and toggle to a rear camera view and look behind them if needed.

"Beyond the houses is a cluster of buildings that could be businesses," Serge said. "I think we should check those first. Your McKnights may have been scavenging for food or medical supplies."

"I agree," Keith replied. "Especially since we didn't find any evidence of them at the crash site."

Their arrival at the wrecked Osprey and subsequent search of the grounds had been an exhausting exercise. The plane's broken-apart fuselage had been empty, the broken rear of the craft stained with blood but no bodies to be found. They'd picked over the area, digging through the snow, spending two hours searching for evidence of the McKnight's direction or if they'd left anyone behind. After an exhaustive search they were convinced the entire family had survived and they got back in their APCs and rejoined the highway.

The lead APC rolled to the end of the exit ramp, slowed in a grind of chained tires against ice, and took a hard right to enter a dismal little town nestled between a pair of hills. Restaurant signs jutted up from the snow-crusted ground, bent by wind, glass broken and filled with white powder, long crystalline icicles pointing downward. Two gas stations bracketed two restaurants, a grocery store, a short strip mall, and a Dollar Saver. A separate roadside motel rested off to the left with only one floor with outside doors and an office at the end, an epitome of a solitary desert landmark if not for the snow scattered all about.

Keith unbuckled himself and stood with his hands pressed against the ceiling of the APC. "Okay, let's check it out. Just leave the engines running. We won't be long."

They parked the APCs on the middle line, lowered the rear doors with a high motor wine, and exited. Lena and Dmitri met them on the right side of the road, dressed in full winter gear: heavy boots, insulated pants and coats, and all-weather hoods and gloves. While each wore sidearm at their hip, they left the rifles inside the vehicles. Somehow, Dmitri stretched even the largest size apparel so that it made him look exceptionally muscular, though Lena's thin form practically swam in hers. Keith breathed in the cool, crisp air, the below zero temperatures already causing his nostrils to stick, eyes squinting, dry and cold. Seeing the mercs with their tinted snow goggles on, he remembered to pull his own over his eyes to cut off the brutally frigid wind.

"It is a long shot," Lena said, head swiveling as she scanned the town. "Based on satellite images and maps, there are at least 16 towns of this size within a hundred miles."

"Yeah, but this one is in the absolute center of our search area," he countered.

"We will split into two teams." Serge pointed to the far west gas station. "Keith and I will start at that end, while the rest of you take the other and move toward us. Move quickly. If there is no sign of them having been here, we will move on to the next most likely location."

All in agreement, they headed in their assigned directions, Keith putting his head down and trudging through the heavy snow to reach the distant building. On the way, he flexed his hands, fingertips still stinging from frostbite despite the strong pain medication in his bloodstream. Flashbacks of his frigid search for Linda McKnight badgered his mind, skin shivering at the thought of wallowing in the freezing river waters. With a low grunt, he shoved the thoughts aside, replacing them with images of him strangling her – followed by her mother. Since arriving at the base with the family, he'd felt himself feeling more rational, but out on the road surrounded by hardened killers it wasn't difficult to imagine slipping back into the insanity he'd felt overcoming him as he had chased after Linda, trying desperately to bring her down.

Bolstered by the warm gear and the pistol at his hip, a surge of optimism coursed through his veins and boots picking up their pace, he soon outpaced Serge to the gas station. The pair circled the building, noting several abandoned cars in the lot, one still sitting at the pump. Using their hands to sweep the snow from the windows, they peered inside to reveal two people sitting in the front seat, a man and a woman, both frozen stiff, skin turned blue and hard.

"This is... concerning," Serge said, face pressed to the glass.

"Yeah, how do people in a car freeze solid so fast?"

"I do not know, but that's what has me worried."

Keith straightened, looking toward the empty wasteland, then off to the north where dark clouds brooded on the horizon. "Back at the base I heard rumors of things they're calling spin-up storms. Nasty pieces of work. They're on you fast and they basically flash freeze everything in a matter of hours. Maybe it was one of them."

Serge's eyes narrowed as he looked off at the storm clouds, then spoke loudly. "The second we see a shift in wind or weather, we immediately return to the APCs. Lena, Dmitri, Mikael. Do you copy?"

The two-way communication devices on their right breast pockets sparked to life with the female merc's thick accent. "We read you loud and clear," she said in a clipped, professional tone. "If the weather changes, we return to the APCs."

The pair resumed their search of the gas station mini mart. The front window was broken out, snow scattered across the shelves and deep into the store and Keith stumbled upon a dead cashier lying frozen behind the counter, huddled in a blanket with days-old frost clinging to his broom-style mustache.

"This one must've survived the first few minutes of the spin-up storm." He stared at the stiffened form. "Poor bastard."

Serge only shook his head and walked across the floor between the stripped shelving, looking over the remaining snacks left behind by the looters when he uttered a sudden gasp. Keith looked up to see him pluck a peanut butter cup candy bar from its box and raise it, a grin stretching his lips wide.

"I cannot believe my luck." The merc leader's tone dripped with rare genuine delight. "My favorite candy bar found in the first store. We cannot get these where I am from."

Keith scoffed, pointing to the stiff wrapper in the merc's hand. "Yeah, too bad it's frozen solid. You can't even eat it."

Serge gave the frozen treat an optimistic look, lips twisting upward in thought. "I will let it thaw and see what happens."

With a shrug, Keith completed his search of the gas station and stepped back outside once more. When his partner caught up with him, the two men turned and walked east through a sit-down restaurant. Inside were more dead bodies, circled in the center with the cold remnants of a fire between them. They'd burned almost all the furniture yet had still frozen into blocks of ice, one mother holding a child in her lap, the smaller hands within hers as she tried to hold them out toward the heat.

Outside, Keith glanced warily to the north, even more untrusting of the bold, roiling cauldron of black clouds in the distance. Over the next hour they checked out the strip mall with its cell phone store and tavern and in the bar, bottles of whiskey and vodka sat frozen, the full ones having exploded into chunks of ice, amber liquid spilling to the floor in crystal shatters.

"This is also too bad." Serge held up a half-full bottle of Kentucky bourbon and gave it a stiff shake. "One does not usually see frozen liquor. Perhaps I will thaw this out too."

"Picking up souvenirs. Do you do this on every mission?"

"Not on every one. But this mission is, as you Americans say, a cakewalk." The merc leader chuckled. "I feel like a tourist."

With a grimace Keith left the tavern with Serge following him, weighed down with his finds. The group met back at the motel in what would have been the parking lot and faced the building, looking over the structure. Many of the doors and windows were broken, though some remained shut and undisturbed. Snow reached a quarter way up the wall, almost covering the doorknobs and slabs of hoarfrost hung over the eaves.

Serge glanced over. "Same groups. Pick an end and work toward the middle."

Keith and his teammate started at the motel's office where the ice crunched beneath their boots but never cracked enough to sink over two or three inches deep. There were signs of footprints partially covered in a new layer of frost, though he couldn't vouch for their freshness and he assumed anyone still in the area was dead, including the McKnights if they'd been around when the presumed spin-up storm struck.

They peeked inside the office window, but the door remained closed, the glass intact with no signs of occupancy, then they came next the hotel rooms. Starting at room number one, they used military shovels to dig around the doors, kicking them in and checking for people. The first five were empty, though the next held the corpse of a man curled up in a bathtub full of ice, arm hanging over the side and blood dripping from a cut wrist in a crimson icicle that pooled on the floor. With twin looks of disgust, the pair exited the room and continued their dismal search. Only when Dmitri's deep voice boomed over the line did Keith grow excited.

"Serge. I found something in twenty-two. Come look, please."

They stopped their digging and hustled across the hard packed snow to room twenty-two and, ducking through the open door, Keith gaped at what he saw. On the pair of twin beds were the frozen bodies of two United States soldiers, both wearing the familiar fatigues, hands resting comfortably over their stomachs, fingers interlocked in a state of peace. Mikael and Lena were inspecting them, the woman glancing up as Keith and Serge entered.

"There are older dressings on the floor," she said. "And if you lift up their shirts, you will see bandages across their belies." She lifted one man's stiff, frozen camo coat to reveal a crisp, bloodstained patch. "They might have sustained these wounds in the Osprey crash. Or, perhaps they were already hurt. Either way, it's a good chance these are your people?"

Keith slid between the beds, glancing from one soldier to the other. Crew cuts were brushed back as stiff as porcupine quills, faces covered with folded white washcloths and he reached in and tapped the collarbone of the corpse on his right. "Someone removed their dog tags after adjusting the bodies in a resting position."

"Yes, that is right," Lena nodded. "It appears they tried to administer aid to them, but they died and were left here."

"And didn't have the time to bury them." Keith bit his dry lower lip as he mulled over the scene.

Dmitri poked his head and shoulders into the door frame, drawing everyone's attention. "I have another to show. Outside."

Something in the man's voice made Keith's feet move, and he was the first out, stepping up from the dug-out entryway to stand atop the snowpack. Serge, Lena, and Mikael climbed out with him, turning to stare as Dmitri remained standing in the recession.

"I was digging and found this." He gestured at his feet.

Keith stepped around the group to get a better view, looking at a bundle of sticks and candy wrappers mixed with the ice chips and detritus the giant had dug up.

Bending and squinting, he picked through the rubbish. "Was this part of a campsite?"

Dmitri shrugged. "This is what I think. Perhaps we can dig. Find more."

Keith swung his military shovel off his back and pointed it. "Good work, man. Let's get digging."

The team spread out, tools in hand, and began chipping away at the tough, brittle snowpack. Putting his back into it, wincing as he gripped the shovel with his remaining frostbitten fingers aching in his gloves, Keith tossed aside a couple hundred pounds of snow. While the mercs worked hard, Dmitri was the real powerhouse, his massive arms swinging the steel shovel with sharp cracks, sweeping broken chunks of ice aside, barely breathing heavily as the others panted and labored with stinging lungs.

Soon, they had a 12 foot circle of snow cut out around the entryway, the excavation revealing a pair of logs and two chairs from inside a motel room. More digging showed the remnants of a fire, stones placed in a circle around it, half burned paper wrappers lingering in the frozen coals. Stepping back, one hand on his hip while leaning on his shovel, Keith surveyed the scene, piecing together the picture in his mind.

"So, they crashed the Osprey a few dozen miles away and walked in a southwesterly direction to reach this little town. They brought their wounded to the hotel where they could use the beds." Looking up, he used his shovel to make a sweeping motion from the northeast to the motel and across the thirty rooms. "They searched the town, grabbed some snacks and supplies, and hunkered down here."

"This is where they decided what camp to go to." Serge stood next to him and inspected the scene with the same critical eye. "But they left behind no clues."

Keith raised his hand. "No, I think–"

Something scraped the hard ice from somewhere to his left, just a snip of sound in the breeze that caught his trained ears. Head snapping up, he pinned someone peeking around the office corner wearing a hood, drawstrings pulled tight so the face hole was only a few inches in diameter. Reflexes kicking in, Keith dropped his shovel and took off in a dead sprint. Almost instantly pain lanced through his feet and up his legs as his frostbitten toes screamed in agony from his heel to his head. He pulled up short, falling into a staggering, limping gait as Lena and Mikael flew by him, boots churning up snow and ice chips. The person standing on the corner twisted and bolted out of sight, soon followed by the mercs. Cursing and hobbling, arms pumping, Keith reached the corner in time to see the chase was already over.

Lena had caught the individual and pinned them face first on the hard-packed ground. Knee pressed to their spine, arm bent behind them, the merc applied pressure and the captive cried out in pain, a woman's cry, nose and lips pressed into the snow, spitting and fighting. Lena only twisted the captive's wrist harder, drawing a louder, pained cry and Keith circled to get a better look, snapping at the merc.

"Ease up a little, would you?"

Lena relaxed her grip and loosened the drawstrings with her free hand, ripping back the hood, revealing the face of a dark-haired woman with light gray eyes in her mid 30s. Gaze shifting to Keith as he knelt in front of her, the captive curled her lip in a snarl, though Lena grabbed her by the hair and jerked her head backward, drawing an anguished yelp that took the edge off her anger. The other mercs circled to stand behind Keith, and when she saw them, her expression melted from scowling to fearful, doubly so upon seeing Dmitri's intimidating physique and stony glare.

"What's your name?" Keith asked, drawing the woman's attention back to him and her mouth clamped shut, looking toward the tundra as if searching for an escape.

"You won't get away." He gestured at Lena. "She'll break your arm if you struggle too hard. Luckily, for you, she listens to me."

"I do not listen to him," the merc spoke flatly, jerking the captive's hair for good measure.

"So," Keith spread his arms, "Let's have your name before she does something I can't control."

With fear-filled eyes, the woman croaked a word, sounding like she hadn't spoken in weeks. Finally, after swallowing hard, she managed something they could understand.

"M... Mary," she said. "My name is Mary."

"Good, Mary. Now, do you live around here?"

She nodded again.

"Were you here before the storms hit?" He gestured, shifting on his pained feet, trying to keep his expression flat in spite of the agony. "I mean, before all this snow?"

"I live just through the woods there on Hayes Road. I only came this far out to scavenge for food." She frowned. "But there's not much left."

"I got one of the last peanut butter cups," Serge held the candy aloft, grinning between it and the woman.

Keith shot Serge a flabbergasted look, shook his head and continued his interrogation. "You would have seen if someone was at the motel recently, yeah? Maybe a family? A group of people, with a fire out front?"

When the woman didn't answer right away, Lena dug her knee harder into Mary's spine, drawing a tight whimper from her throat, a compressed sound with no breath to drive it.

"Y... yes," she gasped. "There were some people here a few days ago. Camped out in front of the hotel. I didn't watch them for too long, because I was scared."

Excited at the information, Keith leaned forward, cupping her cheek with his palm. "It was a family, right? Was there a pilot with them? Anyone wearing military fatigues?"

She shook her head, greasy hair falling into her eyes, lips shivering. "Not a pilot. Doctors I think. They were looking over some kids, checking for injuries."

"Doctors?" Keith's brow furrowed in confusion, then he had it. "Oh, medics. You're saying there were medics with them?"

"Yes," the woman whispered hoarsely. "I told you everything I know. Please, let me go now. I've got to get back... I've got to get back to my boy."

"Where did they go?"

The captive's chin jerked toward the road. "South along the highway."

Looking the way she pointed, his blood pumped excitedly. "Okay, good. Yeah, we'll let you go." He nodded to Lena.

The merc gave the woman's head a shove, pressing her knee once for good measure before standing and backing away. The captive slowly climbed to her feet, head lowered, gaze darting from one person to the next. Feet sliding to the side, she retreated, looking for a gap to escape when Dmitri puffed up, jaw tightening in a clinch of steel. He lunged forward with a grunt, lips drawn into a fierce grimace and the woman yelped and danced back, twisting, half stumbling in the opposite direction before getting her feet beneath her. She ran in a dead-panic, boots pounding across the icy scree as the giant rumbled with laughter deep inside his chest, sounding like a slow roll of thunder.

"Very cute," Keith said as the woman vanished out of sight, then he turned to Serge. "So, the McKnights were here, and we know their general travel direction."

The merc leader nodded thoughtfully. "I agree. They are alive, and seemingly intact. We just need to locate where they went next."

Lena folded her arms across her chest and raised her chin. "Give me an hour. I will find them."

CHAPTER TEN

President John Zimmerman
Havana, Cuba

President Zimmerman steps from the armored limousine into the warm Cuban air, looking slowly left and right, noting hundreds of military personnel lingering on the terraces, rifle barrels sweeping the grounds for signs of trouble. At the top, a long, imposing structure stands erect with a domed roof not unlike the United States Capitol building. Over one hundred years old, perched in the middle of the city, it dwarfs everything in the surrounding area, proud and stoic against a sky streaked with unusually dark clouds. Twelve granite columns stretch across the front of the edifice, gleaming grayish white, the paint along the top chipped and peeled away. The gardens surrounding the building are of European design, comprising wide sections of lawn dotted with royal palm trees and other exotic shrubs. It is *El Capitolio*. The Cuban Capital Building.

He begins his long walk up the fifty-six steps to the front door, heavily armed Secret Service members in military camouflage trailing behind, each heavily armed, only a few feet from their ward as they join the military forces in focusing on protecting the president. Civilian staffers in suits and overalls carry boxes and push carts of goods, swarming around and through the Secret Service detachment, delivering items from trucks and vans parked in the street.

As the president's shoes scuff on the pitted concrete, he raises his eyes and takes in the sky. The dark streaks of clouds stretch in from the north, the fingers of gloom reaching farther south by the hour. The obvious change in the jet stream is evidenced by the muted stillness and occasional bursts of unseasonable winds cutting sharply across the terraced stairs. While he's never before been to Cuba, the chill breeze ruffling his hair feels off, a far cry from the expected tropical heat and soft breezes he's been expecting.

They usher him up the stairs, flanked by the twenty-one-foot tall, greenish-gray statues of *El Trabajo* and *La Virtud Tutelary*, then lead him through the front door into the main rotunda. In the hall, directly beneath the domed cupola, Zimmerman comes face-to face with *La Estatua de la Republica*, the Stature of the Republic. The forty-nine ton, forty-nine foot tall bronze statue dominates the room as it stands tall on an eight foot pedestal, the striking figure of a woman gripping the top of a long spear as she stares at some distant danger.

He stops and admires her beauty for several minutes while his staff wait patiently and nervously behind him. After some time, he turns away and follows an inlaid marble floor framed with gilded lamps on the walls, the group's hard-soled shoes echoing in the cavernous passage. Next comes two semicircular chambers with seats reserved for the Cuban Parliament and Chamber of Deputies, empty now that they've dislodged the government. A set of side stairs brings them to a long hallway of normal size for staff and administrators.

Members of the president's relocation team are busy removing pictures of Cuban leaders from the walls, tossing gold-leaf frames with images of Fidel Castro into boxes and pulling statues from tables. In their place, they raise portraits of former U.S. presidents, NASA milestones, and scenic depictions of United States geography. Still, there is something different about the architecture that can't be fixed with simple changes to the décor. The stiffness of the carpets and rugs and the claustrophobic walls gives the President a sick, sinking feeling in his stomach.

At the end of the hall, his new office awaits. The Cuban Presidential Suite is a long room with tall, white walls, bathed in golden light from elegant wall sconces. Crimson curtains frame the windows, though his staff have removed the rest of the Cuban furniture and décor, both for aesthetic and security reasons. Inside, the Resolute desk stands stoic and heavy, its oaken sides and spread-winged eagle on the front filling him with a pride that lifts his heart. Workers continue to swap out pictures and shift more familiar furniture into place, setting his usual whiskey decanters and glasses on a table, doing their best to make it feel like home.

Circling the thick wooden desk, Zimmerman slips into his chair, gives it a spin and peers out through the windows. While there should be a view of the gardens behind the capital, construction workers stand in his way as they exchange the existing hardware out with six-inch panes of glass, both to stop attacks on the President and to help ward off the inevitable cold.

As he looks on, the staff bring in more chairs—three for Rita, Mark, and Rick—and two sofas are placed against the walls behind them. Maxine approaches with her tablet, halting on the other side of his desk.

"Sir, the Joint Chiefs of Staff are here as well as the new governor."

The window workers are wrapping up and they step away, giving him a view of the gardens and administration buildings beyond it.

Spinning back around, he faces his lead staffer.

"Bring them in."

"First, can you sign a few things?"

Laying her tablet in front of him, she points to direct his stylus to sign a dozen electronic documents. When Maxine is done with him, several more staffers move in to replace her with more things to sign. After forty-five minutes of signing and marking e-paperwork, his hand grows sweaty on the digital pen. Finally, blessedly, they disappear and Rita, Mark, and Rick enter, taking the three seats directly in front of him. Others come in, milling around, some sitting on sofas and talking quietly.

A sense of dread grips the President's chest and he lifts his arms and shakes them to release the tension, expanding his lungs and forcing himself to breathe and relax. The room quiets as people pull out their tablets and phones, receiving the latest updates from Central Command and Zimmerman clears his throat to kill the remaining noise before nodding to General Davidson to get started.

Mark's normally stiff shirt is wrinkled, sleeves rolled up, salt-and-pepper hair unkempt as he returns the nod and turns to glance over those assembled. "Hello, everyone. I think we should all take a deep breath and appreciate what's been accomplished. The Cuban annexation was successful, and we've moved into our new home away from home. Most importantly, we did it with as few casualties as possible, and with the cooperation of the Cuban government – along with the requisite assurances and promises."

"Bribes, you mean." Zimmerman murmurs, barely loud enough to be heard by anyone except the three closest to him.

"It's been a long, tough journey," Rita adds, standing to address everyone, ignoring the President's remark. "We moved the Cuban staff to the centralized headquarters just east of here and have assured them they'll resume their duties as soon as we leave."

Dark thoughts circling in his head, fingers tapping lightly on his desk, Zimmerman releases an impatient sigh. "Look, let's cut through the bullshit. We've invaded a sovereign nation and forced the citizens out of their homes, disrupted their economy and halted their way of life. While the casualties on entry were low, we're still condemning these people to an unknown fate. There won't be a return to normalcy for the Cuban staff. It will never be the same again for any of them. Things are *not* going back to normal."

Both hands resting on the surface of his desk, the president scans the entire room, hardened gaze rimmed with sadness and despair. "When the temperature changes arrive, this place will turn into one giant tomb." A dismal pause settles over them, and he let it sit until people shift in their chairs and glance around at each other uncomfortably. "So, let's get on with it. Tell me who we're invading next."

The advisor remained quiet until Rita speaks up, his Secretary of State clicking swiftly through items on her tablet.

"I'll start with the status of the casualties in our own country," she says, glancing up. "We base these numbers on a count of citizens we've moved to Mexico, what we know of current and future temperature changes, and what is being reported by the scavenging teams who are still deep in the country." She takes a deep breath as she scans the figures one last time before speaking. "As it stands, we've evacuated close to fifty million Americans from the continental mainland. That includes those who self-evacuated and were counted at camps and crossings. The rest are dead or will be if they don't get out soon. Anyone above the fortieth parallel died long ago, and anyone above the thirty-fifth is likely already dead as well." Gasps echo through the room. "Anyone above the thirtieth will be dead in the next week, based on temperature predictions." Her voice shrinks with each statistic. "But the numbers are what were estimated *before* our attempts to close the anomaly. It's bound to become reality sooner than later."

The silence that follows is deafening as the president taps his fingers harder on the desk surface, General Davidson stiffening in his seat. "Mexico, thankfully, is on its last legs, and we've quashed all major resistance."

"I thought they'd surrendered unconditionally." Zimmerman eyes him idly.

"A few groups of rebels gave us problems in the capital, against their government's orders, but they've been dealt with."

"So, we should expect no more trouble from them?" A part of Zimmerman's soul hinges on the general's reply, and he quits his tapping and presses his sweating palms against the desk.

"That's correct, sir. The Mexican resistance is over."

"But a lot of our people are dead," Rita continued, killing Zimmerman's initial exhale of relief. "In fact, well over half the country. Most of Canada is gone, too, and even Pierre has stopped calling. While we haven't been able to confirm it, we think the Canadian government fled across the Atlantic and set up offices in France."

Rick Manglor speaks up for the first time, hair tangled, eyes beyond weary with fat black circles beneath them. His beard has grown out in patches of scruff that he hasn't shaved in weeks. "And that won't do them any good. The weather's turning there as well, though not as severely as here. We've already seen reports of hundreds of thousands, probably millions, dead across northern Africa, Europe, and Asia."

"It's the only thing keeping our enemies and allies from attacking us," the general adds. "Good thing, because they're blaming us for what happened."

"Can you blame them after that shitshow we produced?" John mumbles, guilt spiking his heart for the thousandth time so far in the day. His fingers start their relentless tapping once more. "One more reason to be on guard."

The room grows silent again, the seconds lingering into long moments of discomfort until his quiet whisper breaks through the pall, voice hoarse and husky, betraying his failing confidence.

"Is that it?"

Rita clears her throat and continues. "I'm... afraid it gets worse, sir. Initial projections estimated that this cold snap would descend well below the thirtieth parallel." She shoots a nervous look at the chief scientist. "Now we think it will sink as low as the twentieth."

"That's the top third of Africa, and all of Mexico. And it could last for decades," Rick stammers. "That's why I'm suggesting Hawaii is a no-go."

"Plus, the logistics of transporting our citizens across the ocean would be near impossible," Rita adds. "We need a place that's accessible by land to escort our people. And it needs enough resources to meet our substantial energy requirements."

"We'll need heat no matter how far south we go." Rick shakes his head. "This could get worse than our wildest imaginations."

"Is our location certain to meet our requirements?" Zimmerman steeples his fingers.

"Yes, sir." The general answers. "More oil than we can shake a stick at, and in the last five years they've been overhauling their infrastructure and urban housing. Even with their own government getting in the way, they've put together a fairly stable backbone, perfect for what we need."

"And we're way ahead of the game," the general adds. "Our initial recon teams report their military is in complete disarray, and they'll be easy to move on."

"I'm assuming we've already got ships heading there?"

Mark nods, jaw set with firm resolution. "Three attack subs and several destroyers in the area. Stealth recon has been in the air for the past forty-eight hours, monitoring their movements. We've got them locked down hard."

A folder that had been sitting in front of Rita the entire time slides toward him. It is the same one she'd passed to him the day before, the one he's been reluctant to open. The Secretary of State's hand lifts, her eyes focused on John as if daring him to push it away.

Nervous fingers reach for the folder and he draws it closer, opens it, and pages through, scanning the military projections on casualties and the potential risks and rewards of an attack. He notes points of geographical importance and flicks through the main battle strategy for winning the conflict quickly and decisively. He wants it to be easy, but it has to come from the general's lips.

"We've been running our troops ragged for the last ten days, and I'm seeing reports of equipment failures and low resources. We'd be facing fresh, motivated soldiers who must see what we're going to do next. Are you sure we can do this?"

The general's gaze remains flat. "We have to, Mr. President. If we don't...."

John's eyes drop to the folder. All their hopes are placed in its hastily constructed pages and plans. It is the last of many he'd seen over the past couple months, all of which have yielded mixed results. He draws a long, deep breath, releasing it in a huff. "Okay. Do it. My God have mercy on us for it."

The president shuts the flap and slides the folder back to Rita, its black front marked with red letters.

VE ANX.

CHAPTER ELEVEN

Tom McKnight
Nuevo Laredo, Mexico

Marty's cold gray eyes stared them up and down, his fists clenched loosely at his sides as his two henchmen stood a little ways back from him, both large, big-bellied men with broad shoulders and beards, looking like angry, puffed up bears in their thick coats.

"What do you want?" Tom asked, hand gripping the shiv in his pocket.

"I heard a curious thing."

"Oh yeah? What's that?"

"Rumor has it you two have been going around and doing some trading. Now, that tells me either you're hard up for supplies or you're thinking about ditching this place early, without a single consideration for what I'm working toward."

"I don't answer to you. I answer to my family's own needs, and how I can keep us alive in this camp."

Marty's voice rose in an annoyed growl, his chin lifting, fists squeezing harder. "Are you trying to get out of here or not?"

"We were short on supplies, like you said." Tom gave a breathy sigh. "I was just securing more food and blankets." Stepping aside, he removed his hand from his pocket and gestured at the bins of MREs. "Look, we've got five people to take care of, probably the biggest family in camp. This is maybe two week's worth of food for us."

"Yeah, yeah, spare me the sob story." Marty pointed at the bins in an accusatory gesture. "That's way more than a couple weeks if you stretch them out."

"You don't know what you're talking about." Barbara stepped up on Tom's left, toe tapping the ground, green eyes burrowing into man. "Ever raised three children before, Marty? Growing, hungry kids?"

"I've raised two. Got them all grown up and out of the house years ago. So, yeah, I've got some experience with that."

When she responded, her voice shook with anger, words pressing through clenched teeth. "You don't know what it's like doing it so far from home in a refugee camp, wondering if you've got enough for the next meal. *That's* why we made the trades. *That's* why we went out today. You keep saying we have to escape the government, but the biggest threat to my kids and husband is *you*."

Marty's posture relaxed, some of the tension and accusation draining from his body, though his jaw still worked back and forth. "You shouldn't use your kids as a shield. You're hiding behind them, doing things your own way. Alone. If you would've got on board from the beginning, we wouldn't have to settle things like this."

"Let's get one thing straight." Tom pointed at the ground, using a finger to emphasize each word. "We've nothing to settle with you."

"You're the only family who hasn't joined in, or at least donated supplies to the cause."

Shifting his right foot back, hand squeezing the shiv handle, Tom cycled through his options if things became physical. "My wife just told you we have nothing to donate."

Marty glanced over his shoulder at one of his comrades. "Grab a bin."

The man came forward, ambling toward the McKnights and Tom

crouched and turned sideways, ready to lead with his left foot. "I'm warning you, big boy," he told the enforcer. "Take another step, you'll be eating your teeth for dinner."

In an instant, Tom had transformed from his stand-offish self to someone with nothing left to lose. His voice dripped with violence and ill intent, his eyes a pair of twin fires that stopped the enforcer in his tracks, causing him to back up a step and give his boss a questioning look.

"Marty, take your boys and leave before one of them gets hurt," Barbara spat.

The laugh that came out was laced with nervousness as Marty tried to calculate Tom's change in demeanor. "If you don't give up a bin, feeding your kids will be the last thing you'll need to worry about."

Before the words finished exiting the man's mouth, Tom lunged forward, shiv in hand, reaching for Marty's wrist. Marty saw it coming and yanked his own blade from his pocket, taking a swipe but Tom blocked it with his forearm, then gripped Marty's coat near the wrist, spun him, and pinned his arm behind him. The man yelped in pain, the knife clattering to the pavement as Tom slipped his shiv to Marty's throat. Arching his back, he bent the rebel leader backwards into a defenseless position, the point of his weapon pressed firmly against Marty's skin.

Tightening his grip, Tom growled into Marty's ear. "What did you say about my kids?" He'd spent the last several days tired and weary from sleeping on the floor, being chased across the country, only to end up in a strange land with few friends. Having his enemy in an armlock sent a surge of energy coursing through his body and with a sharp jerk, he pressed the shiv into the man's neck, drawing a cowardly whimper and a trickle of blood.

"Tom, be careful." Barbara spoke softly, looking over toward the fence. "There could be guards on patrol. If they see you with that..."

Marty swallowed hard, barely getting the words out as he tried to reason with Tom. "Hey, buddy. Listen to your wife. How you gonna help your kids if--"

"Shut. Your. Mouth." Tom raised his wrist another few inches, drawing a stifled yowl as something popped in Marty's shoulder.

"We need to wrap this up," Barbara whispered. "People are starting to watch us."

Looking around, Tom spotted folks at the burn barrel in the southeast corner of the camp gazing in their direction, staring with open mouths at the altercation in the pharmacy courtyard. And while the street was relatively clear, his wife was right, there'd likely be guards along at any minute.

In the moment, Tom wanted nothing more than to flick his wrist and slice the blade through Marty's neck, ending the McKnight's threat in the blink of an eye. His patience had officially run out, he was exhausted and no longer in the mood for playing games or tiptoeing around people who intended to do him harm. Looking at Barbara, he gave her a pleading look, begging for her blessing to take Marty out of the equation, but received nothing except a hesitant shake of her head. *Not worth it. Not right now.*

Mind snapping back into focus, Tom glared at the bodyguards. "You two get out of here. Get going. Go!" The pair backed away hesitantly, eyes on their boss.

"Go on." Marty's voice was timid as he tried to speak without causing the blade to penetrate further into his skin. "No sensing risking my neck for a bin of MREs."

The men kept backing up until they reached the edge of the courtyard then they turn and ambled off, hands jammed into the pockets, feet moving swiftly. One glanced back before they turned and disappeared up the street. With the guards out of the way, and the immediate threat to his family gone, Tom jerked the shiv away, pushed Marty forward, and kicked him in the back to send him stumbling. Marty caught himself, stood slowly, and pivoted. Rolling his shoulder, he fixed the McKnights with a genuine glare of hatred as a thin line of blood trailed down his neck and dribbled on his coat.

Tom waved the shiv. "No more warnings. You come around my family again and you'll never see the outside of this camp."

"And let *me* say one last thing, *Tom*." Lip curled upward in a sneer, mustache twisting, the man issued a final demand. "You've got one more chance to join us, or pay the price. Don't make me decide for you."

Tom held the shiv at chest level, pointing the tip at the rebel leader, staring him down as Marty slowly backed away, retreating into the gray afternoon light before slipping into a side alley. As he vanished, Barbara's shoulder's sagged and she leaned against Tom's shoulder.

Tom held her, letting out a slow breath, willing his heart rate to slow. "That was *way* too close."

"No kidding."

"Are you okay?"

"Yeah, I'm fine. But what the hell was that?" Barbara stepped to the side, looking him up and down. "I've never seen you do anything like that before."

Tom chuckled as he tucked the weapon away and stacked the bins, lifting them with a grunt. "I'll tell you about it inside. Right now we need to get this food out of sight."

Barbara knocked gently on the door and shelves slid across the floor on the other side before the girls opened up the entrance. "You guys okay?" Sam asked, voice shaking slightly.

"We're fine." Tom strained, holding the supplies. "Help me get the food inside."

His daughters made room for him to carry the satchel and bins to the table at the back of the pharmacy. Jack was ecstatic to see they'd picked up several more packs of chili mac, but Sam was unfazed by Tom holding up a few pizza ones, jumping back to the subject of immediate concern.

"We saw the whole thing." Sam looked between her parents, hand resting on one bin. "We were standing by the window."

"Marty wanted to have a… discussion with us." Barbara started, when Samantha interrupted, shooting her father a look in the process.

"Looked kinda one way to me. Nice work, dad."

"You should have stabbed him." Linda spoke the words offhandedly as she sorted through the bags of MREs.

Tom couldn't help but snort at Linda's reaction, even as he took her arm and turned her around, drawing her next to her sister. "Probably true, but there's a time for everything, and now's the time for us to lay low and not draw attention. Besides, we can't be hurting people whenever want to, just because we can."

"Dad. Come on." Linda shook her head at him as she pawed through the MREs. "You're talking to us like it's a few months ago. I *shot* Keith, dad. Shot him, stabbed him and dumped him in a frozen river. Sam said she watched Jerry..." Linda trailed off as Sam's shoulders slumped.

"Sweetie," Barbara interjected, "Just because you've heard it before doesn't mean it doesn't bear repeating. Killing someone should be a last resort. Your father was able to defuse the situation out there without resorting to it."

"Next time might be a different story." Sam replied.

"You're not wrong," Tom said, "But we'll burn that bridge when we come to it."

Linda pressed on. "I just want to know when you'll teach us that move. I could have used that against Keith when he grabbed us at the last place."

"I'll have to talk to your mother about that." Shoulder tensing beneath his wife's gaze, he gave them an uneasy grimace.

After a meal of MREs and canned vegetables, Barbara got the kids busy with sweeping and cleaning their small living quarters. With little to do to pass the time, she'd insisted that they at least keep things tidy, both to keep them occupied and to expend a bit of energy in a safe environment. Once they were set up, Barbara motioned to Tom, leading him across the pharmacy floor to where a few old booths rested against a wall from the place's early days as a soda shop. Wind gusted across the pharmacy roof as they sat down, wood creaking and whistling like a ghostly birdsong and a draft wafted beneath the table, causing a cold shiver to run up his spine.

Barbara looked over at the three children for a long moment, then back at Tom. "So, when were you going to tell me you're a ninja?"

Tom scoffed, spreading his hands. "That was hardly a ninja move, hon."

"Maybe not, but it sure took me by surprise. And I'm smart enough to know what a professional move looks like. Executing a maneuver like that requires a lot of skill and practice."

Tom turned over his hands and made circles on the table's surface. "You remember those old missions I did for the government, back when we were first getting the farm going?"

Recognition dawned in her eyes. "Ahh. I should've known you'd had some combat training. That was years ago, though. How'd you remember to do it so well that you could do *that* to Marty?"

Tom grinned awkwardly, taking his wife's words as a compliment. "It's like riding a bike. You get rusty, but you never really forget what you learned. And, c'mon, Marty's not exactly some super-soldier."

Barbara fixed him with a skeptical look, though her crooked grin told him he'd postponed the full truth for another day. "True. Marty's not in fighting shape. He *is* ornery as hell, though, and you wounded his pride like I doubt it's ever been wounded before."

"You got that right."

Backside edging across the seat, she snuggled up next to him, sharing her warmth and settling his restless nerves. She slipped his arm under his and interlocked their fingers. "So, what are we going to do about him? I can't see a guy like that allowing the transgression to pass. Embarrassing him is one thing, but you embarrassed him in front of his men and others in camp. I mean, he's bound to want to get revenge."

"I've been thinking about that." Tom squeezed her fingers and tugged her closer, resting her arm against his chest. "If we're to avoid any unnecessary violence and attention, I think we might have to move our timeline for getting out of here up. Which reminds me." He glanced up at an old battery-powered digital clock sitting on the bar which they'd traded a handful of aspirins for two days prior, and which came in handy for keeping their pre-arranged meetings with Saanvi. "It's getting dark, and we're supposed to meet Saanvi in 10 minutes."

Barbara straightened and unraveled her arm. "Oh, no. You're right. We should get moving if we want to catch her."

As they slid out of the seat, Tom gave her hand an affectionate squeeze before letting go. "And we may need her more than ever if we're going to make an early break."

Covered in their warm weather gear, they put Sam in charge of the store, giving her an extra word of warning about Marty before they stepped back out. Standing next to the lifeless burn barrel, they locked arms and waited until the coast was clear. A crisp chill seeped through their thin layers of material, caressing their skin with icy fingers. Chills ran up the backs of Tom's arms, wind gusting hard from the west, forcing the pair to lean together to keep from being shoved around.

The usual suspects stood around the orange glow of nearby burn barrels, identifying themselves with coat patches sown on out of sheer boredom. Tom remembered his first day in camp when the jackets had been fresh and clean, recently handed out by the military supply team, and it hadn't taken long for them to grow soiled and worn due to their living conditions.

"Okay, I don't see Marty or his guards anywhere. Let's go."

They stepped into the street, glancing right 30 yards where Saanvi usually waited and the medic was there, walking away from the fence, leading Smooch by a leash. With a click of his tongue, he grabbed Barbara's hand and pulled her along, snapping his fingers quickly. The German Shepherd's head swiveled in their direction, eyes brightening, ears perking up. With a high, excited whine, the dog tugged Saanvi back toward the fence. The woman turned, caught sight of the McKnights, and rushed back with a wide smile.

"I didn't think you were coming," she said breathlessly, locking her fingers into the fencing.

"We didn't think we were coming either." With a look in both directions, Tom checked for eavesdroppers but saw no one within earshot. "We ran into a little trouble with the group we were telling you about earlier."

Barbara knelt and placed her palm against the chain-links, accepting licks and nuzzles from Smooch, cooing and making kissing noises to the dog's happy whining and swishing tail. The dog wore a makeshift sweater, holes cut out of the woolen material for her legs to fit through, along with booties that were tied around her feet.

"Can you tell me what's going on with them?" Saanvi fixed him with a hopeful expression. "Who's running the show?"

With a deep breath, Tom rotated his head in both directions, still afraid of getting caught and having to deal with more than just a few thugs. "It's a guy named Marty. He's leading the whole thing, basically forcing everyone to take a side. You're either with him or against him."

Barbara looked up. "Much as we'd like to just remain neutral to protect ourselves, we're the latter. Against him, I mean."

"That's good to hear." Saanvi nodded, looking from Tom to Barbara and then back again. "Whatever you do, don't get caught helping them. Central Command is taking cases of rebellion seriously, and they're punishing people hard."

"No problem there. But he's making it difficult to trade with others in camp."

Saanvi stiffened, shoulders straightening as she gripped the fence harder. "Are you getting the food you need for the kids? Because if you can't, I'll put an end to this right now."

"No, it's okay." Tom shook his head. "We've got plenty of MREs to last us a few weeks."

Barbara glanced up. "Thankfully, some people in camp aren't doing everything Marty says. We were able to get those MREs and keep them despite his bullying. Barely."

"But don't do anything just yet," Tom added quickly. "We want to make our escape first. If they lock this place down before we break out, things will get harder. The revolt... it'll happen within the next 24 hours or so, based on what we've been hearing."

"Got it. I appreciate the information." The medic tapped her fingers on the chain-link. "But where does that leave you guys? If I put my captain on alert in, say, 12 hours, that doesn't give you much of the window to get out ahead of time." The medic leaned closer. "What's the plan?"

"We spotted a weak spot in the fencing on the north block we can use to slip through. It sits by a burned down house that will give us enough cover to hide. Once the coast is clear, we'll break through the fence and get away. The problem is they have one guard on that side of the camp, always on duty."

"There are supposed to be two or three." Saanvi shook her head.

Tom scoffed softly. "They're underperforming then."

"That's not surprising. There's a lot of that going around. But after this revolt, I can guarantee a major lockdown."

"Exactly why we need to get out before that happens."

Saanvi breathed deep, thinking. After a moment, she tapped the cold metal. "Make sure you're at the fence when the revolt starts. I'll clear the guard, but you have to get past the gang."

Tom glanced at his wife and shifted a nod to the medic. "We'll get past Marty and his goons and be waiting."

Saanvi offered a confident smile, tinged at the edges with a hint of nervousness. "Okay, then. I'll take Smooch back."

Kneeling next to the fence, Tom put his fingers through and let the dog lick them. "Hang tight, girl. We're coming for you soon."

The McKnights stood, watching their beloved pet, and the one person who could bust them from the camp, stroll south and disappear between the Army green troop tents.

"Well, I guess we're committed now," Tom said. "We just need to make sure were ready."

The pair turned and headed back to the pharmacy with the night covering them in shadows. Back in the courtyard, they knocked on the front door and listened as the shelves slid away. The entrance opened, spilling out a faint light, and they stepped into what he hoped wasn't their last peaceful evening together.

CHAPTER TWELVE

Specialist Lance Morales
Santa Fe, New Mexico

The shrieking, tearing infrastructure pierced Morales's ears, driving like a wedge down his spine, freezing his blood cold. Soldiers shouted and hollered, crouching low to the ground, hiding from the collapse. Smith grabbed his arm, pulling him in one direction, but Morales fought back, jerking the other way, backing toward the bay doors.

"Come on, man," the lieutenant yelled. "Get into the break room!"

"No!" He shook his head, pointing upward to the rear of the warehouse where light snowfall drifted through the dark, rolling fumes. "The roof is collapsing in back, but not up front. Call the men this way! Get the trucks and equipment pushed forward as shelter! We need to move them!"

Smith stared at him, blinked, then shifted his attention to the back corner of the warehouse. With a tilt of his head to home in on the sound, the lieutenant gave a slow nod.

"I think you're right," he said in a hoarse whisper. "We have to tell the captain." Twisting away, Smith searched for Jones through the crush of dark forms scattering in the glowing orange flames.

"There he is!" He pointed to the tall, red-headed man standing next to his Humvee with the long antennas, gripping an officer's shoulder in each hand, face a mask of grim helplessness.

Morales waded through the crowd, bumped hard by the shoving, shouting soldiers. He grabbed a woman by her coat and threw her past him, then kept going, not worrying if Smith was behind him. His fellow soldiers jostled and knocked him around like a pinball as he surged forward, slamming him against an armored car before he fought his way free.

"Captain!" he shouted, voice raspy from the fumes he'd been breathing, the sound not loud enough to cut through the shrieking warehouse. "Captain! Hey, cap!"

The last note found a silent spot in the noise, drawing Jones's attention as the specialist waved and pointed toward the back of the warehouse. "Get them to the front! Move the trucks! It's coming... ooof!"

Someone slammed into him, cutting off his sentence.

The captain's gaze shifted between the collapsing ceiling and Morales, understanding dawning in his eyes. Grabbing his nearby officers, he jerked them around, pointing toward the roof. Orders flew from his mouth as he pointed to the trucks and then towards the bowing bay doors. The troops caught on, spreading the word, panic turning to purpose and purpose to action. Two men climbed into the nearest Humvees, started them up, and drove them thirty yards to the bay doors. Three more trucks pulled in behind those, Captain Jones standing in the middle of it all, directing traffic with his waving hands.

Morales reeled to find Smith doing the same thing, spinning troops and pointing them toward vehicles. He made a beeline for his excavator, climbing into the cabin and powering the big machine to life. Carefully he put it in gear, spun it on its tracks, and edged it to the front, parking it tight behind the other trucks. With a gasp, he killed the engine and jumped down, dancing back to avoid getting hit by an Army Growler that flew up behind the excavator.

Morales climbed onto the Growler's hood, traipsing over the roof and down the backside, leaping to the next one. From vehicle to vehicle, he staggered and slipped, losing his balance and nearly falling a handful of times. Eyes on the collapsing ceiling, he watched as thick pieces of steel and insulation fell under the weight of tons of ice and snow. An enormous slab of ice broke away, shaped like a dagger, slamming through a Humvee's roof, pinning it to the floor in a massive crash of metal and breaking glass.

Even as the blizzard poured in bearing destruction, the toxic cloud flowed up and outside in a vortex of air currents, clearing the air of the fumes that had been choking them. With the gaps in their shelter came a blistering stiff wind that whipped through the warehouse, knocking soldiers to their knees and sending hats flying off. Morales slammed his hands to his cheeks as his skin felt like it was being flash-frozen and flames from a burn barrel sent a whirl of glowing cinders into the racks and rafters, catching some of the remaining supplies on fire. The flames flared up and expanded, growing into a proper blaze and Morales leapt from the truck, reaching into the rear seat and grabbed an extinguisher. He spun on his toes, looking for his friend and screaming at the top of his lungs as he wove his way toward the flaming racks.

"Hey, Smith! Smith!"

"What?" the lieutenant shouted back from where he stood halfway across the warehouse.

Morales pointed at the racks as flames engulfed old wooden skids, paper materials, and cardboard and Smith grabbed several soldiers, shouting for more extinguishers, pointing at the growing inferno. In the sea of creeping vehicles and chaotic stampede, Morales climbed on a hood, leaping across to another, dancing on the balls of his feet. His boots landed heavily, denting the hoods, slipping and sliding on trickling ice shards.

Finally he reached the main aisle, jumped down, and circled around the first rack, which was already partially collapsed from when the bulldozer had crashed into it earlier. Flames were dancing up to the second level and climbing and Morales pulled the pin on the fire extinguisher, aimed the nozzle, and squeezed the handle. A gust of powdery white squelching agent blasted the base of the skids, mingling with the falling snow and blistering winds. While his efforts partially snuffed the fire, the wind drove the flames higher, stretching them together like fiery tongues.

Morales's cheeks burned as hot and cold wafts of air alternately buffeted him. Squeezed into the thin space between the racks, he crept closer to the base of the fire, cinders flashed towards his face, forcing him to jerk away. The metal racking reacted to the intense, clashing temperatures, bending and grinding against pressures it wasn't built for. A moment later, six columns of fire-squelching agent shot through from the other side. Soldiers stood on vehicles and directed their nozzles at the flames, countering the fire's fierceness.

Morales was caught in a dangerous position, the wind and gusting extinguishers sending the soot and cinders back in his direction, loose material raining down on his head. A big section of smoldering wood separated and plunged toward him and he spun on his heel and dove to the floor, landing hard, catching his chin on the concrete as he kicked and crawled for the main aisle.

Timber and metal crashed around him in a storm of cold flames, the smell of his own burning hair stuffed up his nose. He winced and grunted and gasped, fearful of sucking in flying embers. Eyes closed, he wriggled ahead blindly until his hand landed on a boot, then looked upward to see that it was Smith, and the lieutenant snatched him by his coat and jerked him to his feet. He began a frantic, abusive swatting of Morales's head and neck, knocking him around and beating the flames until they petered out.

Morales threw back his own hood, grabbing the lieutenant's shoulders. "It's coming down! It's coming down!"

As the racks collapsed against one another, the top level dropping in a clatter of smoke and ruins, they sprinted away, clambering onto a truck. They leapt toward safety, skipping from one hood to the other like boulders in a creek. Fire nearly out, the soldiers gave up and scrambled to escape the collapse. Morales slipped and fell, landing on a windshield. Rolling over, he stared at the back of the warehouse where almost all the toxic fumes had escaped. All that remained was the constant avalanche of ice and snow, covering everything in a smoking white mist.

The roof split open like a ruptured ship, hull breached, pieces of fiberglass, metal sheeting, and drywall swinging in massive chunks, plunging, crashing. Captain Jones, in the thick of it, grabbed at soldiers, lifting any that had fallen into the gaps and shoving them toward the bay doors and away from the collapsing section. Morales scrambled to his feet, slipping on the wet hood and nearly falling again. He threw in with the captain, helping the troops retreat under the catastrophic barrage of elements. The wind whipped in blinding flashes of ice and sleet but, to his surprise, it had lost its sting.

The rumbling faded, tapering into nothing. He helped another man up from the crowded floor and stood with his shoulders hunched, gasping on cold fresh air, hating the ache but relishing its pureness after withstanding so much of the smokey fumes. The wind gave one more gust before it died off, leaving a swath of gray light illuminating the warehouse floor. The soldiers stared at the quiet snowfall drifting through the stark grayness, casting their faces upward, taking deep breaths of the crisp air, leaning over and coughing the gunk out of their lungs, spitting it onto the floor. Eyes clearing, the breeze sweeping out the toxicity, Morales turned to Smith with an exuberant smile as the lieutenant clapped him on the shoulder.

"In the future, we should try to avoid warehouses."

A deep belly laugh burst from Morales's chest, forcing him to cough and choke for a good 30 seconds. When it was over, they spotted Jones once again gathering the officers to him. As the pair made their way over, stepping from truck to truck, he placed his hand against his chin and brought it back with a spot of blood.

"Well, that could have been a hell of a lot worse," he said, wiping his fingers on his coat.

"You got that right." Smith chuckled again as they stood on the APC, staring at the captain as he issued more orders.

"Okay, people. It seems the spin-up storm has died down. Don't ask me how or why, but I'm not complaining."

Several of the men and women standing around echoed the captain's sentiments with nods and murmured comments.

"So, what I need from you people is a full damage assessment. I need to know how many trucks we have left and which ones are buried. As we move vehicles outside to clear the warehouse, we can use the excavators to dig out trapped ones as long as it's safe to do so.

"In the meantime, we've still got several trailers left to fill with supplies, and a replacement convoy on the way. So, let's pick up where we left off and keep things moving." The captain turned his bright blue eyes on the gathering crowd, where they stood half-charred and exhausted. "I want us to split up. On one team, I want the big plows and spare troops to get back to clearing the other warehouse. Morales and Smith, you're with me. I've got a special assignment for you. Okay, troops, let's get some fires going again. The fresh air is nice, but we have to remember to stay warm."

Morales gave his partner a confused look, but the lieutenant only shrugged and jumped from the APC to the Humvee's hood. They stood around and waited as the captain invited Brozowsi and LaPlante to joint them. Jones issued a few more orders, watching as the bay doors rolled up, allowing in a brutal wind that caused the soldiers to clench up again, then Smith turned to his assembled four.

"Get inside the truck," he said, dropping between a pair of vehicles and climbing behind his Humvee's wheel.

Smith entered on the passenger side next to the captain while Brozowski, LaPlante, and Morales took the back. Once they were settled, Jones waited until a few trucks pulled out before he started the Humvee and drove out into the rear lot where he parked the truck and produced a logistical map of the warehouses. He spread it across the dashboard, leaning sideways so everyone in the backseat could see.

"What are we looking for, Captain?" Smith asked. "Are we going for another warehouse?"

The captain grinned and tapped his finger at a spot on the map directly behind the bay doors in a wide field. "Nope. We're searching for this puppy right here. It's a bunker they wanted us to find while we were here. They lost contact with the entire facility when the electric and internet died. We don't know what or who's down there, but command wants it found, so that's what we're going to do."

Moralcs glanced between the top edge of the map and the thin sliver of light that showed the ice and snow covering the field ahead. "You mean out there? Captain, that's a whole lot of super deep snow, probably 6 to 8 feet of it at minimum going for a quarter mile or more."

"Big deal," Jones said with a narrow-eyed glance back at the specialist. "Need I remind you that we just uncovered this humongous warehouse? What's so tough about finding a little bunker entrance?"

Morales scoffed, laughing as he shook his head. "I don't mean to sound negative, sir, but at least the warehouses had a shape. Digging around out there... It's going to be like finding a needle in a haystack."

Brozowski and LaPlante both nodded in agreement where they sat next to him, but Captain Jones shrugged, his bright red eyebrows ticking upward. "Don't look at it like you're searching for a needle in a haystack. Look at it like you're digging for ancient, buried treasure. Like the tomb of an Egyptian king and queen." The way he said it made them snicker, and Smith interjected.

"We'll be digging up a tomb, but there won't be any Egyptian kings and queens inside."

Jones dropped a heavy paw on the lieutenant's shoulder. "Come on, you know this is going to be fun."

"Yeah, a hell of a lot of fun. Woo-fricken-hoo."

Morales worked the excavator controls in a well-choreographed dance between his two hands, shifting back and forth, pushing and pulling as he scooped up buckets of snow, spun the entire cabin around, and dropped the load into the dump truck's bed. He'd already dug a good 30 yards into the open field, cutting a six foot deep, twenty-five foot wide trench all the way through to a patch of frozen grass, the faithful Caterpillar engine grinding onward, unfazed by the unseasonable cold, willing to do Morales's bidding until it would eventually draw to a clinking, clanking halt, and die. The machine's tracks churned the grass and snow, turning it into mud as he shifted back and forth vigorously while Brozowski, LaPlante, and Smith worked a small crew of soldiers with shovels and picks who chiseled side paths like moles digging for a fat meal with the help of the smaller excavator, one with a sixteen-inch-wide bucket.

While the map showed the entrance should be about forty yards straight out, they had no landmarks to reference because of heavy snow burying everything. Still, the team worked on as night approached, the light from dozens of nearby burn barrels illuminating the sky with a warm orange glow. The farther he dug his trench through the field, the more he felt alone. The only lights were from the internal cabin and instrument displays and the two spotlights on the outside, pointed at the endless white tundra where the excavator's arm cast a long, ominous shadow.

Behind him, Morales sometimes spotted the headlamps of other trucks driving up to the second warehouse, digging it out beneath the chilling night sky. The fact that a majority of the troops were working on one goal while Jones's group was off on a side mission made him feel even more alone.

He grabbed the radio mic from his dashboard and pressed it to his mouth. "Hey, Captain Jones? I'm running out of fuel. Can you hook me up?"

The captain came back with an immediate response. "I'll have someone run a hose out to you right away. How are you feeling?"

"Like I'm pissing into the wind, but otherwise okay."

"You think this was a dumb idea?"

"No, sir. But I remember what the map showed us, and I've been thinking we're probably digging in the wrong area."

"How so?"

"If you look at how the first two warehouses are positioned, they're farther apart than the map indicated. And I'm sure it's not an exact match of the compound layout."

"All right. Go on."

"Well, I've dug an enormous circle out here, about 30 yards in diameter." Morales sighed. "I'd like to stop digging here and angle more towards the south. I think the bunker is farther than we think."

A pause lingered several seconds before the captain came back. "I'll tell you what. You've been out there digging all afternoon, and you know the area. I never doubted you back in Reynosa and Montcrey, and I won't do that now. If you think it's a little farther south, go for it."

"Thank you, sir."

A pair of soldiers appeared around a curve in the trench, carrying a long fuel hose between them. They each waved, and he returned the gesture, content to sit in the warm cabin while they plugged the hose in and filled the tank. When they were done, Morales gave them a wave and kicked the excavator into motion, left with the trailing scent of diesel fuel being carried off into the night sky.

With a fresh wave of motivation, he drove the machine to bite into the snow like a hungry child eating an endless supply of frosty white ice cream. It took out big chunks and dropped them off to the side, leaving the smaller icy debris for the bulldozer crew to clear. The mechanical whirl of the hydraulics and engine became hypnotic, and over the next hour Morales maneuvered the machine deftly to its own song. Deeper and deeper he cut, falling into a tired trance, going by instinct alone, settling the machine into a slight indention in the grassy field. It was only when his bucket's teeth cracked on a concrete walkway that he grew excited.

Grabbing the radio mic, he pressed the talk button. "Cap? This is Morales. I just hit a walkway, sir. I think I'm close."

"Good work, son. I'll send Smith and the others right away."

Following the new direction, he dug excitedly, loosely and tiredly, the excavator responding like he was leaning on a drunken friend after a long night at the bar. He cut a swath on either side of the concrete as it wound its way to the south before stopping as Smith and his group meandered up and dug behind him, widening the path for more tools and implements to be brought in.

Morales focused on a flat piece of hard-packed ice and snow, bucket crunching as the caterpillar strained to cut through, keeping his motions more rigid and refined in order to avoid hurting any of the nearby men. Gusts of wind seeped into the cabin, frigid air slipping between gaps in the frame, turning his feet and legs numb with cold. Still, his chin remained down, eyes staring at the field of snow that had become his domain. His shoulders ached where they slumped over the controls, instrument panel a blur as he approached the end of his mission.

Soon, he'd dug to the ground and hit something that didn't sound like a piece of walkway stone. He lifted the bucket and lowered it again, the teeth knocking against a heavy, hollow structure. Smith appeared outside his window, tired eyes alight with excitement.

"Did you hear what I heard?" The lieutenant shouted.

"Yep. I definitely heard something. I think this is it. Call Jones up while I clear the entrance."

Just speaking the words sent a chill down his spine. Digging for the bunker hadn't felt like the most productive work before, but it suddenly became the *only* important work. The excavator attacked the snow with a vengeance, bucket falling, cracking through ice, curling, and lifting away mounds of frosted debris until finally Smith waved his hand for him to stop.

Morales raised the excavator's arm and tucked the bucket under. Leaving it idle where it stood, he hopped out, boots touching steady ground for the first time in hours. He staggered a little in the cold, leaning on Brozowski as he made his way to Smith. To his left, he saw the results of his ravenous carving: raised from the flat area was a concrete dais with two massive doors set into it.

Brozowski, LaPlante and their crew started clearing the ice and hard-packed debris off the top until they reached the security panels which they flipped up, hovering over them, using specialized electronic gear to break into it and enter the necessary codes. While they worked, Morales slapped the lieutenant probably a little too hard on the shoulder, a wide grin on his face.

"I just found us some ancient Egyptian treasure," he laughed. "What do you think about that?"

Smith had bundled himself up again, his blue eyes peering out at Morales through a pair of clear coated goggles. "I think you're delirious. You need to get some rest, man, you've been out here for hours without a break."

"And miss the find of my lifetime?" Morales forced a grin, though Smith's words rung true. His knees were buckling, his shoulders ached from hunching over the controls and his eyes burned with exhaustion.

Captain Jones jogged up just as Brozowski and LaPlante got the security code bypassed and the group conferred for a few seconds before one of them hit a button on the side panel, causing the ground to rumble. All eyes jerked toward the cement door on the right as it rose on a big hydraulic arm and they retreated, surprised that something actually worked. Once raised, the soldiers approached and stood around the yawning entryway, peering down a wide staircase that spiraled downward into the darkness with only the dim glow of emergency lights to see by.

Jones stepped to the edge and gestured. "Well, Morales. You found it. You can go first."

Smith tried to get in his way. "I don't think that's a good idea, Captain. He's-"

"I'm fine." Morales pushed past Smith and took the initial steps down, careful not to slip as his soles crunched on chunks of ice toppling inside. Grabbing a flashlight from his coat, he flipped it on and angled the beam downward, stepping carefully and quietly, the heavy footfalls of the others following him, their boots echoing in the oddly shaped chamber.

The stairwell's core was a thick slab of concrete with no doors or markings for the first fifty or so feet until, finally, a notation on the inside wall read *First Level – Administration*. A short time later, they reached a flat landing with a massive steel door facing them which Brozowski and LaPlante got to work on, cracking open the security panel and working their magic with their specialized instruments. Morales stepped back to stand next to Jones and Smith, the shadows of a half-dozen other soldiers on the stairwell behind them.

"They must still have generators or emergency power." Smith stared at the door with a nervous expression.

"The frost hasn't reached this far down. Yet." Morales noted as he breathed out, unused to *not* seeing his breath.

The security panel beeped and the massive slab clicked and popped with an echo that streaked to the top of the chamber. Another pair of soldiers joined Brozowski and LaPlante, all four gripping the thick handle, eight hands heaving it with a chorus of grunts.

The steel slab slid open, silent on its well-oiled hinges, a gust of warm air blowing across their cheeks, carrying with it the faint but certain smells of cooked foods, ozone, and habitation. Everyone leaned in as the door swung wide, peering into a dimly lit hallway with metal grating that stretched twenty or thirty yards into the darkness.

Ears straining, Morales's eyes shot wide as voices called to them. "Hello? Who's there? Are you military? Boy, are we glad to see you guys!"

CHAPTER THIRTEEN

Tom McKnight
Nuevo Laredo, Mexico

The sound of a blaring alarm startled Tom awake from a restless sleep, the noise loud and blaring, shrill all the way down his spine. He sat bolt straight, looking around the room, trying to remember who and where he was. Daylight penetrated through the cracks in the walls, casting dots and squiggles of gold across the floor and next to him Jack and Linda cried out, throwing the covers off, squinting, blinking sleepily in surprise.

The revolt.

Swinging his legs off the sleeping pallet, Tom slipped on his boots and laced them up fast as Barbara flew in from the front of the store where she'd been on watch, movements hurried and stiff though her expression remained calm.

"I think it's happening," she said with a firm nod. "Alarms are going off across the camp."

"It's definitely happening." Tom stood and crossed to his winter gear hanging over a chair by the table. "Get the kids ready to go. I'm going out to have a look."

Barbara shot straight for Jack who, like his sisters, was already half dressed, wearing several layers of light jackets and long underwear. The MREs and supplies were bundled into four homemade backpacks, strung together with straps of leather and string, preparations made the night before. Outside a rifle cracked in the distance, someone yelled and shouts echoed as a rip of gunfire sent chills dancing along Tom's spine, and he threw on his coat, gloves, and hat, and zipped himself up tight.

"Come to the front when you're ready." He told the children, looking to Sam at the end. "Make it fast."

Without waiting for a response, he strode out to the pharmacy floor and retrieved his shiv and pipe off the counter. Hefting the weapons high, he shoved the shelving aside with his shoulder and unwrapped the cable holding the door shut. The door cracked open, muted sunlight spilling into the room, the blaring alarms washing over him in full force, seeming to come primarily from the outside of the encampment. A mist hung over everything, its thickest point five to ten feet above the pavement, clinging to the buildings and foliage and obscuring the view – the perfect conditions for an attempted uprising.

Boots pounded the concrete and a half dozen shadows sprinted through the haze in front of him on the refugee side, running hard for the eastern gate. Adjusting his grip on the pipe, Tom threw the door wider and stepped outside as gunfire popped off again, a sporadic rattle of small arms fire cutting through the brisk morning air, a slight waft of gun smoke arriving on a chilled breeze.

Someone screamed again and a chorus of people shouted back, though he couldn't hear what they were saying. His shoulders clenched tight, eyes narrowed as he homed in on the conflict's direction. "It's coming from the eastern gate, for sure," he said, glancing back to see if Barbara and the kids were ready. "I'm glad we're not heading there."

"You won't be heading anywhere."

He spun left on the balls of his feet, raising the pipe as one of Marty's hulking, bear-sized guards stepped from the alley. The big man appeared puffed up, wearing an extra large vest, arms thick with layers of winter weather clothing, the ear flaps of his hat pulled down and strapped under his chin. At his side, he held a long wooden ball bat with barbed wire wrapped around the end.

"Stay back," Tom warned, hefting his weapon.

"You're a little outmatched," the man said with a grunt, turning sideways, cocking the bat.

"I'd put my money on me."

The man feigned a swing, forcing Tom to shuffle backwards before returning the gesture, taking a swing cut at the man's head. The quick move startled his opponent, causing him to jerk back or have his jaw broken and, pressing his position, Tom swung the pipe two consecutive times, swatting the giant's left shoulder and arm, drawing pained grunts from his shaking jowls.

Tom was about to take another swing when a shuffle of feet behind him made him spin and duck away, his pipe thrown up in defense. A crowbar swept in and connected with a clang, knocking him backwards and off balance and with a gasp, Tom faced his new opponent. It was the other brute who'd been with Marty the day before, both men he'd run off by his threatening their leader's life with a shiv. The new threat wore a red coat to his partner's brown, arms thick with layers of long underwear and coats. The pair slid in beside each other to pin Tom's back against the wall, looming large, limiting his options to move. They were massive brutes - but they weren't fast.

The second man took another swing, but Tom danced to his left, away from the door and his vulnerable family. He slipped by them and spun to draw them into the wider courtyard, crouching, feigning an attack but quickly withdrawing. They rounded on him, crowbar and baseball bat weaving warily in the air, threatening to take his head off.

"Why don't you stay still, little buddy?" The first thug spoke through thick facial hair, mustache thick on his upper lip. "It'll be easier on you."

"That's okay." Tom leapt from his crouch with a swing, taking aim at the raised bat, his lead pipe whacking against wood then swiping at thin air as the slower man finally got out of the way. The other stepped in and drove Tom off before he could land something solid and with a curse of frustration, Tom took two paces back, unable to find an advantage against both at the same time, no matter how slow they were.

The pair shared a look, fat heads nodding like they'd planned ahead, spreading out to flank him again. Tree trunk legs carried them around to either side, trapping him, weapons sweeping in to attack him simultaneously with deadly arcs. He ducked beneath the crowbar first, lunging forward, but the heavy bat landed, smacking him across the small of his back. Grunting in pain, Tom swept his pipe in a backward motion, hitting the thug in the chest with a thud and receiving a surprised exhalation for his efforts as the man grabbed for the pipe, but Tom spun and jerked it away.

The crowbar clipped his elbow as he cleared the trap, numbing it with a flaring pain through his shoulder and neck. With his back toward the pharmacy once more, he feigned another attack, but the pair came at him together, wood and metal launching at his head in a flurry of motion. Retreating, flailing with the pipe, Tom stepped to his right, away from the pharmacy's front door as the blows rained down. Pain erupted all over his body as the men pummeled and clipped him with the ends of their weapons, his jacket tearing on the barbed wire, left forearm flying out to keep the man off him. He fought back, going toe-to-toe for a moment, grunting and growling like an animal as he connected, rewarded with a yelp of anger and shock at his vicious swing.

Dangerously exposed, Tom jerked away, throwing himself backward to barely avoid a vicious swipe, the ball bat's prickly barb catching his chin and slicing the skin in a sharp snap of pain. The men continued to close in, drawing nearer when a furious burst of motion took them by surprise. Barbara flew from the pharmacy's front door and charged at them, clutching a thick piece of wood high, screaming as she brought it down on the second man's head with a crunchy, meaty thwack. His shoulders jerked upward, hat ducking as he staggered beneath the blow. She swung again, but the man had already turned and raised his forearm to block it, but the heavy wood connected with a thud regardless, dust and splinters flying everywhere, the man's face tightening into a grimace as an anguished scream escaped from his lips.

Distracted by Barbara's attack, the man had no chance to defend himself against Tom's follow-up as he whipped his pipe into the man's face with a sick, bone crunching sound. The left eye socket smashed inward, collapsing like a crushed eggshell and the man's chin snapped to the side as his legs buckled, dropping him straight to the ground.

With a feral cry through clenched teeth, Tom turned to find the other man already bearing down on him, spittle flying from his lips, eyes wide with the realization that the odds had drastically changed. The brute snatched Tom's pipe arm with his left hand, holding it away while cocking the ball bat to bring it down. Tom flew against the man, pressing close, grabbing his opponent's weapon arm to lock them in a stalemate, heads butting, faces spitting at each other in rage as they jostled just a few inches apart.

Surrendering to his rage he tensed his neck and shoulders, whipping his head forward several times, smashing his forehead into the man's chubby, bearded face with grunts and growls. Tendons straining, a final scream flew from his mouth as he spasmed one last time, brow crunching the man's soft nose cartilage, driving it into his nasal cavity. Blood burst from the man's face like a popped water balloon, warm liquid splashing everywhere, yet they still struggled, each grasping and pulling for an advantage.

As they fought, Barbara circled behind the man, swinging for his head with her piece of wood, connecting with the back of his skull with an unearthly crunch, tipping the scales that had already been weighed down by Tom's efforts. The gigantic body staggered forward, eyes drifting shut as he stumbled and fell against Tom, sending them both to the ground in a heap. Tom lay beneath the unconscious man, three hundred plus pounds of weight crushing him, and with a twist of his hips and shoulders he freed himself and looked up to see Barbara staring down at them, panting heavily, her face dripping with sweat.

As she saw Tom emerge from beneath the man's body she dropped her weapon, the piece of bloodied wood hitting the ground with a clatter. Tom looked at the man closest to him, then the other one nearby, seeing no movement from either of them. The nearest one was still breathing, albeit very shallowly, and he couldn't tell about the one with the crushed eye socket and temple – not that he cared about the man's condition.

Raising his hand, Barbara slapped her palm into his and she backed up, half squatting to get leverage, pulling him to his feet. They fell into each other's arms for a brief embrace, then turned back to the door, all business, ignoring the fight in favor of sticking to their plan. Barbara leaned in and called to the children while Tom picked up his pipe and looked around for more signs of trouble.

"Let's go, kids," she said, her words a hiss as she still breathed heavy. "Bring the packs with you, your father's and mine, too."

The kids filed through the entrance, Sam and Linda holding their parents' extra packs. Jack ambled out with his own little makeshift pack on his shoulders, wide eyes glancing curiously from the two downed men to his father, gaping at Tom's bloodied chin and the hulking bodies that his parents had taken on and triumphed over.

Swells of shouts filled the air, answered by more rifle fire, the gun play more balanced than before. To the south, soldiers sprinted through a thick layer of mist toward the east gate, rifles cradled in their arms, not even noticing the McKnights.

"Let's go west around the block, like we talked about."

Tom grabbed Jack's hand and pushed him forward as the girls jostled each other, far less shocked at the bodies than Jack was, quickly getting their bearings as they fell in behind Tom and Barbara. Tom guided the group to the block's southern end where they crossed through yards of dilapidated homes filled with shivering trees, the street plagued with abandoned vehicles. With long strides, he stayed on their left, pipe held out and keeping himself between his family and the fence. Bullets flew in from the east side of camp, blowing through the cracked buildings, the soldiers' errant shots taking off pieces of stucco and wood in sharp dust puffs, zipping rounds hitting tree trunks, shredding branches, and sending dry dead leaves floating to the ground.

"Stay down!" he hissed, but it was an impossible command. Between the bursts of gunfire on their right and the threat of the soldiers on the left, the family was vulnerable. Boots crunching on the dry debris, they crept from car to car, from shattered wall to tree, staying hidden and low as the sounds of chaos made a symphony around them. Tom's body ached with the blows he'd received in the fight, back screaming with the pinprick sting of the barbed wire as the adrenaline drained from his system.

He drew his family to a halt at the end of the north block, staring across the road at the burned-out house with the twisted, charred fence. Off to his right, refugees squatted behind a burn barrel and shot around it with rifles they'd managed to get ahold of, no doubt thanks to Marty's machinations. A return round punched through the metal and hit one of the refugees in the chest and cinders flew up from the still burning coals as the man fell backward, the feathers of his coat flying up.

Tom grabbed Jack by the strap of his pack and rushed him across the street, angling left to circle the front of the burned-out building. He dragged the boy past stacks of melted tires and charred wood and garbage, slipping around the corner and squeezing in between the house and the fence. The girls joined them, Barbara forcing the kids to squat low against the chain-link as the mist drifted by, thick, gray and full of shadows.

"It's right there, dad." Sam pointed to a spot on the left where the fire had weakened the barrier. With a nod, he reached out, grabbed the fencing, and gave it a rough shake. Several of the links broke right away, so he gripped either side and yanked it apart like a strong man at a circus, peeling back the edges. Barbara took the other part, each pulling in opposite directions and after straining and groaning, they finally split it wide enough to pass through. Crouched, Tom watched and listened, heart thudding in his chest. With side glances, he caught shadows scurrying in the mist, though he couldn't tell which side they were on or if they were armed.

"Is there a guard?" Barbara asked. "I don't see one."

"I think Saanvi did it. She got rid of the guard."

"Should we go?" Her hand clutched his shoulder, squeezing through his thick layers.

With a deep breath, he searched the surroundings. Errant bullets still zipped and ricocheted off things, but none seemed directed at them. "I think so. I think we can make our move."

He slipped one leg through the gap as if testing the waters, then followed with tense shoulders. Creeping onto the sidewalk, he peered into the impenetrable mist. "There should be some ruins across the street where we can hide." He nodded in the general direction of where he remembered the buildings being, though they were impossible to see in the fog.

With a sidestep, he turned and waved them through. "Okay, let's go."

Sam came first with Jack, the fencing rattling as they crossed to freedom, then Linda and Barbara followed, all with a hunched, frightened postures like animals being released into the wild.

"Where to now?" his wife asked.

"I'm thinking straight ahead." He nodded due north. "We work our way quickly but carefully-"

Hands suddenly clutched his jacket, gripping and spinning him. Tom rolled with the turn, elbow cocked and ready to respond to whoever had grabbed him, but he lowered his arm and grinned when he saw it was Saanvi, the medic's eyes wide but relieved, a tense grin on her lips.

"You made it! I didn't know if you'd make it!"

"It's good to see you." Tom smiled. "We knew you'd come through for us."

"Smooch!" The kids called out in sync, falling around the animal and embracing her as the dog's tail wagged madly, soft whiny barks bursting from her throat as she licked and nuzzled them. The reunion was cut short as a sudden barrage of errant fire buzzed overhead, a pair of rounds hitting the chain-link fence farther east causing them all to duck and cover.

"They're fighting at the eastern gate," the medic said, looking back in the direction of the gunfire. "I sent the guard to help."

"Thank you so much for doing this," Barbara gripped Saanvi's hand tight.

"Yes, we can't thank you enough," Tom agreed. "Which way should we go?"

Saanvi nodded in the direction they were already heading. "I hid some supplies north of here. It's a deserted area with plenty of places to hide. They'll never look for you with this fighting happening." She handed him a piece of paper. "Here are the directions."

"Come with us," he urged, clutching her jacket as rest of the McKnights moved ahead.

"I'd love to go, but I can't." The medic shook her head and pulled back, dark eyes shifting toward the east where the fighting was heaviest. "I owe it to the captain and my fellow soldiers to help them. You're good people, but I can't abandon them in their time of need."

"But after the revolt, assuming it's successful, there'll be nothing here for you," Tom argued. "The camp will be in disarray, maybe even overrun. You could be killed by these assholes."

Still five feet from Tom, Saanvi hesitated, uncertainty mirrored in her eyes, her mouth moving wordlessly as she searched for an excuse. More gunfire erupted, closer than before, and Saanvi cried out in pain as a single shot tore from the mist and punched her in the chest. The round penetrated flesh, bursting from her back in a blast of blood and cloth. Her body convulsed, arms and shoulders thrown forward, a startled gasp ripping from her throat. Hands flying to her chest, she staggered backwards and fell as Tom lunged forward, arms reaching, catching her just before her head hit the pavement.

Holding her shaking form, he stared into her terrified, pain-filled eyes, blood trickling from the corner of her lip, a red spot blossoming on the front of her coat. At first she gazed at the sky, then shifted to meet his face, trying to say something, but it came out as nothing more than a gurgle of blood and spittle on her chin.

Frozen in shock, Tom clutched the woman close, holding her head with one hand. "Saanvi! Tell me what to do, Saanvi. What do I do to help you?!" Right arm supporting her head, he laid her back as far as he dared, trying to keep any more blood from entering her lungs.

The woman shivered and swallowed hard, her eyes blinking rapidly before a sudden calm relaxed her cheeks. She raised a hand to Tom's face, fingers cupping his cheek, blood warm and wet against his skin as her mouth again tried to form words, her breathing growing more intermittent and hoarse as her body convulsed.

"Saanvi," he whispered desperately as he tried to think of a way to help her.

Glancing back with a helpless expression, he saw Barbara's head shaking in disbelief, eyes wide and glassy. Off to the east, the gunfire escalated, more rounds coming toward them, and as he turned back to the wounded medic to start moving her into cover, her hand slipped from his cheek and fell limp at her side as the light faded from her eyes, her whole body sagging to the ground. In a panic, Tom laid her flat, fingers digging inside her hood to feel for a pulse, his heart pounding in his throat, head swirling with dizziness and confusion.

"No, Saanvi! No!" The last twitches of her heartbeat weakened to nothing beneath his fingertips and guilt and sorrow clenched his chest tight as he clutched the lifeless body of his family's savior.

"Tom, we have to go!" Pain flowed freely in Barbara's voice as she called to him. "They're getting closer!"

Nodding absently, he gently released Saanvi's body and turned to follow his family, but stopped at the sound of boots approaching through the mist, Marty and a half dozen of his cronies stepping from the gloom, rifle barrels leveled at the McKnights. The rebel leader's jacket was covered in blood, splatters of it across his cheeks and chin and the man grinned with wide satisfaction. He began to say something to the McKnights when a sound cut him off and he turned, looking into the mist as the sound of a deep, throaty engine grew in volume, roaring toward them, bearing down something emerging from hell itself.

CHAPTER FOURTEEN

Commander Tilly
Somewhere in the Amazon jungle

Moisture ran down a grizzled jaw, clinging to the five o-clock shadow on the man's chin before dripping on the forest floor. Ignoring the distraction, ice-cold eyes stayed focused on their target, peering into the dense jungle through a night vision headset. The rainforest was ablaze with the sounds of life, even in the middle of the night, a cacophony acting as both cover for any human-made sounds and a potential alarm if they were disturbed by said human's movements.

The dark shapes of Commander Tilly's SEAL unit crouched in the thick foliage, silent as ghosts, their warm weather camouflage making them invisible as they waited for orders. Tilly spoke into a microphone that curled from his ear to his lips in a sliver of black, his voice barely audible amid the deafening din that assaulted them from all directions. "Echo One to base. We'll have eyes on target in five. Expect an uplink within twenty."

"That's affirmative," came the reply. "We're on standby. Good luck, Echo One. Now going to radio silence."

With a flick of his finger on his earpiece, Tilly switched to localized communications, the secure channel enabling him to speak to his unit as if he were standing right next to them, the jungle's noise filtered and removed.

"Move on me."

The commander emerged from the cover of broad-leafed plants, stepping through the mass of thick foliage that clung to his sweat-stained clothing. Branches swayed above his head as eleven ghosts rose and followed him in a tight V-formation in the darkness. The ground sloped downward to the left, the sweep of deadfall beneath their boots slippery and dank. They ducked under fallen trees and slid over rotting logs and massive stones on their backsides, swinging over to continue their hastened march.

Night insects continued their chatter, enormous ones as long as his hand buzzing by, fat shapes with stingers and stripes, appearing and vanishing in an instant across the night vision. Creatures twittered and chirped, strange hollow knocks and wild animal cries echoing through the jungle mountains. The dense scents of loam and tree rot filled his nose and clung to his wet skin and a thick flock of bats cut the air above their heads, and Tilly glanced up to see a moon eyed monkey staring back at them.

After another minute of marching, the dense canopy released them into a bright clearing, the pale green of his night vision revealing rolling mountains and peaks covered in a fine gray mist and an endless sea of foliage. Using a hand signal, he ordered the men to halt, and the SEALs shrunk into the forest floor like they were made of mist themselves. Flipping up his night vision headgear, he lifted a pair of binoculars to his eyes, his skin moist beneath the camouflage paint coloring his pale features.

Through the advanced night vision lenses, he spied two communication towers jutting up from the trees a hundred yards away, perched on the hillside, half covered with jungle vines and deadfall. Stuck between them, barely visible in the clinging growth, hung a flag and he tilted up his binoculars to see the yellow, blue, and red colors waving in the moonlight.

Lowering the frames over his eyes, he jogged to the right, sticking to the edge of the forest. "I've got contact just up ahead. Prepare to engage. Branson and McClure, you're on flanks. Alpha has the middle."

The clipped affirmatives sounded in his ear, and Tilly sunk into the foliage once more, giving the flankers thirty seconds to get into position. On his mark, they crept up a shallow slope and dropped, crawling to reach the top of a rise. The towers had fallen out of sight to the left, but he spotted the stone-gray barracks and guard buildings nestled into the side of the hill. As he lay on his stomach staring at the formation, sweat dripped down the sides of his face, his stomach tensing as it always did immediately preceding the first firefight of a mission.

"I've got two marks on the second roof and a pair of box bunkers between the buildings. Branson, pin those gunners while we clear the boxes."

Without waiting for confirmation, Tilly raised his hand and signaled, two SEALs standing to creep past him through the knee-high jungle brush. Tilly then rose to a firing position with members of Alpha team spreading out to either side and after a five-second count, he squeezed off several rounds at the sandbags, the quick soft pops of his suppressed weapon grabbing the enemy soldiers' attention.

The SEAL team's fire rained like a hammer from both directions as the soldiers popped up to see where the incoming fire was coming from, slicing sandbags and flesh, silencing the machine guns before they got started. From the corner of his eye, Tilly spotted Branson and his men swing in from ropes, dropping to the second building's roof, their carbon blades plunging in with quick stabs to neutralize the gunners before they fired a single shot.

Tilly sprinted through the jungle, slipping between saplings, sliding on the wet mossy soil toward the barracks as McClure's team hit the building on the left, having already circled around to their assigned area. Under the brush cover, they waited for the door to fly open, troops rushing outside to join the fight only to run into a controlled spray of the SEALs' rifle fire. Enemy soldiers spun and dove, falling to the ground in shrieks of confusion and pain and McClure sprinted up and soft-tossed a grenade inside the barracks, diving to the side and throwing his shoulders against the wall. A muted boom blasted light and heat from the building's seams, hurling fragments back through the door.

The jungle fell silent but for the drifting leaves and drip of water from the upper canopy. With a satisfied nod, Tilly wiped his arm across his brow to swipe away the never-ending sweat as he strode between the buildings, looking around at the carnage his team had swiftly wrought.

"Secure. Form up and converge on the command post."

The black shapes fell into formation behind him once more, slipping through the dense jungle, boots crunching on plush ferns and wide-leafed shrubs, stamping the soggy debris as they circled the top part of the next rise. Tilly spotted a massive tree laying across the forest floor, at least fifty feet long, partially hanging from tangled vines, crushing mounds of foliage as it sat like a dark lump in the pale green of his night vision. The shouts of foreign soldiers reached his ears, and he motioned his men forward to fall into position behind the thick trunk, rifle barrels resting across the rotted wood.

"Branson, McClure. This is your party. We'll draw them in and pin them in place for you."

The SEALs waited for the contingent of enemy fighters to approach through the brush and over the hill and soon Tilly spotted a group moving toward them in the flitting jungle shadows.

"Hold," he whispered as more shapes appeared, the movements growing thicker and faster as they approached in a run, eager to reach the barracks after hearing the distant gunfire of the attack. The commander used their distraction to his advantage, watching them rush headlong through the dense foliage, not noticing the SEALs concealed behind the massive, rotted log until it was too late.

"Now," Tilly spoke calmly as he sighted down the barrel at a target and ripped off a burst of rounds, the rest of Alpha team joining him, unleashing a barrage of hell on the Venezuelan troops. Enemy soldiers fell like puppets with their strings cut at the same time, crying out, arms waving, rifles rattling to the jungle floor.

A few remembered their training and dove for cover, turning to fire on Tilly's position and the SEALs ducked behind the dead tree, bullets plunging into the soft, porous wood, blowing apart clusters of mushrooms and pulp into the air, creating a layer of dust above their heads. "Anytime now, gentlemen," Tilly intoned, stifling a sneeze.

Branson and McClure swept in from the sides, the soldiers catching the remaining enemy troops unawares in a deadly crossfire and a moment later the forest fell silent, the cries of insects and nocturnal animals temporarily abated by the rifle fire and stinking smoke. Tilly let out the sneeze he'd been holding onto and wiped his nose and stood, rested his backside on the massacred tree trunk, swinging his legs to the other side.

The team reformed and marched in a V shape formation over the dead bodies and across the sloping jungle. The bugs and birds and beasts had come back into their full volume, voicing their aggravation over the invasion and interruption of their domain. Sweat poured down Tilly's cheeks and ran beneath his clothing, making his skin itch. The salt runoff dripped into his eyes, stinging and burning, making him want to take a towel to his face. Tilly ignored the agitations and focused on reaching the command post.

They found the domed-shaped building fifty yards farther through the dense jungle. Like a sphere cut in half, the dome butted against the sheer cliff that stretched a hundred feet above them, its drab gray concrete walls glowing dark green in his night vision, crawling with thick layers of creepers.

A pair of Venezuelan guards took potshots from their sandbag positions beside the building, but Branson's fleet-footed team made quick work of them, utilizing advanced flanking techniques which the enemy never saw coming. Threat eliminated, he strode to the command post door, moving to the left side as SEALs spread around the building.

The commander removed a package of explosives and slapped it on the metal just above the security pad, then stuck an ignition device in the soft clay and slid several feet along the concrete wall.

"We need the leader alive," he ordered. "The rest are KOS."

With the touch of a button, the explosives ignited, snapping the door outward, tearing it off its hinges to land in the dirt. The SEALs filed in, moving tightly together to the left and right. Gunfire rattled the air, striking the concrete wall on the other side for several seconds until they fell quiet and one by one the team members shouted out "all clear" reports.

Taking off his goggles, a waft of cool, dry breeze wicked away the moisture from Tilly's cheeks as vents circulated fresh currents through a room full of workstations and monitors. A series of larger screens were mounted on the wall across the room and the humming fans and smell of electronics ran counterpoint to the natural jungle just outside the door.

Four Venezuelan corpses lay around, two on the floor, and another pair collapsed over the desktops, their blood still dripping into their keyboards. In the back of the room was a fifth man, still alive, being held by his men – the commander of the local squad that they had just obliterated. Dressed in a beige officer's shirt, the man's clean-shaven face was a mask of barely restrained hostility and rage.

With a glance at the Venezuelan commander, Tilly strode to the workstation where two laptops rested on a wide black desk with steel legs, gesturing for the SEALs to bring the man over. He lifted the laptop lids, watching the data flow roll down the screens as he moved the mouse, prompting a sign in warning that requested verification via a biometric reader.

Straightening, he turned to the Venezuelan, speaking in fluent, accented Spanish. "What's your name?"

"I am Commander Jose Rivera of the Venezuelan Defense Force. What do you American dogs want with me and my country? Why did you kill my men?"

Tilly nodded to a biometric pad sitting between the laptops. "All I need is your hand, Rivera." He stepped aside to give the man room. "Just unlock it for me, then step away."

The Venezuelan commander only stared at the SEAL leader with contempt, his eyes widening slightly as Tilly unsheathed a black-bladed knife from a sheath on his leg.

"Your hand will be going onto the reader. Whether or not it's attached to your arm when that happens is up to you."

With a slow nod and hard swallow, Rivera strode to the hand-shaped pad and placed his palm and fingers on it, the device tracing a red ring around the outline. A moment later the lights turned green, and the warning signs on the laptop screen disappeared. While two SEALs pulled the commander aside, another stepped in with a pair of cables that ran outside to their primary transmitter. He plugged the ends into the laptop's USB slots and began typing on the keyboards, talking as he worked.

"Okay, I've just removed all the security required to access the mainframe. Now, all I need to do is merge the data and compress it for sending." His fingers danced over one keyboard, then switched to the other as he kicked off a series of data flows, the lines scrolling upward so fast Tilly couldn't read them.

"You killed all of my men?" Rivera's tone was accusatory, his dark eyes resting on the SEAL commander like he was the devil.

"Yes." Tilly nodded.

"Thirty. Seven. Men."

"And I'd do it again," Tilly responded in an emotionless voice.

"At least tell me how many casualties we caused you. It would hearten me to know my brothers stood up to you."

"I'm not interested in debating you, Rivera. Leave me alone or end up like your men. Your choice."

The Venezuelan's face contorted with rage, spittle flying from his lips as he spat the next words. "You American dogs will not get away with this. There are treaties against this type of unprovoked--"

Tilly whipped his sidearm from its holster and fired a bullet between the man's eyes, dropping him on the spot.

"Get him out of here and wait for us outside." Tilly motioned at the SEALs in the room, who dragged Rivera's body out, leaving Tilly and his tech alone in the room. The commander switched his communication device to a wider band and strolled toward the door, watching as one of his men knelt next to a five-foot tall mobile antenna, the web-like dish standing open in a rough circular shape of 10 inches in diameter.

"Status report."

The tech flashed him a thumbs up sign. "Transmitting data now."

Tilly glanced up, most of the sky blocked by the thick canopy stretching above them. "Base, this is Echo One, we've started the link. Can you confirm on your end?"

"That's affirmative. We are receiving the data stream from your location."

Commander Tilly stepped outside, scanning the surroundings where his soldiers kept watch, feeling satisfied with their overall performance on the mission. Somewhere around the halfway point of the data upload, the radio chirped in his ear.

"Echo One, this is base. Be advised, we are no longer receiving your transmission. Can you check things on your end?"

The commander crossed to the antenna array, squatting next to the operator. "They're saying the transmission failed. Is everything still good?"

The soldier bent and looked at a small panel on the side of the unit. Even the commander could tell the lights were green, and the data flow indicator blinked green. "Everything looks great. We've got solid link to the satellite."

Fists clenched and tapping against his thigh, Tilly strode back to the control post entrance to check things inside, but he stopped before crossing the threshold, keeping perfectly still as the distinct *chuff-chuff-chuff* of helicopters grew to dominate over the sounds of the jungle. Rotors cut through the air, growing louder, drawing him back outside to look toward the sky and the rest of his team joined him, gripping their weapons as they stared upward.

"Are we being picked up at this location, sir?" Branson spoke what they were all thinking, the small, tough soldier standing near the transmitter on the uneven ground. "Wait... no, those are definitely not ours."

"They're Eurocopters," Tilly confirmed. "Cougars, if my ears are correct."

Running lights slid into view above them, spotlights shining through cracks in the trees, beams bouncing off their sweat-glistening faces. The jungle canopy reflected the light as a gusting wind spun leaves and forest debris everywhere and Tilly made out the Venezuelan flag emblazoned on the choppers' undersides. Ropes descended from the Cougars' crew quarters, dark shapes sliding into the surrounding forest and Tilly pointed upward, giving the order.

"Fire on those aircraft!"

The SEALS began ripping off bursts, peppering the choppers' bellies and return gunfire erupted from the forest as the enemy soldiers touched down and took attack positions, firing at them from the dense foliage.

The lights around the transmission equipment and base made for an easy target and several rounds smacked into the delicate equipment, shooting up sparks and sending the SEALs scattering.

"Hold position and find cover!" Tilly shouted, stepping back into the control post as he flipped over to the wider band.

"Echo One to base!" He lifted his voice over the wind and sounds of ricocheting bullets. "We've got a problem here. I have three enemy helicopters above us, dropping troops on our heads. Our transmission gear is compromised. Please advise." As Tilly spoke, he gave hand signals to his soldiers, rounding them up into a defensive formation around the domed structure.

The call came back. "Echo One, we show more tangoes inbound. Advise you to rendezvous at the drop site."

"Understood." He switched to the local secure band. "Saddle up! We're getting out of here! Prepare to break through and return to the rendezvous point."

Rifle gripped tightly, he left the control room and fell into a crouch outside, counting eleven shadows, his men hunkered behind trees and ducking below the thick foliage.

"Move out, on me!"

In a chorus of condensed rifle fire, the SEALs shot east toward the flashing muzzles in the forest. With no time to take measured steps, Tilly charged ahead, head and shoulders down, plowing back the way they'd come. He spotted a muzzle flash to his left, rounds zipping through the foliage at him and the commander responded by firing on the fly, slightly off balance on the mossy, uneven forest floor. His aim true, his target screamed from the darkness, barrel blazing upward as he plunged backward, dead.

The SEALs fell in behind him, shadows encasing them as they ran headlong into the dense night, their tight formation breaking through the line of Venezuelans as they charged at full speed toward the barracks. Those in the rear turned and covered the retreat, moving back in groups to support each other and ensure they couldn't be overwhelmed.

"How the hell did they find us?" Branson asked, his words breathless.

"I don't know," Tilly responded, slowing to a crawl as he sighted two more Venezuelans ahead. He fired, peppering a tree, the rest of the team engaging the same target, their collective rounds biting through wood and flesh to end the threat. They were off and running again in a flash, approaching the original barracks they'd attacked when one of the team members screamed from somewhere close, the groans that followed adding insult to their already FUBAR'd mission.

"Who was that?" Tilly asked, searching the night for more targets.

"Reggie," someone responded. "Hit in the leg, but we've got him."

The SEALs moved slower through the dense foliage and deadfall, forced to carry the wounded soldier and Tilly bumped into logs and sharp stumps, hips and thighs taking a beating as he forged a path toward the rendezvous point. A pursuing Venezuelan helicopter found them as they neared the barracks, pinning them with their spotlights and Tilly guided them through thick patches of forest, hoping to hide beneath the canopy. In the clearing just before the barracks, the Venezuelan helicopter circled around, firing on them and another SEAL screamed, twisting to the jungle floor.

"I want guns on that chopper now!" Tilly shouted, turning his weapon up at the aircraft, sweeping the barrel back and forth, spitting rounds into the sky in a desperate attempt to scare them off. The soldier manning the machine gun flew back, shoulders clenching in pain before he fell from the crew quarters to hang from his tether and the Cougar peeled away. The reprieve was short lived, however, as more Venezuelan ground troops appeared, pouring in behind a hailstorm of bullets.

"Take cover at the barracks!"

Knees high, they sprinted the last thirty yards to the pair of buildings, wrapping around the corners and diving behind sandbags to escape the blistering gunfire. Tilly slipped inside the barracks' blown open door, protected by the thick concrete walls. Poking his head out, he spotted a handful of enemy troops break from the foliage and charge. They came in a staggered, run-and-fire formation, dropping, crawling, and popping up, covering each other expertly as they picked their way toward the SEALs. Their accuracy was uncanny, rounds striking the walls near Tilly's head, spraying brick chips into his face, almost blinding him if not for his goggles.

"Shit, these guys are good!" Branson squealed, firing from around the corner of the first barrack.

The SEALs spat back a withering volley, chewing up foliage and stopping the rush in its tracks, giving better than they received, and after a ferocious few moments the last enemy soldier threw up his arms and died at the edge of the barracks grounds.

Tilly's night vision goggles caught more movement past the clearing, reinforcements entering the fray, and he slipped inside the building, breathing slow and steady as he exchanged a spent magazine for a new one.

"These paratroopers are some tough bastards," someone said. "Definitely not like the first group we encountered."

Tilly lifted the bottoms of his goggles, spilling the accumulated sweat into his lap. "Get loaded and ready to move out."

"They're not Venezuelan," Branson interrupted. "Well, not all of them."

"What?"

"I said, these guys are not all Venezuelan."

Tilly stuck his head and shoulders out to see that Branson had crawled to the edge of the barracks grounds, inspecting the soldier who'd fallen at the edge.

"What's up with him?"

"The insignia on this guy's coat isn't Venezuelan, and he's got light hair and blue eyes. He's not from this continent, that's for damned sure."

"What the hell is he then?"

Branson held up the man's arm, showing a red, blue and white striped flag on it. "Russian."

"Shit."

"You said it."

Tilly clicked his earpiece, connecting to the wider band. "Echo One to base. Be advised. We have engaged with Russian soldiers."

Dispatch came back with a confused reply. "Repeat that, Echo One. Did you say *Russian* soldiers?"

"That's correct. The paratroopers they dropped on us were a mix of Venezuelan and Russian."

"Message received. Continue with your egress."

Branson swung into the barracks with a shocked and worried look. "We need to punch our tickets out of here. I spotted multiple incoming reinforcements. And we still have the choppers to contend with."

Nodding, Tilly gave the order. "Form a defensive posture and retreat to the drop point. Don't stop until you're there. I've got your backs. Beat feet! Fly! Let's go!"

Branson exited the building and fled east with the SEALs as they broke cover and entered the forest, dark shapes pounding across the uneven terrain, ducking beneath bullet-ridden trees and chewed up foliage. Tilly came behind them, backing up as he swept his barrel at the oncoming muzzle flashes, spitting one empty magazine out, tossing it to the ground, and jamming home another. Charging the weapon, he reversed his direction of fire, making it seem like there were more guns covering their retreat, trying only to distract and suppress, not actually hit any targets.

He had no trail to follow, only the pale images in his night-vision goggles showing him where his men had gone. Glancing back, he stayed near his team as bullets flew by, surprised every time one didn't smack him in the face and put an end to him. Eventually, the enemy soldiers realized he was only a single man, and they charged through the tangle at him, the surrounding foliage exploding in a whirling wind of hot dust and shredded vegetation.

Head lowered, Tilly turned and sprinted, leaping deep brush, falling and slipping sideways on the slope. His hip smacked a rock and he stifled a grunt of pain as he scrambled to his feet, keeping the barrel of his weapon out of the dirt. Back on track, he pulled out his GPS as he ran, focusing on the waypoint just two hundred yards to the northeast. Eyes lifted to the sky, he thought he caught the flashing running lights of the Chinook and two U.S. support choppers but the incoming fire distracted him, chasing him through the woods, forcing him to dive into a gully. Rolling to his feet, he picked his way along the muddy earth as it curled up near their drop point.

Exhausted, lungs heaving, he willed himself to keep moving as he crawled out of the ditch, slipping in the mud. Something hissed near his head, and his hand dipped into a slimy pool of muck. With a sneer of revulsion, he sprinted toward what remained of his men. By the time he reached the drop point clearing, the helicopters were just sweeping in. The big Chinook dropped its ladders and hooks to pick up the wounded SEALs while a pair of UH-1Y Venoms cruised over the jungle to engage the Venezuelan aircraft and provide cover for the Chinook.

He spotted seven SEALs either on the ground or being lifted by the pulley retrieval system, Branson strapping Reggie onto a stretcher when Tilly jogged up and they both stepped back as the wounded man flew upward. The air erupted in bright flashes of light, explosions and rattling machine gun fire ripping through the night as the choppers clashed and their lift ropes began to shudder and sway. Tilly started to grab one, but a hail of bullets from the enemy ground troops caused both men to drop and the pair exchanged a nod, raised up, and fired back at the onrushing enemy, blowing through their remaining ammunition.

A thousand miles away, in the Cuban Presidential Office, space heaters rattle as President John Zimmerman leans over his desk, tuned in to the SEAL team's egress through a conference line. Hands wringing, he listens to the explosions and gunfire as a Venom is chewed to bits by enemy fire, the screams of the crew turning his stomach, then sighs with relief as Commander Tilly and the last SEALs are lifted to safety, the Chinook taking heavy fire as it bends away from the drop site to stagger home with the remaining Venom.

The harrowing escape from the jaws of death is bad enough, but the revelation of Russian troops fills him with a deep, unsettling dread. "There's only one reason the Russians would be involved," he murmurs, looking to General Davidson where he sits on the opposite side of the desk, lips pinched tight in surprise and anger.

"According to reports, the Russians aren't experiencing the kinds of temperature changes we are." The general shifts in his seat, rubbing his stubbly chin in doubt. "They'd only be in Venezuela if they were trying to keep us out."

The two shared a dark look, both having the same thoughts.

"Should we proceed, Mr. President?"

The President's eyes drop to his desk, the last vestiges of hope slipping, falling away like sand through his fingers. When he finally lifts his chin, his expression burns with a determination to fight to the bitter end, regardless of the outcome.

Despite the cold in the room, beads of sweat break out on his brow. He nods as implications circle through his mind, then he swallows hard, the decision made. "We don't have any other choice."

"I concur." Davidson's expression mirrors the president's.

"Okay, then." John's fingers squeezed into a fist. "Pull everyone together. We'll proceed."

CHAPTER FIFTEEN

Keith
Somewhere in Texas

The 18 ton Strykers plunged through the snowstorm southwest of San Antonio, sleet gusting off the armored sides as their lowered plows shoved snow from their path. Sixteen knobby wheels ground up icy white flakes as grey clouds chased them ever southward, a pair of hunters in search of prey, armored dogs with their noses down to the ground. The mercenary drivers used camera magnification to scan the distance, searching for blockages of snow and piled vehicles which could put them off course, and twice they'd gone thirty miles down long stretches of highway, only to be turned back and forced to find an alternate route.

The APC's heaters were running at full blast, but Keith sat huddled in the radio chair with his coat bundled tight around him, the older trucks having taken some tough knocks so far on their mission. Deep within the diesel engine's growl was a faint clacking sound, which he associated with suspension damage, and the air that pumped from the vents was only lukewarm.

Serge abruptly spun the wheel to the right, hitting the gas and putting the Stryker into a heavy slide, the armored front-end smacking something hard and metal, the jolt running through the crew quarters before the vehicle settled steadily once more.

"Hey, buddy, why don't you take it easy there?" Keith relaxed his arms from where he'd thrown them out to keep himself from falling out of his seat.

Serge shrugged. "Sorry. Obstacle in the road."

"You couldn't have just slowed down and gone around it?" Keith shook his head, feet planted firmly on the floor to keep his balance against Serge's wild driving.

"In this weather, you slow down, you get stuck. Then, you sit in here until the fuel runs out. Then you die." He turned toward Keith, raising an eyebrow. "You want me to slow down more?"

The agent shrunk into his jacket, saying nothing as Serge snorted and turned back to his driving. A glance back showed Mikael fast asleep atop a bed of backpacks, clutching two cold-weather blankets to his chin like a child on a wintry night, seemingly unbothered by the driving, and Keith felt his regret at joining the mission growing ever stronger.

"Can you read me up there?" Lena's voice crackled from the speakers.

Turning toward the radio console, Keith answered. "We read you loud and clear. Do you have something for us?"

"Another town up ahead we should check. I'm sending you the waypoint now."

"Received," Serge grunted back.

"What's so special about this one?" Keith studied his screen, eyes on the waypoint she'd sent.

"It's about as special is the last one."

"Which means not very." They'd passed three towns on their way to the Texas-Mexico border, each filled with ice and death and the echoes of the old civilization, and none of them with the McKnights.

"This one will be different, I can feel it." Lena's accented voice dripped with mock enthusiasm. "I caught satellite images of our prey traveling this way three days ago, though I could not tell if they entered the town or bypassed it."

Keith nodded, filling his lungs with a deep, hopeful breath. "It's definitely worth checking out."

After two miles they exited the highway onto one of a hundred side roads stretching across the flat state of Texas, all of them snowbound and wind blasted. At the end of the exit ramp, he spotted a sign sticking up from the frost-covered snow that read *Parseville*. Less than a handful of stoplights divided the main roads, signs bent, cables and power lines hanging loose, buried beneath three feet of white.

Serge found an ice-crusted lot to park on and they left the Strykers running as they exited through the rear door. The wind was a demon, whipping their coats against their legs, its bitterness exploiting every gap in their clothing. Like before, they split up, each team starting at one end of the town and working toward the center, leaning against the gusts, pulled their hats tighter and squinting behind their goggles.

Keith's frostbitten toes and fingers ached terribly, causing his teeth to clench in pain as he shuffled through town. Searching for impossible clues, anger fueling his body, he trudged from building to building, disturbing restaurant kitchens, sheds, offices and homes wherever he saw a hint of footprints that might show the McKnights had been there.

The refugees that hadn't evacuated south had raided the remaining pantries, but the food hadn't saved them. Keith and the mercs found groups of frozen corpses holed up inside employee break rooms and kitchens, signs of old fires and beds made of piled sleeping bags. They strode past a tall sign with a horseshoe and *Texas Steakhouse* emblazoned on it and Serge put his shoulder to the door, breaking it open with a crunch of wood. A gathering of thirty stiff frozen people sat bundled up in booths, furniture and partitions dismantled and tossed into a blackened heap in the center of the room. Two bodies lay near the edge, huddled together, candy wrappers and food scraps scattered around their heads, the scent of cold, rotting meat flitting in the air despite the cold, a bleak and nauseating aroma.

"Isn't Texas supposed to be hot?" Serge asked with a wrinkled expression. "I thought it was a desert."

Keith shrugged. "Desert or tundra. Two sides of the same coin." He stared at the frozen dead, piecing together the reasons they'd stayed put. "They must've balked at the evacuation orders, figured they could stick out the storm and take the spoils when things warmed up."

"They were fools," Mikael added.

"Yes."

They left the restaurant, no more informed than before, and met Dimitri and Lena at the APCs. Staring north, Keith pulled his goggles away from his frosted cheeks with a crisp snap and settled them on again. A chill wind blasted them, forcing them to go silent until the gust passed. With a shudder, he blinked into the cold radiating off the winter-rated lenses. In the short time they'd been out, the freezing winds had seeped through his coat, soaking into his muscles and bones. "It's getting even colder. We need to get back inside."

"Much colder than I am used to," Lena said in agreement, trying to stare into the wind but turning her face away.

"Yes, much colder." Mikael added. "And we are no closer to finding our quarry."

"If they're anywhere in these parts, they're either lost or dead. No way could they have gone north if they're still alive – Tom McKnight is too smart to do something like that."

"Then we go south from here on?" Serge asked.

Keith nodded once and they climbed aboard their vehicles and sealed them, leaving on their coats, gloves and hats, desperate to retain any scraps of heat possible. Taking off again, the APCs worked south in a straight pattern, crossing the flat, ice-covered highway, chased by the indomitable cold through the wintry night. The Stryker's tires crunched over ice, passing stubby bumps of cars with layers of hard-packed snow that had grown over them in cocoon shapes, their plows blasting through dense drifts, the frames shuddering with the blows.

Each new town was the same, every stop more agonizing than the last and even the silent giant of a merc dragged his feet when it was time to leave the warmth of the trucks and explore. The enthusiasm shown at the airstrip had worn off in the face of the elements and on more than one occasion Keith had to remind them to do their jobs. By the time they finished searching the city of Encinal, their eyelids hung with sheer exhaustion and refueling the Strykers was a stiff, unenthusiastic exercise that took them a full hour to perform.

Coming in from the snow, stomping his boots up the ramp, Keith realized they were likely done with their search of the surrounding towns. He flopped into the radio seat and eased back, counting the seconds for the mechanical door to shut and cut off the wind. When the clamps finally locked, he let out a heavy sigh and pulled his goggles up to rest them on his forehead. Serge turned in his chair, leaving his headset hanging on its hook as he fixed Keith with a stern look below his frosted eyebrows.

"This is getting tough."

Keith nodded, leaning forward to place his elbows on his knees. "We're not searching any more towns around here, but I don't know what to tell Banks."

As if on cue, a light on the radio console flashed, and he glanced up at the merc before turning toward it. Placing a headset over his ears, he pulled the microphone in front of his lips and answered the call.

"Keith here."

"Any luck?" Banks's voice cracked with static as the wind outside picked up. "Tell me you've picked them up."

"Actually, I don't have very good news." Before Banks could jump down his throat, Keith plowed ahead with his explanation. "Every city within a hundred miles of San Antonio is frozen solid. We've been out searching based on a few clues Lena got from the satellite imaging but if the McKnights hung around, they're dead and buried now."

"You really believe that?" Banks's words were a whispered threat. "They survived the Osprey crash, climbed right out of *that* mess somehow. And you think they'd let themselves freeze in one of those shithole towns?"

"I didn't say that. I'm just saying that if the storms caught them, they're dead."

Banks snorted in derision. "I thought you said these *people* of yours were good. I thought you said they'd have no problem locating our little issue and resolving it."

Keith's glanced around the cabin. Mikael had fallen back onto the packs once more, pressed against a vent, absorbing feeble heat straight from the unit. Serge continued to stare at him, unable to hear what Banks was saying, though he imagined the merc could guess.

"It's too cold." Keith released a sigh. "If we stay out here any longer, we're dead. There's no way the McKnights could be in this area. We need to move south and search there."

Fingers flicked across a keyboard from Banks's end before she came back with a response. "Go to the border camps before they finish their own evacuations." The Colonel paused, clicking a few more keys. "Yes, I think that's the best strategy. If it's as cold as you say it's getting, the McKnight's would have been forced to continue south."

"Any ideas where to start?" Keith placed the microphone on mute and released a heavy sigh, nodding to Serge with a measure of relief.

"I'm sending you a list of holding facilities. The first one on the list is fairly large, located just south of Laredo. Let me know when you receive it."

Eyes fixed to a screen, he watched as a message popped up, indicating a data packet was on its way. The download moved slowly, possibly due to the storm, but eventually downloaded to the Stryker's onboard computer. When the names of the towns came up, he scanned the top ones.

"First one is Laredo, like you said."

"That's the closest and most likely choice." Banks gave an exasperated huff. "Get down there, put boots on the ground, find the McKnights and deal with them. I don't think I need to express what happens to both of us if you fail and this eventually comes to light."

"No." Keith pressed the words between tight lips, voice hoarse from breathing hours of Arctic air. "If they're in the Laredo area, we'll find them. And if they're not, we'll keep looking."

"You don't have an infinite number of chances here." Banks paused, lowering her voice, a note of desperation creeping in. "There are too many questions being asked by those with too much time on their hands. There will be a reckoning soon, and you don't want to be on the losing side when it happens."

"Understood. Let me hop off here, and we'll get going."

"You do that."

Keith cut the connection and sat still, staring at his hands as the truck's heating unit strained and rattled against the unbearable chill. Looking to Serge, he tapped his one good finger on the console and pointed. "We're getting our wish to go south."

"Thank heavens for that." Lena's accent was even thicker in her exhaustion, the hollow-sounding speakers not making it any easier to understand her. "I also received the list of checkpoints Banks recommended. Laredo is eighty miles away."

"I have the waypoint." Serge reached for his headset and slipped it over his eyes. "If the roads hold up, I will have us there in less than two hours."

"Let's not waste any more time." Keith settled back in his seat, grabbing cover from the floor and throwing it over his shoulders, clutching it tight to his chin like Mikael.

"Buckle up," the merc mumbled from where he lay on the backpacks. "It's going to be a long, cold ride."

They reached Laredo from I-35, closing in on the first checkpoint at Killam Industrial Park, leaving the snow behind them, the roads finally clear of the massive drifts of the stuff. The icy winds still challenged the Stryker's heating system, though not like before, and for the first time Keith could feel himself warming up on the inside.

As they approached, Keith looked through the external cameras, spotting a pair of soldiers in a guard booth. Cars were left abandoned on both sides of the entry lane, doors hanging open, tires flat, belongings scattered on the ground, but there were no people in sight; no one was stampeding south toward warmer climates. They'd either made it through already or remained behind, frozen effigies of a dead civilization.

"I'm surprised they only have a single guard booth." Keith half-whispered his concern as he realized how far the evacuations were coming along.

"It is a ghost town like the others," Serge agreed, slowing as they drew near the small building.

The radio console popped to life, a soldier's voice hitting the line with firm authority. "Attention Stryker units. This is Guard Outpost Laredo One. Can you transmit your identity in key codes, please?"

Keith nodded to Serge as he brought the vehicle to a complete halt, with Dmitri drawing the second APC in behind him. Leaning in, the agent hit the talk button and spoke into the microphone. "Transmitting codes now." He clicked a switch on the console to send the data.

"Will they work?" the merc asked.

"Banks gave us everything we need," Keith affirmed. "At least I hope."

A moment later, the guard came back. "What's your destination, Stryker 298? Why are you here?"

"We're heading to the south barracks. Got a weapons delivery run to make. It's a last bit from the, uh, Asheville Armory. Orders are to deliver it to the captain there."

"Affirmative, Stryker 298. You're free to pass." There was a pause, and the soldier on the other end came through with a slight chuckle. "Any chance you can you take us with you?"

"Negative on that, guard post," Keith laughed. "I'm sure they'll pick you up soon and relocate you boys to a nice sandy beach."

"Roger that, Stryker unit. Good luck with your drop."

Serge edged the APC past the guards and into the warehouse district beyond. The massive lots were empty, abandoned tents flapping in the wind, some uprooted and drifting in the air, two broken down Humvees sitting parked side-by-side near a long, squat building. A pair of generator units rested on trailers nearby and MRE packaging and empty plastic water bottles rolled across the pavement.

"They're already abandoning this post," the merc said. "Not looking good for you Americans."

"They know what's coming," Keith murmured. "Cold, cold, and more cold."

The trucks wove slowly to the south, slipping between abandoned cars and at least two more broken down military vehicles. Turning a camera to the sky, Keith watched helicopters lifting off with cargo containers hanging from ropes, then looked to the GPS screen, using his fingers to zoom in on a map of Laredo. Using the street maps, he navigated for Serge, guiding them closer to the nearest border crossing.

At one point, a pair of soldiers stood in front of an unidentifiable smoldering heap blocking the road, forcing them to swing west along the Rio Grande. They rejoined the highway as it swung them back southwest to a bridge that spanned the waterway where they stopped at a checkpoint station halfway across that was fitted with automated wooden arms that blocked their path. Keith retransmitted his security codes to the guards, and they waved the APC through, though before he gave Serge the go ahead to continue, he fired off a quick question to the guards.

"Hey, guys. Can you give me the location of the internment camp?"

"Uh, which one is that, Stryker unit?"

"I'm not actually sure. We're supposed to meet a captain..." He referred to the list of camps Banks had fed them. "A Captain Godwin. You know him?"

"He's a she," the guard replied. "And yeah, Captain Godwin is in charge of the internment camp south of Nuevo Laredo. You can find her down there."

"Great, thanks; that's exactly where we're supposed to be heading." The wooden arms lifted, and the APCs pulled off down the expressway where they cruised for a mile to the exit for Nuevo Laredo. "Go left here," Keith directed, and the vehicles took a long, curved exit ramp and headed south toward an approaching city. Smoke drifted up from a sea of block structures on the horizon, gathering in the sky below the gray clouds and the wide road narrowed into a two-lane main drag that ran through the center of town.

"Just stay straight," Keith said, clenching the edge of the console. "Let's see if this takes us there."

They cruised past dilapidated houses until the lifeless streets exploded with action, flooded with cars and people. People of all walks of life were busy packing possessions into car trunks or backseats, blank stares on their faces as they were forced to move yet again, their race and creed making no difference in the face of the onslaught from the north.

Soldiers stood on corners, directing a line of traffic onto the main highway heading south. They ignored the APCs, their massive presence and military stature giving them the run of the road. Using the map, Keith guided them down thin alleyways where the Stryker's armor brushed tree branches and brick, plowing abandoned vehicles aside, avoiding jams where they could, taking side roads and shortcuts as they worked their way south. The haggard, zoned-out citizens watched them pass with the blank expressions of herded cattle and soldiers shouted through bullhorns as they broke up vicious fights driven by resentment and confusion.

"They are all at each other's throats," Lena commented through the radio link.

"Wouldn't you be?" Serge responded.

"The camp must be around here somewhere." Keith's eyes flitted over the screen impatiently as he pointed a side camera at the sea of pale brick houses. With a frustrated slap on the console, he growled, "Stop here. Let me out."

Pulling his hat tighter, bundling up like he had so many times in the past two days, Keith waited for the rear door to lower before climbing out and circling to the front of the APC, making a beeline for the first soldier he saw. Back in the truck, Mikael rose from the pack he'd been laying on and took Keith's radio chair, watching the agent as he waved Serge forward.

"You think he will find the camp?" Mikael asked, Serge replying with a silent shrug as the pair worked the external cameras with a tiny joystick, having a look around at the decaying situation. In a side alley, a pair of families fought over the last spot on a military truck, fathers pushed and shoved each other, children squalled and mothers tried to make sense of the confusion, arms thrown protectively over their kids as they awaited an uncertain fate.

"This..." Mikael frowned. "This is worse than I expected to see. Even in the slums and the poverty there is some semblance of order. Here there is nothing but chaos tied up with string, bursting at the seams to escape. I do not like it."

"Completely FUBAR, as the Americans say," Serge agreed as he watched Keith stride up to the soldier, waving to get his attention. "Let's see what Mr. Wonderful can find out."

Mikael scoffed, snorting a laugh. "I used to think he was good. But sometimes I think he's still in basic training."

"I know what you mean," Lena said, overhearing the conversation. "Do you remember Tripoli?"

"I remember it well." Serge nodded. "Agent Keith was a much better man then. Arranged the drop-off and pickup points with ease. Very professional. Now, he seems filled with dangerous emotion. Like his mind is not all there."

"Perhaps he is getting old," Mikael agreed, "or the McKnights took some fight out of him. He did not even want to go on this mission to begin with. Imagine that, being afraid of a family, of children." Mikael spat derisively.

"Perhaps his edge is gone after losing a few fingers and toes," Lena suggested. "It happens. I worked with a man who had his left hand amputated. Afterward, he was never the same. Retired to a small village in Minsk and became a baker."

Mikael snickered. "But I thought Keith was supposed to be some big hero."

"Look, it seems our hero found some information." Serge gestured ahead.

They turned their attention back to Keith where he was backing away from the soldier, waving for the trucks to follow him around the corner.

With a shrug, the merc guided the Stryker after him as the agent walked three blocks to where another soldier barked orders at civilians. At first, the soldier rounded on him, screaming into his face to get back in his car, which drew chuckles from the mercs. Then the trooper saw the two massive APCs backing Keith up, and he instantly became more helpful. After listening to his questions, the soldier raised his mitten and made chopping motions off to the west. Keith nodded at him then sprinted to the truck, waving for Serge to let him in. With a sigh, the merc punched the button, and the door began its slow descent, boots pounded up the ramp with a gust of icy wind and Keith stepped over the packs to exchange positions with Mikael.

With a sweep of his hand, Keith unbuckled his hat and pulled it back, blue eyes alight with excitement. "They say the camp is just two blocks to the West. Turns out that particular soldier worked on the prisoner list, and he remembers a family with the name of McKnight being checked in around four days ago." Keith smiled wickedly, settling back into his seat, rubbing his hands in front of the heater vent. "I think we found them!"

"Yes, yes, that is wonderful. I just hope he is not mistaken."

"Come on, man! Go!" Keith said, hitting the dashboard with both hands, ignoring the pain shooting up his arms, a wide grin broadening on his face.

The APCs kicked forward, leaving what remained of the traffic behind and entering a part of town cut off from the rest. Whipping the Stryker down a dirt road in a squeal of knobby tires, Serge circled blocks of dilapidated homes toward a cluster of green army tents off to the left and the APCs trundled through the trash-ridden streets, crossing a set of train tracks into an area that appeared to be even poorer than the neighborhoods they'd passed earlier.

A thick mist hung in the air and abandoned buildings stretched around them like ruins, looking like they'd been unoccupied for years. Boards covered the windows, frames leaned at odd angles and walls lay collapsed, the wood riddled with dry rot and holes.

"Yes. This is it. We must be getting close." While Keith had been riding waves of confidence and doubt, a sudden sense of hope made his pained fingers tick, wishing more than anything that Tom McKnight would appear before him so he could smash the man's face in. Revenge and redemption were just within his grasp.

Serge drove them closer to the cluster of green, tops barely visible through the fog as he brought the Stryker to a squealing halt in front of the nearest tent, tracking a sudden rush of soldiers that flew past. One man stopped and gestured at the APC crew.

"What's he want?" the merc asked.

"No clue."

With Mikael peering over his shoulder, Keith maneuvered the camera around, watching as soldiers sprinted through the morning haze toward a block of trashed houses encircled by abnormally new-looking chain link fencing and razor wire. Beyond the fence, an old pharmacy sat in the block's center, a pair of men lying in the weed-ridden courtyard. Muffled reports came from outside, and Keith looked over at Serge.

"Is that gunfire? Hit the external audio."

As soon as Serge pressed the button, the obscured sounds grew distinct, revealing themselves to indeed be gunfire accompanied by shouting. People chanted and hollered in a cacophony of noise, followed by more single rifle shots, the back and forth gun play familiar to him.

"It's a revolt." He frowned. "Prisoners must be trying to escape."

"The American soldiers have lost control of the camp?" Mikael asked, grinning, a hand resting on his sidearm as he looked over at Mikael with a raised eyebrow. "Maybe this will be fun after all."

Keith listened for another several seconds as chaos reigned around them and more soldiers ran past, gesturing for the APCs to enter the fight. Serge's head moved back and forth, eyes unreadable behind his headset. "What do you want me to do? Should we help them and then recover the McKnight's?"

"No. Turn around. Let's drive around the camp and look for them." Keith slapped his hand on the console. "If I know Tom McKnight, they're probably leading the damned escape themselves. Come on. Go!"

Serge pulled the APC in a tight circle, causing soldiers to dive out of his way. Dmitri followed him, and soon the pair of APCs trundled around the outskirts of the camp, skirting the fencing, looking off to their left as soldiers fired into a broken down part of the gates on the eastern side. A dozen or more camp occupants shot back from positions on the opposite side of the fence, hundreds more huddled around them, armed with pipes, knives, bats and scraps of wood. Others slipped through cuts in the chain link, escaping past the thin Army line, a few receiving fire from the guards as they ran.

Via the camera, Keith scanned across the firing refugees, looking for signs of the McKnights. "They'll be two adults and three kids, one of them small."

Squinting, he stared into the rising mist, vision obscured by the drifting haze and distracted by the occasional stray rounds that plinked harmlessly off the Stryker's armor. When he couldn't identify them right away, he made another circling gesture. "Take us around the bend ahead."

Serge whipped the Stryker to the left, squealing around the corner. In a break in the fog, Keith gaped at a scene playing out forty yards ahead. A small group stood in the middle of the road, backing away from another, larger group – not soldiers, though – armed with rifles and handguns. The smaller group was bundled up tight, faces barely visible in their hoods, but Keith made out five forms, and a swirling in his gut confirmed what he already suspected.

"Hit them!"

"Hit who?" The merc driver let his foot off the gas and the APC lurched.

"The people with the guns!" Keith turned and gripped Serge's shoulder. "Aim for the riflemen, but don't harm the family! It's the McKnights!"

"Just... run them over?" Serge's expression wasn't one of hesitation, but of confusion, wondering if he had heard the instruction correctly.

He slammed his fist on the console, screaming the words through a clenched jaw. "Yes! Hit them! Run them over!"

Serge shrugged. "Okay."

The mercenary leader pounded the gas pedal and the Stryker flew forward with a jerk, its engine revving, bringing them to thirty, then forty miles an hour. Eighteen tons of metal roared toward the larger of the two groups as they gesticulated at the smaller group, hearing the massive vehicle coming and turning their useless weapons on it far too late. Two shots pinged off the armor before the truck's plow slammed into the rebels, bouncing them like pin balls to skid across the concrete, rolling and pitching, arms and legs flailing as their guns flew loose, crushing as many beneath the wheels as it knocked away. One man farther out than the others tried to dive out of the way, but Serge banked into him with a sickening crunch of bone. Another stood with his eyes wide, a deer in headlights as the Stryker's plow cut him in half.

"Stop!" Keith yelled and Serge brought the APC to a screeching halt. Keith toggled to the rear camera, seeing that they'd pulverized most of the group. Two people were crawling away, one with a hip and leg twisted impossibly out of the socket while others lay unconscious on the pavement. A handful were creeping toward the APCs with their rifles already firing, obviously in pain but still able to put up a fight.

"Come on, man! Get that back door down!" With a frustrated grunt, Keith spun out of his seat, pulling his right glove off and snatching his pistol from its holster. Knocking Mikael aside, he clambered to the rear and stumbled onto the ramp as it fell far too slowly for his liking.

Squatting, edging toward the growing sliver of light, he ducked as bullets ricocheted off the armor. His boots carried him to the pavement where he landed with a pained grunt, the ache from his mangled toes screaming up his ankles to his hips, but he didn't care. Nothing mattered except getting the family. Nothing at all.

He raised his pistol and fired it at an approaching survivor, putting a bullet into the man's throat, sending him gurgling, spinning to the asphalt as Mikael and Serge flew out after him, their own rifles popping off, scattering the forces like roaches. Wide eyes whipping left and right, Keith searched for the McKnights, but they'd slipped away again.

"Serge, Mikael! With me! Do *not* kill any of the family!"

The pair broke off their attack on the civilians and fell in behind Keith, seeming reluctant to give up the fire fight but professional enough to stick to their assignment. Errant gunfire flew toward them and something exploded off to Keith's left, but he kept his head down and focused, angling for the dense cluster of shattered homes to their right. He caught the flash of a jacket swinging into an alleyway forty yards along a deserted street and headed in that direction. Picking up the pace, wincing from the pain in his feet, he sprinted to the spot and plunged into the alleyway only to find it blocked with old furniture piled atop a rusted out washing machine.

With a cry of rage, he slammed his hands into the pile of debris, knocking it off and diving over the washer's smooth surface, swinging his legs around to land on the balls of his feet. He stepped out of the alley to face a string of broken homes, doorways and windows open and yawning. Shoulders rotating, direction uncertain, he listened for a clue to where the McKnights might have gone when glass crunched off to his right, followed by a dog's muffled yelp.

"How the hell is that mutt still breathing?" Keith growled to himself, hobble-running across the street toward an open door. Ducking his head and shoulders inside, he listened for more sounds and was rewarded with crunching debris. Heel-to-toe, he walked carefully through the room, sliding right into a hallway that divided the house.

Eyes narrowed, he peered into an entryway that was far too dark. Far too quiet. Memories of the small town and the bitch of a child came back to him, his vision starting to cloud over with red, the wounds flaring up in pain and he forced the anger down, determined to keep a clear head. Not this time. Not like last time.

As he walked ahead, a thick piece of wood swung at his chin and Keith jerked back in reflex. The board missed his face but slapped his raised gun hand, sending the weapon clattering off the door frame to land in the hall. Fingers on fire with pain, mouth twisted in an agonized grimace, he watched as a boot heel flew from the darkness and landed squarely in the middle of his chest, knocking him into the wall. Before he could recover, the wood whacked the archway in an overhanded swing, bringing a pile of rubble down in a crash to block the entrance and Serge and Mikael arrived and stepped over him, rifles pointed at the debris.

"I will go back outside and trap them." Mikael turned and took off the way he'd come, leaving Serge and Keith to break through the blockage.

They pulled off the loose boards and tossed them down the hallway, pushing the rest of the plywood and drywall over. Keith grabbed his gun off the floor, shoved Serge aside, and threw his feet over the pile, sliding to the other side, risking impalement on debris to land on his heels with a jolt. Growling, eyes watering in pain, he rushed out the back door in a blind-red rage, all rationalization gone again, focused again on the hunt.

An old concrete wall surrounded the yard with several holes in it. Instincts on fire, he staggered straight ahead, dodging a rusted swing set, plunging through the gap to come out in the street. He stood there panting, fingers and toes wailing their displeasure, chest heated with fury when Serge jogged up behind him, barely winded, shooting Keith a dark glance, Mikael close on his heels, speaking first.

"They did not come around this way. Did you see them?"

"No." Keith gave a breathless, frustrated sigh, chest still smarting from the kick, pride wounded more than his body. Serge reached out and dusted off the front of Keith's coat, causing him to jerk backward, swatting at the mercenary.

"What the hell was that for?!"

Serge smirked. "You have a boot print on your chest. Come, let us go back to the Strykers. We can pursue them from behind our armored protection. It is getting too dangerous out here."

Jaw churning, chewing on his anger, Keith spun on his heel and strode stiffly back to the APCs.

CHAPTER SIXTEEN

President John Zimmerman
Havana, Cuba

Zimmerman paces across the presidential office in his new thermal boots, the footwear replacing his hard-soled dress shoes, a necessity in the ever-increasing chill. Gloved hands slapping together, he hunkers down in a heavy coat, the space heaters in the room rattling with clacking fans and the smell of burning dust. The extra heat is necessary in the hundred-year-old building with its high ceilings and poor ventilation.

Cold clings to the stone, creeping through to turn the air frigid and unforgiving, the extra insulation and retrofitting to the building doing little to stop the never-ending advance of the cold. The President comes to the window and looks down at the Marines interspersed throughout the courtyards and gardens, all of them wearing thick winter gear and standing near burn barrels, trying to stay warm while performing their duties.

"That sounds like a solid plan," he says to General Davidson, where he sits across from the President.

The big man has more meat on his bones than the rest of them, but he's bundled up just the same, as are Rick, Rita, and Maxine, all of whom also have a space heater near their feet. The general turns and shifts in his seat so he can see the President as he paces back and forth across the room. "Key to all this will be securing the oil refineries in the Orinoco Belt, on the Northern coastline."

The President nods. "We have the transports and supplies for that, right?"

"Despite the fact that every supply chain we've ever had is screwed up to the max, we're somehow getting it done. We're pulling all ships out of the North Atlantic and bringing home the South China Sea patrols and even those in the Baltic and Indian Oceans." The general shakes his shoulders in a sort of half shrug, as if he's reached a rope's end. "We're consolidating our assets, and that should give us enough firepower to protect the oil platforms and keep the Russians out."

"What about the refining plants inland?"

"We'll cover those with ground forces, inserted via sea and air. Once everything is secure, we'll immediately begin working on processing it into fuel and upgrading any facilities that need it. It won't be perfect for a hell of a long time, but it will give us enough to fight and stay warm."

The president paces to the other side of the room where he rubs his hands together as he stares at a picture of George Washington crossing the Delaware in the freezing cold, an ironic smirk tugging the corner of his mouth upward.

"The idea is to hit them hard, and go all-in," he said, turning back to his advisors. "We need the Russians to understand we won't be deterred, and we're staying in South America for the long haul. It's *ours*."

"That's been communicated to all who need to know it, sir."

"Once the Venezuelan and Russian troops know we mean business, they'll destroy every platform and refinery they can. Those must be secured right away."

The general nods, his heavy jowls shaking, his face having grown thinner over the past few days, covered with an excessive growth of stubble. "Scorched-earth policy, sir. That's what I would do if I were them. But that won't happen. We've got teams training round the clock, and they'll be prepped and ready to go. It will be the biggest air drop and naval maneuver since World War II."

Hands clamped together, the President nods and returns to his desk, circling to his seat and easing down. A female staffer comes in armed with a pair of pitchers and looks at the small group. "Tea or coffee?"

"I'll take some tea," Zimmerman says with a nod. After it's been poured, he gives the woman his thanks and sips from his cup, relishing the bitter, sobering taste. The others take a black coffee each, Rita with her hands wrapped around the mug to suck up the heat.

"The secondary mission will not only be to secure key infrastructure, including housing, power plants, and city centers, but to ensure those aren't destroyed. We can't have a repeat of Mexico. We need shelter for our people when we bring them over."

Davidson nods. "We learned a lot from Mexico, sir. We're going to hit the military complexes hard and keep the fighting away from the populated regions as much as possible. We've also upgraded our plan to cut off their key infrastructure and supply lines and get them to surrender within 24 hours. We won't fight in the cities unless the Venezuelans and Russians force us to."

"This will be huge for us," the President says. "Once those two objectives are reached, the last thing we'll need is to transport our citizens in. Rita?"

The Secretary of State draws her hands away from her mug and folds them in her lap. "While the General prepares for the invasion, I'll be working with administrators on the ground in Mexico to get our people ready. Part one will be to move half our entire civilian population to the border of Guatemala, where we've established over a thousand major camps. They'll be leaving by bus and troop transports from Chiapas, south into neighboring countries, all the way to Panama. We'll be using the rail systems whenever we can, obviously, but it's going to be messy. We'll get it done, though."

"What about protection? The people down there won't be happy with us using their roads and highways."

"For those going across land, we're working with General Davidson and his commanders to secure helicopters and jets for cover on the trips down. Each convoy will be fitted with plenty of firepower to defend themselves."

"It won't be easy, Mr. President," Mark interjects, "but we'll be able to hold our own against anything they can throw at us. We're already sending warnings to all the countries we pass through, threatening severe retaliation should any of those convoys be attacked."

"Good. Rita, what about the rest of the refugees? How are we getting them there?"

"We've secured major ports along the Gulf of Mexico and have already begun the transport of half the remaining population to those cities...." Eyes shifting upward, she stops and lets out a soft sigh, followed by a subtle gasp.

"Are you okay, Rita?" The president asked, leaning across his desk.

In an uncharacteristic moment of caring, the general puts his arm around her and pulls her close, squeezing her shoulders in a comforting but brief embrace. "It's fine," Mark whispers. "We're all very tired, but within two weeks we'll be working toward a new future."

She gives a nod, looking up and smiling. "Thank you." She laughs and looks to the President. "I haven't worked this hard since going for my doctorate degree, and I was 20 years younger with twice the energy. I can barely keep my eyes open."

"You're doing an outstanding job," Zimmerman adds, feeling his own frustration and weariness rise. "All of us are about to collapse. Just a little while more and we'll be through the worst of this."

Putting forth a confident smile, burying her exhaustion, Rita continues. "Like I was saying—as with the land convoys, we'll have the ports protected with yet more personnel provided by General Davidson. Cargo ships and a small fleet of cruise vessels 'donated' by every cruise ship company in the United States will begin transport of our citizens once the Venezuelan landing sites are secure."

"It's not like anyone's going to be taking vacation anytime soon," the General laughs, "so it didn't take much convincing for them to hand their ships over."

"It will take multiple trips, upwards of months' worth, but we think we can get the majority moved pretty quick. Protecting them at sea will be an endeavor, though General Davidson has promised destroyer escorts every leg of the way."

"Good." Zimmerman turns to his scientist. "How about it, Rick? Can people survive until the boats pick them up?"

The disheveled scientist nods as if he's been expecting the question, shifting forward in his seat. Since the last attempt to collapse the anomaly, his job responsibilities have diminished, yet he's still called upon for temperature predictions and general atmospheric and weather advice.

"It's going to get pretty cold pretty fast, Mr. President," he says. "Like we spoke about before, the twentieth parallel will be hit by deep freezes of near Arctic temperatures. We're already seeing major drops in the cities we just now settled in. It may remain slightly warmer on the coast, given the relatively temperate waters there, but it's not something we should count on."

"You think we need to get our citizens off the Mexican coast in an expedited time frame?"

"Unfortunately, yes. The chilling waters in the Mid-Atlantic will create sheets of ice forming as far south as Florida which will cause potential hazards for ships leaving from the southern tip of the state. Add to that the rapidly advancing cold and... well...."

Zimmerman nods. "If we don't get them out of those Gulf cities, they could be stuck there?"

"Exactly, sir. I discussed this with Rita, and we both agree. There may not be enough time to beat the ice."

"It's not that we don't *want* to do it," she replies with a single nod of apology. "We just can't guarantee they'll make it before the routes get congested or the people freeze to death."

"No, it's something we should consider." After a light tap of his fingers on his desk, the President points back and forth between the two. "Can you put together a plan to get half the citizens in the coastal cities down to the convoy camps on the Guatemalan border?"

Rita nods. "We can do it, but we'll need to use the spare fuel reserves."

"Then that's what we'll do." Zimmerman looks at the General. "But if we burn through the spare fuel, we'll need a fresh supply quick or the whole shebang will be dead in the water. That's why it's critical for us to get those oil refineries locked up."

"Consider them ours, Mr. President." The man looks exhausted, the bags under his eyes dark with sleeplessness.

"Get a few hours rest first, Mark," the President scoffs, but his expression is sober. "That's an order."

"Yes, sir."

"Rita? Rick? Do it. Pretend like you have all the fuel and resources in the world to get those people relocated. We'll figure it out on the other end. I'm not leaving any of our people to die."

"We'll do it, Mr. President." Rita nods assuredly.

"Good. The invasion will start in one week. We need this to work like clockwork. Now, on to other-"

A rattle of gunfire rips through the courtyards below and Rita and Maxine both cry out and dive to the floor as Rick sinks lower in his seat. Zimmerman instinctively leaps from his desk, sliding toward the window to have a look outside when General Davidson grabs him, spinning him away from the window as Secret Service agents burst into the room, securing the exits.

Another spattering of shots crack the air, rounds pinging off the concrete on the other side of the wall as the US troops respond, the automatic rifle fire causing Zimmerman's insides to clench tight. Shouts and the muted sound of a grenade blast go off near the edge of their encampment, not a massive explosion but enough to send trails of dust drifting from the old wooden ceiling.

The response from the US troops is brutal, an impressive chorus of firepower as bursts are rattled off, a siren wailing like a banshee as the Iron Dome silos are activated.

Boots sprint along the hall, and the office door bursts open. A half dozen more Secret Service agents fly in, more heavily armed and armored than the first who came in, carbines lifted and heading straight for the windows, plastering themselves on either side of the newly installed bulletproof panes.

The head of security leans forward and peeks outside to have a look at the grounds. The thick glass is struck with three quick shots, the impact of the high caliber rounds punching an inch into the bullet-proof material and caroming off, leaving burnt divots in the composite material, causing the man to jerk back behind cover.

"What's happening?" Zimmerman directs his question at his head of security.

"There's been a slight breach of the defenses by a guerrilla group, but it's currently being contained. I'd say you're at no risk," he gestures at the window, "but they've obviously penetrated far enough inside to get a line of sight on us. Just sit tight, sir."

The President lets himself relax against the wall. With nothing else to do but sit and wait until the fighting stops, he listens to the gunfire exchange outside, topped off by sharp explosions, each causing him to wince. After the last few concussions, the shooting all but dies out. A few more rounds pop off, the sounds of shouts and revving engines, then the noise finally trails off to a halt.

"We good?" the President asks.

Mark and the security lead both nod at nearly the same time, listening to a feed through their earpieces.

"Yes, sir," the general says, backing up from Zimmerman to allow the President to move around again. "The threat has been neutralized."

"Thanks, guys." Zimmerman slouches against the wall and takes a deep breath while Rick helps Rita and Maxine off the floor while the security forces file out of the room except for two, the black-garbed agents staying around to watch through the windows.

"There'll no doubt be more," Mark says, patting the President on the shoulder before shuffling to his seat. "We should expect it at this point."

With a stiff stride, John steps to his desk and eases into his chair, huffing with uncertain relief, spreading his hands across the surface, bracing against it like an anchor. "I suppose it's the price we must pay for what we're doing."

"It's the price we'll pay for keeping our citizens – and our country – alive," Rita's tone takes a noticeably dark turn. "And woe be to anyone who doesn't think we're ready to pay that price."

CHAPTER SEVENTEEN

Tom McKnight
Nuevo Laredo, Mexico

Jack's hand gripped tightly in his, Tom led his family from the rough Nuevo Laredo neighborhood into a better part of town. Spread out around them were blocks of upgraded Spanish revival and adobe style homes with multi-level patios and rustic wooden trellises. The fog had lifted, revealing deserted streets and abandoned cars, dirt roads giving way to pavement and gravel with boxy courtyards surrounded by brick, stucco, or latticework walls on either side.

Explosions and the staccato rips of small arms fire filled the air, drawing closer as the fighting spread. Bullets flew out of nowhere, nicking the walls and zipping by like angry insects as screams penetrated the haze, the two sides battling in the gloom. A US military bullhorn roared for the rebels to give up their weapons, though they never did, and if anything the order only caused the battle to grow louder, more frenzied, threatening to spread outward through the town.

After the shock of seeing Keith, knocking the man down and barely escaping, Tom had guided Barbara and the kids to where he hoped their supplies waited.

"Saanvi said they'd be just north of here." He lifted the paper directions in one hand and grabbed Jack up with the other, carrying him so they could move faster. "It says to find the missionary home on Miguel Hidalgo Street."

"What kind of a missionary home?"

Tom swung Jack to his left side so he could see better. "I don't know, but it should be on this street."

"*Missionary* home? Like, a church? Or a house?"

"Or that," Tom said, pointing to a large, odd-shaped structure in the middle of a block of smaller ones. The light gray stucco with blue trim stood out above everything else, and a crucifix was displayed on the topmost peak. "That's got to be it."

The family angled across the street as the sounds of fighting grew nearer. Underpinning the gun fire were the roars of APC diesel engines prowling the neighborhood behind them. Barbara jogged ahead and opened a dark wooden gate nestled into a white outer wall. Beyond it was a small inner courtyard and a thick oaken front door on the building itself.

Tom strode up and grabbed the plastic yellow ribbon Saanvi had tied around the porch post, ripping it off and holding it up for Barbara to see, then he twisted the doorknob, shoving hard with his forearm to open the door wide and shined his flashlight into a wide foyer hall. When he hollered inside, no one answered, so he gestured for his family to enter behind him, still carrying Jack in his arm. Barbara ushered the girls in along a short, tiled passage to the back of the house where an open living room greeted them as Smooch trotted in behind them, looking around curiously. Tom placed Jack down, giving him a pat in Sam's direction, pointing across the room.

"Girls, can you take your brother over there while your mother and I search for the supplies?"

Standing straight, hands on his hips, he looked over the ornate fixtures in the chamber. Metal sconces and biblical images hung from the walls, along with at least a dozen crucifixes and Tom blinked at the peaceful reverence, his breathing slowing as his nerves calmed.

"That was Keith back there," Barbara said as the pair stood in the center of the room.

"Yes, it was." His voice dripped with contempt. "And it looks like he brought some friends with him."

"We can't let him get us. We can't let him get to the children."

"I know." He nodded, looking around as he searched for the gear Saanvi had promised. "Let's spread out, honey. Search for backpacks and other supplies. She must have stacked them around here somewhere. They shouldn't be hard to miss."

The kids stood by a modest couch pushed against the wall, facing a small tube television sitting on a stand. Almost every archway in the home was rounded, the end tables laden with ornate metal lamps and old fashioned lanterns.

"No flashlights, okay kids?"

They all nodded, but Linda spoke up. "Can we help look?"

"No," Tom replied. "I don't want any of you near the windows, especially not the front ones facing the fighting. Stray bullets are flying everywhere." He was already leaning into the kitchen, though he saw nothing on the floor, and when he threw open the pantry, it was bare. "As soon as we find the gear, we're leaving."

Barbara strode across the living room to a suite of back bedrooms while Tom glanced into a closet, then returned to the foyer to check upstairs. Wide tiled stairs with an ornate wrought-iron banister circled up to the next landing and as he ascended, he studied a series of black-framed pictures running up the wall to the top. They were mostly of a middle-aged man wearing a priest's collar, posing with people in remote locations across the world. At the landing, Tom caught the faint scent of cooked meat and laundry detergent, something the man might have been in the middle of doing when the evacuation orders came. He turned right down the hallway, peering into a bathroom, then into a spare bedroom with a perfectly made bed, cross hanging above it, Bible lying on a desk in the corner.

The window faced the front of the house and the encroaching gunfire, so Tom carefully approached, keeping the wall between himself and the fighting. Leaning forward, he glanced outside, overlooking the street and its tiny yards and crowded parking before turning back to the room, mumbling, "Come on, Saanvi, where did you put the stuff?"

He backed into the hallway and searched the master bedroom and an adobe-colored prayer room overflowing with potted plants and a skylight that illuminated a massive crucifix perched atop an ornate staff. Stomach doing anxious flips, Tom walked back to the landing and shouted down.

"Barbara, have you found anything yet?"

"No!" she called out. "Not yet."

"Maybe it's the wrong house."

Linda yelled from below, but her voice wasn't coming from the living room. "Dad! Mom! I think I found it. It's out here!"

Confused, Tom started down the stairs, then turned back into the hall, taking two strides to reach the master bedroom, walking past the meticulously made bed to the window. Head against the glass, he peered into a two-car driveway where his daughter stood behind a Humvee. At first glance, the vehicle didn't look like much, certainly not new with spots of rust and old tires, an early model likely out of service until recent events had brought it back.

Hands held out excitedly, he called. "Awesome! Stay there."

Stomach flipping with growing exhilaration, he flew down the stairs to the bottom floor, swung around the banister, and shot out through the double doors at the rear of the house. Jack and Sam had joined their mother and Linda at the vehicle, peering inside, hands pressed against the glass. Tom checked, too, staring at the things piled in the cargo section.

"I count six backpacks in there," he whispered breathlessly. "And a couple of rifles and pistols. Good job, Saanvi."

"Six backpacks." Barbara stepped back with a frown. "She wanted to come with us."

"I know," he said with a sinking stomach, remembering the medic's last haunting look, then he slid along the side of the vehicle, popped the door, and slipped behind the wheel. "I'd say this is it, wouldn't you?"

"Definitely," his wife replied. "Kids get inside with Smooch, now!"

With a rush of feet, the McKnights got in, Barbara in the passenger seat, the children filing into the back, the German Shepherd laying across the floorboards.

"Wow, this is so cool," Jack said, looking around with wide eyes. "It's a real army truck."

Tom pushed the start button and the old diesel engine shuddered, sputtered, then rumbled to life rattling and thundering from beneath the hood, its noise heightened by spotty exhaust pipes running up both sides of the front windshield.

As he adjusted the rearview mirror, Tom glanced back, throwing out a command. "Kids, get down, right now. You too, Barbara. There'll be bullets flying everywhere, and I don't want you to get hit. This thing's got some built-in armor, so try to use it, okay?"

She agreed with a nod, turning in her seat and sinking, motioning for the kids to duck. Tom searched the courtyard shared with the house next door, seeing two older model vehicles sitting with flat tires. While Tom could see the street directly in front of him, his view to the sides was cut off by the privacy walls penning them in. Above the encroaching explosions and small arms fire came the growling of APC engines, the diesel growls closing in on them from what sounded like two directions.

Tom shook his head, gritted his teeth, and put the vehicle in drive. Testing the brakes, he edged to the end of the courtyard and peered to his right, seeing an empty street, but on the left one of Keith's APCs rumbled slowly toward them, bearing down. Its front profile was a thin cut of metal, menacing and sharp, the mounted gun on top swinging around and pointing directly at them.

Tom slammed the gas pedal, shooting into the lane as a hail of rounds tore into the wall where they'd just been. Brick shards flew against the Humvee's roof and rear glass as the rubber shrieked on the pavement. Tom whipped them hard to the right, clipping a compact car and sending it spinning away, then he straightened the Humvee in a squeal of tires, punching forward to the next block and swinging into the first left turn he saw. Throwing his weight behind the wheel, he slid the vehicle hard, tossing Barbara and the kids against their doors, clearing the corner as more rounds streaked across the road behind them, tearing into a nearby house. Windows shattered, stucco exploding everywhere as tree branches were blown to pieces, dropping to the ground in shredded green and brown slivers.

The children screamed and Smooch whined as Barbara shouted, trying to keep her balance. "Are they crazy?! I thought they wanted to bring you in alive?"

Tom didn't answer. Shoulders low, he pressed himself against the wheel, glaring at the streets ahead, the neighborhood carved up into mostly straight lines with some back alleys and hidden driveways. Before he could make a decision, a second APC unit spun around the far corner, its eight wheels spinning at full speed, the bulky armor leaning and falling onto its suspension with a bounce.

Barbara flew into him as he whipped the wheel hard to the right, kids screaming in unison as the oncoming vehicle unleashed a brief volley of bullets at their tires. Tom had already cut across the next corner, splitting a pair of thick trees, the trunks absorbing machine gun rounds. The chaotic swerving pushed him toward a brick wall and Tom adjusted again, jerking the wheel hard left, throwing the McKnights back the other way. The Humvee clipped the wall with its right fender in an explosion of bricks, sending shards and dust flying out ahead of them.

Dragging grass, parts of the wall, and stripped tree branches behind it, the Humvee screeched across the road, engine growling as he pushed the pedal to the floor. A glance in his rearview mirror showed the two APCs swing in behind him, machine guns sweeping the ground, chewing up pavement, nipping at his tires.

"They're trying to take out the wheels!" Tom's voice was a horse, throaty hiss. "They definitely want us alive."

"Well, you could have fooled me." Barbara's tone rose to a fevered pitch, reaching back, hand thrown over Jack's knee. "Are you kids okay?"

The three nodded vigorously, eyes wide, clutching each other, slumped and terrified with Smooch at their feet. Tom searched for a way out, swerving back and forth, dragging the wheel in long, hard turns, taking one street after the other, pushing the old Humvee to its limits. The suspension shuddered, windows rattling in their frames and sometimes, when he hit the accelerator, the engine coughed before finally catching.

The rounds finally stopped firing, though, giving him a minute's respite, a moment to breathe and think. The next time he checked his rearview, only one APC hung behind him. "They're trying to flank me," he said, lips pressed into a thin line, skin itchy with sweat even in the intense cold.

Head lifting, eyes scanning back and forth like a hawk, Tom searched for a way out for a long moment before finally finding it. The Humvee angled toward a gravel road that led up to a neighborhood filled with blocks of construction and abandoned projects. Huge mounds of soil lay everywhere, piles of wood and debris, stone and insulation, dumpsters full of garbage from the old, torn down buildings. They climbed the steep rise to a grid of dirt streets, the lanes just wide enough for two large vehicles to pass.

"Slow down, honey," Barbara said, looking back. "You're kicking up a dirt trail."

"Crap." Tom eased up on the gas, cutting the dust trail drastically.

"This is perfect terrain for the Humvee," he mumbled, "but it's a little tight for them. I can turn faster than they can."

His wife only nodded as she peered through the windows, the big truck cruising past tarps flapping in the chill breeze, piles of construction materials, excavators and bulldozers sitting idle amongst the half-framed homes. The hulking vehicle eased over the rocky, dirt-frozen ground, the suspension shaking gently on its struts, the squeaky frame loose with missing bolts and parts. Tom rolled the window down, ear to the outside, listening as the APC engines growled up the gravel road after them, the sound bouncing off the surrounding hillsides, making it impossible to pinpoint their location. He leaned forward and back, trying to see through the gaps in the construction, directing them up a rise to a nest of houses scattered there.

"Maybe we can spot them from up here," he said. Reaching the top, he swung left onto a dirt lane, cruising, raising in his seat and craning his neck to look below. The road took him right, deeper into the neighborhood, on another nameless street, the Humvee's wheels shifting on potholes filled with crumbled blacktop, and he slowed more, the diesel engine thrumming softly beneath his feet.

"Hey, guys. Help me. You see anything?"

From the corner of his eye, he saw the family raising and looking everywhere through the windows, Barbara shaking her head and Sam's curly locks shifting around her shoulders.

"Wait, what was that?" Linda asked from her middle position in the back seat where she had completely turned and was staring out the Humvee's rear window.

"What?" Tom glanced back and forth between the road ahead and the rearview mirror.

"Oh, shoot. I guess it's nothing. I thought something moved around the last corner."

"You mean up on this level with us?"

"Yeah, but it was nothing." Her voice quivered, shivery and uncertain.

"Don't say that. It could have been them. Keep looking." The APC engines had gone quiet and he took another soft turn, pointing the Humvee toward the center of the neighborhood. Their rattling, shaking vehicle went two more blocks before he finally drew it to a stop in the middle of the street. They sat idling as he wondered if he should pull into a garage or if he should get out and try to find a vantage point to search for their pursuers.

As he was deciding, a wide section of tarp wavered and fluttered off to the left. Doubled up on itself, the opaque material was stretched over a passage that cut between two homes, yet it couldn't hide the massive dark shape behind it. There came a punch of sound, and the plastic exploded outward, the sheeting flying up as an APC shot from beneath it, kicking up frozen dirt and gravel as it banked toward their Humvee.

The roaring engine sent the kids screaming, a spike of adrenaline straight into Tom's veins. He double-pumped the gas pedal to keep the vehicle from sputtering and catching, then he punched it hard, the Humvee rocketing forward, the family thrown backward in their seats.

The APC slid out of the passage, skewing sideways, barely clipping the back of their Humvee as they sped forward. A quick spray of rounds chewed up the ground behind them, and Tom took the first hard left to get out of the way, but the turn put them right into the lap of the second APC. Its massive form sat in the road, thick armor looming over the Humvee like a bully and for a fleeting moment he thought about shooting the gap to get around it, but the APC angled across the road, driver sensing what he was thinking and blocking his escape.

A slam of his foot on the brakes brought the truck to a skidding stop. Thrown forward against the wheel, Tom jerked them into reverse and hit the gas, tires spinning, icy mud spraying the fenders, clattering like rain on a tin roof. The Humvee backed into the intersection as the first APC reached it. Wheels churning, he wormed around the charging vehicle, slipping by, and the APC missed them and rammed into the nearby construction materials, slamming into a pile of bricks and beams, riding up it until its huge front tires were left spinning helplessly, unable to get traction.

Tom didn't wait to see more. He spun the wheel, throwing their rear end into a stack of shingles, sending the packages flying before reversing direction, foot pounding on the gas, the Humvee shooting up the street with the second APC roaring in on his back bumper. The diesel engines growled in challenge to each other, Tom pressing the pedal down to the floor, stretching his speed to forty then fifty, the Humvee's suspension shuddering over the dirt road as he pulled away, every dangerous turn putting their lives in jeopardy.

The children clutched each other in the back seat, forearms pressed against the armored insides, feet resting on Smooch. Tom drove for several blocks, leading the APC on, keeping to the right side of the dirt track, inching forward, teasing the bigger vehicle to keep up. As he hoped, the APC pounded after them, eight tires carrying 12 tons of steel smoothly across the road, the pointed nose of pushing against the Humvee, bending the back frame, spider webbing the glass as easily as a foot crunching a tin can.

Tom hit the brake and spun the wheel, cutting a sharp right, the Humvee's wide base taking the turn, tires digging furrows into the dirt. The APC broke past, unable to follow the shorter arc, its trajectory carrying it into a corner lot where it smashed through a home, barreling into the 2 x 4 framing. Stucco sheathing split and exploded like eggshells, insulation and wiring materials dragging behind. The tires slid on swaths of slick siding and plywood, its front end jumping the stoop, plunging into a basement with a rough growl of metal on concrete, wheels left spinning in thin air. The rest of the home collapsed on the armored car in an avalanche of debris, the wide flat roof dropping in a rain of shingles and brick.

With a metal-bending squeal, Tom barely kept the Humvee on the road. It slid across the street and to the edge of the concrete courtyards and patios, slicing through stacks of building materials and tarps, clipping pallets of siding, slamming into garbage barrels. The tires vibrated on their axles as the vehicle bounced over the sharp, uneven terrain, Tom fighting to get them straightened back out. Not waiting to see if the APCs were back on his tail, he slowed, taking turns at speed, getting more and more lost.

"Tom, there's the exit road!" Barbara shouted, pointing to the road they'd come in on.

He gunned the Humvee, racing onto the gravel lane and down to the lower part of the neighborhood. The truck growled and clawed its way through the streets, searching for an exit. Barbara leaned to the side, spun in her seat, both hands on the headrest as she stared back through the cracked glass. "I think we lost them, honey. I think we got away!"

"Nice driving, Dad," Sam said as she deflated with a slack expression of relief.

No one had gotten hurt, miraculously, and something was grinding in the truck's frame, the engine still coughing and sputtering, but as he pulled out of the Nuevo Laredo neighborhood, Tom considered them lucky. *Very* lucky.

"Stay strapped in, kids," he growled, eyes flitting from the road to the rearview, half-expecting to see the impervious, dogged APCs on their tail. "We've got a long way to go, and we can't let up."

"Pull over here!" Keith screamed, fists slamming on the console, the pain an afterthought, more of a friend to him than a discomfort. "This is where they crashed."

The APC came to a grinding halt, back door dropping to the ground and he rushed outside, glaring at Dimitri's Stryker as it shifted back and forth to free itself from its stuck position. Spinning on his heels, he turned and ran to a dirt pile and climbed to the top, staring into the neighborhoods below, following the Humvee as it shot west along the cold Nuevo Laredo streets. Serge and Mikael flew up behind him, clambering up the dirt hill to stand next to him.

"There he goes, dammit!" Keith spat, pounding his fist into his palm, setting his fingertips on fire.

"Is he heading to the highway?" the merc leader asked.

The agent leaned forward, eyes narrowed as the vehicle took a turn north and then swung west once more. He lifted his gaze, glimpsing the highway in the distance, a long stretch that wound far to the south.

"Yeah, I think that's where they went." He nodded slowly. "That's where I would go if I were him."

After the Humvee disappeared from sight he turned and slid down the dirt hill, stalking to the APCs just as Dmitri freed his vehicle and backed onto the road.

"All right, people! Let's move it out!"

They clambered inside, shut the door, and pulled off to give chase once more. Keith settled back in the comm chair, frustration simmering like a rash beneath his skin. Tom McKnight had been within his grasp – quite literally – then somehow escaped, found a vehicle – where the hell had that come from anyway? – and managed to evade *two* armed vehicles hunting him down.

No matter. As persistent as the McKnights were, Keith was more so. He'd continue hunting them, chasing them down wherever they went to roost, and eventually he'd catch them. He'd catch them and rain hell upon their heads.

CHAPTER EIGHTEEN

Specialist Lance Morales
Santa Fe, New Mexico

"Hello? Who's there? Are you military? Boy, are we glad to see you guys."

Morales and Smith exchanged an uncertain look, Smith stepping around the captain, calling out. "This is the United States Army. Who are we speaking to?"

Shuffling footsteps greeted them from the dark hallway, and several figures came into view. Morales didn't draw his weapon, not with the four other Army rifles pointed down the hall, but he shifted to Captain Jones's right side and stared into the darkness.

The first two people stepped into the light, a man and a woman, each wearing loose-fitting military-esque fatigues with a special unit emblem on the arms that he didn't recognize. The woman was short with inky black hair hanging to her shoulders, her cold blue eyes picking over them beneath stark eyebrows. The man next to her was a swarthy type, his loose dark locks falling into his face, a growth of beard lining his firm jaw. A handful of others came behind them, clothes disheveled, shoulders slumped, not the postures of strictly-trained and disciplined members of the military. Morales read their haggard, uncertain eyes bearing the weight of being trapped under tons of snow and felt an immense pity for their situation.

The man stepped forward into the emergency lights. "I'm Chet Peterson, part of the special unit here at the FEMA facility." He gestured to the woman and those assembled behind him. "This is Shae Roberts and the rest of my team. Who am I talking to?"

The captain met him briskly, offering his hand. "I'm Captain Jones, United States Army, Special Scavenging Unit. We formed less than a week ago and were sent north from Mexico to transport supplies from this facility down south. How long have you folks been down here?"

"Since the big freeze started," Shae replied, raising a dark eyebrow. "We barely made it inside before the really icy stuff hit." Her eyes flashed past them and up the stairs. "What happened to the others?"

"You mean everyone up in the warehouses?" Jones asked.

"Yeah."

"All dead. It looks like they tried to hold out up there, but the spin-up storms were a little too much for them." The captain's gaze shifted back and forth between the bunker leaders. "Can you tell us why they stayed up there and didn't come down here with you folks?"

A mixture of emotions Morales couldn't read flashed across Chet's face. "I told them not to stay up there, but they insisted on sticking it out and waiting for rescue to show up. I guess they weren't counting on the spin-up storms to hit as hard as they did." He stepped forward to emphasize his point. "I saw the writing on the wall, so I got my people out of the warehouses and into this bunker as quickly as possible. We must be the only ones left alive on the grounds, right?"

"At the moment, yes," Jones replied. "But we haven't checked all the warehouses yet." The captain stood back and looked them over. "How many of you are there?"

"About a dozen. The rest of the group is downstairs where we set up some sleeping quarters." Shae gazed across at the array of soldiers who had lowered their weapons, eyes flashing from face to face. The corner of her mouth ticked up in a bone-weary smile. "You guys wouldn't be offering rides south, would you? We wouldn't mind a one-way ticket out of this frozen wasteland."

"We're just here to ferry the supplies and that's all." Jones kept his hands on his hips. "And we don't have room for stragglers, I'm sorry to say. Nobody told us there might be survivors, but I'll call it in and see what we can do." He turned to a staff sergeant. "Radio in, let them know what's going on and ask for guidance."

"I'll send a message to headquarters." The soldier replied then pivoted and moved toward the back of the landing, taking a radio off his belt and ascending the stairs as he spoke into it.

The captain nodded to the bunker team. "You folks up for some loading?"

Chet and Shae exchanged a glance, the man speaking up. "We're not full military, just a special hybrid unit. I'd like to keep my group separate from your units. You people look like you just came off the front lines. I don't think-"

"Don't worry," Jones interrupted. "We don't bite. Well, maybe Smith does." A humorous chuckle came from the soldiers, though the bunker team only shared uneasy looks.

The captain continued. "If anything, you can show us where the warehouse supplies are and get us a full inventory. We'd like to see what we're moving. Would make our lives a hell of a lot easier."

Chet shrugged and nodded. "Yes, sir. We can at least do that much. And if helping out will buy us a ride home, we'll do it."

Jones stepped to the side and gestured. "Morales. Smith. Take a small team and go with these two. Locate the supplies and manifests and determine a load-out order. And we need to know where the cargo elevators are so we can dig the doors clear."

"Yes, sir," Morales said, stepping with Smith over to the pair as the staff sergeant came running down the stairs with an update. "Headquarters responded. We can't carve out a transport unit for passengers back with our convoy, but the third transport wave will have some APCs with room to spare for survivors. That one should arrive in a few days."

"Thanks, Staff Sergeant." The captain turned to Chet and Shae. "How's that sound?"

"Perfect." The man grinned. "You've got our full cooperation, sir."

"All right. I'll let you get to work. In the meantime, I'll be overseeing operations in the warehouses."

Jones took his staff sergeant upstairs, leaving Morales, Smith, Brozowski, LePlante, and eight soldiers with the bunker crew. Lieutenant Smith jumped ahead with Chet, while Morales fell behind with Shae, followed by the mix of soldiers and crew. Together, the group moved deeper into the dark depths of the sub-floors, boring into the ground, circling a central core of concrete, the walls marked with bold letters. Boots tromped on the stairs, echoes banging in the enclosed space, the sterile smell of moist, warm concrete lingering in the air.

"Sub-floor 1 is dedicated to storage pods," Chet said, loud enough for everyone to hear. "Sensitive electronics are on Sub-floor 5. In between are larger warehouses, at least 10 on each level."

"How big are these spaces?" Morales asked as they moved past Sub-floor 2.

Shae scoffed. "The ones we found are huge."

"You don't know the square footage?"

"No," she said with an apologetic glance. "Well, the exact specs are in the system. I might be able to get them for you."

"Great. Thanks."

They stopped on the third landing labeled *Warehouse 3L,* where Chet paused at the door.

Smith turned to two of the soldiers. "Brozowski and LePlante. Why don't you take Meyers, Jennings, Johnson, Isaacs, and Richardson down to the next level? Check out the radio gear and see if there's anything we can salvage." Lieutenant Smith pointed to three soldiers to stay with them. "Stevens, Griggs, and Rupert. You're with us."

Brozowski and LePlante nodded and gestured for their team to follow.

Chet motioned at his four other bunker crew members. "Take them downstairs, boys. Shae and I will see after the lieutenant and his people." The bunker leader turned and pulled open the heavy metal door, stepping into another long hallway that stretched at least 500 feet, lit by pale circular bulbs nestled into the ceiling. "This way, folks."

As they walked, Morales's eyes roamed over the concrete walls, tracing over each warehouse door as they passed.

"The entire place is connected by a slick intercom system," Chet explained. "You can call to any room using the internal speakers. You just have to know how to work the buttons, but it's pretty easy."

"There's a hell of a lot of rooms down here." Morales glanced over several square security pads next to a few of the doors, their keys glowing green. Chet and Shae didn't stop at any of them. "What about the ones with the security pads?"

"We haven't been able to get into them." The leader threw his reply over his shoulder. "No one on our team has the codes, and those who had them either never arrived at the bunker or were in the warehouses when the snows hit. And, according to your Captain Jones, they're all dead."

"So, there were people down here originally?" Morales asked.

"Yep," Shae responded. "There was a staff here when we showed up, but some left as soon as the snow started falling. I guess they didn't want to be buried alive."

Morales flashed Smith a look, raising an eyebrow as they trudged along, their boots thudding on the tiles all the way to the end of the hall.

Chet paused and turned, spreading his hands at Shea. "Do you remember where food storage was? I get confused between those rooms and refrigeration units every time." He shrugged and glanced at the lieutenant. "This place is like a damn maze sometimes, more cells, cubicles, and compartments than you can count. But it's all organized. You'll see."

"Left up here." Shea gestured at a branching hall, a flash of annoyance in her eyes. "Sorry, I would've brought my inventory tablet if I'd known we were going to get to work right away. You guys didn't even text ahead. We didn't know you were coming."

"No problem." The lieutenant waved her off with a crooked smile, hiding his true aggravation that Morales might not have noticed if they hadn't become best friends over the last couple months. "Let's just get through what we can," Smith continued. "I just need an idea of what we're looking at so I can report back to the captain."

"No problem," Chet agreed. "Let's go."

Smith dropped back by Morales and let the other three solders walk up front as they strode through a series of intersections. The group took two left turns and another right, confusing his sense of direction. When the others weren't watching, the lieutenant leaned in to Morales, mumbling out of the corner of his mouth.

"Do you have a bad feeling about this?"

"Yeah. They don't seem to have anything together," Morales replied. "No codes to any of the secure rooms."

"And no clue about their inventory."

"And their story seems a little sketchy."

"Keep your eyes peeled, okay? Look for a chance to break away if you can. Have a look around yourself."

Morales nodded secretively as Chet brought them to a flat gray door marked Food Stores, 6-3L. "Oh, here we are." The bunker leader opened the door, stepped aside and gestured for them to enter.

Inside, he gaped at the massive room filled with endless buckets of freeze-dried fruits, vegetables, eggs, and other dry rations. It wasn't as big as the initial warehouse they'd broken into, but just three or four rooms like 6-3L would easily surpass it.

Shae stepped out between the rows, pointing toward the rear. "It looks like there's a centralized cargo lift in the back corner that connects with several surrounding warehouses."

Morales spotted the massive steel door and nodded. "Those will be extremely convenient once we start bringing up supplies. Do they work?"

"To be honest, we don't know," Shae replied. "We haven't had to use them because we haven't moved any product, but I'm sure you boys can figure it out."

"You've got some lights out up there." Smith pointed up to the rafters, steel beams crisscrossing in blue paint, at least two big white lamps with aluminum hoods blinking sporadically.

"Yeah, we've had little time for repairs," Chet said. "We were more worried about securing the facility, making sure we were prepared to stay here for the long haul."

"Your radios are down, right?" Smith asked.

Chet's eyes flashed to Shae as an uncertain smile tweaked the corners of his mouth. "They work, but we haven't been able to reach anyone in weeks. I guess the spin-up storm took out our radio tower or something. You want to see some of the other storage areas?"

"I want to see everything you have access to. We'll have Brozowski and LePlante dig at those security keypads later."

The small group left Food Stores 6-3L and walked the entire warehouse sub-floor, poking their heads into at least six other large storage facilities packed to the brim with supplies of every kind. One offshoot section of the hallway was completely blacked out with even the emergency lights dark and dead.

"What's going on down there?" Smith asked. "You've got a total blackout."

"It was like that when we arrived." Chet cleared his throat. "We suspect a possible wiring problem, or blown fuses. I have someone looking into it, but they've had no luck yet."

"There's got to be a load of goods down there." The lieutenant squinted. "We should prioritize working on getting this section of the warehouse up right away."

"Yes, sir."

Morales peered through the darkness, eyes narrowed, lingering behind the group as they walked on. He spied a smidgen of light glinting off several metal doors along the dimmest part of the hall and suspicion pricked at the back of his mind, but the party was moving on, forcing him to catch up with them or be left behind.

The next room was filled with batteries, racks of deep cycle rechargeable batteries pressed against the left-hand wall, and tens of thousands of smaller appliance batteries sitting in wooden cases on the shelves. There were chargers, spools of cabling and connectors, and solar panels by the thousands. Morales's jaw dropped as they strode across the echoing space. Two dozen massive Xtreme worksite generators were neatly parked in the center of the chamber, resting on their own trailers, ready to be lifted upstairs and driven off by Humvees. He also counted 50 High Max mobile generators rated for 36,000 continuous watts each lined up in 10 rows of five along with smaller civilian generators, too, enough to easily power a small city.

"Well, this is exactly what we need," Smith said with a grin. "Do we have the diesel to run it?"

"The, uh, fuel tanks are upstairs installed near the cargo door," Chet replied in sheepish tone. "I think the pumps are above ground. Just make sure you guys are careful not to hit them."

Morales nodded, wishing he'd known that earlier when he was up digging around in the snow in an exhausted half-daze. "We'll take that into consideration."

"You know how much fuel you've got?" Smith asked.

Again, the two leaders shrugged at each other. "We're not actually sure," Chet replied. "We've been poring through the inventory system, but it's not as easy to navigate as we thought."

The lieutenant rounded on the man, hands on his hips, neck craned forward with a hard expression as he threw off any semblance of understanding. "You guys work here, but you don't have any of the security pad codes. You don't know how much of anything you have, or where it is. You can't even get into the computer inventory. Wait, I thought you said you could before. Am I getting mixed messages here?"

Chet held his ground, giving Smith a faint nod. "Look, the actual warehouse managers, the ones who would have all those access codes, weren't around when we got here. Or they bolted when the storms hit."

"One manager promised to come back," Shea explained, eyes darting between the three men. "But he never did, and we couldn't go get him after the snow started piling up. Back in the control room, we tried to hack into the databases and get full access to the inventory, but we could only read the non-restricted lists. The rest were off-limits."

"And there are no tunnels connecting this building and the outside warehouses?"

"That's right," she nodded. "At least as far as we know."

Smith scowled at the pair with a degree of menace. "I know we just got here and everything, but you people don't have your shit together at all. I can understand about the security codes and inventory, but you've got entire sections of the facility without lighting. That should have been fixed right away. It's almost like you don't know what the hell you're doing."

Chet's body froze, shoulders stiff as he swiped a lock of hair out of his eyes. He shot a stone-cold glance at Shea, and Morales squinted at them, wondering what the answer would be.

"Like I said before, Lieutenant Smith, we're not soldiers," he said. "We work here as part of the civilian unit, part-time, too. We were never given full access or had enough training to run the entire place. Our jobs consisted of packing and stacking things. None of us are electricians, but we've been working on it. We got 6-4L lit up, didn't we, Shea?"

"Hell yeah, we did," she responded. For the first time, the woman's shoulders sagged, the raw weariness in her eyes showing as she mumbled her words. "And, man, we're tired. It's just 12 of us, and most haven't slept for days."

"It's true." Chet agreed. "Not to mention being stuck down here. It's damn claustrophobic. Believe me, guys. It hasn't been a picnic for us."

"All right, fine," Smith said with a dismissive wave. "We're sorry you had to go through all that, but we really need to get a handle on what's here and get it moved south as soon as possible." He looked around the room. "I'm thinking we're going to have to hack into those secure warehouse rooms and do an entire inventory ourselves, from scratch." The other three soldiers with them groaned in response, and a tight ball of dread formed in Morales's stomach.

The lieutenant shrugged and exhaled sharply. "Unless Brozowski can hack into the inventory system, too. It'd be nice to check any security camera footage, see if we can figure out what happened here before you guys showed up. Anyway, let's keep going."

Morales caught another strange look between Chet and Shae before they stepped ahead to lead the group on. As the team left the battery room, he lingered behind, pretending to kneel and tie his shoe. He watched as the three soldiers walked beside Shea, asking her questions, Smith fully engaging with Chet as they moved to another section of the warehouse.

Legs slowing, boots quiet on the tile floors, Morales allowed himself to drift farther and farther back. Hands behind him, he strolled nonchalantly, pretending to study the doors and the wall markings, arrows pointing backward to various other sub-floors. The group rounded the next corner, and the specialist stopped cold. He waited a moment, then backed down the hall, finally turning and marching forward with quick steps.

He traced back the way they'd come, twisting door latches and peeking inside the storage rooms they hadn't checked. Stopping at the first security pad he saw, he tried out the codes he'd heard Brozowski and LePlante whispering to each other earlier. He punched the numbers into the keypad but had no luck and the second try didn't work either.

Morales glanced over his shoulder before rushing ahead to the beat of his quickening heart. Reaching the darkened intersection, he tried to penetrate the gloom, but all he could see was a spot of light at the far end of the hall; the rest was pitch black. With one more glance back, he strode forward through the darkness, emergency lights above his head as dead as night, not a single monochrome blinker or exit sign anywhere. None of the security pads were working, their normally green glow gone. In passing he grabbed random latches and turned them, but every door remained locked.

Feet shuffling, boots clacking on the tiles, he approached the faint hint of light he'd seen earlier. Time was running out, and he was certain Shae and Chet would notice he was missing at any moment. At the end of the hall, one emergency bulb illuminated three doors. Two sat on the right, neither with the security keypad on them while another stood on the left, its security pad lit with soft green keys. Two steps took him to the keypad, shoulders hunched forward, finger raised and frozen over the buttons when his nose twitched.

A stench wafted up from around the edges of the door, sweet and familiar, subtle at first, mingled with the heavy perfume of pine-scented cleaner. It was the smell of death, the intense reek climbing up his nasal passage and tickling the back of his throat. With a hard swallow, Morales punched in the first security combination he remembered. Each button made a quiet beeping sound, soft against his fingertip but when he hit *Enter* the pad turned red and left him locked out. He tried the second code, punching in the numbers and blinking in surprise when the keypad beeped with an upward-lilting click. The door popped open a quarter of an inch and, stomach rising through his throat, guts squirming, he opened it and stepped in.

The stench hit him first, a sucker punch to the chin, head jerking to the right as he threw up his elbow to protect himself and try to keep from expelling the contents of his stomach all over the floor. It was a large storage room with shelves lining the rear wall, mostly cleaning supplies, rags, and brooms hanging from racks. Boxes full of plastic bags and even a tile polishing machine sat at the back between the last two rows and the space was dimly lit by a pair of dull yellow bulbs beneath aluminum hoods.

The dim wattage cast a weak glow across a dozen corpses lying in a haphazard line in the middle of the floor. They were completely naked, left in awkward positions, rigor mortis capturing their tortured forms in stiff poses. Their chaffed skin was stretched and bloated in the early stages of decomposition, covered in blood and grime, the yellowish light gleaming off the tiny dots of moisture.

Gaze falling to the floor, Morales saw that someone had doused the tiles with pine-scented cleaner and bleach, rags soaked and pressed across the bottom of the door. Sickened, Morales hesitantly approached the bodies. The victims had been beaten, skulls crushed, bones broken, jaws knocked sideways, hanging loose from their faces. Without warning, the rations he'd eaten earlier in the day exploded from his stomach and he spun, reeling as the food and water and coffee spewed from his mouth and splashed across the bleach-slick floor.

Stumbling around it, careful not to get his boots messy, he moved to the wall, leaning forward as he waited for his guts to settle. Belly empty, he turned back to the bodies with a colder eye, approaching with a focused squint. While they were mostly without clothing, he spotted a woman at the far right end wearing the tatters of a military uniform. She had on army green socks pulled up to her shins, a tight-fitting sports top covering her chest and dog tags on a thin chain around her bruised neck.

Morales crept to the other end, studying the faces of the people lying still. They were clearly military with buzzed hair cuts and chiseled features, the women with their hair pulled back into tight buns, wearing minimal makeup. It was a military work crew if he ever saw one.

Chet and Shae being in charge made no sense. They didn't know anything about the facility or how much inventory they had, and had failed to fix simple things such as lighting, not to mention every answer they gave was vague and conflicting. They'd seemed more than a little surprised to see the soldiers at all, in spite of their original assertion. Morales stared at the puddles of cleaner, cracking his knuckles as the pieces came together in his mind, then he launched forward, gripping the door handle and throwing it open, stumbling, staggering into the hallway, almost slipping from his wet boots.

He bolted back the way he'd come, slowing as he reached the corner where he'd left Smith and the work crew, peeking around to make sure no one was around to see the direction he'd just come from. Coast clear, Morales began a fast walk along the hall, covering several hundred feet quickly, turning to where they'd disappeared.

It was a hallway like the others, doors on both sides, lighting running along the center of the ceiling. About midway down, he heard voices babbling from a room on his right. The door stood propped open, and he approached cautiously, stomach churning, pressing his palm against the surface with his hand lingering near his side-arm before he stepped inside.

Inside was a boiler room with pipes of various sizes and diameters running across the ceiling and far wall. Valves and pressure gauges sat at even intervals and touchscreen computer monitors placed in the center with schematics of the plumbing and steam systems highlighted in white on the screens.

Smith stood in the middle of the room near Shae and Chet with the soldiers standing off to the side while three members of Chet's team lingered behind the warehouse leader, shirts off, grease on their skin, at least two holding massive wrenches.

"There he is!" Chet said, regarding Morales with a grin. "We were about to come looking for you."

Eyes falling so he didn't give himself away, he nodded and made a show of zipping up his coat, coming to stand on Smith's other side. "I had to take a leak. I've been in an excavator all day, and I hadn't made yellow snow for a few hours." The group chuckled, yet the hot, moist air remained thick with tension, or maybe it was all in Morales's mind.

He nodded at the service workers and the pipes. "What do we have here?"

"It's part of the boiler system," Smith said, explaining what he must've just been told. "They've got heated water that flows around the entire place, and steam systems that run the conveyors and cargo elevators, and provide some of the power."

"These are the guys I was telling you about, the ones making repairs." Chet turned sideways, gesturing at the three men who were covered in sweat and stains, one with a thick beard growth uncharacteristic of a military employee. While they'd certainly been working, Morales doubted they were experienced workers, and he couldn't keep his eyes from flitting over the big wrenches in their hands.

Before they caught him staring, he glanced away, elbowing Smith in the side. "Hey, man I need to talk to you for a second."

Looking annoyed, the lieutenant squinted. "Can it wait until the tour is done?"

"I just had an idea about where the main cargo bay is, based on what I've seen of the layout so far. I think I can dig it up, but I wanted to see if you agree with me on the location first." He shot Chet and Shae a grin. "Boring military crap."

As he and Smith stepped to the back of the room to the gentle hissing of pipes, the other three soldiers strode up to chat with the bunker team, arms crossed as they engaged them in friendly conversation. Morales turned to face the group, putting his back to the corner, the lieutenant facing him.

"What's up?" Smith asked.

"Don't react to what I'm about to say in any way, okay?" The specialist's tone was flat.

"Yeah, okay."

"No, I need you to promise me not to react."

Smith grimaced, annoyed by the lack of direction in the conversation. "I think you know me by now, Morales. Just spit the damned thing out."

"All right." With wild gestures of his hands, Morales pointed upstairs and along the hall in a show of conversing about cargo elevators and loading strategies. "I wasn't in the restroom just now."

"I figured that. Go on."

"I searched that dark hallway. There's a room at the end where the lights work." He winced uncomfortably. "That's where the, um, real bunker crew is."

The lieutenant shifted from one leg to the other, jaw tightening as he fixed Morales with his customary stony look. "What do you mean by that? Are they having lunch down there or something?"

"No, sir. They're dead, but not dead like the ones we found in the warehouse. Not frozen. Beaten. Bludgeoned. To a pulp."

The gears behind Smith's eyes rolled out of control, anger, confusion, and resentment clashing on his face, but he quickly wiped the look away, forming a neutral expression despite that the information was undoubtedly burning his brain to pieces. "That would explain why these guys don't know jack shit," he whispered.

"Exactly." He glanced up to see Chet looking over. The man's face remained relaxed, but his eyes held an odd hint of wariness Morales had previously mistaken as exhaustion. "Whoever these people are, they took control of the bunker somehow, killed the original crew, and have been living off the supplies ever since."

"The place never felt good to me," Smith said with a head shake, lips pursing as he realized their predicament. "I don't care what the situation is, these jerks are too frikkin' clueless to pass as actual military."

"What do we do?"

"We need to get our people regrouped as soon as we can, if they haven't already been attacked."

After receiving a nod from Morales, Smith turned and gave a single clap. "All right, folks. Tour is over. We're going to reconvene and arrange to get this stuff moved out."

Before the warehouse crew leader could respond, Morales grabbed the door and held it for the other three soldiers, gesturing for them to go outside. Smith followed them, with Chet and Shae behind him, but the workers with the wrenches didn't come out. As he walked by, the lieutenant whispered from the corner of his mouth. "Keep an eye on our rear, would you?"

Morales nodded, smiled, and clapped one of the soldiers on the back.

"So we'll go find Brozowski and LePlante," Smith said as he caught up with the rest of the group, masking his suspicions behind the guise of urgency. "Then we'll start the inventory and get load outs arranged."

"They should be down on Sub-level 4," Shea mentioned, studying the lieutenant carefully as she guided them. "It'll just take a minute to get there."

Conversations were low as they moved through the halls, Smith hurrying them along, cautiously trying to avoid appearing like he was concerned. Morales lingered behind, glancing back, looking for the shirtless workers. There was no sign of them by the time they reached the stairwell, though that didn't mean they weren't there, trailing the group, waiting to make their move.

The others passed through the doorway, but he waited a moment and only after hearing no footsteps and seeing no shadows moving in the hall behind them, he entered the stairwell and quickly caught up with the group, tromping along the metal stairs to the next landing. Chet beat Smith to the door, holding it for everyone in a game of musical politeness. The hallway beyond was exactly like the one upstairs, long and starkly lit, the tiles hard beneath his boots.

"So what do you do for the military?" Chet was suddenly at Morales's side, shoulders relaxed with a smile on his face. "You're not a big, stupid grunt like some of these other guys."

Stevens, Griggs, and Rupert laughed good naturedly, having formed a loose friendship with the bunker crew, though as far as Morales was concerned, that was a good thing. It would keep the impersonators off guard when the soldiers made their move, but they would have to regroup first.

"I'm a driver, actually," he replied. "I'm rated to drive almost any military vehicle, including most forklifts and bulldozers. Stuff like that."

"What about helicopters and jets?"

"Unfortunately, no. I can't fly," Morales chuckled. "I'm a grunt, probably lower on the totem pole than these guys."

"That's right," Griggs said, rifle bouncing against his back. "You'll always be a chauffeur, Morales." Chuckling, Morales started to reply when they came to a stop, having reached an open door at the corner of the hallway, entering to see three big refrigeration units purring inside. Four of Chet's people stood with two soldiers from Brozowski's group, Meyers and Jennings, but neither Brozowski nor LePlante were anywhere to be seen.

"Looks like you guys found our seed stores," Chet said, stepping past them to one door and throwing it open. "When I first discovered these, I hoped they were full of beer. Boy, was I wrong."

His comment got another round of chuckles from everyone, though Morales continued to notice the exchange of glances between Shea and the other bunker crew as they adjusted their positioning, moving to stand closer to the soldiers.

Smith took a radio from his belt. "I'm not sure if this will work, but I'm going to try calling Brozowski and LePlante." As soon as he clicked the button, all he received was a scratch of feedback and static noise. "Attention, those in Smith's team. If you get this, move to Sub-floor 4, to the refrigeration units at the end of the first hallway."

"Yeah, radios don't work in here so well." Shae shook her head, striding to an intercom on the wall near the door. Her finger raised to one of the buttons. "Want me to call down to them?"

"Nah, we got this." Smith shook his head and gestured at Jennings. "Hey, Jennings. Why don't you run down and grab Brozowski and LePlante from the communication floor? We've got some stuff for them to check out. Hurry it up. Bring everyone up."

The soldier nodded, spun, and exited the room, and Morales's spirits rose despite the thrumming tension in his body though his expression fell just as quickly when Meyers strolled inside the refrigerated room and started perusing the shelves. The big, toe-headed kid looked out at them with a wide, Nebraska-sized grin.

"Boy, my dad would love it in here. He used to have a shed full of seeds, and we planted new ones each year in the garden. By the end of the summer, I knew every type of seed there was."

Morales glanced at Smith, eyes widening, and the lieutenant waved the soldier back. "Yeah, yeah, Meyers, we've heard the stories before. Come on out of thre."

"Seriously, guys," Meyers went on, scoffing in amusement and mock disbelief. "You need to check this out. This is the most awesome display of seeds I've ever seen. There're tons of corn, potatoes, beans, even honey producing flowers. Wow, this is real Noah's Ark stuff. Come here, Morales!"

"No thanks," Morales called back, separating himself from the group, walking over to a bulletin board near the door where someone had made a sheet of climate settings for the seeds. Big digital consoles showing the refrigerators' temperature and humidity hung on the walls, and he pretended to study them as Shea meandered over and put herself between Morales and the others, both groups shifting positions casually. "He's right, you know. It's an amazing display. You should check it out."

"I was never really into farm stuff. I'm a junk food fanatic myself." He glanced back at the refrigerator, grimacing even more as Rupert walked in behind Meyers. Outside the coolers, it was Smith, Morales, Stevens, and Griggs versus Chet, Shae, and three of their people. All it would take was one of the bunker crew to slam the door shut to even the odds, and that wasn't even considering the maintenance workers who could walk in at any minute.

Morales glanced at the lieutenant, waiting for him to pull out his sidearm and arrest the group, but if he jumped too soon, it might put Brozowski and LePlante in danger. Still, the decision had to be made, and it had to be made quickly.

"Hey," Smith called to his men, trying to sound casual despite the note of tension in his voice. "I'm serious, get out here where I can see you. Can't have you in there screwing off--"

The other woman in Chet's crew threw her shoulder against the refrigerator door, slamming it shut on the soldiers inside while the two other crew members grabbed Stevens and Griggs, going for their weapons. Shea lunged for Morales's holster, but he spun in time to crack her across the jaw with a left hook, the woman crashing to one knee as a flurry of motion exploded in the room. Pistol whipping out, Morales tried to shoot her, but she struck his hand with her forearm, knocking the gun free. They dropped down, grappling for the weapon on the floor as it slid and bounced against the wall. Morales lifted his hand and slammed it down, finally pinning the gun to the tiles, fingers clutching the pistol but she collapsed on his arm, clinging to him like a banshee.

Smith grappled with Chet, the lieutenant grabbing the thinner man by the shirt, sweeping his legs from under him and slamming him to the floor. Unfortunately, the rifle they'd jerked away from Briggs swung around and pointed at Smith's temple, freezing him in place. Stevens's rifle had been taken, too, the barrel jabbing into Morales's ribs as the man holding it glared down at him darkly.

"Drop the weapon or the lieutenant gets his head blown off!" the one on Smith yelled.

Morales froze with his hand on the grip, looking back at the crews' faces, their expressions having turned from helpful to furious in a handful of seconds. Releasing the weapon, he held his hands out and Shea snatched the gun and leapt up, firing it once into the ceiling before leveling it at him.

"Get off the floor, asshole. Move it!"

Morales stood slowly, palms raised, eyes on the woman with his pistol, and without warning she cocked her fist and struck him across the jaw, leaving his chin stinging from the blow. "You should know better than to hit a lady," she snarled, backing to the center of the room, gun pointed at his chest. "Against the wall. All of you."

Hands raised, Morales did as he was told, working his jaw back and forth. Stevens and Griggs put their backs to the bulletin board with him as Chet stood and grabbed Lieutenant Smith by his jacket, throwing him in Morales's direction. The soldier caught himself before he slipped and fell, raising slowly, chin lifted in defiance as he stared holes in the impostors.

"You keep that attitude up, buddy," Chet said, grabbing one of the rifles, "and I'll wipe that look right off your face with this."

The soldiers trapped inside the refrigeration unit were pounding on the door and Chet walked over and pounded back. "Hey, you boys want to keep it down in there? If you annoy us enough, we might have to kill one of your buddies."

The pounding on the door fell silent, and the intercom exploded with the huffing, panting voice. "This is Larry down on five. I'm looking for Chet. Chet, are you there? Everything good?"

The bunker leader stepped to the other side of the door, pressing the intercom button. "This is Chet. Yeah. All's well. I'm on Sub-level 4 in the seed storage room. What's going on?"

"We heard the gunshot, and the Army boys panicked. We've got a pair pinned behind some equipment. They won't come out. What do you want me to do?"

Chet backed away from the speaker, gesturing at Smith with the end of the rifle. "Tell them to surrender, or we'll do to you what we did to the other shits that ran this place."

CHAPTER NINETEEN

Tom McKnight
Nuevo Laredo, Mexico

The Humvee flew over what was just barely a highway through a desert that had become gentle curves of flat, white-dusted tundra in every direction. Tom's feet were cold as he kept the accelerator pedal pressed steadily to the floor, weaving back and forth over icy spots and slamming through the rare drifts that were a foot and a half high. The snowfall accumulation wasn't as bad as what they'd seen near San Antonio, but things were getting worse by the hour.

"This place must've gotten hit with a storm right before we came through," he said to Barbara. "Look at the wind."

Even as he spoke, a gust of chill air skimmed the ground in front of them, blowing a soft patch of snow into their windshield. The road vanished in a dusting of white before the windshield wipers swiped it clean and Tom bent the vehicle around a stiff curve, the highway banking right to cut between a pair of hills covered in scrub and snow. The Humvee's knobby tires slid sideways, the rear end shifting dangerously, slinging itself toward the middle of the road, and had someone been coming the other way, they would've crashed into them.

"Forget about the snow, Tom. Please slow down. There's been no sign of Keith or those APCs since we left Nuevo Laredo."

"Right," he said, easing the speed down to thirty, leaning back and trying to relax. The winter driving kept him on edge, and every few moments he learned a new lesson on how to keep the two and a half ton vehicle on the road. "Sorry. Better?"

"Yeah, thanks."

Despite the heater kicked up to full blast, the cabin was still chilly. Cold air filtered in through rust spots in the floorboards and cracks around the doors, his toes as frozen as ice cubes on the pedals. The kids huddled in back with Smooch, covered in blankets, a pile of children and dog, shivering as they munched on snacks from their backpacks. The cracked rear windshield whistled and leaked, and not even the piece of duct tape Samantha had placed on the surface helped much.

"Boy, these things weren't meant for comfort, were they?" she said with a grunt as the bouncy suspension jostled her around. "I'll tell you, Tom, I'm about to abandon you and join the kids in the back."

"I wouldn't blame you at all. I can barely feel my feet or my rear end, and my hands aren't doing any better." Still bundled from head to toe, his body was warm except for his extremities, the thick gloves covering his fingers no match for the frigid chill that surrounded them.

They hit a slight incline and Tom pressed forward, not wanting to get stuck. Tires spinning, kicking out snow in arcing wakes he turned the wheel to the right, hugging the inside lane. The Humvee gave off a soft clatter of noise, every part rattling on the frame but still it held together, and they came over the rise and down the other side in one piece.

"Oh, Tom. Look!" Barbara pointed out the front window, off her side where an exit ramp branched off the main highway. Beyond that, nestled into the snow-covered trees, were three buildings that comprised a rest stop area. He saw a gas station with a mini-mart and two garage bays off to the side, what looked like a Mexican eatery, and another adobe style building that could have been a hotel. The signs were in Spanish with English letters written smaller beneath them.

"We're definitely not in the United States anymore," Tom said, tracing over the words.

"Let's stop and get our bearings," Barbara suggested, turning to face him in the seat. "We don't know where we are or where we're going. This highway could be leading us anywhere."

"As long as it's not north, I don't care." He slowed as they approached, creeping, keeping the tires moving fast enough to avoid getting stuck in the mounds of snow. "You're right. We should at least stop and see if there's something we can scavenge. We'll need all the diesel, food, and water we can find. I'm just a little worried because of what people back in camp were saying about the annexation."

Barbara nodded, looking on at the establishments with keen interest. "Yeah, I don't think the people around here would appreciate a family of Americans busting in on them right now. For all we know, they might consider us sworn enemies. Especially driving this sort of vehicle."

With a deep breath and a sigh, Tom turned the wheel toward the exit and trundled down the ramp. At the bottom, he didn't bother stopping, but spun in a short arc, drove straight for another 200 feet, then angled left into the gas station parking lot. The big Humvee swung in beside the diesel fuel pump and came to a skidding halt and Tom sat with his hands on the wheel, fingers wiggling, head on a swivel as he looked for movement. Peering toward the mini mart's wide glass, he found the insides dark and impregnable, the front section of the store lit by the dismal gray winter light, fading to darkness at the rear.

"I don't see anyone, so I'll take Smooch inside and clear the place. Be right back."

Tom popped his door and got out, shouldered one of the rifles Saanvi had left in their supplies and opened the back door for the dog to jump down. The German Shepherd walked in a quick circle, limping slightly but looking much healthier than she had when he and Samantha had first found her. Smooch's fur was growing back on her wounded shoulder, and the singed hair from the house fire was filling in, too. Saanvi had fed the animal well, her chest and belly round and thick, and after another month of healing she'd be as good as new.

Tom slammed both doors shut, leaving the truck running, treading through the snow to the mini mart with Smooch on his heels. He paused at the front door, putting his hands to the glass and peering inside. The new perspective wasn't much better, his gaze only able to penetrate a few yards into the back of the store.

"Okay, girl. Let's check it out." With a flick of his wrist, he grabbed the door handle and pulled the unlocked door open, stepped in with the dog, pushing the door shut behind him to lock out the wind. The air was chilly, frosty, his misty breath blossoming into the darkness, hanging for a long moment thanks to the absence of a breeze. Flashlight shining toward the rear, he moved straight down the middle, looking through the remaining snacks still sitting on the skewed shelves.

There was hardly anything left, just a few of the less popular candy bars, energy snacks, and chip bags. A cooler sat in back and when he opened the door, the foul smell of sour milk poured out from several broken plastic bottles, white liquid sprayed and frozen on the glass. The dog whined, and Tom reached down and rubbed her head.

"I know, girl. It's pretty gross in there."

Still, he took three frozen bottles of water out, their caps having exploded, setting the blocks of ice on the bright red pressboard counter next to the old cash register. If anything, they could thaw them out and drink them later and use the plastic containers to help collect and melt down snow after that. Circling to check the cash register, he saw the door was open, the money having been cleaned out. "No dinero," Tom mumbled as he slammed the drawer shut, only to have it pop open again, some mechanism on the inside frozen or broken by those who had plundered the place.

The bathrooms were dirty, borderline disgusting, with the faint scent of cold sewage wafting in the air. The mirrors were smeared with muck, sink stained with iron deposits and the pipes had long since burst. Whatever piping materials they'd used likely couldn't resist such freezing weather – after all, since when did anyone so far south expect such frigid temperatures?

Exiting the restrooms, Tom stepped along the hallway to the end, pushing through the door into the garage area. The petrol scents of axle grease and motor oil permeated the space, and his flashlight revealed one bay taken up by an old Ford F150, while the other was empty. He did a slow circle of the place, stepping over hydraulic jacks and tires, walking past cabinets, tool chests, and work benches littered with tools. Soiled rags were draped around and piled on a bench near the back and a wood stove with two flat plates on top sat along the right wall, its rusted pipe angling upward to disappear into the ceiling. On the left side of the second bay, a fuel tank shared the wall with a row of metal shelves stacked with cans of oil, paint, and grease.

"Well, it looks safe to me. Time to put the kids to work."

Smooch gave another soft whine, faithfully sticking to Tom's heels as he returned to the store. From the inside, he knocked on the door glass and waved to get Barbara's attention. His wife raised in the seat, nodding at his motioning and the truck doors popped open, the children rolling out of the backseat, bundled up, kicking snow all the way to the front door. Holding the door open, he ushered them in and took his wife's hand as she followed behind.

"It's safe in here. Doesn't seem to be a lot of food, but there's a fuel tank in the garage and some spare oil cans that might come in handy later."

Barbara nodded. "This is good. There could be some things in here we can use later on. Kids, why don't you go around and start collecting whatever you can find, okay? Anything edible, even if you don't think you'll like it, gather up. We can't afford to be picky."

"I put some bricks of water on the counter," Tom pointed over toward the register. "Just set everything beside those."

Sam snickered, repeating his words with a sarcastic mumble while nudging Jack, who giggled in response. "He said 'bricks of water.'"

The children got busy walking through the store, noisily and busily checking under the rows of crooked shelving, stooping to reach to the back where they discovered the looters had left a veritable treasure trove behind. Barbara strode over to one shelf filled with paper towels and napkins and grabbed some packages, placing them on the counter with the rest of their goods.

"For when we don't want to use cacti to wipe," she said with a playful wink and grin.

"At the very least, we can use it for kindling." He narrowed his eyes at his wife. "You're in a good mood."

"I guess I am," she replied, traipsing by and giving him a kiss on the cheek.

Hands stuffed into his pockets, he followed her along the aisles as she picked through what remained of the store. Stopping at the medicine section, she snatched up aspirin packets, lip balm, and lotion. "These'll come in handy for our noses and hands."

"I guess you're right. Those are things I wouldn't have thought about, but it makes sense. The air is getting drier by the day."

"Exactly."

"So, why the good mood?" Tom gave her a friendly smirk. "You're really that happy we finally got our vacation to Mexico?"

Linda heard him from the other side of the store and laughed, while Barbara shot him a crooked smile, batting her eyes. "You always take me to the fanciest places."

Jack rounded the corner, holding up canned dog food as the German Shepherd followed him, sniffing and licking at it. Around the sides, one of the cans had broken, and the meaty frozen morsels had popped out. "You think we can thaw this out so Smooch can eat it?"

Reaching down, Tom took the split can from the boy and held it up. "I guess it's possible. I don't imagine it would be bad for her. How many other cans are there?"

Jack spread his mittens wide. "I'd say a bunch. Like, 12."

"All right, put them in a plastic bag, and we'll take them with us."

"Outstanding!" He spun and flew back to the dog food section to collect more, Smooch following him with a click of claws on the tile. Once Tom and Barbara had taken everything worth taking from the medicine aisle, they dropped it off at the counter, their tiny stockpile growing by leaps and bounds.

"It's amazing what we can do when we work together." Barbara's bright spirit suddenly switched off like a light, her expression shifting and uncertain.

Tom took her by the shoulders and fixed her jade green eyes with a questioning look. "Hey, honey. What's wrong?"

"Nothing at all." She circled her arms around his chest, squeezing him through his thick coat and layers of long underwear and shirts. "I'm just happy we're together. Even when we were in Asheville, it didn't feel like home."

"I know exactly what you mean." Tom embraced her back, letting his chin rest on the top of her head. "Even in the camp, it was hard to be ourselves, but I guess we're adjusting to the new reality. I didn't realize how much stronger I am when I'm with you guys."

Barbara melted into his arms, falling against him completely, sighing into his coat. Lifting her, he swung her around and set her on the floor again as Linda came up with a can of beef barley soup in each hand. She took one look at her parents and rolled her eyes before she placed the cans on the counter.

Laughing, Tom let go of Barbara and chased after his daughter. "You think you'll get away without a hug?!"

Linda squealed as she rushed to the end of the aisle with her father chasing on her heels. They rounded the bend, and she ran into Sam, giving Tom the moment he needed to snatch her up, lift her from the ground and swing her with her feet flying out.

"Jeez, dad! What are you doing? Let me go!" Yet, even as she struggled, she laughed and kicked without trying too hard to escape. Releasing Linda, he feigned a lunge at his eldest daughter, who jumped back, finger in the air, pointing and warning. "Hey, hey! What's gotten into you guys?!"

"I guess it's that we're finally free and not surrounded by a bunch of armed guards or people trying to kill us," he said, grabbing at her hands and chuckling as she away. Tom sobered up, standing straight, fists on his hips as he watched his family gathering supplies in the store. "I missed goofing around with you guys."

"I want a hug, too!" Jack flew into his father's arms, laughing, clinging to his bag of dog food as the cans clattered inside. Tom lifted him up, heart swelling with elation for the first time since they'd showed up at the Nuevo Laredo camp. The tension unwound from his shoulders, the gut-turning nervousness fraying and giving way. With

Jack placed back on his feet, he found his wife and wrapped his arms around her again, lowering his voice as the kids returned to searching. "I'm not kidding about feeling free. It's like a huge weight has been lifted off my shoulders."

Barbara nodded, grinning, glancing outside at the idling truck. "Too bad we can't just stay here and get warm. Have some family time away from that damn camp, Marty, Keith... all of it."

Tom followed her gaze outside, staring at the Humvee, not particularly thrilled about getting back in the driver's seat. They'd seen no signs of pursuit since the town, and he was relatively certain the pace he'd set had allowed them to outdistance the APCs. A sporadic dusting of snowfall suddenly picked up, a wash of flakes whipping back and forth in what remained of the daylight and he felt a sense of peace wash over him.

"Hey, you know what? Why don't we stay here? I think we're far enough ahead, and it looks like a storm is coming in, anyway. We don't want to get caught in it."

The pair walked to the window and looked outside, Barbara putting her gloved hands to the glass. "What about our tire tracks? Won't they see those?"

Tom shook his head. "I think our tracks will be almost invisible within the hour, and I know the perfect spot to park the Humvee."

"On top of the weapons she got us, Saanvi packed a small cooking stove in with the supplies," Barbara said. "We could use that to get warm."

"I can one up you on that. There's a wood-burning stove in the garage."

Barbara's jaw dropped in awe. "Are you serious? An actual wood-burning stove?"

With a shrug and nod, he replied, "Yeah, it's back there. There're some pans and skillets lying around, too."

"And we have a few cans of food we can cook up," Barbara's smile grew.

"Sounds like a plan." Tom moved toward the garage door at the end of the hall. "I'll bring the Humvee in while you guys carry those supplies to the back. Line them up on the workbench and we'll get this party started."

Tom crossed through the garage and found the manual release for the second bay door. He popped it open, dragged it up by the handle, wheels squeaking and protesting as it grudgingly rose. With the wind and sleet whipping across his face and flying into the gaps of his clothing, he jogged through the ever-thickening snow and got behind the Humvee's wheel. A moment later, he was pulling it inside, easing the truck to the back, leaving plenty of room for them to gather around the stove.

Tom climbed out and stood at the bay door, staring out, dancing motes of white powder drifting in front of his eyes, growing stronger even as the daylight faded to night. The cool scent of winter mixed with the petroleum smells of the garage, his nostrils flaring as he watched their old tire tracks filling bit by bit, masking their route.

He reached up and grabbed the bay door handle, pulling it down on its squeaky wheels until it struck the floor with a soft impact. Locking it, he called over to Linda, and together they covered the garage windows with old rags and duct tape. Saanvi had packed a pair of electric lanterns in with their supplies, and Barbara turned them both on and placed one on the work bench near the stove.

"Hey, Sam, do you think you can get us a fire going?"

"We need some kindling and wood." Samantha strode to the stove, hands on her hips, bending lower, opening the door and peering at the coals the last person had left. She reached down and grabbed a stick from the floor, using it to prod around in the belly while Tom pointed to a stack of logs on the shelf behind the stove, grabbing a couple of large pieces and carrying it over while his wife brought a napkin pack.

"Can you use this as kindling?" She asked.

"That might work," Sam replied. "But ideally, we'd use some smaller sticks. I think there's some down here on the floor."

"Well, you've proven you can make a fire just about anywhere." Barbara placed the napkins on the floor and took a step back, watching her daughter build the fire with an expert hand.

"I learned how to do it when Dad and I were on the road."

"I guess I didn't realize how independent you were," she said with a glance over at Tom. "You're quite the survivalist now."

Tom strode over and put his arm around his wife's shoulders. "We've all had to learn some new skills, right?"

Linda gave an affirmative nod while Jack brought his bag of dog food cans over to the fire and set it down.

"Hey, kids. Let's find some chairs and pull them up to the stove. I'm sure Sam will have things pretty warm here in a minute."

Tom pulled up a rolling tool chest while the children went back into the mini mart and grabbed two foldout chairs from the storeroom. Barbara dug up a pair of truck pads in a cabinet, and together they placed them in a semicircle around the stove. The heat from the Humvee's cooling engine had taken the edge off the chill in the small space, and Sam was working diligently on the fire.

Sticks went in with a small cluster of kindling, then she placed a match carefully inside, leaning forward on her knees to blow the resulting cinders into a spark of flame. Two more larger pieces of wood were thrown in, orange tendrils of fire catching and licking upward and at the first crackle of smoke, she dropped in a bigger log, adjusted its position, and stepped back to see her handiwork.

The McKnights relaxed in their seats, Tom on the truck pad with Barbara on his left. As he squatted and lowered himself to the floor, every joint creaked and groaned with discomfort. Shoulders stiff, feet gnawed through with cold, he placed his hands behind him and leaned back, putting his boots closer to the growing fire. Sam settled back onto the toolbox, ready to jump in and stoke the flames when it was needed and Smooch rested at the end of the truck pad, turning in a circle and lying at Tom's right hand while Jack and Linda sat in the foldout chairs.

After several minutes, the small flame was a roaring fire, blossomed in a halo of warmth, smoking wood masking the mechanic shop smells. Feet stretched out toward the open stove, Tom's boots soon grew warm, and he had to pull his legs back to keep them from growing uncomfortable.

"Awesome fire, Sam. Good job."

"Thanks, Dad. I learned from the best."

"What else can you do?" Barbara asked, sliding her hand over to hold Tom's.

"Not much," she sighed. "I can cook soup, but that's about it."

She rose off the toolbox and picked up the sack of frozen items they'd brought in, lining up waters, cans of food, and other iced goods around the stove.

"It'll probably take a few hours for these to thaw," she said, stepping back to her seat. "But Smooch will be glad when she can eat some real dog food. We weren't able to give her much on the road."

"But I bet Saanvi fed her well." Tom stroked the Shepard's fur. "She looks way better now. Her weight seems to have picked up."

"I'm just happy we still have her. I'm still shocked she survived the house fire," Barbara added with a fond glance at the animal. "That girl has been through quite a lot."

"The best friend ever!" Jack gleamed, leaning in and giving Smooch a big embrace before he settled back in his seat.

They relaxed for a short time, allowing the warmth to radiate outward while Barbara and Linda went through their supplies of snacks, thumping cans of soup into two pans, placing them on the steel plates as the stove grew hot to the touch. Soon, the salty-rich smells of beef and chicken broth filled the air, a welcome relief after so many of the same MREs in a row.

"Not the greatest meal, but the best we can do under the circumstances," Barbara said, her eyes picking lovingly across her family.

"Fit for a king, I'd say," he replied. "Better than we've had in a long time."

"Too bad Jerry couldn't be here." Sam's glum tone cut through the quiet, and Tom absently rubbed Smooch's head as he thought back on the young man they'd traveled so far with. "He was a pretty good guy, and I know he would've been a big help if he were still here today."

"I would've loved to have met him," Barbara nodded. "We owe him an enormous thanks for helping you guys."

"The kid had his problems." Tom tilted his head, eyes filled with a sense of loss. "But he had a good heart, and he kept us going when things got tough. It burns me up that he lost his life because of Keith. It was so stupid and random, and I get sick just thinking about it."

"I miss the Everetts," Linda added. "They were so fun."

"Darren was my buddy." Jack was suddenly crestfallen, his previously happy face sinking with the memory of the loss of his friend. "He liked to show me shark teeth and other stuff they found."

Tom laughed, glassy eyed. "Remember when he brought over that metal detector? The guy was finding all kinds of stuff. Old bullets, coins, he even found some lead shot in his field from when they'd used his property as a training ground for infantry during the Civil War."

"Darren loved all that sort of stuff." Barbara sighed deeply. "What a tragic, pointless loss."

"And Marie cooked some awesome dinners." Linda's smile widened as she stared at the fire, seeming to see visions of the past playing out in the flames, then her face slackened as a single tear streaked down her cheek.

A silence hung over the group as they got comfortable, the old stove driving the numbness from Tom's feet and fingers, replacing pure survival with memories of their lives and the lives of others.

"Here's to all the people we've lost." Barbara raised a water bottle, and everyone else lifted their drinks with him.

"To Marie, Darren, and Jerry," Tom said in a lofty tone. "Good friends who we'll miss dearly."

They clicked their bottles and cans together, drank, then fell once more into a somber silence. Tom's eyes went distant, the flames hypnotizing as they danced and wavered. "And let's not forget our good friend, Saanvi. If it wasn't for her, we'd still be back in camp, dealing with Marty."

"Or Keith and his new friends," his wife added, her own jade green eyes falling prey to the fire's movements.

Silence filled the space as Barbara and Linda got everyone a bowl of soup and spoons from the dishes they'd found lying around. The quiet lingered as they ate, the broth and vegetables and big chunks of meat hitting their stomachs with a satisfying warmth. Finishing his meal, Tom placed his bowl aside and slid to his elbow. Laying lengthwise on the truck pads, his wife stretched out in front of him, her sandy hair brushing his nose and cheeks. Arm resting over her waist, hand relaxed, his fingers rested on her stomach as the fire warmed the floor.

Linda fished out a piece of jerky from a side bag, smiling as she chewed. "What's that grin for?" Tom asked.

"I was thinking this is just like home, except we don't have the big screen TV and a movie playing."

"And the popcorn," Barbara interjected.

"Oh, boy, do I miss popcorn." Samantha leaned forward with her stick and shifted the wood inside the stove's belly, kicking up cinders and producing even more heat. She circled to the stove's rear, found the sliding vent, and opened it one notch, allowing more air to circulate through, making the fire even hotter. "I'd give anything to be back on the couch with a cover over me and my favorite movie with you guys." As she retreated to her seat, her light green eyes gazed lovingly over her family, trademark curls falling over her coat in ringlets. "But I guess this is better than nothing, right?"

"Way better than nothing," Linda agreed with a nod as she popped another piece of jerky into her mouth and unzipped her coat, the stove rapidly turning the small building into the warmest place the family had experienced in quite a while.

"I miss the farm, too," Linda jeered. "The week you guys were at the conference, we harvested all the crops and Mom taught me how to can the food. She said I was better than you, Sam."

Samantha let a scoff slip free, lips crooked, smirking. "I seriously doubt that, you twerp. I was the best at canning in the family."

"I don't know." Barbara raised her eyebrows doubtfully. "Linda was pretty good. We'd finished with all the produce and were about to make some freeze-dried potato flakes when things started heading south."

"Next place we go that has canning equipment, it's on," Sam growled at her sister who pointed back, accepting the challenge, nodding as she chewed.

"You're on. It's going to be a good old canning competition between me and you, girl."

"But where will we do that?" Jack said, slapping his thighs as he kicked his feet. "We don't even have a home or a place to go. What are we going to do?"

"I can't tell you where that'll be." Tom stared at the white-hot coals in the oven. "But I do know one thing. We need to get to where it's warm and safe from the cold. South. Far to the south."

"Is that where the rest of the Americans are?" Jack asked. "South? Did the Army people take them there?"

"Hard to say," Tom shrugged. "We probably have millions of citizens there who were evacuated by our government and whatever's left of the Mexican authorities. I'm not sure we can call ourselves a country anymore except in spirit. We're all just human beings, trying to survive and stay warm."

The quiet of the mechanic shop blanketed them in a pleasant cover, the crackling stove with its blazing heat giving the McKnight's a semblance of peace, though said peace was overshadowed by the constant threats lurking just out of sight.

Voice lifting, Tom spoke to the children. "Your mother and I will take first watch tonight, kids. Linda and Jack, grab the sleeping bags out of the Humvee and stretch them out in front of the fire, then get ready for bed. Just like at the camp, you'll stay dressed, ready to move at a moment's notice. You can take off your boots and jackets, but keep your cold-weather clothing on. Okay?"

Jack and Linda nodded and hopped up from their chairs, hurrying off to get the gear while Tom enjoyed another few minutes of warmth with his arm wrapped around his wife's waist. His eyes shifted back to the fire, wondering what the next day would bring.

CHAPTER TWENTY

Navy Admiral Ben Spencer
Venezuela, South America

The sky was bright blue, the sun shining through cloudless skies, reflecting off the ocean waves in shimmering streaks of light. The water stretched flat and calm in every direction, no signs of storms or foul weather in sight. Schools of fish banked away from the massive fleet as it neared, eight sleek ships plowing through the water at full speed, leaving towering wakes behind them and marine turbulence trailing in aqua blue streaks. To everyone aboard Carrier Strike Group Eight, it was a beautiful day.

At the center of the fleet was a heavy aircraft carrier, the USS Harry S. Truman, a Nimitz-class warship powered by two nuclear reactors, ultra advanced sensors, a suite of electronic warfare decoys, and enough armaments to take out entire nations. The vessel was supported thirty-five hundred sailors, pilots, and assorted crew and atop the main tower, a dozen radar arrays and sensory dishes spun, searching for enemy ships and aircraft in the area.

The vessels surrounding the Truman were formidable in their own rights. One Ticonderoga-class cruiser, four Arleigh Burke-class destroyers, and two Oliver Hazard Perry-class anti-submarine frigates comprised the bulk of the task force while three Los Angeles-class attack subs lurked beneath the waters, running silent.

With the bridge windows open, the command crew enjoyed a warm breeze blowing through, carrying the heavy scent of the salt sea. Coming from the growing cold of the Cuban base, Navy Admiral Ben Spencer took a deep breath of the tropical air, his gaze stony as he studied the distant ocean. The carrier group was cutting through the Caribbean Sea toward Barcelona after deploying from a port in Puerto Rico to spearhead the invasion of Venezuela.

The Admiral was on hand to assist with Operation Heat Strike, the Navy's jab at the Venezuelan coast. Once they arrived, they'd give air support for the landing parties and act as a distraction to confuse the Venezuelan Army. The crew bustled around the bridge, tactical displays and control columns in the back of the room manned by experienced sailors. Shoes shuffled and voices quietly called out changes to engine speed and direction, keeping them on course per the captain's orders.

Captain Rogers sat in his chair to the admiral's right, monitoring a tactical display of controls, radar screens, and maps. The man leaned slightly forward, pulling down a mic that hung above them, placing it in front of his lips. "Air control, launch the Hawkeye. I want to know what's on that Venezuelan coastline."

"Yes, sir," came the controller through the tiny speaker on the console.

The captain raised a pair of binoculars to his eyes and peered ahead toward the Venezuelan coast where Barcelona lay in wait. Spencer raised his own lenses and studied the distance with a furrowed brow like he was reading a book. Past the lead battle cruiser and destroyer was a solid line separating the sky from the sea, the two differing shades topped off by a bank of white clouds. The shore was still out of range, though soon they'd see it, reaching the point of no return when the Admiral would give the final go ahead for the operation to begin, putting the fate and hope of an entire nation entirely in his hands.

"What do you think, Captain?" He lowered his binoculars and looked aside.

Captain Rogers was a middle-aged man of fifty-two. Dressed in casual Navy trousers and a windbreaker, he struck a relaxed but stoic pose in his seat, sunglasses perched on a wide, hawkish nose, shoulders hunched forward.

"It looks good so far, but I expect some resistance from the Venezuelans. They won't leave their coast unprotected." The man spoke in a commanding voice, keeping his tone low enough so only the admiral could hear.

From the deck, the twin turboprop Hawkeye took off in a burst of burring propellers. It lifted into the air and banked left, rising in altitude with its massively round dish perched on top. The array held transponders, radar, and a Mini-DAMA SATCOM system. As it rose higher, it began feeding data into the Naval Tactical Data System, filling their screens with information. Spencer and Rogers both glanced down at their tactical displays as the first sweeps were made. Almost immediately, six large blips appeared just beyond their battleships' gun range.

The captain leaned forward, expression never wavering. "Tactical, give me a reading on those marks I'm seeing. What am I looking at?"

"We see them, sir," came a voice through the overhead speaker. "One second, and I'll get an identification on them."

A brief pause lingered over the bridge as tactical determined what types of ships were waiting for them.

The admiral looked over at the Rogers. "Whoever they are, it looks like they're guarding the coast closely. Look at that formation. You think it's Venezuelan?"

"No clue," the captain replied. "If it is, they'd be foolish to challenge us in open water. But let's see what tactical comes back with."

The question was answered a moment later. "Sir, we're seeing six Russian vessels out there. There's a Kuznetsov-class carrier, one Parchim-class anti-sub destroyer, two Grisha-class corvettes, and a Gepard-class frigate."

"Russians," the Admiral snorted derisively. "Trying to beat us to the punch."

"That's a big part of their forces," the captain replied. "That confirms the intel. They're definitely working with the Venezuelans."

The admiral squinted and raised his binoculars, still unable to get a visual on the Russian ships. "The Kuznetsov is one of their only three carriers. They're serious."

"If we attack them, do you think they'll launch nukes?"

"At what?" Spencer scoffed. "The whole northern United States is frozen, and most of Russia, too. There's nothing left to bomb – nothing that doesn't have resources that they're already trying to secure. No, we'll win this war conventionally, but we have to strike first and hard. I just wish we had a little more backup."

"We only had the one East Coast strike group available for this fight," the captain confirmed. "We couldn't commit any West Coast ships."

"It'll take weeks for them to arrive." The decision loomed, the moment of no return hovering like a dark cloud. The Admiral squeezed the binoculars in his hands, gripping them so tightly the frame creaked. "We can't wait for them to get here."

"Is that a go to begin Heat Strike?"

A deep bite of doubt froze his mind. The conflict in front of them could ignite World War III. It wasn't a decision to take lightly. "No. Let me talk to the President one last time."

The Admiral stepped away from his position at the glass and strode to a small steel case lying open on a utility table, guarded by two Marines who stood like statues on the wavering deck. Inside the case was a communications array with a direct feed to the president and Spencer picked up the receiver and put it to his ear, not needing to dial any numbers. After two brief rings, John Zimmerman's voice greeted him on the other end.

"Hello, Admiral. How goes it?"

"Things are going well, sir. We're approaching the Venezuelan coast on calm seas."

"Have you given the authorization to move ahead with Operation Heat Strike?"

"Not yet. That's what I was calling you about. We've confirmed that the Russians are here, and in force. Pings on radar."

COLLAPSE

"That's what satellite imagery showed us. What's your take on the situation?"

Spencer looked out through the front window of the ship's bridge out into the open waters, imagining what was waiting for them just a short distance ahead.

"I say we punch through. We've got them outclassed and outnumbered, and they won't be expecting us to move in force. We can knock the hell out of them. Then we'll start the landings. Once we get those refineries stabilized, we'll be in business."

A pause came over the line as the President weighed his options and the admiral's advice. Spencer took a handkerchief and dabbed at his brow. He'd been a Navy man his entire life, from the time he was eighteen until his seventy-second year on the earth. While scoring high marks in battle tactics and simulated maneuvers, his true love was for process and procedure, the uniform and what it represented. He'd enjoyed many years being at the top of his game astride the mighty United States Navy, all culminating in what would be the biggest fight of their lives.

"I authorize Operation Heat Strike." The President spoke with a flat finality. "Give 'em hell, Admiral. May God bless you and those sailors."

Spencer hung up the phone, spinning on his heel and marching back to the captain. He held the man's eyes, giving him a terse nod. "We have the go. Engage Operation Heat Strike."

A flurry of motion began as the Captain relayed the confirmation of their orders. Jets lined up on the deck, preparing to lift off and crews swarmed them in orange or yellow jackets, moving like a well-choreographed unit. They guided an F-18 to its starting point with the catapult officer watching from a control pod on the deck, connecting the nose to the slingshot hook with a clank of steel. Steam shot up in thick gouts as internal cylinders below filled with pressure and the pilot engaged the jet's engines as they released the catapult, hurling the jet along the deck. Its nose flew up, ejecting cyclonic winds behind it as it lifted into the sky. The voice of the flight deck operator boomed from loudspeakers, echoing across the water between the ships as more F-18s and F-35s were lined up and launched in twenty-second intervals. Their turbo engines shrieked as they swarmed upward, quickly forming strike groups.

"Captain, this is tactical. We have two squadrons up and two more coming online."

"Has the enemy scrambled any aircraft?" Rogers asked, leaning forward in his seat, neck craned as he scanned for ships on the horizon.

"None that we can see, sir. Should we have our squadrons wait for the others?"

"No. Their primary objective is to neutralize their air support before it can take off."

"Roger that, Captain."

Spencer looked upward as distant formations banked in a wide arc toward the Venezuelan coast, rising even higher into the clear blue sky. The admiral and captain dropped their eyes on the horizon, sometimes glancing at the tactical screen, watching the warships as the fighter squadrons approached. Hand resting on the touchscreen, the admiral could zoom in on the triangular shapes to pick out individual fighters, familiarizing himself with the units.

"I've got visual on the Russian warships," someone said on the other side of the bridge. Both the captain and admiral lifted binoculars to their eyes, watching the distant specs of the Russian destroyers waiting for them.

"Have they seen us yet?" Spencer asked. "It doesn't seem like they're moving... Wait, there they go, getting into defensive positions surrounding their carrier. They're probably scrambling planes."

As if to confirm his suspicion, the tactical display showed smaller triangles appearing on the screen around the Russian fleet, indicating the formation of the enemy squadrons.

The captain peered through his lenses, lifting them away from his eyes to glance at his screen, his voice riding high with anticipation as the fighters started their bombing runs. "I wonder if they even have satellite capabilities to speak of anymore. Seems we caught them with their pants down," he murmured, lips tight around the words. "Come on, guys. Nail that deck."

In the distance, Spencer spotted thin lines of counter fire, anti-gun ordinance exploding in the air, flak flying from the destroyers' guns. Explosions lit up the Russian carrier's deck, one massive strike blasting across the base of the tower. A launching jet was caught up in the concussion, spinning toward the deck's edge. The aircraft tilted, wing catching the pavement, flipping it right off the side of the deck and into the sea.

"Yes!" Spencer spat quietly.

"This is tactical. We can confirm two direct hits on the enemy carrier. We've lost one fighter."

The Captain confirmed it by glancing at his screen, noting a squadron was down one jet. As the US ships drew closer to the fight, ships became visible to the naked eye, smoke and fire trailing up from the carrier as the Corvettes and frigates circled it in a protective formation.

"We've got another jet down, sir," came tactical. "The Russians got half a squadron in the air, and more are coming up. Also, we're picking up the signatures of two Akula-class attack subs advancing on our position."

"Engage them with our own subs," the captain commanded. "And get the frigates into position to take them out."

"Understood."

Within minutes, US planes angled downward and fired missiles at the ships before sweeping upward, harassed by antiaircraft guns and the growing number of Russian jets on their tails. A US fighter banked toward them, wings tipping back and forth, tail dropping as it shot into the sky to avoid an air-to-air missile that missed and plunged harmlessly into the sea. The Russian destroyers fired furious barrages into the air, at the risk of hitting their own jets, doing everything they could do to stop the brutal US air assault.

Soon the sky was filled with streaks of tracer fire, bright red even in the daylight, the black shapes of planes swinging, dancing, diving in and out of formation, one explosion after another. A jet fell from the air, spiraling, wobbling, exploding on the ocean surface, though the admiral couldn't tell if it was a US or Russian fighter. Glancing down at the tactical display, he saw it was one of their own, cringing at the loss.

But the Russian squadrons were quickly being taken apart, the deck of the carrier beginning to smoke and catch fire.

Still, the Russians continued to launch planes only to be hit by F-18s in strafing runs. The 50 caliber rounds tore through their wings, buckling them, sending them spinning downward to crash in a spray of salt water and smoke. The ones that made it a few thousand feet into the sky faced the clawed talons of the US reinforcement wing.

As the US destroyers closed on the enemy ships, a massive explosion ripped the ocean surface a quarter mile behind them, directly in front of the Truman. A geyser of spray shot as high as the deck, jolting the admiral from the hypnotic scene of the air fight.

"They're coming for us now," the captain said grimly as he shifted in his seat, ordering the deck officer to turn the carrier out of harm's way. The bridge crew exploded into action, calling and reaffirming the navigational adjustments.

The massive engines grumbled in the ship's guts. Vibrations shook the decking and ran through the admiral's boots as the ship began a slow rotation.

"Get those frigates on the subs!" he barked. "We need--"

An enormous explosion rocked the hull, shaking the floor, throwing everyone to their knees. Sailors grasped railings, clinging to their kiosks as they fought to stay upright amidst thick binders of manuals and tactical information spilling from overhead bins. Thrown against his console, the admiral stared off to his left where the deck dipped 10 feet, bowing in the water, a massive geyser of billowing orange soot and ocean spray flying up. The bridge crew scrambled, repeating the captain's continuous orders to get the ship turned away to safety.

In a tight grouping, the anti-sub frigates circled an area a mile ahead of the carrier. Depth charges were lobbed off the sides to splash in the water, a dozen, then two dozen, sinking fast, detonating when they reached their programmed depth and sending blisters of air bubbling up to explode in sprays of white foam.

"Captain, this is tactical control. Our subs are engaging an Akula that slipped through undetected."

"No kidding? How the hell did they get within a mile of us?"

"They shouldn't have, sir. It looks like a suicide run--"

Another explosion ripped the carrier's hull, shaking the admiral from foot to jaw, sending a shock of dread through his belly. His old stubborn will flooded to the surface, and he glared down into the ocean as if he could locate the enemy sub with his bare eyes.

"Get that submarine, Captain," he growled.

"Damage report?" Rogers was half turned in his seat, staring at the smoke coming off the side of his ship.

"There's minimal damage to the hull, Captain. That last one just glanced off us, and we're sealing off the affected sections."

"Good. Now, as the Admiral suggested, someone take out that damned sub!"

"We've got a feed from two of our boats. They're on it, and we're launching torpedoes as well."

Billows of steam hissed from the frigates' decks as racks of torpedoes launched. Like arrows, they flew free from their tubes in a hiss of pneumatic ejection, plunging into the sea, motors spinning up and carrying them toward the charging enemy submarine.

"Sir, our destroyers have their battleships within reach."

"Engage them," Admiral Spencer growled, clutching the console. "Throw everything we've got at them!"

The captain nodded and passed the orders to the fleet. Out on the ocean, in the thick of the fight, the US ships launched their long range surface-to-surface missiles. Streaking through the sky, they blotted out the sun as they raced toward their targets, the impacts blowing the Russian boats sideways, throwing sailors to the deck, many on fire, spinning and dancing as they leapt over the side into the sea. Massive holes erupted in their sides, sooty black smoke racing upward. The engine compartments caught fire and burned away the oil and fuel as ammunition detonated freely, blossoming flowers of raging flames, blowing sailors to pieces, chunks of them splattering across the ocean surface, chum for the sharks to eat.

The Russian carrier was already listing heavily to port, men and women leaping off the sides in life jackets, lowering the wounded to lifeboats. Fifty planes still sat on the deck or down in the hangers, never launched. The high whine of a US rail gun threw hyper-velocity projectiles at the Russian Corvettes, the rounds chewing the fast ships to pieces, puncturing deep into their hulls with a sickening rip of steel, destroying their critical infrastructure before they could respond.

Spencer narrowed his eyes as the missiles flew toward them in streaks of gray. The US anti-missile arrays launched projectiles into the sky, intercepting the incoming rockets, filling the air with pops, bursts, and ear-shattering explosions as debris rained into the sea. A handful of Russian missiles broke through, slamming into the US ships, spreading fire and death deep into their hulls. None of them reached the carrier and the next barrage of US rockets put the Russian vessels to sleep, all of them dead in the water. Over a mile out, where the anti-sub torpedoes had prowled, the water exploded in black foam, the sea swirling and pitching as a swath of oil spread like blood across the surface.

"This is tactical," the cabin speaker piped. "We got the Akula, and the other Russian subs are retreating. The leader of their battle group would like to discuss terms of surrender."

"I want a full damage report ASAP." Rogers stood with his thighs pressed to the console, binoculars pinned on the scene playing out before them.

Out on the water, orange lifeboats blossomed on the ocean surface as the Russians tried to save their sailors. "Let's send rescue parties," Spencer said, eyes shifting to the captain. "No sense in those men dying out there for doing their duty."

"We'll see it gets done." Rogers gave a confident nod.

The admiral watched as the sky cleared of debris, the smoke drifting in thick clouds. F-18s and F-35s landed on the wobbling ship as the repair crews below tried to get a handle on the damaged sections. Rescue helicopters launched from the deck, Seahawks and Hueys lifting into the air, bending toward the destroyed Russian vessels.

Within 30 minutes, shaken and dazed Russian sailors began arriving on the carrier deck in torn, oil-stained, and bloody uniforms. Marines sectioned them into holding areas, laying the injured on the deck for the Truman's medical team to triage. Under Captain Roger's guidance, the fleet cruised through the obliterated Russian ships. Admiral Spencer stared down into the waters, the frigates and destroyers listing, horrific tears in their hulls, slabs of steel peeled back and smoking, the bowels of the lower decks exposed.

A debris field of flotation devices, garbage, oars, pieces of shattered wood, oil and fuel was scattered across the ocean's surface, corpses floating in the nightmarish stew. As for the big carrier, all that remained was a rear section of the ship, broken off from the main hull, still drifting in an inferno of burning petrol, occasional pockets of ammunition blowing off like fireworks. As the bridge returned to normal, the admiral and captain directed the carrier unit into a defensive position on the Barcelona coast, just out of range of any land-based guns.

When things had calmed, Spencer strode to his phone and gave the resident a call.

"Speak to me, Ben. What's happening?"

The admiral let out a long sigh, the pent-up tension he'd been feeling starting to loosen. "We punched through and forced a surrender from the Russians but sustained a few battle scars. We're now in a defensive position around Barcelona, awaiting instructions."

"That's fantastic news, Admiral. Well done to everyone there."

"No problem, sir. Just doing our jobs."

"Hold tight while we contact the Venezuelan government and try to enter negotiations. If we can do this without more loss of life, we will. Standby for further instructions."

The President hung up, and the Admiral placed his own handset in its receiver before returning to Captain Rogers's side. The man had retaken his stoic pose in his seat, sunglasses pushed back into place as he adroitly juggled repositioning the ship with assessing damage reports filtering in from the other vessels.

His dark lenses turned toward the Admiral. "What did he say?"

"The President expresses his thanks to both of us, and he wants us to sit tight while they negotiate with the Venezuelans."

The Captain nodded, and both men raised their binoculars to get a look at the Venezuelan shore where a bustle of tanks and earth moving equipment showed that the South American soldiers were digging in deep.

CHAPTER TWENTY-ONE

Tom McKnight
Somewhere in Mexico

A hand rested on Tom's foot, patting it above the thick layer of blankets on top of him. Curled on his side, fists jammed into his chin, he breathed into the covers. While it was chilly so far away from the fire, he'd longed to lie on something softer than blankets and a hard floor, plus he'd wanted to be in a suitable position to jump behind the wheel if they needed to leave quickly. The Humvee's back seat had seemed like the perfect spot, the old crusty seats better than nothing.

"Tom, wake up. Tom?"

Keith.

With a jerk, Tom's eyes went wide to find Barbara standing in the open door, hands resting on his legs. "What's going on?" he whispered harshly. "Is it Keith? Did you see someone?"

She shook her head and leveled her green eyes on him, her hair out of its ponytail and hanging loose from her hood. "No, I didn't see anything all night. The snow is still falling, but it's tapering off. It's about eight, give or take. I thought you'd want to get up."

"Yeah, thanks."

With the swallow and a nod as his racing heart began to slow, Tom lifted the covers free, precious warmth escaping as he sat up and scooted to the edge of the seat. Legs thrown out, Barbara between his knees, he kissed his wife on the chin and reached for his boots from the floorboard.

She slipped her rifle off her shoulder and leaned it against the Humvee. "I'll get the children up and see what we can drum up for breakfast. Why don't you go keep watch while we do that?"

"Sounds good." Tom bundled himself up in his thick coat and hat, laced his shoes tight, climbed out of the back of the Humvee, and grabbed the rifle. "Morning, kids!" he called, waving as Linda and Jack ran up and gave him a brief hug in passing.

Sam was still lying beneath a pile of covers in front of the stove, resisting her mother's attempts to wake her up. Barbara was kneeling at her side, shaking the girl's shoulder, but she only pulled the blankets tighter to her chin, grumbling something about only wanting a few more minutes. With a smile, Tom stepped across the garage and through the door, entering the mini mart. He walked to the window where his wife had positioned a rolling chair near the glass, nestled behind a shelf where it was easy to watch the road and parking lot for any signs of the APCs.

The snow was still falling, but softer, less of a storm and more like something he would've wanted to see on Christmas Eve. Big fat flakes drifted down and had covered their tracks completely so that the entire parking lot was one even surface of white. The gas station awning had dipped lower, the middle section bowing from the weight of accumulated snow. Beyond the end of the lot, out in the flat desert, small groups of trees were clustered with bent branches, bushes sprouting through the bone frost that had settled over the land.

It didn't take much to imagine the frozen ground beneath it, the dirt freezing, wildlife and insects destroyed by the abrupt change in seasons. Off to the right, across another flat piece of land miles long, mountains and hills rose, their once green and brown sides turned to frosty slopes, a gray mist rolling overhead, drifting over the landscape.

A man stared back at him in the glass, a reflection of himself that made him wince. His face was gaunt, cheeks pulled thinner beneath his firm brown eyes, the growth of hair lining his jaw thick and long, the start of a woodsman's beard which would suit him well given the new reality they faced. He put his hands against the glass, taking in the beautiful scene as his brain came awake and his body threw off the sluggishness of sleep. The rest had done him some good, the sharp snow vivid in his sight, the zombie-like exhaustion that had plagued him the previous day all but gone. Soon the smells of food drifted through the hallway and his stomach rumbled, complaining with hunger.

The door at the end of the hallway opened and Barbara poked her head through. "Hey honey. Why don't you come in and grab some food? We combined all the leftover soup." She shrugged. "I guess it's more of a stew."

"One of us should probably stay out here to keep watch," Tom said, shifting his gaze back to the wintry scene stretching out before him.

Her crooked smile warmed him, loving eyes regarding him with an adoration he'd sorely missed in his weeks on the road. "Honey, it won't make a big difference if you spend 15 minutes having breakfast with the kids. It could be the last one we have for a long time."

"Yeah, that's what I'm afraid of," he replied in a flat, somber tone. "I want it to last."

"I do, too. But if you don't hurry, Jack's going to eat it all." She laughed. "That boy's appetite has been growing by the day. Come on, honey. Just a few minutes. Sam's already made you a bowl."

"Okay."

Tom left the glass, striding along the hall to greet his wife with a kiss and a brief hug. They strolled hand-in-hand around the beat-up Ford back to the stove where the girls had found some more bowls and dishes with antiquated floral designs tucked into a cardboard box. They'd used water and some dish soap to clean them and had poured three or four large spoonfuls of mixed soup into Tom's. Barbara grabbed it off the bench it'd been sitting on and handed it to her husband, followed by an old, dented spoon.

"Thanks, honey."

He took his breakfast over to the truck pads and sat cross-legged, watching Jack kick his legs as he happily dug into his share. Linda sat curled in her foldout chair, feet beneath her, knees to her chest as she ate and his eldest daughter sat on her rolling toolbox, feet dangling over the side, the blaze roaring from the stove's belly displaying the fruits of her morning labor.

"You're the fire girl now," Tom told her with a nod before he stuffed a spoonful of the hearty beef stew into his mouth.

"I guess it's kind of my thing," she responded with a shrug. "I'm not sure why, but I love doing it. I got up three times overnight on my own without anyone telling me, and I kept it going."

"You're taking responsibility for something, and that's a good thing," Tom nodded. "Thanks, Sam."

"No problem, Dad. I like helping." Samantha smiled, taking a last bite of her stew and placing her bowl next to her, dusting her hands off, resting them in her lap. "So, where do you think Keith and his buddies went?"

"I have no clue, but I'm not complaining," Tom said as he dug through his last few bites. "I'm just happy they didn't show up overnight. They either fell way behind or they took a different route."

"Which leaves us with the problem of what to do next," Linda added from her curled position.

Dishes rattled as Barbara got her own bowl of stew and sat by Tom. "I could've gone for some coffee before we decided anything. But, I'm not sure we'll ever have any. At least nothing fresh."

"I'd kill for a cup of coffee right now," Linda agreed with a sigh, looking to her mother. "What do you think, Mom? I mean, about what to do now? Dad already said we'll be moving south, somewhere warm, but where?"

His wife gave him a sideways glance, passing the buck to him without a word being spoken and, nodding, he offered a simple answer. "We'll go as far south as we can. I'm talking all the way to South America."

Sam scoffed. "Dad, South America is a long, long walk, unless you think that Humvee will take us there."

"No offense, but that thing is a piece of junk." Linda chimed in.

"That piece of junk saved our lives yesterday." Tom gave her a disapproving look. "And it might save our butts again. We should be thankful we have it."

"I *am*, but it won't get us to South America. I'm a kid, and even I know that."

Tom shrugged. "Not necessarily. These things are tougher than you'd think. But even if you're right, we'll just take it as far as we can and then we'll find another form of transportation."

"Do you really think we'll have to go that far?" Sam asked. "Isn't there someplace closer, past the winter storms, or maybe a military camp that's not as bad as the last one?"

"No more camps." He shook his head firmly. "Absolutely not."

"I just want to go home," Jack chimed in, still kicking his feet as he looked between his parents. "Can't we go home and put everything back together?"

Barbara smiled at him, reaching out to take his hand in hers. "Remember what we talked about before? About what home is about?"

"Home is...." Jack thought for a moment. "About the people, right?"

"The people, not the place." Linda nodded.

"Exactly," Barbara replied. "And look around this room. We're home right now. We have each other, for the first time in... I don't want to think how long. We're finally home. Here. In this old mechanic's bay in a strange country just trying to survive." Barbara glanced at Tom, eyes glassy with emotion as she continued. "Our old place isn't what it used to be. I don't think we can ever go back. We'll have to find a new place, like your dad said. It might be all the way in South America, far away." Her eyes lingered on each of her children in turn. "The important thing is that as long as we stick together, as long as we love each other, we can call anyplace home."

"I agree with Mom," Linda said, mirroring her brother's expression of hope. "She's right. We have to stick together. If we do that, everything will be fine. Think of all the stuff we went through, but we're here now."

Tom surreptitiously wiped a tear from the corner of his eye as he drank from a bottle of water, prouder of his family in that moment than he could recall. They were drifters, nomads searching for a home amidst the chaos of a new world, fighting the universe every day just for a place to lay their heads, to find a moment of peace, to share a meal on a cold winter night. But they were together. They were already home.

Samantha pushed her curls back from her face. "But what about all our animals?" she asked. "I never even said goodbye to them. I thought we'd be going back home. I mean, to the house. Are you saying we'll never see the farm again?"

"I know it really sucks, guys," Tom replied. "I had hoped we'd be able to sometime. But we have to keep moving south... Or die. We don't have a choice. Truth is, everything a hundred miles north of the border's frozen solid. Nothing can survive up there without extreme levels of gear and preparation. Not even our stockpiles could have gotten us through it. There's only one way forward, and we're going to have to do it together. You feel me?"

Sam slowly nodded, turning her head to look at her parents through tears in her eyes. "Of course, we're going to give it a hundred percent. We have to at least try."

"How about you, Jack?" Barbara held the boy's hand up and swung it affectionately. "Can you be brave, too, like your sister?"

"Yeah," the boy said, his voice husky, staring at Sam and his mother.

Linda stood from her chair, finishing her last bite of stew, and brought the old plate back to the stove. She placed the dirty dish in the box and tossed the spoon in behind it. "What do you guys say we get going? We've got a long way to go."

Tom and Barbara exchanged a look, nodding and smiling at each other, his heart lifting at his children's bravery. "Yep, okay. Let's get up and get moving, guys. Pack up the sleeping bags and clean the pots and pans and dishes. We'll take some of those with us in case we need them on the road. Put these chairs back, though, and make sure we douse the fire out before we leave. If Keith and his friends come by, we want it to look like no one was here, especially not us."

The family got moving, cleaning up after themselves, packing away the gear and stowing it in the Humvee's rear. Tom checked the fuel tank in the garage and realized the rusted lettering read "Diesel" and he ran a hose from the tank to their truck and siphoned it from one to the other, completely filling up the Humvee. Saanvi had left them two Jerry cans of fuel, so he topped those off and filled a couple more gas cans he found lying around the garage, sticking them in with their supplies. Within thirty minutes they'd packed everything up and were ready to go. Tom started the Humvee and stood by the manual bay door release, enjoying one last feel of the warm air inside the repair shop.

"Ugh. I dread doing this."

Closing his eyes, he popped the latch and threw the door up on its creaking, scraping wheels. An icy wind burst in, brushing across his cheeks, slipping into the cracks of his clothing, that dreadful winter freeze sending chills over his skin. Back behind the Humvee's wheel, he started it, the engine coughing to life, spitting once, then finally idling. The kids climbed in with Smooch, settling in with a blanket pulled over their legs. Tom backed out of the garage, lurching into 8 inches of hard-packed snow. The tires spun as they circled backward and pointed the nose of the truck toward the exit. Barbara, still outside, reached up and grabbed a rope hanging from the bay door, dragging it down to slam it shut, then she turned and jogged to the Humvee, jumping in on the passenger side and buckling herself in.

Brushing snow off her jacket, she shivered and flipped on the heater asa Tom threw it into drive, gently gassing it, guiding the vehicle through the parking lot and up to the highway. The tires spun as they slipped onto the road in a long sweep, rear end sliding to the left before jolting straight again. The knobby wheels kicked out sprays of snow as the old military truck plowed on, white flakes whisking against the windshield, glancing and spinning off the glass, the wipers sweeping off the rest.

With his seat pushed all the way forward and lifted to its highest setting, Tom stared at the road, enraptured in focused concentration. The wind followed them from the north, gusting at their backs, whistling through the cracks, the bigger blasts rattling the windows in their frames. With the heater turned to high and the fan clacking noisily, Tom sighed with gratitude for what it gave them, the bleeding warmth from the vents enough to keep the worst of the frost and shivers away.

As the highway wound south, Barbara pointed out gas stations and buildings off to the sides of the road. What once might have been adobe type structures with flat roofs had turned into squarish igloos, their chimneys long gone silent, owners evacuated to warmer climes. There were signs for motels, markets, taverns, and restaurants and if the places had been lonely before, they'd grown even more so with the storms. The occasional neighborhood they passed had a few desolate streets, all dark and foreboding and abandoned. Vehicles had become white bumps in the roads, snow-capped, a deep hoarfrost setting in across the landscape.

"Everything is gone," Tom said. "Frozen. Dead. And we're well into Mexico. I wouldn't have imagined the cold would drift this far south, but the North Atlantic Current must be almost negligible. All that warmth is trapped below the equator... but how far?"

"Mother Nature sure is pissed off," Barbara agreed, staring at the winter wonderland with a fearful resolve. "Did you ever think in a million years it would actually get this cold?"

"Not even when we were back traveling with Jerry. I figured in the worst-case scenario, the frigid weather would stop around the US-Mexico border, but it's clearly gone beyond that."

"Did Banks's little project she forced you into have something to do with that?"

Tom snorted. "Undoubtedly. I told them it was a bad idea."

Silence soaked into the Humvee's cabin as they drove another hour, then two, the storm shifting between levels of voracity. Sometimes it was a harsh slicing of sleet and hail, other times a soft flurry of fat snowflakes. Barbara reached across and let her hand linger on Tom's leg, patting it before withdrawing to her own lap where she pressed her arms together and shivered. Tom looked at his rearview mirror, glancing up like he'd done a hundred times over the past two hours, fixing his gaze to the road behind them, blinking, watching. *Was that... no... can't be.*

Shifting the wheel right and left, searching for traction, he glanced at the road and then the rearview again, peering back into the vast grayness. There came a flutter, a glimpse of definite brightness in the drifting haze before it vanished in the shadows, then the blink of light returned, staying. They were headlight beams for certain, a pair of yellow eyes in the gray and white.

"What is it, Tom?" Barbara asked, catching his worried glances. Turning around in her seat, she draped her arms across the back and stared through the cracked rear windshield. "Oh, I see what you mean. Is that them? Is that Keith?"

"I don't think so," he replied. "I see one set of headlamps, but I can't tell if it's an APC or not. Wait..." His stomach felt like it sank through the floor. "It *is* them. There're two pairs now."

Barbara muttered something under her breath, loud enough to stir the kids in the back. The girls turned groggily, climbing their seats to look outside as Tom started pushing the Humvee harder, driving them through the snow at upwards of forty-five when the distant echoes of machine gun reports cut the winter air. Puffs of snow and ice blossomed behind their rear tires, rounds ricocheting off the pavement and zipping by. Cringing, he pushed their speed even higher, engine grinding hard, slewing the vehicle around a long bend in the road, briefly losing the APCs in his rearview mirror. He brought the truck straight again as it flew over a ridge and down the other side.

"It's definitely them," he said, releasing his held breath in a whisper. "Or someone else out here has a real dislike for American military Humvees."

"Can we outrun them?" Barbara asked.

"We've got a pretty big lead on them still," Tom replied, "but they've got the firepower to shoot out our tires. These run flats won't mean jack if they punch a couple rounds into them; they'll tear up the axle and that'll be all she wrote."

As soon as the APCs reappeared, more rounds ripped through the air, streaking across the ground behind them. One clipped the rear left side to blast out the taillight in a flash of sparks and shattered polymer. The girls screamed, Jack flying awake with a gasp, Barbara leaning into the back seat to put her arms around them.

"Get down, kids!" Tom growled. "Take your seatbelts off and get down as low as you can."

Sam and Linda dragged Jack to the floorboards with Smooch, huddled behind what he hoped was enough of the Humvee's protective armor.

"You, too," he told Barbara as his hands gripped the wheel, slithering the truck back and forth in a tight pattern to keep the APCs' aim off. "Stay as low as you can."

Barbara slunk in her seat, still peering around the headrest to watch their pursuers. The enemy headlamps were closer than before, maybe three hundred yards away, the hulking shadows gaining by the second. They were real, their mounted guns visible as they spat flashes of light, grinding through the snow with immutable power.

"I don't think we can outrun them," Tom said. "The Humvee is faster, but they're plowing through that snow and ice like it's nothing."

"What are we going to do?"

"We have to get off the road." Stomach queasy with nausea, fear riding up his spine, he began looking for an exit off the highway.

"Will it work?" Barbara asked frantically. "If they can catch us out here in the straightaway, what makes you think we can escape on some side street?"

"I don't know!" Tom slammed his palms on the wheel. "I just know that if we stay on this highway, we're screwed. If we take the exit, we can hide somewhere..."

An exit ramp came up almost faster than he could turn off, with no sign to show it was even there, but the small commercial buildings and tall town signs caught his attention and he whipped the Humvee's wheel to the right, cutting back toward the ramp. They fell off the road into the V-shaped gully, smashing through a line of dust covered shrubs to throw tufts of snow into the air. The truck's suspension tilted, unsteady for a frightening moment, Tom thinking they might wind up in a ditch before the knobby tires snagged the shoulder of the pavement and pulled them back left again, slamming straight, driving to the end of the ramp.

Tom brought the truck to a sliding finish, turning the wheel right yet again. The Humvee veered onto a thin roadway, straightened, and shot toward a stretch of low-rise buildings. They ground past a corner gas station and supermarket, the parking lot covered in a foot and a half of snow, the accumulation engulfing cars that sat half on the road and half on the sidewalk.

The Humvee tore into a small neighborhood of one-story, flat roofed homes, many with tin walls or sections plugged with plywood and swaths of stucco siding. Gnarled trees stuck up from the ground between the houses, their once exotic looking leaves having turned brown and weathered, branches weighed down with clinging snow. Along the walkways, thick tufts of grass and shrubs had wilted dead beneath the frosted layers of white.

A glance in his rearview showed the APCs just reaching the exit ramp so Tom took the first immediate left, sliding into a side street that led deeper into the endless maze of squat, narrow roads. He wove a convoluted path between the dense blocks, circling with three hard left turns before taking a right through more snow swept squalor.

While he couldn't see them, the soft yellow glow of the APC headlamps filtered up from the ground over the buildings like a pair of halos in slow pursuit. Tom's cold toes worked the Humvee's accelerator and brake pedals, moving it through city blocks, taking hectic turns, wheels spinning beneath his hands. In the distance, he spotted a cluster of taller buildings, enormous warehouses and looming complexes, windows gaping and dark, icicles clinging to brick walls like crystalline cocoons. Tom imagined all the nooks and crannies that could hide them and he angled the truck in their general direction.

"Now I know how a rabbit feels trying to lose a fox," he mumbled to himself, focusing on the mechanics of driving over his emotions, drawing strength from the repetitive motions. While not an expert driver, Tom had gotten used to the old Humvee's little quirks. He'd learned that the steering had a certain amount of play, and it was slightly harder to turn right than left. His shoulders and arms anticipated the motions, forearms tightening, hands gripping the well-worn wheel.

The big diesel engine ground faithfully beneath his demands, coughing and sputtering as he rounded a bend and hit a straightaway. The tires pounded over a twenty-foot-long bridge that spanned a shallow gully, rattling the wooden planks and causing the entire span to shudder. With cringing shoulders, he half expected the thing to collapse under the Humvee's weight. But it held, and in less than five seconds, the truck trundled to the other side, plunging into another densely packed neighborhood.

"I'm not sure they can drive those APCs over that," he said as he glanced into the rearview to see the APCs headlamps turn toward them. "At the very least, they'll have to take it slow."

"I hope so," Barbara replied, whispering as she peeked up to watch out the back window.

Pushing along a narrow lane, he swerved back and forth to get around spurs of accumulated snowdrifts. The vehicle exploded through a drift, sliding left into another hard, snow-blinding turn. Tom straightened the wheel with big sweeps of his arms, wrestling the Humvee as they fell into a cluster of taller buildings, five to thirteen stories high. They passed a gray-stone structure with frosted glass windows, a hotel, and a hospital. Spotting a service alley between the latter two, he angled into the parking lot and pushed the vehicle through the gap, hoping it would be too narrow for the APCs to follow. Coming out the other side, he shot along the entrance lane and into a cluster of streets that divided the warehouses into messy square blocks.

"Where are we?" Barbara asked, shifting in her seat and throwing her eyes frantically in every direction.

"No clue," Tom wiped a bead of sweat from his brow. "I'm just hoping following us will be just as confusing for them."

A massive courtyard came up on his left, snow-covered stairs rising ten feet on all four sides. On each corner were hollowed out pavilions, concrete structures that might be for a market or town gathering, the pastel pink and orange colors showing in bright patches through the frost. At the head of the courtyard stood a massive church, its old gray stone matching the glum sky, the steeple looming high above them. Tom didn't slow a bit. He ran the vehicle right up the set of stairs, tossing the McKnights around in their seats with surprised cries as the big tires climbed the stone with ease. The Humvee streaked across to the courtyard's other side and down the opposite stairs then he circled back and climbed into the courtyard from a third direction, crossing his own tracks before flying past the church to plummet into the street.

They hit with a lurching impact, tires digging deep furrows in the snow as he swung them south again. Brain in overdrive, Tom guided them between the taller buildings, sometimes stopping in the middle of a lane, slamming the vehicle into reverse, and backtracking in the other direction. If the APCs followed them, they'd run into a blank field of white, the Humvee's tire tracks disappearing as if they'd been sky lifted out of the city.

A few minutes later, satisfied his misdirection was complete, Tom slipped the Humvee through a side alley and along a short hill between some ritzy looking haciendas. On the other side, they entered another commercial area with corner stores and what might have been a pharmacy. The buildings flashed by, their bold-lettered signs unreadable in Spanish.

"I need a place to hide us." The buildings all started to look the same, squeezed together in gray and green facings, many as tall as ten stories high.

"We need to find one with a gate," Barbara said, eyes tracing back and forth across the road. "Or a garage. Like that one there."

Tom immediately saw what she was looking at. It was a pale brick building with a rust-colored garage door wide enough for the Humvee to fit. It appeared frosted shut, ice and snow crusting the edges. Pulling the truck to a sharp, skidding stop, Tom and Barbara got out and circled to the door.

He grabbed the latch, but it was frozen stiff. "Okay, we need to loosen this thing up."

Right boot flashing out, he began kicking along the bottom, fists pounding the sides to knock off the loose ice and snow. Together, they came back to the latch, and he twisted it several times, finally getting it to turn with a rusty groan.

"Grab the handle," he said, "and I'll lift from the bottom."

Barbara did as he asked while Tom slid his hand under the rubber seal. On the count of three, they heaved, and the door ground upward a few inches.

"Again." He slipped his fingers all the way under to get a better grip.

After another count they jerked the door up a few feet, ice and snow falling on their heads. Getting beneath it, each on a knee, they both put their shoulders under it and stood. Together they drove the groaning, protesting door upward, tall enough for the truck to fit. The inside was almost empty, just a few shelves pressed up against the walls, buckets and maintenance materials stacked in the corners.

Tom jogged back to the vehicle, climbed behind the wheel, and took a wide turn into the courtyard, sliding the Humvee into the garage, the armored sides fitting easily. He killed the engine, hopped out, and went to help Barbara get the door shut. They stood together, peering out into the frosted landscape as he looked at their tire track back the way they'd come, all the way to the end of the street.

"As soon as they get past the bridge and figure out where I misdirected them, it'll lead them right here. It's just a matter of time."

"What about the snow?" Barbara asked. "Think it'll cover our tracks?"

Tom lifted his eyes to the oppressive gray sky where the snowfall was picking up, flakes dancing in a flurry to the ground. While some were landing in the tracks, the cover offered by the surrounding buildings meant that there were less to fall directly in the tracks, unlike the relatively open area at the last place they had stopped.

"I don't know. Maybe..." he replied, pulling Barbara close in an embrace. "All we can do is hope, though. Come on, let's get inside, out of sight."

CHAPTER TWENTY-TWO

Simon Sharp
Santa Fe, New Mexico

Private First-Class Simon Sharp jogged along the snowy path to the bunker stairs. The passage walls weaving through the snow towered over him like a maze in an Arctic fantasy world. Morales had outdone himself to uncover the underground bunker, the mysterious discovery the subject of intense discussion for the soldiers back in the warehouses. Everyone seemed to have a different idea of what was inside, some guessing it held military secrets available only to Jones and higher-ups while other speculated that vast quantities of supplies were buried there, ready to be transported south. Sharp was eager to see it for himself, which was why he'd volunteered to check in on the bunker crews.

The path to the door in the ground was marked with orange ribbons nailed into the snowy walls, impossible to miss in the stark whiteness. Boots crunching through the snow, he rounded a bend that brought him before the massive, circular opening, edges frosted with ice, a set of stairs leading into the bowels of the hill. Seeing no one on guard at the top, he clutched his rifle to his side and descended, boot heels stomping the steps in quickstep fashion, looking for Smith or Morales.

When he came to the first landing, he opened the hall door and peered in. The passage stretched on forever, pale light illuminating countless doors. Hearing no voices, seeing no one, he let the door fall shut and went down to the second level. He stepped into the hallway and jogged to the end, looking both ways along the intersection. There was nothing but a maze of passages and doors in both directions, and no sign of the lieutenant or specialist. With a frustrated huff, he reeled on his boot heels and ran back to the stairwell door.

"All right, guys," he mumbled, "where'd everyone go?"

As he proceeded to the third landing, he noticed the air turning warmer, remembering something about how caves always kept their relative temperature. They were never too cold or too warm. Still, he imagined the frozen temperatures would eventually work their way down at least some distance through the Earth's crust, just like it had seeped into his clothing and muscles to chill his bones.

When he reached the third landing, he whipped open the door in agitation, about to call out, then stopped as he spotted three soldiers standing near his end of the passage, rifles in hand, arms tensed as they tilted their heads, listening to someone speaking over the intercom. Grinning, he charged along the hallway, striding up to the team, slowing to listen to the strained voice coming from the speaker.

"... Specialist Morales here. All Army units come to Sub-level 4 to the refrigeration unit at the end of the hall. We're being held there. We need everyone to surrender right now, or they'll execute Lieutenant Smith."

The speaker made a crackling sound before cutting off.

"Did you guys hear that?" one soldier said to the others, his face a mix of anger and uncertainty.

"Yeah, that was Morales," a soldier named Isaacs replied. "Did I just hear him say they want us to surrender?"

"Surrender to who?" asked the third man, a big soldier he recognized as Richardson. "Surrender to the bunker crew? Screw that. We don't surrender. Why would Morales tell us we need to surrender?"

"Morales said if we don't, Smith gets executed."

"So, what the hell? What do we do?"

"Hey, guys," Sharp said as he came up, his tone curious and uncertain. "What's going on?"

The three soldiers spun at the same time, harrowing expressions written on their faces. The first one who spoke, a man named Johnson, swung his rifle around to point it at Sharp's chest before recognizing who it was and lowering his weapon. "Hey, man. Get out of here. Go tell Captain Jones what's going on."

Private Sharp squinted, once again looking at each in turn. "I don't understand. What are you talking about? Tell the captain what?"

"Didn't you hear Morales?" Johnson jerked his thumb toward the speaker in the wall. "The bunker crew aren't what they seem."

"You mean the people we found here?"

"Yeah, man. We thought they were from FEMA or a special unit or something, but they've got Smith, Morales, and the rest of the team trapped on Sub-level 4. That's why you have to go tell Jones."

The private absorbed the information, his mind reeling with the true reality of the situation, eyes widening as the danger dawned in them. He stepped up, unslung his rifle, and held it in a tight grip across his chest. "We can take them, guys. We're armed and they're not."

Johnson shook his head, lip curling in a snarl. "Dude, they've got a gun to Lieutenant Smith's skull and have captured at least three or four of our other soldiers. Maybe everyone who went down there. You don't think they've taken our boys' weapons?"

"Why don't you guys come out with me? We'll tell Captain Jones together. Then we can attack the situation as a team."

"We don't have time for that. They know how many of us came in initially, and they're asking for us by name."

As if on cue, the speaker cracked to life once more, and Morales's voice piped over the line, again sounding unnaturally strained, like someone was holding a knife to his throat or a gun to his temple. "Come on, Johnson, Isaacs, and Richardson. They know you guys are

COLLAPSE

here, and if you're not part of the headcount in five minutes, they're going to blow Lieutenant Smith's head off."

The speaker cut off again and Johnson dropped a heavy hand on Sharp's shoulder, causing the skinny private to slouch. "See what I mean? We don't have a choice. We can't let our men die. Buzz off, Sharp. Go tell Jones what the situation is, but make sure he knows these people aren't messing around. You got that? We'll go surrender to help buy some time. You bring Jones and take these bastards out, got it?"

The private nodded vigorously, eyes darting across his buddies, a nervous sweat sprouting on his brow despite the chilly air. "Don't worry, guys. I'll get some help. We'll get you out of here, okay?"

The soldiers bobbed their heads and waved the private back through the door where he slipped away. Then Johnson, Isaacs, and Richardson turned to see three men come striding around the corner and along the hall, shirtless with thick pipe wrenches in their hands.

One of them, a giant with a grey goatee hanging from his jaw, pointed at Johnson, who stood in front of the door as it fell softly shut behind the fleeing private. "I'm assuming you heard the announcement?"

"Yeah, we heard it," Johnson nodded, voice filled with contempt.

"Then let's get this over with. Give us your weapons, or Smith gets a round to the head. It's about time we got upgrades."

The two insurgents behind him chuckled, their wide shoulders flexing with the heavy wrenches in their hands. Johnson glanced at Isaacs and Richardson before he unslung his rifle and placed it on the ground.

Back upstairs, Morales took his finger off the intercom button and turned to Chet. "They'll be here, don't worry."

"They better be here within five minutes." Chet pointed the barrel of his weapon at the other three soldiers standing on Morales's left. "Or we'll end Lieutenant Smith. Your buddies will be next, then you."

Morales glanced at Shae, where she held his pistol on him from a few yards away. Several other members of Chet's crew had come to the room, bringing Brozowski and LaPlante with them. Their weapons were stripped and in the wrong hands and Rupert and Meyers were still locked inside the refrigeration unit.

Standing on Morales's left, Lieutenant Smith stood with his fists clasped at his side, shoulders tense, veins pulsing in his temples. "Who the hell are you people, anyway?" he asked. "You're not some civilian group who stumbled on the bunker randomly. Everything about this seems a bit too planned to me."

"Glad to see you're not a dumb grunt," Chet replied. "You're right, we're not civvies. We're with The United Front, New Mexico branch."

Smith shook his head and made a disgusted sound. "Son of a... you're a bunch of damn agitators, insurgents, filthy rioters and troublemakers. Terrorists. Weren't you people the ones who shot that woman and her child in St. Louis?"

Chet's jaw locked in anger, shifted back and forth, his friendly blue eyes taking on a harsh and hostile gaze. "We didn't cause any of that. That was police brutality. The bastards always handle things with a heavy hand."

Smith continued. "And you're behind a bunch of other stuff, too. Last I heard, the FBI was investigating you for a string of pipe bombings."

Morales noted the militia group leader tensing, shoulders growing tight as the rifle slowly raised to Smith's belly.

"I don't think it matters much anymore," he interjected with a halting gesture. "What I am curious about though, is how you people discovered this place."

Eyes lingering on Smith for another angry second, Chet shifted his attention to Morales, causing his coiled guts to turn cold. Still, he didn't cringe or shy away, keeping the focus on him. Jones would eventually figure out what was going on, but until then, he had to keep the situation calm or risk having his people shot and killed.

"We saw what was happening in the North Atlantic." The leader said. "We got the reports and our sources said things were a hell of a lot worse than the government assholes were saying on the news.

"We tried to organize and take over, but the police and military were gone so fast there was nobody left to fight. Many of our people got caught up in the fascist forced evacuations, and we couldn't track them all south. We've known about this place for a long time, and we had all the entry codes." The man glanced at Shae. "We brought everyone we could find, but we didn't realize they'd already changed the security codes on most of the warehouse doors."

"I thought you guys could hack all that stuff?" Morales asked.

Chet scoffed. "All the people here are muscle, but not a single one of them is a tech-head. Our techs are probably frozen dead by now or gone south. Idiots didn't hurry up and join us when they had the chance."

Morales shared a quick glance with Brozowski before continuing. "So, you guys were planning on waiting out the apocalypse down here?"

"At least until you showed up. I guess things have changed."

"And what do you expect to accomplish now?" Morales asked, homing in on the big question. "What do you want out of us? You want us to get out of here and leave you alone? Seal up the bunker? We can do that." A lie, painfully obvious to most, but the ego of The United Front was well known, and if Chet was anything like his more notorious comrades, he'd be too self-absorbed to realize Morales was simply fishing for information.

"Something like that," Chet said. "But it won't do us any good if we can't get into the locked rooms."

Morales raised his hand, looking between Smith and Chet. "We can help you. I'll figure out how to get you access to the locked areas, but you have to let us leave. You can't kill us. And if we seal you guys back in here, you can't kill the other convoy drivers that come along."

"Don't you get it?" Shae said, her voice cracking. "We're not interested in killing. Just leave us the hell alone!"

"That's why you've got our guns on us, right?" Smith snarled. "You just want to be left alone?"

Ignoring Smith's swipe, Chet continued speaking to Morales, treating the specialist as though he was in charge of the situation, a position Morales was more than happy to take on if it meant Smith was less at risk. "And if we let you go, you'll just run to Captain Jones and tell him who we are. He'll launch an assault, no doubt." The leader swept his rifle across the lot of them. "Or, who's to say you won't bomb us from 10,000 feet?"

The door came open, and the three pipe workers they'd seen earlier guided in Johnson, Isaacs, and Richardson. They'd taken the soldiers' weapons, and the militia leader pointed for the new soldiers to join their comrades against the wall. Morales gave the newcomers a nod, realizing all of the soldiers who'd remained in the bunker were gathered in the room. Chet could execute them and no one would be the wiser for who knew how long. Long enough for them to mount up a defense against Jones and the rest, bottlenecking any attack and rendering it next to useless.

With an icy feeling radiating from his belly, Morales faced the insurgent leader again. "It doesn't have to go like that. You could let us leave in exchange for access to the supplies in this bunker. I could tell the captain the cargo lifts aren't working, and we need to get some specialists up here to fix them. But after a few hours, we'll claim they're irreparable. Something about needing a special tool we don't have on hand. The captain will cut his losses and pull us out. By then, we'll have moved on to another camp, and you'll have the place to yourselves." It was a bald-faced lie, all of it, but Morales had few cards left to play.

"It's not like it matters anyway," Brozowski hissed. "You can't live down here forever, especially after the big freeze hits--"

Morales gave Brozowski a sharp glance, but Shae immediately stepped over and put her weapon to the man's forehead. "What was that, grunt? What was that about a big freeze?"

"N-nothing," Brozowski stammered, both eyes crossed as he stared at the pistol barrel. "It's just, you know, getting super cold out there. We don't want to stay around too much longer."

Eyes narrowed, the woman adjusted her grip on the weapon, pressing the steel cylinder harder between his eyes. "You better come clean, buddy, or your friends will be wearing your brains on their jackets."

"What Brozowski is saying," Morales interjected, "is that we're well below the freeze point here in New Mexico. Above us are Arctic temperatures, with spin-up storms hitting every few hours or so, freezing everything, and killing anything. What we're hearing is that this cold won't end. It'll be around for a long time."

Shae's ice-blue eyes narrowed beneath her thick eyebrows, gun shifting from the stammering soldier to settle against Morales's temple. "So, what you're saying is that if we stay here, if we seal ourselves inside this bunker, we'd be stuck forever?"

Morales looked to Smith, who stared at him with an even expression, giving him a slight nod of approval to continue. Negotiating with a domestic terrorist outfit wasn't exactly operating by the book, but given their situation he'd start handing out free lap dances if it meant getting his people free, then Jones could come up with a plan to burn out The United Front. Unfortunately, Brozowski's ill-timed admission about the upcoming freeze had ruined his plans.

Looking back to Shae, he nodded in the affirmative. "We're not a hundred percent sure, but there's a good chance that if you stay here, you'll be here for the rest of your lives. Sealed in."

"Like a tomb," Chet snarled, bringing his gun up to Smith's head. "And you assholes would've left us down here."

"Hey, wait a minute! You wanted us to leave!" Morales took a step toward the two men when Shae grabbed his arm, digging the rounded end of her weapon into his temple even harder. "Take one more step and see what happens." The woman's voice was a tense grumble pressed through clenched teeth. Morales froze and kept his hands raised. Eyes closed, he recalled the corpses in the room from earlier with their bashed-in skulls and twisted limbs.

"Like I said," he quickly added. "We don't know for sure—"

"Shut up and get back in line." Shae sidestepped to face him, dropping the gun from his temple and jamming it into his chest, forcing him to retreat to Smith. She spun to the militia leader, expression anguished. "We have to change our plans. We can't stay here."

Chet was already nodding, eyes falling to the floor before lifting to the soldiers. "Yeah. There's no way in hell we're sticking around."

The pipe worker with the gray goatee spoke up. "I say we grab some of the convoy trucks, fill them with supplies, and bus our asses the hell out of here."

"We head south then?" Shae asked, shooting him a glance. "It's got to be warmer there, right?"

"Yeah, that's what I figure," the man said. "Get to warmer weather as soon as possible, outrun these spin-up storms. What do you think, Chet?"

"You can't do that either," Smith interrupted with a growl. "You'll end up getting caught, or the Captain will come after you. People will lose their lives. Your best option is to give yourselves up."

Chet grinned widely, looking over the soldiers with a mischievous gleam. "We've been taking risks for years. Things aren't any different now. We'll take our chances with a few of your trucks and all the supplies we can carry. At the first signs of screwing us over, we'll mow you down. Now, strip those uniforms off, boys. We're going to need them."

Morales groaned and slapped his freezing hands together as he, Smith, and the rest of the soldiers moved bins of supplies from the elevator platform to a trailer. The militia had connected it to a Humvee that was idling nearby and were prepared to pull out and drive away from the convoy. Two hours had passed since the militia group had taken control of the secret bunker, and the Army crew was fast at work, loading three trucks and a Humvee full of supplies.

Standing nearby were five United Front members in stolen uniforms, covered head to toe in military cold-weather gear. The rest of the soldiers were in the bowels of the bunker, piling stacks of stores near the cargo lifts. The mid-morning sun was trying to push through the endless gray clouds, their edges marked with black burns. Every time the icy winds kicked up, Morales's eyes lifted upward, expecting the next spin-up storm to roar down on their heads.

"You just had to go and tell them about the weather, didn't you?" Smith chastised Brozowski. "If it wasn't for you, we'd have these jerks sealed up and could be sitting around thinking of a hundred different ways to end them. Now, here we are doing their dirty work."

"Sorry, Lieutenant." The soldier's expression was sheepish as he hefted a large plastic bin with military stenciling on the side, slipping on the circular platform as he staggered over to the trailer to place it with the rest.

"Don't be so hard on him," Morales said, shifting supplies around. "I don't think he realized who we were dealing with until it was too late."

"Once a dumb grunt, always a dumb grunt," the lieutenant snapped in a surly tone.

"Need I remind you? You're a grunt, too."

"Yeah, but I'm one of the smart ones." Smith snatched a bin off the top of the pile and carried it over to the trailer. "And I could use a damn cigarette."

Morales rolled his eyes, following the lieutenant, slamming his bin next to Smith's.

The snow was still falling fast enough to create a layer of white on the crates of supplies. A militia member was always standing nearby with a rifle, dusting the tops off and monitoring the soldiers. Within a few minutes, they'd cleared the cargo platform and stood waiting to be sent back downstairs for more. A United Front guard stepped on with them and punched a button on a control panel. A high-pitched beep went off, then the platform grumbled and lurched, Morales's knees buckling as they sunk straight into the sub-floors, passing all the way to the fourth level where more supplies awaited them.

"I think they're going to get away with this," Morales mumbled low to Smith. "I was a little skeptical at first, but we've got one truck already loaded, and Jones and the rest of our boys are still in the second warehouse."

"Yeah, I was doubtful, but the bastards are efficient." The lieutenant looked back at the militia woman standing behind them, covered head to toe in military gear. "They look just like us, dammit. Even if Jones sends guys over here for a status update, they'll never know they're talking to the wrong people. Hell, it might even get some of our men shot."

Johnson stepped around and stood between Morales and Smith, nudging them both with his elbows. Under the grinding sound of the hydraulics and sliding plate, he turned slightly, glancing at the guard. "Hang in there, guys," he murmured. "There's help on the way."

The specialist refrained from reacting, but the lieutenant shot Johnson a narrow-eyed glare. "What the hell are you talking about, soldier?"

"Just before they captured us, Private Sharp came into the bunker looking for us. We sent him off with instructions to let Captain Jones know what was happening. I think he got away without them seeing him."

Smith stiffened where he stood, his arms held out from his body like he was ready to fight. The lieutenant stared straight ahead, head turning toward the militia member standing behind them with one of their rifles. "Is that so?"

"That had to have been over two hours ago," Morales whispered from the corner of his mouth, his own heart pounding with renewed hope. "Hopefully he got to the Captain."

"Jones'll eat these jerks' heads for lunch." Smith's grin widened manically. "We just need to be ready when the time comes."

"Hey, you three!" the woman snapped. "Shut the hell up. No talking on the platform!"

The big steel dais reached Sub-floor Four, coming to a jarring stop, the men standing on it wobbling for a moment before stepping off. Chet and Shae were waiting for them, dressed in thick military fatigues, the size mismatches easily hidden by the heaviness of the clothing.

"All right, Army boys," Chet said, pointing to another skid of supplies. "Let's get the rest of this loaded up. Hup, hup! Let's go!"

CHAPTER TWENTY-THREE

Private First Class Simon Sharp
Santa Fe, New Mexico

Private Sharp leaned against the door he'd just come through, turning, reentering the key code on the other side and hitting "Enter" to lock it. After leaving Richardson, Johnson, and Isaacs, he'd trotted up the stairs, intending to head outside and over to the warehouse. But he'd turned back at the sound of two enemies standing guard on the landing above him, their harsh whispers and snickers about having captured the GIs sent waves of dread through him, weakening his knees.

Going downstairs was off limits, so he spun and slipped into the Sub-floor 2 passage, shutting the door quietly behind him, sprinting to the next hall, taking a right, and running even farther, fatigue causing his boots to hammer on the tiles. Unsure whether the enemy had heard him, he crossed to the first secure room he saw and punched in the code with his fingers.

He'd gotten two sets of codes from his time working with Brozowski and LaPlante in the original warehouse when he'd been on technician duty which was one reason Captain Jones had sent him to find Morales and Smith. The private wasn't a brutish worker, and he couldn't run any of the trucks or loading machines so they'd assigned him messenger boy duty, ferrying orders around to the various lieutenants and specialists when the radios got spotty. The captain hadn't asked him to come straight back, with the work on the second warehouse moving fast and furious and no one else was aware of the betrayal happening at the bunker.

Lungs strained, heart hammering, a deep sense of isolation settled on his shoulders. Inside the room, he slid onto his backside, letting his fists rest on his knees, squeezing his sweaty palms, head lowered as he realized he was cut off from his team. During his time with the military, he'd relied heavily on the members of his unit to get through the rigors of basic training and the nightmare of Mexico. All the blood, sweat, and tears, the callouses and bruises, the brief but brutal fights in Reynosa, Monterrey, and Mexico City.

The men being held by whoever had taken over the bunker were his friends and fellow soldiers, the guys who relied on him to come through. He relied on them, too. Without them, he had no one to command him or shout an order into his face, no squad leader or lieutenant to give him flack for screwing up, no one to pat him on the back and lift him up and be there at his side. It had always been tough, but the private thrived on the comradery and teamwork. There'd been few things he'd ever done alone, but cut off from his team he had to think of a way to either reach the captain or, barring that, pull off some kind of miracle on his own.

The underground bunker was massive, several floors of warehouses, hundreds of rooms, side halls, and equipment areas, all buried beneath tons of earth in a quiet claustrophobia. Sharp squeezed his hands one last time, took a deep breath, and tried to remember his training. He needed to make a list of things, mental or written, minor tasks that, when accumulated, would lead him to a bigger goal.

Calm down. Focus.

Sharp took a deep breath and thought. Johnson had told him to go back and find the captain, because people had taken Smith and the others hostage and were about to execute them. The bunker crew, the people they'd found underground, had not been waiting for rescue at all. They were dangerous, and they'd captured his friends and posted guards at the top of the shaft to make sure no one got in or out. So, there were two options. Sharp could try to get past the guards and return to the warehouse to alert Captain Jones, or he could break the guys out himself.

The bit of critical thinking calmed his nerves and he took another deep breath, stood, and dusted his pants off, then he scanned the room, bringing an instant smile to his face. He was standing in a mess hall. Not exactly a military version, but close enough. Basic tables were placed around the area, each with four plastic chairs. The buffet line cut across the middle of the room, clean glass partitions and empty cases telling him it hadn't been used in quite a while.

Glorious memories of basic training and of the staging camp before the Mexico invasion flooded back. Sharp had always seen the mess hall as a haven of quiet relaxation, where he could grab a meal and joke around with his buddies. It was probably his favorite place to be besides his rack, and it filled him with a sense of comfort, steadying his queasy stomach.

With a quick glance backward at the door, he strode between the tables toward the banquet line, angling to the left where he squeezed through to the kitchen area. Two prep tables sat in the middle of the red-tiled room, one with a knife block and chopping board on it. Shelves stood pressed against the walls, stocked with big cans of tomato paste, pickles, soups, and boxes of candy bars.

Starving, after a ten-hour stint of loading trucks with almost no break, Sharp made a beeline for the shelves. He grabbed two of the candy bars, ripped open the packaging, and double-fisted them like he was chugging beers back in college. As he stuffed his mouth with the sugary sweets, he strode around the room, thinking about what he was going to do. A small part of him realized he'd have to fight the bunker crew to bust his friends out, regardless of whether he tried to get past the guards or free them himself. It wouldn't be a simple task. He'd only been average on the gun range, and he wasn't great in hand-to-hand combat so there'd be no running around the place, shooting it up like a cowboy or snapping opponents' necks like Chuck Norris.

The answer flashed in his mind. Knife work. That was something he was efficient at, a skill he'd practiced a lot. Being of smaller stature, he'd worked extensively with blades of every size and shape, often defeating larger men in basic training. "But this is reality," he mumbled to himself around mouthfuls. "Can you use any of those moves in real life, buddy?"

He stopped at the knife block and set his half-finished candy bars down, then removed his jacket. He slid two thick-bladed knives from the block, each six inches with sharp points, testing the edges with his thumb before taking a few experimental swipes. Satisfied, he tucked them under his belt near his hips, handles jutting up for quick access. Candy bars back in hand, Smart resumed his chocolate binge, walking around and exploring more.

He found an empty sack with a strap on it and placed it on a table. With no idea how long he'd be inside, or how long his mission would last, he'd need supplies. There might be times where he had to hide for several hours, or a day, so having food and water handy would be helpful. Even if Captain Jones found out about the hostage situation, he might not be able to do anything about it right away. He'd need someone on the inside, working behind the scenes to cut off the head of the snake.

"So that's what it's going to be, Sharp?" He grumbled, speaking to himself in third person, voice full of toughness. "You going to break your buddies out?"

In the pack, he placed the rest of the box of candy bars, a box of pilot bread crackers, a can of peanut butter, and a can of jelly. He tossed in a butter knife, fork, and a 12 pack of bottled water from the storage closet in the back. With the supplies on his shoulder, and a modest array of weapons in his belt, Private Sharp crept from the mess hall, peering along the passage before stepping out.

Taking a right, he moved deeper into the facility, watching the walls for a map of the place or to gain some sense of where things were. The air simmered with a quiet tension, the only sounds his breath and his boot heels gently falling on the tiles. Keeping to the left side of the wall, he crept through darker sections where the lights were dim or missing. With one six-inch cutting blade lifted from his belt, he switched to the opposite side of the passage, holding the weapon in his front hand.

Turning a myriad of corners, he slipped along multiple passages with his shoulders to the wall, knife glinting in the emergency lighting. Still, he struggled to make sense of the surrounding maze. With a quiet sigh, he stopped for a moment, squatting and closing his eyes as he thought back on the whirlwind of training he'd gone through over the past three months.

He'd done basic training in Fort Knox, Kentucky, before returning home to Covington while awaiting his deployment orders. As the days passed, he'd wondered if they'd ever call him. Then everything had happened with the anomaly, the news reports about the North Atlantic current dragging to a standstill, cutting off the warm waters from the south and bringing with it frigid temperatures. What followed had been an apocalypse no one ever expected. His deployment orders came swiftly, and he returned to a military that had changed drastically in a few weeks. With new recruits flooding in by the thousands, they'd pushed his unit out to a massive warehousing complex with three underground bunkers similar to the one he was standing in. During that time, he'd completed several inventory runs for their trainer, the layout of the place sticking somewhere inside his head.

"I remember the orders from Lieutenant Anderson," he whispered to himself, the memory floating forward from the back of his mind. "I was supposed to go to the armory and get .50 caliber MK211 ammunition and deliver it to the range for gunnery practice that afternoon. But what floor was the armory on?"

Sharp shook his clenched fist, face wincing as he thought back to that day, tried to recall what he'd eaten for breakfast. It had likely been oatmeal and toast with a cup of coffee. Then he mentally traced his footsteps outside to meet up with his squad out on the range. There'd come the orders from the Lieutenant, and his aggravation that he'd been the one having to run for the ammo. It was only because he was a newbie, the youngest in the unit, and they'd punished him by making him fetch anything and everything.

"I came down the steps, just like I did today. At the second landing, I took a right and walked to the end of the hall. Then…" The directions solidified themselves in his mind as butterflies danced in his stomach.

A smile widened on his face. Not only did he think he knew where the armory was, he also remembered some hidden stairwells and other interesting facets of the building. If the layout was the same in the bunker as it was back where he'd been before, he could move around undetected and no one would be the wiser.

Sharp turned back the way he'd come, slipping to the other side of the hall, shoulders brushing against the wall as he held his blade in a forward position, ready to strike like a snake.

"I'm coming for you, brothers. Hang in there. I'm coming."

CHAPTER TWENTY-FOUR

Keith
Somewhere in Mexico

"Here! Stop right here!"

Keith leaned forward over the radio console, staring at the external camera screen from his spot in the Stryker's communication chair, maneuvering the joystick to peer through the city streets. When Serge didn't immediately pull in where he wanted, he slammed both fists on the console and cursed under his breath. "What are you doing, man? Pull up those stairs and into the courtyard. Follow the tracks!"

The merc leader shot the agent a dark glance and then whipped the wheel to the right, sending the APC rocketing up a set of short, snow-covered stone steps at 35 mph. The front end crashed onto a flat courtyard about 40 yards square. The merc slammed on the brakes, catching the tires in the snow and ice, sliding them to a fast and shuddering stop in the middle of a large marketplace.

Three other sides of the plaza had similar stairs, even at the north end where a massive grey cathedral stood slightly off to the right. The thick, grey walls and steeple were covered with sleet, decorative statues, and figurines all along the top portion. The four market corners were concrete pavilions with stone tables and wooden benches where traders might have once sold their wares.

"Lower the back door! Lower it, now!"

Keith leapt from his seat and shoved past Mikael as the rear door crept open. With a single thick coat on and a thin pair of gloves covering his fragile fingers, he jumped before the door completely opened, landing in the snow, circling to the front and staring at the crisscrossing Humvee tracks snaking off in every direction.

For the last thirty minutes they'd been trying to follow Tom McKnight's blighted path, his backtracking and weaving throwing the mercs into a state of confusion. Standing in the center of the marketplace, Keith glared at three sets of tracks going in opposite directions, all Humvee tires, none of them any fresher than the others. Hands on his hips, he stomped around in the snow, moving from one set of tire marks to the other, following them where they plunged down the stairs and out into the neighborhood streets. Glaring up at the big church steeple, he wondered if some supernatural force was trying to tell them something.

"Perhaps we can park the Strykers at separate ends of town and wait them out."

Keith turned to see Serge lingering behind him, rifle cradled gently in his arms, Mikael standing a few yards away.

Lena and Dmitri exited the back of their idling APC and came to join them. Rifles in their arms, barrels pointed at the ground, they stared with bitter eyes at the even colder surroundings. Breath drifted from their mouths to be consumed by the hungry cold.

"No. We will *not* do that." Keith snarled. "Let's split up, actively pursue them, and whoever finds them first will call in."

Serge shook his head, a crooked grin beneath his hood. "You're being too impatient, my friend. This family, this Tom McKnight, is reckless and smart. That is a dangerous combination."

The agent whirled on the merc, fist clenched at his hip. "They're just civvies. You said so yourself. What, are you afraid of them now?"

Serge raised his finger and shook it at Keith. "None of us are afraid, but we understand when we are facing an enemy with great instincts and ability. That is not an insult to anyone." A shrug lifted his shoulders. "It only makes it more of a challenge for us, one where we must take our time and do things correctly."

"Serge is right." Lena jerked her chin at the man, locks of her blonde hair hanging from her hood. "You are underestimating them like you did before, as evidenced by your injuries. Your missing fingers and toes."

The mercenaries snicked, even Dmitri showing a big, dumb grin as Mikael kicked at the icy ground with the toe of his boot. Keith glared at them in turn, gaze lingering on Serge before shifting to Lena. "You people think this is funny? You think a *family* will win this? They may have beaten me before, but they won't win. There're on the run, and they're scared. I won't let Tom McKnight's little slalom course beat me, and you should feel the same way."

"Oh, we do," Serge said. "We'd just rather do this more methodically than you." He shrugged again. "We prefer methods that work to ones that lose fingers and toes."

"Luckily, we're not on your dime," Keith snarled, gesturing for them to follow him to the APCs. When they didn't immediately come, he stopped and turned back, finger raised and pointed at them. "Were splitting up. Serge, Mikael, and I will move north. Lena and Dmitri, you go east. We'll search by grids. I want to check every track until we find them. Is that understood?"

"We're splitting up, but we're not going to actively hunt them." Lena jerked her thumb behind them. "Serge, Mikael, and Keith will head to the overpass just north of us. Dmitri and I will go back the way we came. Once in position, we will lie in wait."

The merc leader agreed with a calm, careful nod. "And we will be ready when they come out."

"You're ignoring a direct order." Keith stepped up to Lena and put his face two inches from hers, knowing he was pushing his luck with her but not caring. "Do that, and you won't get the rest of your payment."

Lena shrugged, her jade green eyes watching him carefully. "You are not in charge of this mission. We were hired by Banks, and you were only to come along and observe." Her gaze shifted to Serge. "The final decision on how to carry out the plan is up to us."

Keith spun to face Serge, squinting in accusation, the man only staring at him with his cold, impenetrable eyes. "Bastards," he growled, stomping up the APC's ramp, shoving his way to the front, and falling into the radio chair.

Serge climbed into the APC and slipped back behind the wheel with Mikael dropping into a seat, watching Keith with amusement. After the door was up, the merc leader put the vehicle into drive and pulled it off the market square, trundling down the steps and into the street with a clatter of equipment inside the crew quarters.

The APCs split up, Serge's vehicle cruising north along the narrow roads, making their way to the massive overpass Lena had mentioned. The merc leader found the entrance ramp and climbed the vehicle up the wide arcing overpass to the very top, putting them a hundred and fifty feet in the air with a perfect view of the city's center.

He parked the Stryker and left it running, using the external cameras to look around, fingers toggling the magnification as he peered across the city. Keith merely sat in his seat, arms crossed, jaw clenched in anger as he stared at the radio controls, thinking through what had just happened.

"We are in position," Lena said over the speaker, and the merc leader replied that they were, too.

Mikael relaxed back in a crew seat. "Now, all we have to do is watch and wait."

Keith tapped his heel on the floor of the truck. "You know, if McKnight slips out on a side road, he'll be gone for good."

"He will not slip out on a side road," Serge assured him in his thick accent. "Do not worry. This will be like the rabbit hunting I used to do on my uncle's farm. If we dig around for them and make too much noise, they will only dig deeper so we can never find them. If we wait patiently, we will be in a suitable position to smash their heads when they come out. It's simple."

"And just how long is this supposed to take?"

The merc shrugged. "As long as it takes."

"Listen to Serge," Lena said over the comms system, and Keith caught the slight hint of amusement in her voice. "He knows what he's talking about, and he has been hunting people many years."

"And I haven't?"

"Apparently not someone like Tom McKnight," the woman responded, her amused tone cutting through the line to stab him in the chest. The agent bowed his head, jaw working back and forth, throat clenching tighter and tighter until a low growl rolled from his gut.

Slamming a fist on the console, he leaned forward and tapped the necessary buttons to make a call to Banks. Fingers throbbing, every press of a key like a spark of lightning up his wrist, but he didn't care. The mercs were out of control and needed to be brought back in line.

"Are you calling your boss?" Serge asked, his tone incredulous, then he raised his voice to the speaker system, his tone flat. "Lena, he is calling his boss."

The sultry woman returned. "What? Keith, why would you do that? What can Banks do for you now?"

"She can pull the plug on the weapons caches," the agent nodded, fingers lancing with pain as he tapped the console, waiting for the connection. "She can have those shut down, and you'll get nothing."

Serge shifted and lifted his visor, the slight grin on his face turning harder. "Your plan was not good. What we presented is better. We can just wait them out here, no problem. No risk to us, except it might be a little boring. Bringing Banks into this is unnecessary."

Keith stewed in his chair until the connection finally died, a roar of snow and wind eliminating the possibility of contacting anyone.

"Damn it!" he shouted, the tendons in his neck bulging with anger, face turning hot. Pressing his fingers into the console, driving pain to his hands like a nail, he shifted his furious glare to the merc leader. "Let me tell you the first mistake about your plan. As we wait for them, it'll grow too cold for any of us to survive. Remember what it felt like in Texas? The Strykers could barely keep us warm then. Once it hits down here, we'll be done for. Do you really want to wait for that to happen?" The agent shook his head vigorously. "No, we need to move now before it's too late."

"You are one man, my friend." Serge smiled at him. "How are you going to force us to do what you want?"

Dmitri's deep voice chuckled over the speakers in harmony with the svelte woman's higher tone. Serge still grinned, his humor sending a spike of rage through Keith's chest. Snatching his headset off, he slammed it on the console, giving the merc a brief glare before he settled back in his seat in frustration.

"We will monitor things, including the weather, from the warmth of the Strykers," Serge pressed on with his mocking amusement. "You can sit on top of the truck if you want, or rest, or have a snack. Just do not touch my candy."

The agent stared at the merc for a handful of seconds. With a disgusted sound, he jerked out of the seat, rummaging for his equipment and weapons. He shrugged on his cold weather coat and his extra pair of gloves, then he gathered a small pack of supplies. Pistol holstered at his side, he snatched a rifle from its place on the wall.

"Where are you going?" Serge asked. "Did we hurt your feelings?"

"What is he doing?" Lena spoke over the speakers.

"I'm going out there to do this myself," he responded, stuffing a couple of spare magazines into his waistband and pulling his goggles over his eyes.

Serge chuckled and tossed him a radio, Keith catching it with a wince. "We will keep a look out," he said. "If you see Tom McKnight, flush him toward us, and we shall take him out."

"Finally, you're making sense," the agent snapped.

"You don't have to do this." Lena's voice held a somber, half-apology before bursting into a giggle. "But if you want to lose more of your extremities, please, go ahead."

"To hell with you people! Lower the door." Keith picked up his things, shoved past Mikael, and jumped out.

"Keith!" Lena called in a mock sing-song voice. "Come back, and let's talk!"

"He's already gone." Serge stepped to the door, watching the man tromp angrily through the dense snow. "He is going to do what he wants with or without us."

"Do you think he'll flush these McKnights out?" Lena asked.

Serge's head bobbed, lips pursed. "He probably will, yes. Right into our hands. It would be a shame, though, if he died in the process. Wouldn't it?" The mercenaries' chuckles resounded in the frozen winter air.

Anger fueled Keith's body like an internal nuclear reactor, and he fed on the wrathful energy like a vampire, grimacing into the ice-cold wind as it blew snowflakes against his goggles. As he left the mercs behind, all he could think of was *good riddance*. They did nothing but mock him anyway, none of them with an appreciation for his resilience and strength in the face of adversity. It was poetic, being alone again, hunting the McKnight clan through the freezing cold over hours and days, chasing his prey wolfishly across the tundra. Never bending. Never wavering.

Pain filled every ounce of his body, muscle and bone, his frostbitten fingers and toes laughing at the powerful painkillers he'd taken an hour ago. He kept his hands tight to his sides, fists squeezed closed, conserving his warmth and strength. Mind fraying against the coming storm, body bound by fragile threads of sinew and cartilage, Keith took solace in his own intense desire for revenge. The purity of the thought was all that remained, turning the sour bitterness in his stomach to raw fire, the malice in his blood, warmth.

The agent was still alive, still trudging on, held together by willpower alone.

CHAPTER TWENTY-FIVE

Tom McKnight
Somewhere in Mexico

Tom stood at the window, fingers dividing the second-floor blinders, looking back and forth along the street, taking in the wintry afternoon scene. It had been an hour since they'd parked inside the garage, and he'd seen no sign of the APCs, or Keith. While the skies remained gray and angry, the snowfall had let up some, a soft pattering against the windows of the old industrial building.

After parking the Humvee, they'd found a storeroom leading off the garage, filled with canned grease and machine parts he couldn't identify. Beyond that, they'd climbed one floor of rickety stairs to reach an open warehouse space, just to get off the street and get a better view of their surroundings. Lips pressed together, he allowed the blinds to fall back and turned to face his wife and family.

Barbara stood in the middle of a wide factory floor, boots spread shoulder-width apart on the stripped hardwood. The ceilings stretched tall with round columns placed every twenty feet. Old milling machines and parts converters lay around like iron hulks, tons of weight squatting on the bowed flooring, cobwebs hanging from the spindles and wheels, metal filings everywhere, the whole place smelling like dust and cold grease. The three children sat in chairs, lined up perfectly, eldest to youngest, left to right, Smooch sitting dutifully at Jack's side. They remained bundled in their coats, hats, gloves, misty breaths puffing into the air.

The kids stared at their parents with expectant eyes, still nervous after the rattling ride into the city. Sam sat quietly, eyes raised to her mother, hands folded into her lap, back stiff, shoulders square and ready to run at any second. Linda held Jack's hand, only slightly more relaxed, but only because she was trying to keep her brother amused. Barbara stepped closer to Tom, her head swimming inside her hood, lips cracked and dry from the intense cold, her goggles frosted around the edges.

"It's been an hour, honey," she said, shifting her rifle on her shoulder. "We've seen no sign of them. Can we leave?"

Tom entertained the notion of getting back in the Humvee and driving off, but something nagged at the back of his mind, something that told him it would be a dangerous move.

"This is Keith were talking about here," he huffed. "I can't believe he'd give up so easily. He has to know we're still hiding somewhere in town."

"Your false tracks probably threw them off. Maybe they're lost and gave up or moved on."

Shaking his head, Tom crossed to one of the gigantic machines, running his hand along a curved part as he passed. At the back window, he parted another blind and looked across the street to the lines of dark buildings behind him. The lifeless panes of dingy glass stared back at him, chilling him to the bone. But it was their drooping, sagging roofs and the undisturbed snow resting between them that left an uneasy feeling in his gut.

He turned and strolled back to his wife. "The snow is slowly starting to cover our tracks, but the storm is tapering off."

"Yeah, the one time we want it to storm hard, and it won't."

Barbara shook her head dismissively. "Damned if you do, damned if you don't."

Tom took a sharp intake of breath and then cleared his throat. "Something tells me if we go out there, we'll be falling into a trap. It might serve us better if we go up to the next floor and have a look around. I think this goes up four or five stories, so I'll take Smooch with me."

"That doesn't make sense, Dad." Sam stood in her big coat with her hands pressed to her side. "You need a human up there, not a dog. Let me come with you and I'll watch from the other windows. I'll be your second set of eyes."

"That's not a good idea, honey." Tom placed his palms on her shoulders. "We need to think about your safety, and you being up there with me-"

"That's BS and you know it. We've done this whole big journey with me doing dangerous stuff all the time. Being a lookout is nothing in comparison. You need me up there to look around with you. Mom can stay here and keep an eye on Linda, Jack, and Smooch."

Tom looked back and forth between his wife and daughter, eyebrows raised in question, eyes directed toward Barbara. "What do you think, honey?"

Barbara shrugged. "Your call."

"I'll stay ducked down," Sam said in an imploring voice. "They won't even notice me. I'll just look around the edges and report what I see." The girl was already walking toward the access door to the stairwell, and she stopped and looked back. "Are you coming?"

Tom gave an exasperated sigh and shook his head. "I guess I am. You guys keep Smooch down here in case Keith or any of his friends show up." Finger raised, he met their eyes so they understood. "Just be ready to leave at the drop of a hat, okay? If either me or your mother say to get to the truck, you go ASAP." The kids nodded.

"Be careful," Barbara added. "Both of you."

Tom went first, stepping past Sam through the old metal door, its hinges shrieking up the shaft. The stairwell was wide, a typical U-shaped pattern, with no windows letting in a single speck of light. The hardwood creaked as they stepped over to a wooden banister with pale aqua paint flaking off. Adjusting his rifle on his shoulder, Tom retrieved his flashlight from his coat and shined it up to the next landing. With an assured glance back at Sam, he started up with tentative steps.

Fingers sliding up the handrail, he kicked aside piles of paper and garbage, sweeping the debris out of Sam's way. The first landing was empty but for the trash and a single door with a simple frame. Tom walked over and pulled the knob, opening the door a bit, peeking into a similar room as the one downstairs. The space was filled with old machinery and parts, gray light spilling through the smudged glass. It painted a dismal picture of what might have once been a robust factory with workers and machine sounds, smoke and motion and life, though it had become nothing but a skeleton of the past.

Sam's stifled shriek sent Tom spinning on his heels, flashlight aiming at his daughter on the landing, rifle sliding from his shoulder to a firing position. Legs stiff, eyes wide behind her goggles, she pointed to the floor where her boot had uncovered a frozen rat.

"Jeez, Sam," he said, clutching his chest. "You almost gave me a heart attack."

Sam let out a long exhale, stepping over the animal. "Sorry, Dad. Startled the crap out of me."

He shook his head. "That's okay. But come on. And no more scares."

They moved up to the next landing, finding their way blocked by a desk and office furniture, trash piled on top along with dog-eared cardboard, water stained with mold. The place smelled like old dust and lost time, the smells of abandonment, the building left behind.

"Careful up here." Tom shifted boxes aside and lifted an upturned chair from the desk, setting it on the landing. "The last thing we need right now is to get hurt."

"I know. I've got this."

Tom leaned forward, fists together on the table surface to test its weight, then he climbed up, crawled across on his knees, and put one boot on the other side, holding his hand against the wall to balance. Adjusting his rifle on his shoulder, he moved up a couple of steps and gestured for Sam to come over. She crossed easily enough, stepping down to where he'd been standing, nodding that she was ready to continue. They passed the next two landings and came face to face with a pile of piping and wooden framing spilled onto the steps. One hand out, he stooped and raised a little, craning his neck, peering up and looking for a way through.

He handed her his rifle. "Stand back for a sec." Sam accepted the weapon and backed to the lower landing, waiting for Tom to clear the steel, aluminum, and junk, dragging it out with a screech of metal and stacking it along the wall.

Tunnel opened, he took his rifle back from his daughter and pushed it ahead of him, crawling through the prickling debris and drooping drywall. His coat caught on a nail, snagging him for a moment, and he turned back and freed himself before moving on. Once past the jagged rubble, he ascended a few steps and turned. "Come on through but watch out for the nails."

Sam nodded and climbed carefully, kneeling, crawling on one hand while using the other to hold off the sagging debris. "Ugh, this stuff is gross," she said, standing, dusting her gloves and coat off.

"Are you okay?"

"Yeah, I'm fine. Not a fan of this place, that's all."

With a faint nod, Tom turned and shined his light up to the final landing on an aqua-tinted door. Tucking his flashlight away, he cradled his rifle in his right arm, opened the door, and stepped in two paces.

It was an open warehouse room like the others. Wooden slats stretched the length of the floor, three windows on both sides with large frames cut into four panes. There were more of the same abandoned machines they'd seen on the lower floors, stinking of oil and grease and the faint scent of something dead. Sam started to walk ahead, but Tom reached out and held her back.

"Wait a second. Let me check things out first. No sense in showing ourselves to anyone who might be watching."

Raising his rifle to a firing position, pointing it out the first window on his left, he peered through the scope, his view limited because of the narrow angle. They were elevated slightly higher than most of the other buildings, but not high enough to see above the entire city, or into the streets unless he walked up to the glass.

The scope swept across the flat rooftops with red-tinted shingles, some covered in gravel and blacktop, overhanging slabs of snow and icicles in a thick layer of whiteness. He swung the rifle around to the right and pointed the scope out the nearest window, catching sight of roads between buildings. One wound up into a hillside where the snow had yet to cover. There were a few scraps of land visible, distant patches of brown, at the edge of the scope's range.

He leaned forward, inching the rifle barrel farther north, squinting into the glass and watching the crosshairs move across the desolate landscape, the city devoid of life and enemies.

"Okay, you can come in," he told her as he kept looking.

The girl started to push past him, to walk to the other windows, when Tom threw his arm across her chest and shoved her backwards out of the room, stopping only when they reached the stairs.

"Dad! What are you doing?" Sam grabbed at his coat, catching his jacket before she took a tumble.

"Sorry, Sam!" He pulled her back into the doorway. "I thought I saw something. Just wait here, and I'll be right back."

Creeping up, angling to the right, he switched the rifle to a left-handed grip, easing it ahead and peering through the scope with his left eye. Shifting forward, a bead of sweat trickling down his neck, he zeroed in on what he thought he'd spotted previously. Toward the north, a tall overpass towered over the city, higher than most of the buildings in the surrounding area, with an unobstructed view of their spot in particular.

The crosshairs brought the hulking form into view, the dark shape of a Stryker crouching beyond the concrete barrier, its massive gun pointed downward, two men sitting on top, back-to-back. One held a pair of binoculars in his hands while the other faced their building, scanning the area with a rifle scope, idly sweeping it back and forth. Because of wearing heavy winter gear, he couldn't tell if either of the figures were Keith, but they were definitely lying in wait. As he looked on, the man with the rifle swung it in his direction, the barrel moving rapidly to line up with the window. Tom jerked back into the doorway once more, tripping over Sam where she lurked behind him.

"Is someone up there?"

"One of the APCs. Two people, too."

"Did they see you, Dad?"

Sliding around to the landing, he sunk into a sitting position and shook his head. "I don't think so. No, I'm sure they didn't. But I have no clue why they're there. The other APC must be close by, or roaming the streets."

"I guess that kills any plans to leave, huh?" Sam knelt on the floor in front of him, eyes dancing across his face.

"Yeah, we're definitely not going to pull out any time soon. We've got enough supplies to last a couple of weeks, but the cold is what will kill us."

"Could we wait for another big storm to hit? I mean, maybe we could find a map somewhere and take a side road out under cover. They'd never see us leave."

With a grunt, Tom pushed to his feet, gesturing for Sam to stay where she was while he slunk back inside the room. He edged closer to the window, staying back out of the direct line of sight from the APC, and raised his weapon once more. A gentle wind whipped snow against the glass as he leaned forward slowly, painfully, giving up as little of his body as he could until he had the APC back in view.

The overpass was a quarter mile away, and the two men sitting on top had turned to face south, though they weren't looking directly at his building. The one with the rifle elbowed the other in the arm and pointed toward the streets. His partner edged forward on his knees, bringing his binoculars up to follow where the man was pointing. The second one saw something and then nudged the first man back. He made a circling motion with his hand and jerked it toward the streets once again.

Tom stared at them for a moment, wondering what they were gesturing at, until he realized. Someone must be down in the snow, searching the area for the McKnights, hunting them, flushing them out.

CHAPTER TWENTY-SIX

The Mercenaries
Somewhere in Mexico

Serge and Mikael had exited the Stryker to watch things from the top of the APC, the extra couple feet of height giving them a better view of their surroundings. The merc leader's hands and toes were chilly, but the air-activated hand warmers they'd broken out, stuffed into their clothing after Keith had left, kept them warm enough. The pair were sitting back-to-back, Mikael with his binoculars and Serge with the rifle and scope, gazing back in the other direction toward Lena's APC where it sat on the street amidst the buildings. They wore their earpieces so they could keep in constant contact with each other, though there was little to discuss of importance. The town was destitute. Everything from the ricketiest home to the ritziest hacienda had been abandoned, citizens having left their possessions behind, abandoning their homes in desperation.

"This reminds me of my hometown," Serge said. "Or like one of those movies where all the people simply vanish."

"Yes, I have seen an American movie like that," Mikael replied with a raised eyebrow. "But it was a Russian original though."

The merc leader laughed. "Every tragedy is a Russian original. The terrible story of our lives." He glanced around at the Mexican town once more. "I cannot believe so many people left here so quickly."

"I wouldn't be here myself if it weren't for this mission," Mikael agreed, "and if you weren't my trusted companions. We stand to gain a lot of equipment and supplies if we pull this off. And after we're done making the sales, I expect to be in a nice warm boat off the coast of South America within a week."

"I'll be right there with you, my friend." Serge nodded. "First, we have to capture these McKnight's."

Mikael chortled, shoulders shaking. "Yes, we must save them from Keith."

The merc leader chuckled. Mikael always got him laughing no matter how grim the situation. And they'd all seen some grim situations in their time together.

"Do you see him yet?" Mikael asked.

"He's down there playing in the streets," Serge said. The merc scooted to the edge of the APC, boots dangling over the side, rifle pointed into the lonely city roads, past the church and marketplace where Keith had passed earlier. "Let me find him again."

Squinting through his scope, Serge poked and prodded into dark alcoves and deep stoops, housing complexes with gated yards, courtyards with vehicles crowding the streets, everything snow-packed and white except for the occasional glimpse of the agent's tracks. He caught movement off to the left, and he guided his rifle toward the southeast, moving past a lonely figure trudging through the snow.

"There he is," Serge said. "I have him lined up. Should I take the shot?"

Mikael snickered, spinning on his backside, and drawing himself up to sit next to the mercenary leader. Binoculars to his eyes, he began searching. "I don't see him. Where is he? Don't shoot him until I can watch."

Serge laughed, following the agent's path as he stumbled along a narrow street within the shadow of taller buildings. The man was small against the backdrop of frozen abandonment, staggering, slipping, arms windmilling as he clutched his rifle to his side. "Do you see that cluster of buildings southeast of our position?"

The other merc gave a light gasp. "Ah, I see him down there now. He's standing in the intersection. I think he is looking at us." The merc pointed and laughed. "He's in the middle of a warehouse area, perhaps the manufacturing center of the city. What in the world is he doing? He looks drunk."

"The man is frostbitten all over his body. I think even his brain," Serge replied as his scope followed Keith's staggering progress through the knee-high snow. "I have to admit, I admire him a little."

"Admiration for that idiot? Look at him. He can barely stand."

Lena's sultry voice came through their earpieces. "You boys get to have all the fun, watching that clown stagger around. I would like to request that we change positions. I want to see, too."

"No way, Lena." Serge made a derisive scoff through his frosted lips. "It is boring and cold out here, and Keith is far too entertaining. Ah, damn. He just crossed out of sight behind a building. Hopefully, he will come out the other side."

Every step he took was a fresh experience in pain, his boots pounding through a foot of snow, painful waves reverberating into his ankles, knees, and hips. It was like wading in quicksand made from dry ice, his frostbitten toes on fire, feet sore and twisted from having to walk unbalanced. Tottering and swerving, he clasped his rifle to his side to keep it from rattling, flashlight in his other hand, shining it into the darkest corners of the desolate city for a sign of his prey.

The never-ending shade of grey daylight left everything captive in a perpetual shadow as he moved through a residential district, cutting into back alleyways and side streets there. The Spanish-style homes began to look the same to him, the buildings like sentinels. Shoulders hunched beneath the gaze of black windows, he passed gardens snowed over and windswept, trees bending toward the road with branches like wretched claws. Looking side to side, he searched for any signs of life, any indication that he wasn't alone in the abandoned city.

But it had become a place of shadow, a land of ill omen, and Keith was on his own, more so than he'd ever been in his entire life. A light snow began to fall, the flakes drifting on sudden gusts of wind. He plowed ahead, driving through the snow with his knees, gazing up at a large cluster of warehouses that had been his original destination. As he approached, the old buildings loomed massive over him, thick brick structures that looked like they'd been built in the 1970s.

The dark doorways invited him inside, wanting to chew him up like toothless maws. Shattered windows gaped and screamed, though no sound came out. He thought he caught movement in the front door of one warehouse, and he froze, crouching lower, peering through his frosted goggles. In a flash, he unslung his rifle, grasped it in both hands, and charged up the stairs to fly across the threshold.

Flashlight pressed against the barrel, stock raised to his shoulder, he swept the weapon back and forth over a massive open warehouse space. Back in the shadows where his light beam barely reached, hulking machines squatted like sleeping giants, hydraulic arms poised as if frozen in time. Pipes and hoses and gauges covered their thick steel forms. Flywheels and gears stretched belts between them, sitting stagnant and unturned for weeks. Off to his left, snowflakes drifted through a hole in the ceiling, fluttering in his light to fall softly on the old hardwood floor. But there was no one there, certainly not the McKnight's.

"Damn," he sighed. "Now I'm seeing things." He gave a quick shake of his head, palm pounding his temple briefly. "No, it's just my nerves and this cold, and Serge's useless ass."

Keith backed out of the warehouse, stepped slowly down the stoop, and rejoined his footprints out in the street. With a last glance at the dark doorway, he resumed his search for the McKnights. The thick snowfall sucked up the sound of his boots as he crunched through the top layer of frost, busting it to pieces like candy brittle. He had no idea where the McKnights were, or if they were still in the city. He only knew he couldn't stand the company of the mercenaries any longer and needed to be out on his own, fighting, doing something despite his growing weakness. The cold and snow were sucking the life out of him, yet a fire still burned deep within, the part of him that wouldn't accept defeat or failure.

Reaching an intersection, he glanced left over his shoulder to see Serge and Mikael just specs where they sat on the APC at the top of the overpass. They looked down at him and pointed, probably laughing at him, following his progress with their scopes and binoculars. He resisted the urge to flip them off and instead staggered forward quickly, ducking behind another high-rise factory monstrosity, five stories high and inlaid with frosted windows like ancient gems.

Playful breaths of snow gusted against his face, causing him to glance aside and bow his head. Then he threw his eyes up, gazing up into the grey sky, shining his flashlight beam upward as flakes danced in the light. While the weather played, his body sang with pain. It was no longer the honed killing machine it had once been. He was well beyond top form and had extensive wounds. Doubt entered his mind, tickling his stomach before trickling through the rest of his limbs.

Still, he trudged on, arms swinging wide to keep his balance, boots lifting over the snow and pounding down again. He stopped in the middle of a four-way intersection that had once been a well-lit city street. The lamp posts were dead, the electric gone, devoid of life like everything else. He turned in a full-circle, staggering sideways, held up by the snow, stopping when something caught his eye on the south-running lane.

He stumbled ahead a few steps, bending, eyes focused on a brick alley and a set of tire tracks that crossed in front of him. They were thin and shallow, moving from right to left, not exactly the width of Humvee prints but wide enough to be distinguishable. Willing himself forward, Keith staggered the twenty yards to the tracks, lifting his goggles and glaring anxiously down, raking his gaze back and forth three or four times.

Were they the Humvee tracks? Yes... yes. It was the only answer. There was no one else around. Hand coming up, he wiped the frost from his nose and mouth and breathed hesitantly. With the spurt of determination, Keith put his goggles over his eyes and took the left passage between two buildings, certain he was closing in on his prey.

Driving against the snow and a wall of pain he'd built for himself, he sucked gouts of ice-cold air, freezing his nose and lungs.

Farther up, the tracks angled right along a dark alleyway lined with steel doors and an emergency stairway zigzagging upward. A spattering of windows looked down at him, amused at his sudden vulnerability, waiting for him to keel over in the snow. Despite his pounding heart, frozen throat, and every limb crying for relief, his flesh and bones still served him. Swaying and tottering, Keith plodded into the next street, watching the Humvee tracks go half a block before turning right and disappearing beneath a big steel garage door.

The space was wide enough to hold a truck inside, plenty of room for his quarry to hide like a rabbit in a hole. Suddenly, he was alive again, the most living thing in the entire damn dead city. He was a wolf in the snow, a brother to winter, and he was there to take his prey and complete the cycle of life and death. He unslung his rifle, gave it a tap with his palm to knock off the loose frost and ice then he took several deep breaths and crept toward the door.

CHAPTER TWENTY-SEVEN

Tom McKnight
Somewhere in Mexico

"Come on, Sam. We need to get back downstairs. Now!"
Tom flew down the steps in a blind panic, taking them two at a time, Sam's lighter footfalls following. He slid beneath the pile of pipes and wood, snagging himself again on the big nail, pricking through his coat to scrape his skin, crying out, part in pain and part as warning to his daughter. Then he was falling down the stairs, boots flailing, rifle rattling, his backside bouncing three steps before he regained his footing. He didn't wait for Sam to catch up, but kept moving. A couple of flights later, he came to the desk with all the debris sitting on top. He threw himself across it, boots first, kicking aside a box of papers to send them tumbling to the floor.
As soon as his feet landed, he heard the smash of the front door and a gunshot from below. Nostrils flaring, Tom grunted sharply, pushing forward, eyes wide with terror and realization, staggering and falling to the next landing. Tom spun and leaped in a blur, body flying,

spanning the entire length of steps, boots slamming on the hardwood. From his crouched position, he launched himself toward the machine room door, shoulder low as he crashed through it, throwing it back against the wall with another resounding bang.

His jaw fell, knees weak as he caught sight of Barbara on the floor, clutching her chest, gasping, blood soaking her coat, flailing to grab her pistol she'd dropped in front of her. As Tom looked on in horror, she pointed, bloody hand shaking, finger quivering. He jerked his head around and saw Linda, Jack and Smooch wrestling with Keith. His daughter's lips were pulled back in a grimace as she clutched the man's rifle, elbows locked over it and clinging like a monkey to a branch while Jack hung on Keith's coat, screaming, right fist striking out repeatedly, as ineffectual as a gnat but just as irritating to the larger man. Smooth had latched onto Keith's leg, but the thick winter fabric rendered him impervious to her teeth.

Tom jerked his rifle to his shoulder, leaning in, aiming at his nemesis, but Linda and Jack were in the way and he growled, the noise punching from his throat with raw emotion. "Get out of the way, kids! Get out of the way!"

They either didn't hear him or were so enraged by what had happened to their mother that they only felt their own crying hearts. Shifting the barrel slightly left, then right, then up, Tom realized in a split second he couldn't take a shot without putting a round into the back of his daughter's or son's heads. With a hiss of frustration, he tossed his rifle to the ground, diving toward the struggling trio. He grabbed Linda by the shoulder and threw her off then took Keith's gun barrel in his left hand, cocking his right fist, delivering a punch to Keith's jaw that rocked him backwards.

The agent ripped the weapon out of Tom's hands, falling to the floor, pulling Jack along with him and sending Smooch flying across the floor to smash into a pile of scrap with a high-pitched yelp. Sitting there dazed, head shaking, Keith swung the weapon around and fired at Tom, but Tom had seen the move coming, and he dove to the side before the round could connect with anything but air and wood and metal above.

Tom tried to roll forward and get to Keith before the man could do any more damage, but the agent was on his backside, kicking away, retreating with his gun clutched in his lap. Back slamming against the wall, pushing himself up to stand. Keith had no place left to go, so the rifle came up, barrel pointed at Linda before shifting to Tom. He stepped forward with a rictus grin, finger on the trigger when Sam's cry cut through the din, resonating with unrestrained rage.

"No!"

Tom's looked in her direction where she stood, holding Barbara's dropped pistol. A grimace stretching her lips wide, Sam squeezed the trigger twice, firing two rounds into Keith's chest. The first pinged against his armor and he slammed into the wall, howling in pain. The second round hit the drywall with a sharp puff of dust and Keith spun away, rifle clutched to his chest, looking for the exit as Smooch got back to her feet with a bark, charging at him. Sam fired again, willing the round to kill him, but Keith only grunted and arched his back, hammering his way through the door, stumbling outside and into the snow, Smooch snapping at his heels as the door closed in her face.

A moment's hesitation struck her as she debated between chasing after the man and staying, but she made the decision quickly, shouldering the door aside as it tried to swing shut, ordering Smooch to stay put as she stepped out into the growing snowfall. The agent was hobbling along the street, glancing back as he clutched his bruised chest. Sam stopped at the top of the steps, slipping a little, raising the weapon and centering to shoot. A squeeze of the trigger sent another round flying, zipping to his left, barely missing him. Hearing the gunshot, Keith put his body into overdrive, plowing forward with his knees pumping, heading for cover.

As he hobbled and staggered, he grabbed the radio from his pocket, slamming the transmit button. "Serge! Lena! I found them. I found the family. Come on, get down here!" Only static greeted him in response.

Back on the stoop, Sam tried to aim, tried to fire one more round, but the man had become a shadow in the snowfall, the wind sweeping white dust through the streets to obscure her vision. It was no use. He was gone.

With a pained expression, dreading what waited for her in the warehouse, Sam screamed a curse into the wind and spun back inside. Her father had stripped off her mother's coat and cut her shirt open with a knife, leaving her bloody wet skin exposed to the freezing air as his fingers danced over her abdomen, looking for the wounds. Throwing herself to her knees, opposite Tom, Sam saw her mother was unconscious, and she grasped her hand and looked to her father.

"What can I do, Dad? Tell me what to do!"

Jack was screaming in the background, crying and reaching for his Barbara, but Linda held him back, trying to cover the boy's eyes and turn him away from the bloody sight while she stared on, weeping. Smooch sat near the pair of them, Linda squeezing her with a free hand as the dog whined, adding to the mix of noise and confusion.

"Find a place to make a fire," Tom said, fighting a wave of panic and memories of the past swirling unbidden as he swabbed away the blood from Barbara's stomach with her shirt. "There's got to be a stove or something around. Something that would have kept the workers warm on cold days."

"I'll look, but won't the smoke give us away?" Sam implored.

"I don't care!" Tom roared at her, his calm demeanor shattering. "If we're going to save your mother's, we need a heated place to work. Go! Now!"

Sam leapt to her feet, knees shaking as she stared at the unconscious figure, her mother's chin and cheek smeared with blood. Then Samantha turned on her heel and ran into the back of the warehouse, searching across the wide-open space until she spotted a door at the far end on the right. She jogged past the machines, paint flecked and rusted, saws and pressure fitters, racks of rollers that reached from one end of the warehouse to the other. At the door, she jerked the handle, pulling it back with rough resistance as it scraped across the old floor. Sticking her head and shoulders inside, she saw it was a break room of sorts with tables and vending machines. But as her father had suggested, they had a stove in back with a single small door and vent going up into the wall.

The girl immediately started gathering scraps of paper and wood framing that had fallen. It wasn't much, so she jogged back across the warehouse and out to the stairwell, where she and her father had run across all the junk to get to the top. She grabbed two pieces of wood and shoved them into a box of old documents, snatching it up by the handles and carrying it two flights of stairs to the bottom floor.

As she passed, she shot a look at Linda and Jack. "Grab some paper and wood, whatever you can find! Bring it to the back so we can make a fire for mom! Hurry, and keep Smooch with you!"

Linda nodded and gave her brother a tug, pointing his shoulders toward the stairwell door. A whisper in his ear was all it took, and the two ran upstairs to gather more scraps, Smooch trailing behind them. Back in the break room, Sam opened the stove, threw in some wadded pieces of paper and grabbed the stick matches out of her pocket. With shaking hands, she lit the match and set the kindling aflame, watching the wavering orange tendrils lick toward the top of the stove. She fed it a little more and then added a small piece of wood, then more scraps, then more wood. The fire caught, grew, and began putting out some serious heat. Sam turned to exit, almost running into her brother and sister as they were bringing in more boxes of paper and pieces of wood.

"Put it over there by the rest of the stuff," she said as she squeezed passed them and jogged to where Tom was still working on Barbara.

Standing over them, she couldn't tell how many times her mother had been hit or where. Feet shuffling, fists pressed to her sides, she was caught between running away and screaming. Instead, she strode over and knelt by her mom, keeping her voice firm. "Okay, I got a fire going in the back room. What can I do next?"

"Help me get her next to the fire." Tom rose and put his hands beneath Barbara's arms, his expression stoic, eyes hard to read behind his goggles. "Grab her legs. Come on, hon."

Nodding, her insides shaking, Samantha stood and moved to her mother's feet, grabbing her boots and lifting them off the floor. On a count of three, they raised Barbara up and waddled through the warehouse. It was almost impossible to hold her mother's feet with gloves on, but Sam hooked her fingers beneath her mother's ankles, using her arms to pin the boots against her waist. After setting her down once to readjust, they finally got her into the break room and placed her in front of the stove on the cold, hard floor. The air was already warming up, the area filled with the scents and sounds of crackling wood. Jack, Linda and Smooch stood off to the side, Jack and Smooch having calmed down as Jack embraced his furry companion while Linda stood by them stoically.

"Kids, go to the Humvee and get some blankets," Tom said, fighting to keep the panic out of his voice. "And grab a sleeping bag, too."

Tom moved back to his wife's side, staring down at the abdominal wound on her left side, a few inches below her ribs. From what he could tell, it was only one shot, one bullet that had entered one side and gone out the other. That was a good thing, but if the round had hit any internal organs on its way through, he wasn't sure what he could do. Blood was still leaking from his wife's body, pooling on the surrounding floor in a big red stain, barely contained by his shirt that he had removed and ripped into pieces, putting them on her wounds. Handing Samantha a few strips of cloth, he took deep breaths, still fighting against the past, refusing to base future expectations on past tragedies.

"Sam, get on your mother's left side and hold that rag beneath the exit wound. That's it. Press hard. We want to stop the bleeding." While she did that, Tom did his best to keep pressure on the entry wound. He nodded at his hands. "Now, put your other hand where mine is and apply force on the top and bottom. I'm going to rip up some more rags."

Letting Sam take over the pressure responsibilities, Tom stripped two more shirts off, leaving him with just a long John top as protection from the cold. The sound of cloth ripping filled the room as the chill seeped into his skin, the stove's heat barely keeping it at bay. Soon, he had a pile of rags lying in Barbara's lap, ready to go in case they needed them. Feet shuffled into the room and he looked up to see Linda and Jack with bundles of blankets in their arms. Linda dropped a sleeping bag by the stove and held up a box with a red cross on top. "I found this packed in there, too. It's a first aid kit, right?"

"Yes, it is. Please set it down beside me and open it up. I want to see what's inside."

Jack dropped blankets on the sleeping bag, backing away from the horrific scene of his mother's shallow breaths, bloody smears streaking across her fire-lit, glistening skin.

"Come on, kids," Tom growled. "Focus up. Stop staring at your mother and make a bed for her. We need something to lay her on."

Wordlessly, Linda and Jack spread the sleeping bag out next to the stove. On top of that, they placed a blanket, then Tom asked Linda to take over pressure duty while he and Sam stood at the woman's head and feet again. On a count of three, they lifted Barbara onto the pallet they'd made, folding a towel beneath her head as a pillow. Still keeping pressure on the wound, eyes watering in the warming air, the McKnight family huddled around Barbara's still form, stoking the fire, praying for the bleeding to stop.

Back on the overpass, sitting atop the APCs, Serge glanced at Mikael as he swept his rifle back and forth. "I haven't seen Keith in a few minutes now. I wonder where he went?"

"Maybe he froze to death," his partner replied, pulling his coat tighter around his shoulders. "The storm is picking up, and it's getting colder, I think."

"We can only hope." The merc leader searched for a few more minutes, guiding the rifle back and forth, peering through the scope at what streets he could see, moving back to the last location he'd seen the agent. "I don't know. Maybe we should go look for him."

"Careful, Serge. You sound like you care about the man."

"I am just as amused as you are with him, but it would be bad form to let him die out in the cold. Banks might not like that. We should at least give him the benefit of the doubt. Lena can..." Something caught his attention off to the east, a little left of their position. "What's that?"

"What's what?"

The merc leader pointed in the direction he was looking, a thin tendril of gray rising from a squat warehouse, drifting out of a pipe in the side. "It's smoke. Someone lit a fire in one of the buildings. Someone is alive."

Mikael shrugged. "Perhaps Keith got too cold and couldn't make it back to us. So, he made a fire."

"He may be trying to send smoke signals," Lena's voice piped through their headsets, and the mercs laughed, Serge especially so as he imagined the agent huddled in a tiny room somewhere waving a cloth over a fire. Before his grin could grow any wider, the merc leader sobered up.

"Keith has a radio. He would have called us to let us know what he was doing." He stood atop the APC and aimed the rifle back down toward the smoke, the snowfall swirling around, obscuring his vision.

"Unless the radio signal is poor." Mikael looked up. "The storm is picking up quite a lot."

"I think, more than likely, it's the McKnights who made the fire," he frowned. "Why they are doing it, I don't know." Serge watched for another moment before he sat and slid down the APC's front end on his backside, feet kicking as he dropped into the snow. Mikael followed him without question, boots thudding on the snowy pavement next to him.

"Lena, we're going on foot to check things out."

"Would you like us to assist?"

"Yes, please." Serge walked to the end of the overpass, taking an exit ramp down, following Keith's fading boot prints. But a violent gust kicked up, lifting white powder from the ground and throwing it into his face, and he had to turn to the side and wait for the chilly gust to pass. "On second thought, let's move in with our vehicles. We will approach under the cover of the storm and then attack as soon as it lifts."

"Command received," Lena replied. "Will meet you in ten minutes."

As Serge and Mikael marched back to the APC, he glanced toward the gentle smoke seeping upward from the chimney, wondering what had come over Tom McKnight.

Made in the USA
Columbia, SC
23 April 2024

349531b7-257f-4e33-8ed3-c88948ff24f0R01